"I'm scared, Liam. I don't know what's going on, or what I'm supposed to do."

"Don't worry, Gabby," Liam said over the phone. "We'll make sure you and Mia are safe."

Gabby glanced in the rearview mirror, thankful that Mia was finally sleeping. There was a black pickup behind her. Was that the same one she'd noticed earlier?

"Gabby? Are you...there?"

The call was breaking up.

Gabby gave the car all the gas she could and flew back up the hill. All she had to do was get to the nearby sleepy tourist town and she would be fine.

She glanced again in the rearview mirror. The black pickup was still there.

"Liam..."

"What's...on...Gabby..."

The car behind her smashed into her bumper. Mia woke up and started crying. Gabby fought to keep the car on the road...

MOUNTAIN GUARDIAN

LISA HARRIS

&

USA TODAY Bestselling Author

SHARON DUNN

Previously published as *Sheltered by the Soldier* and *Night Prey*

LOVE INSPIRED
INSPIRATIONAL ROMANCE

LOVE INSPIRED®

INSPIRATIONAL ROMANCE

Recycling programs for this product may not exist in your area.

ISBN-13: 978-1-335-60099-8

Mountain Guardian

Copyright © 2021 by Harlequin Books S.A.

Sheltered by the Soldier
First published in 2019. This edition published in 2021.
Copyright © 2019 by Lisa Harris

Night Prey
First published in 2010. This edition published in 2021.
Copyright © 2010 by Sharon Dunn

This edition published by arrangement with Harlequin Books S.A.

For questions and comments about the quality of this book, please contact us at CustomerService@Harlequin.com.

Love Inspired
22 Adelaide St. West, 40th Floor
Toronto, Ontario M5H 4E3, Canada
www.Harlequin.com

Printed in U.S.A.

CONTENTS

Lisa Harris is a Christy Award winner and winner of the Best Inspirational Suspense Novel for 2011 from *RT Book Reviews*. She and her family are missionaries in southern Africa. When she's not working, she loves hanging out with her family, cooking different ethnic dishes, photography and heading into the African bush on safari. For more information about her books and life in Africa, visit her website at lisaharriswrites.com.

Books by Lisa Harris

Love Inspired Suspense

Final Deposit
Stolen Identity
Deadly Safari
Taken
Desperate Escape
Desert Secrets
Fatal Cover-Up
Deadly Exchange
No Place to Hide
Sheltered by the Soldier
Christmas Witness Pursuit

Visit the Author Profile page
at Harlequin.com for more titles.

SHELTERED BY THE SOLDIER

Lisa Harris

I will lift up mine eyes unto the hills, from whence cometh my help. My help cometh from the Lord, which made heaven and earth. He will not suffer thy foot to be moved: he that keepeth thee will not slumber.
—*Psalms* 121:1–3

To those longing for strength when hard times hit.
May you find your protection in Him.

ONE

Gabriella Kensington balanced her eleven-month-old daughter Mia on her hip while fighting to get the key into the sticky lock of the back door of her townhouse. The next time she went out, she was going to have to buy a can of WD-40 and fix it. She considered setting the two plastic grocery bags hanging from her wrist down on the porch, but the three inches of snow that had blanketed the city last night from a late fall cold front had left the mostly uncovered surface both slippery and wet.

But she'd worry about that another day.

She wiggled the handle, heard the click, then finally opened the door. Heat from the house rushed out and filled her lungs with warmth.

Gabby stepped inside as an unexpected chill sliced through her. Setting the two plastic bags of groceries onto the counter, she glanced around the kitchen, managing to knock one of the bags over in the process. A grapefruit rolled off the counter and onto the floor, but she hardly noticed.

Instead, she stared into the living room that opened

up from the kitchen. The entire room had been trashed. Papers had been dumped from her desk. Drawers pulled open and their contents dumped. Books and photos lay scattered across the hardwood floor. Mia started fussing. Gabby had no idea if whoever had done this was still somewhere in the house, but there was no time to find out.

This can't be happening.

But the frightening text she'd received two days ago, demanding her to stop asking questions and threatening her and her daughter, only served to confirm her worst fears. Adrenaline pumping, she hushed her daughter who was struggling to get down. She couldn't take any chances in case someone was still in the house. Not with Mia. Instead, she raced back to the car, fumbled with the straps on the car seat while Mia's fussing grew louder.

"It's okay, sweet baby. Nothing's going to happen to you. Mama's going to make sure of that."

A lump swelled in her throat as she slid into the car. She wanted to pray, except she knew God didn't always answer prayers. If someone was after her, she was on her own.

Hands shaking, she turned the key in the ignition. The car refused to start.

No…no…no…

"Not now. Please…not now."

She glanced back at the house, terrified that at any moment someone was going to burst out of the back door and come after her. If someone had still been in the house, she had no doubt that they'd heard Mia crying. She turned the key again to start the engine. Her father had tried to convince her to replace her jeep with something more reliable, but it was going to take her another year to save up. Now she couldn't help but wonder if she should have tried to make it work.

A third try and the engine caught.

Letting out a strong huff of relief, she pulled out of the driveway, her heart still racing. Calling 911 was the logical option, but something made her hesitate. The letters her husband had written her before his death while still deployed had left her shaken. And this happening so soon after she'd questioned his commanding officers made her wonder if she'd managed to ask the wrong person, triggering something she was at a loss of how to handle. Which meant if someone was after her, she had no idea how far their arm might reach. She stopped at a red light, then glanced at the leather bag with Will's letters on the floorboard of the car. That had to be what they were after. She swallowed hard. No. She was sounding paranoid. But Will had been paranoid, too. So maybe her fear stemming from the last letter he'd written her wasn't that far off after all.

I think they realize I've been looking into the paper trail. I need to go to someone with what I have, but I have to make sure the evidence is solid. Some of these contractors are the kind of people who wouldn't hesitate at defrauding our government. The kind of people who wouldn't blink at killing anyone who got in their way.

The light turned green and she headed north toward the freeway. She'd memorized the details of Will's letters. They had mentioned contracted workers, so she'd assumed that going to someone in the military was safe. But clearly, she'd been mistaken. And now she couldn't afford to trust the wrong person again. It wasn't worth risking her daughter's life. But either way, she needed a plan and the best option seemed to be to get as far away from here as she could.

But where? The digital clock on the dash said it was a quarter to three. She could call her parents, but what could they do? They were currently enjoying Florida's balmy weather and couldn't exactly help her. She had friends that would take her in, but there was no way she was going to put someone else's life at risk. And until she figured out who was behind this, she'd never be safe. Will was dead, and she had Mia to protect.

Her mind shifted gears as she upped her speed and merged onto the freeway. There was one person who might be able to help her. She glanced at the phone laying in the console next to her. One person who might have the answers to whoever was behind this.

Liam O'Callaghan.

She tried to push the name out of her mind, and instead glanced at the line of cars behind her as each mile took her farther way from danger—and closer to the town of Timber Falls near where he lived. She hadn't heard from Liam for several weeks. He and Will had been deployed together, then Liam had spent months in both inpatient and outpatient rehabilitation with injuries from the blast that killed her husband. Over the past year and a half, he'd called at least once a month to check on her and make sure she was doing okay and had even come to see her several times. But she hadn't missed the hint of guilt in his voice each time. As if what had happened to Will was somehow his fault. And she was clearly a reminder.

She placed the call on the cheap smart phone she'd picked up yesterday before she had a chance to change her mind again. But instead of him answering, it switched to voice mail.

"Liam, this is Gabby." She paused, wondering if she was doing the right thing. Wondering why she felt so hesitant in asking for his help. She tried to shake off the tension in her voice. "Listen… I need to talk to you. It's important. Please. Call me back as soon as you can on this number."

Gabby hung up the call, then glanced into the rear-view mirror at the back seat where Mia sat in her car seat, playing with her stuffed giraffe. At least she'd stopped crying. When Gabby had found out she was pregnant, everything had seemed so perfect. She'd had the perfect marriage, perfect family, perfect life. Then in one life-altering moment, two uniformed officers had shown up at her front door and everything changed.

Her phone rang, pulling her back into the present. She pushed the call-answer button on the steering wheel. "Liam?"

"Gabby…are you okay?"

"Not really." She didn't want to tell him what was going on—that would only make the situation more real—but neither could she put the life of her daughter at risk. "I need help, and I didn't know who else to call."

She glanced back into the rearview mirror. Mia had thrown down the giraffe and was fussing again, but Gabby couldn't stop the car. Couldn't take any risks that might jeopardize her baby's life more than she already had.

"What happened?" he asked.

She swallowed hard, trying to dismiss the feeling she was being followed. "I got home this afternoon and discovered someone had ransacked my place."

"Wait a minute... Have you called 911?"

"I was scared and panicked. Afraid someone might still be in the house."

"I understand, but you need to call the authorities."

She hesitated. "I can't."

"Why not?"

The last thing she wanted to do was get Liam involved, but what other option did she have?

"Gabby...what's going on?"

"There's something I need to talk to you about. There have been other threats—"

"Threats? Is that why you have a new number?"

"I was afraid someone might have been tracking my phone, but I'd rather discuss everything in person."

"Where are you now?" he asked.

She glanced at the clock. "I'm about twenty minutes from Timber Falls. If you could meet me in town—"

"Of course. Or you could come out to the ranch."

"I don't want to get your family involved."

"Will was my best friend. I promised him if anything ever happened to him, I'd make sure you and Mia were okay. I owe him my life. My family understands that."

She looked around, her chest still heaving. Sirens wailed from a wreck on the other side of the highway.

"Is there a chance anyone is following you?" he asked.

"I don't think so, but I can't be sure. Traffic's pretty heavy, and it's starting to snow."

"I'm out at the ranch, but I'll head to town now. It will take me at least thirty minutes, but you can wait for me at the sheriff's office on the edge of town. It's well lit. You can't miss it."

"Okay."

"Do you remember meeting my brother Griffin?"

"Yes."

She'd met his entire family at Will's funeral, and while most of that day was a blur, she remembered being impressed with the four brothers and their parents, whose ancestors had first settled in this area three generations ago.

"I'll call him. Griffin's a deputy and on duty today. I'll give him a heads-up."

She drew in a long, slow breath, trying to gather her nerves. "I'm scared, Liam. I don't know what's going on, or what I'm supposed to do."

"Don't worry. We're going to find a way to make sure you and Mia are safe until we figure out what's going on."

She glanced in the rearview mirror, thankful that Mia was finally sleeping. Poor baby was missing her nap and was exhausted. Her gaze shifted slightly as something else caught her attention. There was a black pickup behind her, following too close. Had she seen the same vehicle earlier?

Her fingers gripped the steering wheel. Five seconds later, the road straightened and headed down another narrow mountainous stretch. She pressed harder on the accelerator as she sucked in a deep breath and tried to talk herself down. No one had followed her out of her neighborhood. This was nothing more than her imagination playing tricks on her.

She gave the car all the gas she could and flew back up the hill. A stab of pain shot through her head, and she realized she'd been clenching her jaw. The stress from the last few days had managed to consume her. She kept her eyes on the road, her hand steady on the wheel as she passed a sign to Timber Falls. All she had to do was get to the sleepy tourist town and she would be fine.

"Gabby? Are you…there?"

The call was breaking up.

She glanced again in the rearview mirror. The black pickup was still there. "Liam…"

"What's…on… Gabby…"

The car behind her smashed into her bumper. She fought to keep the car on the road as she pushed on the pedal. Mia woke up and started crying.

For the first time in months, Gabby prayed God would intervene.

Liam pressed on the gas pedal, pushing the speed limit down the narrow two-lane road that led from the O'Callaghan Ranch toward Timber Falls, the nearest town from his family's ten-thousand-plus acre ranch. He called Gabby back.

Nothing.

He tried to ignore the list of uncertainties simmering beneath the surface. He needed to stop worrying. Phone service around the ranch and the road leading into Timber Falls had always left holes of no reception in spite of recent upgrades over the past couple years.

It didn't mean something had happened. This had been his life the past few months. Waiting for the ball to drop, dumping another tragedy on him. His mother kept reminding him that he wasn't living. And yet, he knew he hadn't really been living for a long time.

Not since Will had died and Liam had been life-flighted to Germany, almost losing his own life alongside his best friend.

He tried to shake off the memories and instead focus on the road. The last thing he needed to do was run into a deer on the long stretch of winding road toward town. Gabby was fine. One of them had just gone through a no-service patch. He'd meet up with her, see what she needed, then go on with his own life.

Because if he were honest with himself, seeing Gabby was the last thing he wanted to do. Months of therapy had finally gotten him to the place he needed to be physically, but emotionally the scars were yet to completely heal. And seeing Gabby again… He knew it was only going to be a reminder of what happened that night to his best friend. But he couldn't let emotion rule his thoughts. He owed Will his life on more than one occasion and if that meant ensuring Gabby and her baby were safe, then he planned on doing anything in his power to keep them that way.

Memories from the night of Will's death refused to leave him alone, bringing back the all-too-familiar panic. They'd been ambushed that starless night only a few miles from the base while out on a routine patrol in Afghanistan. But there was nothing routine about what had happened that night. By the time he got to Will, his friend was already dead.

Mercifully, his memories of that night were few and far between. The following minutes and hours had dragged by as comrades fought to get him to safety. Over a year later, there were still moments when he wished he'd died instead of his friend. Will had a wife and daughter. He should have lived. And yet, for some reason God had taken Will and let Liam live. The guilt of that loss had yet to let go of him completely. But if he could help Will's widow, it seemed the least he could do to make amends.

He tried to call her again, but for a third time, the call wouldn't go through. This time he called a different number.

"Griffin?"

"Hey," his older brother said. "I was just planning on calling you. Are we still on for tomorrow night—"

"Yeah, but listen. I've got a problem, and I'm going to need your help. Do you remember Gabby Kensington?"

"Of course. Will's wife."

"Yes. She's on her way into town now to see me. I'm not sure exactly what's going on, but apparently her house was burglarized. She's scared, and our call got disconnected."

"You know how sketchy phone service is in the passes leading up here. I'm sure she's fine."

"I know, but I'm still worried. I'm on my way into town now, but you're closer than I am."

"What kind of vehicle is she driving?"

"She owns a yellow jeep."

"Don't worry. I'll head south out of town right now and see if I can find her. Keep me updated on your location and we'll meet up. In the meantime, try to keep calling her, but send me her number so I can try as well."

Twenty minutes later, Timber Falls began to show above the horizon. He'd grown up in this town. Graduated from the local high school. And for the past few weeks, it had been the place where he could work on the family ranch alongside his older brother, Caden, while he continued to heal. He wanted to go back to active duty, but the doctors still hadn't approved him. Which left his future in the military hanging in the balance.

Liam's phone rang, jerking him from his thoughts. "Griffin?"

"I found her."

"Where is she?"

"First of all, she and her daughter are both fine," Griffin said, answering Liam's next question before he had a chance to ask it. "We're heading back into town now."

"What's going on?"

"You did the right thing to call me, because there are a couple things you need to know before you see her."

Liam felt a shot of adrenaline rush through him. "What do you mean?"

"I haven't had time to take an official statement yet, but someone rammed into her from behind while she was on her way here." Griffin hesitated. "From the way she described it, this wasn't an accident."

"But she's okay?"

"She's fine. Just meet me at the sheriff's office."

Five minutes later, Liam parked in front of the square brick building on the edge of town, then hurried inside.

"Liam…" Angie Baker, the department's secretary, looked up from her computer as he stepped into the lobby. "I just got off the phone with Deputy O'Callaghan. He's almost here."

"Thank you."

He started pacing the white tiled floor while Angie went back to her computer. The clock on the wall ticked by the seconds. But he couldn't find a way to shove aside the guilt. If anything happened to Gabby, he'd never forgive himself.

"You're going to wear a hole in the floor." Angie stood up and grabbed a file from a tray. "Can I get you some coffee?"

"No. I'm fine." He stopped pacing and forced a smile at the offer. "But thanks."

Ten minutes later, Griffin finally walked into the lobby from the back. The two of them might be brothers, but while Griffin had brown hair, brown eyes and a knack for management, Liam had blond hair, blue eyes and an affinity for strategizing and problem solving. Though their looks and even personalities might be different, there was one thing they had in common. They both had a strong sense of duty and justice neither could ignore.

"Griffin…" He didn't even try to curb his impatience as he crossed the room. "Where are they?"

"I took them directly through the back door to the conference rooms. Thought she might be more comfortable there. I also asked Mom to come over from the clinic, so she could check them out."

"But Gabby's really alright?"

"She's shook up, but yes. Apparently, the car that

hit her spun out in the snow, and she managed to lose them."

"Do you have any idea who hit her?"

"I've got a deputy looking into the incident, but the chances of us finding them are slim in this weather. What about you? She didn't say much except that she'd been threatened before. Did she give you any clue as to who might be after her?"

"No. That's why I need to talk with her." Liam weighed his options, then made a decision. "I'm going to take her out to the ranch until we can figure out what's going on. A burglary is one thing, but almost getting run off the road means all of this isn't random. And from what I can tell, she doesn't think so, either. I've known Gabby for several years and she's not the kind of woman to borrow trouble. Something is very wrong."

"I agree." Griffin pulled off his deputy hat and scratched the back of his head. "You can come back with me now. Then as soon as she's given her statement and Mom has cleared them medically, you can take them out to the ranch. If we need her for anything else, I'll know where she is."

And he'd be able to ensure she stayed safe.

A minute later, Liam walked into the small conference room where Gabby was standing near the window. He crossed the room, then pulled her into his arms and hugged her. "Gabby... I'm so, so sorry."

"I'm fine, really. Just shook up."

She looked at him with those big brown eyes of hers. He'd gone to visit her half a dozen times since Will's death seventeen months ago, but his own physical therapy had kept him out of the loop for the most part. She'd changed little on the outside, but he knew the emotional toll had been high.

"Wow...she's grown up so much." He knelt down next to the car seat where Mia slept, with her chubby fingers wrapped tightly around a stuffed orange giraffe. "She's adorable and so much bigger than the last time I saw her."

"That's what babies do. They tend to grow up. She turns one this month."

"It's hard to believe that much time has passed." He stood up and faced her again. "Griffin told me you were hit from behind. Are you sure you're fine?"

"Yes, though I've been told that your mother's on her way to check us out."

"We'll need to have your car looked at as well, and what about the phone you thought they might be using to track you?"

She pulled it out of her purse and handed the phone to him. "Maybe I'm just paranoid, but I saw something a while back on TV about apps that can be installed to track someone without their knowledge. I didn't want to take any chances."

"You did the right thing. I'll pass this on to Griffin and see if someone who works with their IT can look at it. And Gabby... I promise we're going to find out what's going on."

She nodded, but he didn't miss the fear in her eyes.

"Do you have any idea who's behind all of this?" he asked.

There was a long silence before she answered. "I think this has something to do with Will's death."

Liam worked to process the information, surprised

at her answer. "Will's death? He died in an explosion halfway around the world a year and a half ago. How can this be related?"

She shrugged. "I recently went through the rest of Will's footlocker. I found some letters he wrote that I'd never seen before. He was worried about something. What if it wasn't just another attack? What if it was just meant to look that way?"

"Wait a minute. You mean that someone—other than terrorists—wanted him dead?"

"I think he stumbled upon something illegal while he was over there. Will hinted that contractors where involved, but I think he was afraid of the repercussions without solid proof of what was going on. And whatever it was got him killed. Because when I start asking questions…" A tear streamed down her face. "Liam, I think they're after me."

TWO

Gabby watched Liam's face, worried about his reaction. She knew Will had been his closest friend. They'd lived in a war zone together, and in turn, they'd developed a bond that only soldiers understood. On top of that, Liam had been there the day Will died.

"I don't understand." His jaw tensed as he caught her gaze. "Why would someone come after you in connection with a soldier who died seven-thousand miles away in the Middle East. It doesn't make sense. Will never said anything to me."

"Maybe not, but that's what I need to find out. Because there is a connection. I decided to start asking a few questions about things Will told me in his letters, and not only was I sent a threatening text message to stop asking questions, but now this happens."

"You said he was looking into something. Something…illegal?"

"Yes, but unfortunately, he never gave specifics."

"Why wouldn't he have told me if something was going on at the base? We talked about everything."

"I don't know. But he was definitely looking into some illegal activities."

He wasn't totally buying her theory. She could tell by the look of doubt in his eyes and the frown on his lips. He and Will had been close. She got that. She also knew there were things Will told him that he would have never told her. And yet, for some reason, this was different.

"Tell me more about the letters," he said.

"After he died, there were things I never went through in his locker. I just…couldn't. I was four months pregnant, then suddenly a widow… I was overwhelmed. A few weeks ago, I decided it was time to go through his things. I found several letters Will never had a chance to send. Someone must have added them to his personal belongings. In them, his tone had changed. He was looking for proof that someone was defrauding the government."

"Contractors."

She nodded.

"Who have you spoken to?"

"I contacted several officers he worked under, hoping they might have answers."

"But there was nothing specific in what he wrote? No names?"

She shook her head. "I'll let you read through the letters, but the only name mentioned was Casada. Someone he seemed to trust. Will thought the man might have answers for some reason."

"James Casada. He was a contracted worker."

"I guess I was hoping since you were there you'd have some answers, too."

He walked toward the window and stared outside. The snow was picking up, making her doubly thankful she and Mia weren't still out there.

"I'd like to look at the letters if that's okay, but I don't have answers. I know that things have been hard since Will died." He turned back around to face her. "Losing Will was a horrible tragedy that neither of us will ever be able to forget."

"It was horrible, but what better way to silence someone? No one would ask questions. It would simply be another unfortunate loss that happens far too often."

"I also know how easy it is to keep searching for an explanation when someone dies."

Gabby felt a ball of anger begin to bubble inside her gut. Hadn't she spent the last year and a half trying to combat those feelings? Weekly counseling sessions with her pastor, dozens of books on grief, along with advice from half the people she ran into while she tried to work full-time and raise Mia.

"I'm not just looking for answers." She bit the edge of her tongue. Healing was raw and personal. She knew that. Knew how easy it was to snap back a response that she'd later regret. But you couldn't just throw out grief with the trash and expect everything to simply switch back to normal. Healing was a process and losing Will had changed her forever.

"I'm sorry." He stepped in front of her and rubbed the back of his neck. "All I meant was that nothing can change the fact that he's gone. We know how he died and digging for answers is just going to hurt more."

"Maybe. But then why did someone ransack my house and follow me here? This all has to be related."

"All I know for certain is that Will died in an ambush. We all knew our jobs were a risk, but it was a choice he made every day in order to serve his country."

"I understand that, but what if there was more involved? Because I believe there was."

She'd been around Liam enough to know he was far more methodical than impulsive. His questions weren't a dismissal of what she believed, but rather his way of working through a problem.

"Do you have his letters with you?" he asked.

"I'm not really sure why, but I've been carrying them around in my car. Now I'm glad I did."

"Do you think that's what the intruder was after?"

"It makes sense. The only problem is I don't know what they think is in them." She blew out a slow breath. "I thought maybe you'd see something I didn't."

Liam pulled out one of the chairs and sat down in it. "Will seemed distracted before he died. But to be honest, I thought it was because he was ready to get back home. It just seems odd he never mentioned something like this was going on."

She caught the fatigue in his eyes, making her second-guess her impulsive decision to come here. He had enough of a burden to carry without her adding to it. He might not have died in the explosion, but he carried the physical scars as reminders. Months of therapy had healed most of them, but she understood all too well that it was often what couldn't be seen that hurt the most.

"You know, I'm sorry," she said, taking a step back. "I shouldn't have come. I just thought maybe you'd spoken to him and that you might have some of the answers. But you don't know anything, so—"

"Gabby, no." He stood up and bridged the distance between them. "You did the right thing. Of course, I'll help. I'll do anything I can, but in the meantime, I want to get you somewhere safe. I'll take you up to the ranch. I've been staying there the past few weeks while waiting to get approved for active duty. You'll be safe there, and it will give us a safe place to figure things out."

She caught the sincerity in his voice, but that didn't sway her response. "I couldn't impose. I'll just stay at the hotel here in town. I can't just drop everything, either. I've got my job—"

"Forget it. My mother would never forgive me if I don't insist you come. And in fact…" Liam turned toward the woman who'd just stepped into the doorway of the room, wearing a flowered scrub top and matching pants. "You remember my mother."

"Of course. It's good to see you again, Mrs. O'Callaghan."

"Please call me Marci."

"Alright, but I'm sorry you had to come down here. I'm fine. Really."

The older woman set a small padded medical bag onto the table. "Even at low speeds, there can be issues with whiplash and back injuries after a car accident. It's not something you should play around with."

Liam shot Gabby a smile. "If I were you, I wouldn't argue with my mom."

Mia started fussing in the car seat.

"I'm sorry, but I've forgotten your baby's name," Marci said.

"Mia."

"That's a beautiful name. Liam…why don't you entertain Mia while I look at her mama. I'll check her over next."

Gabby glanced at Liam. "You don't mind?"

"Of course not."

She handed Liam Mia, her stuffed giraffe and a small tub of Cheerios.

"We'll just wait for your mama in the hallway, won't we, Mia?"

Gabby turned back to Liam's mother while he stepped out of the room.

"You said you didn't have any complaints?" Marci asked.

"Besides being chilled to the bone, I feel fine. It could have been so much worse."

"Any bruises or cuts that you noticed?"

"No. I've got a slight crick in my neck, but it honestly isn't bad enough to even take Tylenol."

"Any trouble moving it?"

Gabby turned her head to the right, then the left. "No. None at all."

"No pain or dizziness?"

"Nothing."

She glanced at the hallway where Liam was pretending the giraffe was an airplane. Mia laughed, all smiles.

"He's really good with her." Somehow, she'd expected Liam to shy away from kids, but apparently she had been wrong.

"Liam might be a soldier who's served on the battlefield, but he's always had a soft spot for kids."

Gabby smiled, filing that information away with what she already knew about him.

"What about your parents?" Marci asked, slowly

moving her hand down Gabby's spine. "Do they live near you?"

"They did until about a month ago. They're used to wintering in Florida, and I insisted they go this year. They'll be back for the holidays and some skiing this winter."

"It's got to be tough, raising a child on your own."

"Thankfully, I'm a graphic designer and able to work at home. And Mia's an easy baby. Most days anyway."

It had taken her a while to convince her parents to take their yearly winter in Florida, but for some reason, doing things on her own this winter had been an important step forward for her.

"At this point," Marci said, "I don't notice anything to be concerned about, but some injuries can take several days to show up, especially in your spine or neck. If you have any numbness, swelling, back pain or headaches, you need to let me know immediately."

"Thank you. I appreciate it."

"How old is Mia?"

"She turns one in a few days. I can hardly believe it."

"Seems like my boys were that age not too long ago, though that's not exactly true."

Gabby laughed.

"Do you have any brothers or sisters?" Marci asked.

"I'm an only child."

Mia threw her giraffe onto the floor and started fussing.

Liam made his way back over to them. "I think someone needs her mama."

"You're good with her, but she's getting sleepy, and

I have a feeling she won't be herself until she gets a proper nap."

Mia just nuzzled her head into Gabby's shoulder while Marci quickly checked her out.

"From what Griffin told me, the accident was very minor, but you'll still need to watch Mia for anything that seems off like vomiting, not sleeping and unusual crying. I'd also suggest you do a follow-up with your pediatrician when you get home."

"I will. Thank you."

"I was serious about coming out to the ranch for a few days," Liam said. "I can make sure you're safe, and it will give us time to figure out who hit you."

"Your family's already done so much. I couldn't impose. I could get a hotel tonight—"

"That's out of the question. Besides, we have plenty of room. Right, Mom?"

"He is right. You'd be more than welcome to stay with us."

Will had told her about the O'Callaghan family and their ranch that sat nestled beneath impressive views of Pikes Peak and surrounding mountains. From everything she'd heard, she knew the place would be stunning. But as much as she wanted someone like Liam to take care of her, if he didn't have the answers, she'd have to figure things out on her own.

"Besides, I'll bet you could use some time away," Liam said. "It's a beautiful place. And if you're up for it, I could take you riding tomorrow. The fresh air of the mountains always makes me feel better."

"That would be nice."

There was nothing she'd rather do than spend the day

in the mountains, away from all of this, but that wasn't why she was here.

Liam caught her gaze. "We'll talk more later. Just come for now."

She glanced toward the door, hoping she'd made the right decision. Hoping whoever had hit her wouldn't be able to find her.

"I'm going to keep you safe, Gabby. I promise. Whoever's after you won't find you at the ranch."

"You can't promise that."

"Maybe not, but I can do everything in my power to make sure you're safe. Griffin's trying to find the person who hit you, but in the meantime, I think we should head out to the ranch."

"If you're sure."

"I am." He reached out and squeezed her hand. "We're going to figure out what's going on. But first you need to get a good night's sleep. You look exhausted."

She let out a low chuckle. "Thanks."

"I didn't mean it that way."

"I know."

His smile managed to break through some of the pain in her heart. She could trust him. She had to. What other choice did she have?

The next morning, Liam sat out on the wraparound porch of his parents' ranch house, nursing a cup of coffee and watching the sun rise over the mountains. As beautiful as the scenery was, he couldn't shed the worry that had settled in his gut. He still needed to read Will's letters, but even if his friend had discovered corruption within one of the contracted firms, that didn't mean he'd been murdered. But then how did that explain the threatening text, the break-in and car wreck?

Had Will's death really been the perfect cover-up?

He shifted his thoughts back to the view. The O'Callaghan ranch had been his home his entire life and in his family's possession since the early 1920s. The thousands of acres included irrigated meadows, pastures, ponds for fishing and livestock. On top of that, there was some of the best elk hunting in the country. When he'd been deployed overseas, what he'd missed most had been Sunday dinners, hunting with his father and three brothers, and white Christmases. Three things that he might be getting more regularly if the army didn't sign off on his going back to active duty.

He pushed away the reminder as Gabby stepped out onto the porch wearing her long red coat, a scarf and boots, and holding a mug of coffee.

"Good morning," he said, jumping up to straighten a cushion on the chair next to him. "I see you found the coffee?"

"Your mother found it for me, actually." She sat down next to him, then took a sip of her drink. "This is just what I needed this morning. And she insisted she'd listen for Mia while I enjoy the sunrise."

"How did you sleep?" he asked.

She shot him a smile before sitting down next to him. "Like a rock. Mia managed to only wake up once, and she's still sound asleep. I don't think I realized just how tired I was."

"I'm glad you slept. Both of you. Everything always seems better when you have a good night's rest behind you."

He wasn't going to tell her how little he'd slept last night. He'd tossed and turned while going over every conversation with Will he could remember, trying to figure out what he'd missed. If Will had stumbled on something that had gotten him killed, he should have at least been aware that there was a problem. Why hadn't his friend come to him?

He pulled her phone out of his pocket and handed it to her. "Griffin dropped by earlier this morning and asked me to give it back to you."

"Did they find something on it?"

He hesitated. "There was spy software installed."

"Spy software?" Gabby let out a sharp puff of air. "How could they do that without physical access to my phone?"

"It's clean now, but apparently it is possible to install it remotely through a cellular or Bluetooth connection. Griffin's guy installed a security app to protect it from now on."

"Thank you. I just... I'm having a hard time processing all of this."

"I don't blame you. I am, too."

Gabby slipped the phone into her coat pocket then stared at the tree line in the distance. "Will told me how much you loved this place and wanted us to come for a visit after the two of you were finished with your deployments. I knew it was beautiful, but all of this...the colors of the sunrise...the fall leaves...the mountains... This truly is stunning."

The house was surrounded by aspens that turned golden every fall, as well as blue spruce and Douglas firs. With the sun slipping above the horizon, he couldn't imagine a more peaceful setting. But even with the pull of family and home, a part of him had begun to feel antsy and ready to go back to active duty.

"There's a tributary from the lake called Wayward Creek that runs through the part of the property," he said, pointing to the left. "It's one of my favorite places. And no matter what you like to do, hunting, fishing, snowmobiling in the winter, hiking, you can do it here. We even go ice fishing when the ponds are frozen over."

"Ice fishing?" She pulled her mug of coffee against her. "While my parents love their Florida winters, I admit, I prefer the snow and the cold. Though I've never tried ice fishing. That might be a bit too cold, even for my blood."

"I should take you one day, though…though I'm sure you're going to be ready to get home as soon as we figure out what's going on." He quickly tried to backtrack his invitation, wondering why he'd said that. Gabby wasn't here on holiday. She was here because her life had been threatened. And that didn't include excursions with him out on the ranch. She needed his help, which meant he needed to stay focused.

"What's the likelihood of falling through the ice?" she asked. "I think that would be my biggest fear."

He shifted his mind back to the conversation. "My father taught us the importance of both having fun and being safe. But it happens. As long as you check your safety equipment and have the necessary gear in case of an emergency, you should be fine. Though my brother Reid fell in one winter while we were playing a game of hockey with skates, sticks and pucks. Took all three of us to drag him out, and we never told my father. We'd been lectured on the dangers of playing on the ice, and we knew he'd be furious."

Gabby laughed. "Somehow, I have a feeling that the four O'Callaghan brothers managed to get into a lot of trouble growing up."

"Well, we learned our lesson that time. We dragged him back to the house, stuck him in front of the fireplace and made him drink about a gallon of hot coffee. The only real issue after that was that he didn't sleep that night from all the caffeine, but we were just grateful he was okay."

He'd realized just how close they'd been to losing Reid, which was why he'd always believed God had stepped in that night. He glanced at Gabby. She'd pulled her long dark hair back in a ponytail and for the first time since she arrived, she looked relaxed. But what if he wasn't able to keep her safe? There were no guarantees in life. Hadn't he learned that the hard way? Reid had survived that day out on the ice. But on the battlefield, Will hadn't. If someone was after Gabby, how was Liam supposed to stop them?

He took a sip of his coffee, wishing he could somehow drown his worries. His training had taught him how to fight and how to survive, but it had never completely prepared him for what it was like to watch someone you cared about die. The emotional wounds he'd suffered had ended up being far worse than the physical ones he'd received.

She reached out and brushed her hand against his arm. "Thank you for bringing me here."

"It's not a problem at all. My mom's always telling

us there's too much testosterone when we're all home, though I know she loves every minute of it."

"I'm sure she does. How often do the O'Callaghan brothers get to all be home at the same time?"

"Except for yours truly, pretty often, actually. You know Griffin. He's the oldest and one of the deputies in town, so he's around a lot. Next in line is Caden, who was an army ranger until he was honorably discharged three years ago. He now runs the ranch with my father and lives in a small house next to my parents' home. Reid's one of three full-time firemen in Timber Falls and lives there, and I'm the youngest."

"I don't think I knew that."

"The baby of the family, as they like to constantly remind me. I'm the one who's spent the most time away, but no matter where we are, we all always manage to find ourselves back at the ranch."

"I like your parents."

"My father considers retiring every year, though something tells me he never will. At least not officially."

She let out a low laugh, but her smile quickly faded.

"You okay?"

"For now, yes. It's almost too easy to forget the reason why I'm here." She pulled a handful of letters out of her pocket. "But as much as I'd love to just enjoy the sunrise, I need you to look at these."

"You're sure you don't mind?" Part of him felt uncomfortable reading through Will's personal letters to his wife.

"It's fine. I've organized them in chronological order."

Liam pulled out the first letter in the stack. "I used

to tease Will for sending as many handwritten letters as emails. And do you know what his answer was?"

"That I loved handwritten mail?"

He nodded.

Gabby let out a sharp breath of air. "Now I can't help but wonder if it was also a way to write out his concerns without leaving a digital trail."

He started through the letters in order by date, surprised at how many memories they evoked. If he closed his eyes, he was there again, catching Will writing letters to his wife by flashlight in the tent in the middle of the night.

Why didn't Will tell me what was going on?

Twenty minutes later, he set down the last letter. "While my mom's watching Mia, would you like to go for a short walk? The fresh air always clears my mind and helps me think better."

She nodded, and they started down the path that led east of the house toward the creek, the reality of why she was really here at the forefront of his mind. Even with the idyllic scene of the red barn in the background and several horses in the corral, he couldn't ignore it. Someone had broken into her home, then tried to run her off the road. She needed answers and he was determined to get them for her.

"You were right. Will clearly stumbled onto something and didn't know what to do, but with no specifics, it's hard to know where to start. And just because he was tracking down some corruption doesn't mean he was killed over it."

"When I married Will, I thought I knew what I was getting into, but the reality is that you're never ready for long deployments and so many months apart," she said. "It was hard, but we were determined to make it work. In the back of my mind, I always knew that losing him was a possibility. What he did was dangerous, and I accepted that, but now... I guess having Mia makes me look at things differently. And this... I have no idea how to deal with this."

"There are a lot of things that you simply can't completely prepare yourself for."

Like losing someone you love.

"What did you think about the letters? What am I supposed to do?"

The phone he'd just given her back started dinging, and she pulled it out of her pocket to check her messages. A moment later, her face paled.

"Gabby...what's wrong?"

"It's a bunch of photos." Her voice broke as she spoke. "Liam..."

"Photos of what?"

She handed him the phone. There were half a dozen photos of her and Mia, snapped at several different locations. And after the photos was a chilling message.

We told you to stop asking questions. We know where you are. Don't go to the police. You will regret it.

THREE

Gabby spun around and started down the path back toward the house, her heart pounding. "I can't stay here. If they know where I am—"

"Wait a minute." Liam ran to catch up with her. "Look again at the photos. Where were these taken?"

"I don't know." She stopped, tears welling in her eyes as she pulled open the photos again. "In front of my house…the grocery store with Mia…getting into my car…it looks like the gym parking lot."

"They were following you. That is clear, but there are no photos of Timber Falls or the ranch."

Her brow narrowed in surprise. "You're right."

He took her hand and caught her gaze. "I think they're bluffing, because they don't know where you are. If they did, they'd show up here, not just send you photos."

"Maybe, but I still don't understand any of this." She worked to hold back the dam of tears about to break loose. "If they've been following me back home, why didn't they confront me then?"

"I don't know. Maybe they wanted to make sure

you knew something before they did anything. This all began after you started asking questions."

"Yes."

"So it makes sense that someone's trying to find out what you know. And in the process scaring you to make sure you don't go to the authorities."

"Well, I am scared." She could hear the panic in her own voice but at this point, she didn't care. "Will is dead, and I have a child to protect. If anything happens to Mia, I'll never forgive myself."

Liam pulled her against him. "Nothing's going to happen, Gabby. Not to Mia. Not to you. I won't let it."

She nestled her head into his shoulder as he wrapped his arms around her. There was something calming in the warmth of his embrace. Something that made her want to stay in this moment for as long as possible. She missed feeling secure and cherished. Missed having someone to face life with. A partner for her. A father for Mia. Not that she was looking for someone to take Will's place. She was just so tired of doing everything on her own.

"I'm sorry." She pulled away from him abruptly and wiped her eyes. "I didn't mean to fall apart like that."

"You have nothing to be sorry about. You've been through a lot this past year and a half, and none of it's been easy."

"No, it hasn't, but my losing it isn't going to help put an end to all of this."

She started back to the house beside him. "I called James Casada two days ago. He lives in a suburb of Denver. Will indicated he trusted him. I thought it would be a good idea to talk to him in person. Maybe he knows something."

Liam stopped on the path and turned to her. "Did you get ahold of him?"

"Yes. He was out of town but was flying back to Denver last night. He told me he'd be working at home all day if I wanted to come by. I almost forgot I'd thought about going to go see him this morning."

"What if he's somehow involved in this?"

"You read the letters. Will trusted him and believed he could help."

"Which is what scares me. Someone thinks you have answers, and if they intend to silence you…"

"The problem is I don't really know anything."

"Maybe not, but someone thinks you do."

"I've gone over this in my head a hundred times. But you were there with him, Liam. You had to have seen something."

"Will worked some with Casada. Always spoke highly of him. And as I already told you, Will seemed preoccupied, but you were pregnant, and I thought he was just ready to get home." Liam shoved his hands into his pockets. "Is there anything else from Will in your house that might have answers about what he was working on, or maybe something they were after?"

"Not that I know of. But he had to have discovered something. Maybe someone is simply trying to guarantee that whatever they're involved in doesn't get found out."

"Let me go talk with Casada alone," Liam said. "See if he knows anything. You can stay here with Mia. You'll be safe."

"I can't just hide." While a part of her wished she could let him do this for her, she knew it was something she needed to do. "I've come so far in my search for closure over Will's death, but this… I need to find out what's going on. I need to talk to him myself."

They walked down the path flanked by aspen trees with gold leaves shimmering in the morning breeze, and the mountains rising up beyond them. She wanted to enjoy the scenery. Wished she could see God's hand in her own life as much as she saw it in the beauty around her. But instead, everything that had happened had left her with far more questions than answers. About loss. About fear. About God.

"But that said, my concern is for Mia." She broke the silence between them. "I can't do anything to put her life at risk."

"My mom's already volunteered if you need someone to watch her. If you feel comfortable."

"I do, but—"

"She's safe here. I promise. My dad will be here. Plus, it's Griffin's day off. He's promised to come by again later today and check on things."

"Okay." She drew a deep breath, wishing she felt as courageous about going to see Casada as she hoped she sounded. "Liam…thank you, but I still feel bad about getting you involved in this."

He shoved his hands into his pockets. "I haven't done anything really. And if Will were in my place, he'd do the same thing."

"I know, and while you might not know it, you've done so much for me. The times you've called me. Coming to see me when you weren't in therapy. The gifts for Mia. I owe you a lot."

And that wasn't all she owed him for. Now she'd dragged him into a dangerous situation. One she had no idea how to get out of on her own.

A wave of guilt shot through him. She was wrong. He should have called her more often. Made more of an effort to ensure that she and Mia had everything they needed. He couldn't imagine how difficult it had been for her as a single mom. He knew she'd been surrounded by her parents and friends and church family. Somehow that had allowed him to justify the times he hadn't picked up the phone to make sure she was okay. It had let him justify the fact that he'd been too busy with physical therapy. Too busy trying to get his own life back on track. But those had only been excuses.

He stared out over the mountains as they walked. Despite his desire to help her, what he really wanted was to leave the past where it belonged. In the past. Because while he didn't know what it was like to lose a spouse, he did know what it was like to lose a fellow soldier and best friend.

Having Gabby here was forcing him to remember things better left forgotten. But the past wasn't something that would simply disappear. He'd have to face it head on if they wanted to figure out what was going on.

An hour later, they were saying goodbye to his mother and Mia. He watched as Gabby held her daughter and smothered her with kisses while the little girl laughed. He handed Mia her giraffe, surprised when she threw it back at him. He held it out to her and she squealed as she grabbed it from him.

Liam smiled and snatched it back from her chubby fingers.

Mia laughed and lunged for him.

He grabbed her, surprised that she'd come to him so willingly.

She poked at his face with her finger. He responded by giving her a raspberry on her neck.

"We're never going to get out of here if the two of you keep playing." Gabby's tone was firm, but he didn't miss the twinkle in her eye.

He handed Mia to his mother. "We'll be back soon."

"She'll be fine." His mom settled Mia in on her hip. "Liam's father is here, so between him and Griffin you have nothing to worry about."

"I know." Gabby gave her daughter one more kiss. "Thank you."

They headed out toward his truck, while he prayed he was making the right decision. Putting Gabby's life in jeopardy was the last thing he wanted to do. And yet, if they were going to figure out why she was a target, neither could they sit around and wait for the truth to emerge.

"Mia's adorable," he said, unlocking the vehicle and sliding into the driver's seat.

Gabby dropped her purse onto the floorboard, then buckled her seat belt. "She's the best thing that's happened to me. When I think I can't go on, she gives me a reason to get out of bed."

He glanced at her as he started down the narrow two-lane road toward town, suddenly wondering what it would be like to have a family of his own. Someone to share his life with. To laugh with. Someone who'd support him while he was deployed and be there for him when he returned.

He shoved away the random thoughts. Gabby was beautiful. There was no doubt about that. And he loved her passion and heart, but she was his best friend's wife. And even though Will was gone, there was way too much painful baggage between them to be anything more than simply friends. Still, something told him it would be far too easy for the lines of friendship and his concern for her to blur in his mind. Something he could never let happen.

"Do you remember anything more about James Casada?"

Gabby's question broke into his thoughts. "I wasn't around him much, but he always seemed honest and was a hard worker. I understand he was married at one time, but I believe his wife died a few years ago. That's part of the reason he was working overseas. He might have a couple adult children, but I'm not sure."

"Did you like him?"

"A lot of those contract guys are rough around the edges, but James was different. He seemed to be more like a…grandfather. Tough, but friendly, and he always had a story to share. He mainly worked in security for convoys that were carrying supplies between bases. A couple times, he was part of the detail that provided personal protection for the higher ups. And while he was six four and two-hundred-plus pounds, there was a gentleness to him that always took me off guard. I liked him. Everyone liked him as far as I know."

"Do you think Will would have wanted me to talk to him?"

"I don't know."

"But are we doing the right thing?"

He paused before answering her question. "What other choice do we have?"

Just over an hour and a half later, Liam pulled in front of the house where James Casada lived. He'd enjoyed the drive through the mountains with Gabby, and the time to reconnect. But that's all this was. A couple of friends catching up. They'd talked about Will, he'd answered her questions about his rehabilitation and laughed at her stories about Mia, and he'd found himself surprised by how comfortable he felt with her. How much he enjoyed being around her.

"You ready for this?" He turned off the motor, then glanced at her.

"Yeah." She tugged on the end of her ponytail and nodded. "Let's go."

The yard in front of the one-story house had low maintenance ground cover and a few woody shrubs. Gabby rang the doorbell, then pulled her coat tighter around her. The sun was out, but the temperature had yet to climb out of the mid-thirties. A few seconds later, she rang the bell again.

"That's strange. He said he'd be here."

Liam glanced around the front of the house. There was no car in the drive, but Casada probably would have parked inside the garage. Nothing seemed off or out of place, but that didn't erase the uneasiness he felt. If the man knew something, he was a potential target as well.

"Mr. Casada?" Gabby tried the handle. "Liam, the door's open. Something's wrong."

He took a step forward. "Stay here."

"Liam—"

He squeezed her hand, then slowly opened the door. "James? Is everything okay? It's Liam O'Callaghan."

No answer.

Something was definitely wrong.

"If my phone was tapped. If they knew I was coming…"

A second later, Liam caught movement and turned. A figure rushed at him from behind the front door, slamming something into the back of his head. Stars exploding behind his eyes, he pivoted and swung at his attacker. But he couldn't fight the darkness sweeping through him as he collapsed onto the floor.

FOUR

Gabby heard her own scream as Liam slumped to the ground, but she couldn't move. A second armed man grabbed her, pinning her arms tightly behind her and pulling her backward toward the wall. She squirmed, trying desperately to get away, but his iron grip only tightened against her flesh.

A wave of nausea flooded through her. She glanced up at her attacker, and time seemed to momentarily freeze. Even with his ski mask, she could see his piercing brown eyes and the spiderweb tattoo on the side of his neck…

"You're such a fool." She could feel his breath against her ear as he spoke to her. "We already told you you'd regret nosing into something that's none of your business."

A shiver of terror coursed through her at his words. She'd ended up doing exactly what she'd promised herself she wouldn't do. Will had been a born warrior, sworn to obey and protect his country, and in the end, it had gotten him killed. What if coming here ended up putting her or her daughter in further danger? If these men had their way, the same thing was going to happen to her and Liam.

Her attacker gripped both her shoulders. "What do we do with them? If they really do have evidence—"

"She wouldn't be here if she'd found it."

"Maybe not, but this is going to lead back to us. That was never the plan."

Liam groaned on the floor as he struggled to get up. Sirens wailed in the background, shifting her gaze to the front window. Her attacker loosened his grip slightly at the distraction. She stomped on his foot with her boot, managed to jerk one arm away, then grabbed the lamp sitting on the end table beside her.

"Gabby!" Liam shouted her name. "Run."

Swinging with all her might, she slammed the lamp into her attacker's head. Glass shattered. Her attacker groaned, then stumbled backward, giving her the second she needed to pull away from him. She ran across the living room toward the one unblocked exit that she assumed led to the kitchen. She and Liam had no advantage against bullets. And she had no doubt the men intended to shoot them, which was probably what they'd done to Casada.

"We need to go," one of them shouted. "Now."

She stopped at the edge of the hardwood floor of the kitchen, then stumbled backward. James Casada lay still on the floor, eyes open and a gunshot wound through his forehead, blood trickling down the side of his face. But there wasn't time for regrets or grief. She glanced around the room for a cell phone.

A door slammed open, hitting the wall, and she spun around as Liam stepped into the room.

"Gabby…they're gone." Liam ran toward her. "Are you okay?"

"Yes, but…"

"Looks like they decided to cut their losses and run when they heard the sirens. And at least one of them will be leaving with a pretty good shiner."

She nodded, barely hearing him. Her legs were shaking. She felt as if she were going to throw up. How had this happened?

"He's dead." She turned back to Casada. "What if they come back?"

His hand squeezed her shoulder. "Are you okay?"

"No. They killed him." She pressed her hand against her mouth, biting back the bile. While Liam and Will had seen the terrors of war, the only dead bodies she'd ever seen had been faked on television, and even that was something she preferred to avoid. Give her a sappy romance movie any day over a cop show and reality TV. "They could have killed you…"

She fought to take in a deep breath, but the air wouldn't fill her lungs. She was responsible for this. If she'd never called Casada, never tried to involve him, he'd still be alive. And now she'd risked Liam's life on top of everything else.

"Gabby, the police are going to be here any moment now."

She looked up at him, her eyes wet with tears. "And you're bleeding."

He reached up and touched the side of his face. "It's nothing. I'll be fine."

Maybe he would, but she didn't think she'd ever be

okay again. She needed to do something to fix everything that had just happened.

"Wait…" She grabbed a paper towel from the roll sitting on the counter, wet it at the sink, then started to dab at the blood, still unsure where the blood was coming from.

He took her hand to stop her. "I'm fine. We need to go out there now. Because while I'm not sure how we're going to explain what we're doing here, I'd rather not get caught hovering over a dead body."

She glanced toward the front entrance. Car doors slammed. The police were here now, which meant they were finally safe. But if that was true, why did she feel so terrified? She dropped the paper towel into the trash, then followed Liam out the front door.

Officers were surrounding the house, their weapons drawn.

"Let me see your hands," one of the officers shouted at them. "Both of you. Now."

She raised her hands in the air, praying her legs wouldn't give out and willing her heart to stop racing. Her mind wanted to pray. To beg God to put an end to this, so she could go back to taking care of her little girl. But her heart wasn't sure He'd listen to her after all this time.

Two uniformed officers patted them down, searching for weapons, then combed through her bag.

"Let me see your ID."

Gabby slowly pulled her driver's license out of her wallet, then handed it to the officer.

"Liam O'Callaghan and Gabby Kensington." The officer turned to Liam. "You're military?"

"Captain Liam O'Callaghan. US Army."

"We received a 911 call that there had been gunshots coming from this house."

Liam nodded. "We came to visit the man who lives here. James Casada. I met him when I was deployed in the Middle East. Two men were here in the house when we arrived. The door was open, so we went in, but he was already dead. The men fled when they heard your sirens."

A female officer approached them. "Their story fits. The neighbor across the street told 911 a couple matching their description showed up after she heard a gunshot and called 911. Said she was still on the phone with the operator when she saw two masked men escape down the street right before we showed up."

"Cordon off the house and get a BOLO out on the suspects. Turner and Sterling, go interview the neighbors." He turned back to them. "I'm Lieutenant Baxter with DPD. What can you tell us about the intruders?"

Liam shook his head. "Nothing as far as facial features. They both wore black ski masks. But I can give you a description of their clothes."

The lieutenant pulled out a notepad and pen.

"One wore khaki pants, a gray T-shirt and gray tennis shoes. The other one wore jeans and a black jean jacket and cowboy boots."

Gabby was amazed he remembered anything. In the middle of the attack, her mind had frozen and now any details she'd seen had vanished.

"Did you have physical contact with the men?"

Liam reached up and touched his face. "One of them

hit me with something from behind before we even knew anyone was in the house."

"The paramedics just pulled up. I want you both checked out to ensure you're okay, then we're going to need a full statement from each of you."

A minute later, Gabby was answering questions from a paramedic, wondering how she'd managed having to be checked out by medical personnel twice in two days. "Miss Kensington? Does anything hurt?"

"I'll probably have a few bruises on my arms where he grabbed me, but that's all. I'm fine. Really."

Physically, at least. Emotionally was a whole different matter. She tried to concentrate as they ran through their list of questions and focused on her answers, but she couldn't settle her mind. These were no idle threats. Yesterday's accident made that clear. But did that mean they'd stumbled across the people who'd killed Will?

"Looks like you're okay, but it's probably a good idea to go to your own doctor for a thorough check-up, and if you need to talk to someone about what happened—"

"I will. Thank you."

She nodded. All she wanted to do was to get away from all of this and get back to the ranch and Mia. She sat on the curb outside Casada's house, her hands still shaking while the paramedics finished looking over Liam.

Everything seemed to move in slow motion around her. An officer yelled something across the front lawn. They were searching the house, trying to find the motivation behind what was going on. She pulled her phone out, needing to make sure Mia was okay, and called the number she'd programed into her phone for Liam's mom.

She let it ring until it switched to voice mail. "Marci…it's Gabby. I just needed to check on Mia and make sure everything is okay there. We've run into a bit of a snag on this end, so we might be gone longer than we planned. Just…just call me when you get this please."

She hung up, trying to convince herself there was nothing to worry about. Mia was fine. Glitches in cell phone service were common. Liam had told her that. If they'd gone for a walk or a drive, they wouldn't get her call. Which was okay. Liam's dad was there; plus, his brother Griffin had promised to stop by. And from what she knew about his family, you couldn't ask for better protection for her daughter.

She was just getting ready to try calling again when Liam climbed down from the back of the ambulance and joined her on the curb.

"You okay?" she asked.

"I've got a bit of a headache, but thankfully there's no need for stitches. What about you?"

"I'm fine, too."

"You don't sound okay."

She shot him a half smile. "You're the one with a goose egg on your head."

"I'm supposed to watch for any symptoms that might pop up, but they don't think it's a concussion. Just a nasty bump."

"I tried calling your mother but couldn't get through."

A flicker of concern registered in his eyes as he

pulled out his phone. "I'm sure it's nothing. Signal out there can be spotty."

"I know."

"I'll give Griffin a call. Make sure the sheriff's office knows what happened here."

She grabbed the edge of Liam's sleeve, her adrenaline still racing, and leaned toward him. "But we can't tell them the real reason we're here. Not yet. This wasn't over. The text earlier told me not to talk to the police."

We know where you are.

Stop asking questions.

Don't go to the police.

You will regret it.

It was going to be a long time before she could forget the threats. A long time before she didn't see Casada's lifeless face staring up at her. All she cared about right now was protecting her child, and if it meant not telling the police everything, then it would have to be that way. Because she wasn't taking any chances.

Liam hesitated as he tried to form a response. While he understood her fears, figuring all this out on their own was no longer an option in his opinion. "I don't think we have a choice, Gabby. We need help to figure out what's going on. The authorities have the resources—"

"You're wrong. They threatened me again. In the house. Threatened Mia. I can't let them hurt her. Please. They said no cops, and if we go in there and tell those officers what happened I have no doubt that they'll follow through. The only reason we're alive right now is because a neighbor called 911 and spooked them, but this is far from over."

Which was exactly what had him worried.

"Then what are we supposed to tell the police?" he asked.

"Only what we have to. Casada was a friend of yours. We came by to visit him. That's all they need to know at this point. I want to keep Will out of this."

"And the fact that Casada's lying in the house with a gunshot wound to his head? How do we explain that? They're not going to just believe that our showing up when we did was a coincidence any more than I do."

"We came here to visit him, and he was already dead. Which they know. We were just paying an old friend a visit. There doesn't have to be anything more to our story."

Liam stared at his phone. "We need to find out the truth, Gabby, and I'm pretty sure that withholding evidence isn't the right way. How are we supposed to do this on our own? We don't even know what those men are looking for. And until we figure things out, you and Mia won't be safe."

"These people don't play games. We've both seen that firsthand now."

"All the more reason to tell the police what's going on. They need to know you've been threatened. You don't have to tell them everything, but we need to let them help us figure out what's going on."

She shook her head. "The men were searching the house."

"I know."

"They won't stop until they have what they want.

Until they ensure there is no one left to spill their secrets."

"I'll make a deal with you. We leave out Will's connection, for now, but you let me keep Griffin in the loop and see what he can find out. Quietly."

She hesitated before giving him an answer. "I'm not sure we should. Not yet."

"If you change your mind?"

"I'll tell you."

An hour later, they finished talking with the police. Gabby was exhausted. He could tell by the look in her eyes. He needed to get her back to the ranch where she could take a nap.

"We appreciate your cooperation in this matter," the lieutenant said. "We have your contact information and we will be in touch in case we end up with any more questions. All we need now is a signature on your statements and for you to double check that your contact information is correct."

Liam signed his name, then slid the paper back across the table to the officer. He hadn't lied. The only thing he hadn't mentioned was the threats Gabby had received and the possible connection to Will's death. He led Gabby outside to where his truck was parked, staying silent until they got into the vehicle.

She slid on her seat belt. "Thank you."

"I'm still not sure we did the right thing."

"They know enough. But there's something else I'm worried about. I've tried calling your mother three times now and no one answers. What about Griffin?"

He hesitated, knowing she wasn't going to like his answer. "I haven't got ahold of him yet, but I reached out to the Timber Falls sheriff's office. They said he was out on a call, and they'd have him get back to me as soon as possible."

He was positive it was nothing, but he wasn't sure she'd believe the same. She was scared and had every right to feel that way.

She was quiet as they took the highway south and headed out of Denver. He tried asking a few questions but finally gave up, realizing she wasn't in the mood for small talk. Instead, he used the scenic drive to come up with his own plan. He understood her fear of telling the authorities what was going on, but they needed help. Griffin could discreetly use his resources and try to find out about the men who'd attacked them, as well as James Casada.

"How's your headache?" she asked, breaking the silence between them.

"Better, thanks. Pretty much gone, in fact."

"I'm glad."

"Me, too." He glanced at her profile, wishing he could fix everything for her. "Gabby, what happened this morning was traumatic, and it's okay to feel scared."

"I know. I guess… I'm just more worried about Mia right now. She's totally dependent on me and yet I feel so helpless. Like there's nothing I can do to stop this. And that's what I'm supposed to do."

He knew that what had happened today had to have brought up a surge of emotions about losing Will. She was strong, but everyone had a breaking point. A place where they needed someone else to step in and help pick up the slack. But she also had a stubborn streak. Maybe that was a part of being a single mom when everything automatically fell on her. It had been a long time since she'd had someone to care for her and protect her. Which was exactly what he intended to do.

"I'd still like to read Griffin in on what's going on. Let him discreetly use the department's resources to see if he can find out who's behind this and keep us updated on the police investigation into Casada's murder."

He glanced at her, trying to gauge her reaction, but he couldn't tell what she was thinking. "Gabby?"

She nodded. "Okay. But only him for the moment."

"Agreed."

Liam's phone rang, and he pushed the answer button on the steering wheel.

"Mom?"

"I saw I missed a couple calls from you and Gabby."

"Yeah. We've been trying to get ahold of you."

"I'm sorry. We're fine. Your father needed to check on a couple fences, so we decided to take Mia with us. She loves the truck. I hope the two of you weren't worried."

"As long as you're all okay, that's all that matters. We're headed back to the ranch now, actually. I've got the call on Speaker."

"I just listened to your voice message, Gabby. What's going on?"

"We'll fill you in on everything once we get back to the ranch, but we're okay."

His mother had come to terms over the years with the fact that she had four adult sons who all had dangerous jobs. But he knew for a fact, as much as she tried to hide it, that it didn't mean she didn't worry. And she spent a lot of time on her knees in prayer.

"What about Griffin?" Liam asked. "Have you seen him? I've been trying to get ahold of him as well."

"He was out at the ranch with us until about an hour ago. He had to go out on a call."

"Okay. We'll meet you at the house shortly."

He hung up the call, then reached out and squeezed Gabby's hand. "Relieved?"

"Very."

"But?"

She let out a low laugh. "How did you know there was going to be a *but*?"

"Just a guess."

"I know I shouldn't let my mind automatically go to the worst-case scenario, but it's hard not to worry and question. Especially after all that's happened. I feel like I'm waiting for the next catastrophe to hit, and then praying I can deal with it." She stared out the window at the mountains in the distance. "Do you believe in prayer?"

"I do. I've seen enough horror in my life to know that without my faith I couldn't go on. But I've also learned that there are times when we feel like we're in the wilderness. When God's presence seems far away."

"And what happens when you can't find your way back? I believe God is out there. Know He still cares, but I've had a hard time praying these past few months."

"I've been exactly where you are and still too many times find myself there again. But Gabby, He's not out there, watching down on you from above. He wants His presence to be in you. Constantly with you. Even when things hurt the most. Maybe especially when things hurt the most."

The phone rang again, interrupting their conversation as Griffin's name showed up on the caller ID.

"It's my brother, but I'd like to continue this conversation."

She nodded as he picked up the call.

"Griffin? What's going on?"

"Sorry I missed you. Where are you?"

"Almost to Timber Falls, headed back to the ranch," Liam said, quickly filling him in on what had just happened.

"I hate to throw another wrench into the works," Griffin said, "but I need you to stop by town on your way. I've got some new information you're going to want to hear."

FIVE

Gabby stared across the sleepy diner on the outskirts of Timber Falls. At almost half past one, the lunch crowd had already headed back to work, leaving half a dozen empty tables.

Liam had tried to get her to order something, but she knew she couldn't eat despite the menu boasting comfort food. Her stomach was still tied up in knots, her adrenaline still racing. Even knowing that Mia was safe, and that Liam was determined not to let anything happen to either of them, she couldn't shake the lingering terror. It was the unknown that scared her the most. Not knowing who was behind this. Not knowing when or if they were going to strike, and how far they were willing to go. Becoming a single mom had changed the way she looked at everything. And it made it hard to let someone else in.

"Are you still okay with meeting with my brother?" He picked up one of the cheese sticks he'd ordered.

She glanced at the door. "I want to get back to Mia as soon as possible, but I'm just as anxious as you are to find out what he knows."

"You can trust him."

"I know. I just…" She took a sip of the hot tea she'd ordered, hoping the drink would calm her nerves. "There is something that's bothering me."

"What's that?"

"Why didn't they just shoot us like they did Casada? They had every advantage. We were unarmed and they both had guns. And they certainly had the opportunity."

"To be honest, I thought the same thing, but I don't know."

"I get that they were spooked, but why run knowing we were probably going to end up talking to the police. Aren't we a liability?"

"They were masked, so they knew we couldn't identify them, and I'm also guessing they could be working for someone else. And here's another thing to throw into the mix." Liam wrapped his hands around his coffee mug. "I'm not a police detective, but what if they hadn't intended to kill Casada."

"What do you mean?"

"It seems to fit with their behavior. There was an unopened box of donuts on the counter next to a set of car keys. They would have known Casada was home. Maybe their plan was to scare him into not talking to you, but then things went south when Casada fought back."

"That makes sense. I thought they could only track my location, but they had to know I was going to be there this morning."

"It's possible they were able to monitor your conversation and knew you were coming," Liam said.

She worked to put the pieces of the puzzle together

in her own mind. "What about Will's death? How does it fit in then?"

"We still can't be sure at this point if his death was planned or simply an accident."

She jumped as the bell on the front door rang and a couple walked in. She shook her head. "Sorry."

He smiled at her. "For what?"

She held out her hands above the table. "I'm still shaking and jumping at every noise. My heart is racing and I... I just want this to be over."

"I know." He reached out and took her hands. "You're not the only one caught off balance. I might be military trained, but that doesn't mean this situation doesn't rattle me, too. The only thing I could think about was getting you out of there alive."

"I did. We both did."

The door jingled again, and this time she managed not to jump. Griffin stepped into the diner, but today he wasn't wearing his uniform. Instead, he had on jeans, a plaid shirt, and a tan jacket and boots, looking almost as handsome as Liam. And making her wonder why none of the O'Callaghan brothers had married. It was something she just might have to ask Liam if the subject ever came up.

Griffin slid into the booth where they sat in the back of the diner. "Are you two okay?"

"We are. And thanks for meeting us here and not at the station," Liam said.

"No problem." He glanced at Liam's appetizer plate.

Liam nodded at his brother. "Help yourself."

"Thanks, but I think I'll order something as well. I was planning to eat lunch at the ranch, but I got called out." He signaled the waitress and asked for a burger and fries.

Gabby just wanted to get to the point. "I'm assuming you found out something about my accident."

"I did, actually. But I'm not sure what to make of it."

"What do you mean?"

Griffin pulled a small plastic bag out of his pocket and laid it on the table.

"What is it?" Liam asked.

"It's a tracking device."

"Wait a minute… Where did you find it?" Gabby asked.

"On your car. I'm actually surprised we found it—it's so small—but the problem is this isn't some run-of-the-mill tracker you can buy off the internet. This one is military grade."

"They bugged my phone and my car?"

"I had our IT guy disable it, but yes." Griffin leaned forward. "You know I want to help, but I'm going to need to make sure I know everything that's going on."

Gabby glanced at Liam who nodded at her. He'd been right about one thing. She had to trust someone. "Besides the accident on the road coming here, there have been threats, both toward me and my daughter. I've been told not to go to the authorities."

"What do they want?"

"It started with a threatening text, then I showed up at my house yesterday and it had been trashed."

"What do you think they were looking for?"

"Evidence. Will had been following a paper trail of some contractors he believed were defrauding the government."

"Have you seen the evidence?"

"No. Which is part of the problem. If Will did have evidence, I have no idea where it is."

"And yet someone believes she has it," Liam said.

"So, yesterday they run you off the road, because they were trying to scare you into giving it to them?" Griffin asked.

"That's my best guess."

"Tell me more about what happened in Denver?" Griffin asked, salting his fries. "How does your visit play into all of this?"

"We went to see a man by the name of James Casada," Liam said. "He worked with Will, and we believe he was someone Will trusted. His name was mentioned in one of Will's letters to Gabby. We were hoping he might have some information that would help."

"Did he?"

"When we got there, he'd been shot and the two men who killed him were in the house."

"I guess that would explain the knot on your head?"

Liam nodded. "You should see the other guy. He's got quite a shiner."

Griffin grabbed for a fry, then stopped. "If they were armed, how did you get away?"

"A neighbor called 911 after the first shots. The two guys ran as soon as they heard the sirens."

"Can you identify the men?"

"They were both wearing ski masks, so not their faces. I did give a description of their clothes to the officers, but that's all we've got."

"It's a start. What about you, Gabby? Did you notice anything?"

She waited to answer until after their waitress set down Griffin's burger and fries, and they reassured the woman they didn't need anything else.

"I wish I could remember something, but everything happened so fast."

"That's okay. You'd be surprised how many witnesses don't remember details after a trauma like that," Griffin said. "The only other new information I've got right now is the statement of a couple who saw the accident and called it in. While they didn't get a good look at the man in the vehicle, they did manage to get the model and color, along with a partial license plate, which we were able to track down."

"Did you identify the driver?" Liam asked.

"The car was stolen two nights ago."

"So another dead end."

"Unfortunately, yes."

"There's something else. It's just a theory, but what if their intentions weren't to kill Casada," Liam said, "but just to scare him, ensuring he didn't talk to Gabby?"

"And things got out of hand."

"Exactly," Liam said. "Their plan has definitely been to scare Gabby."

"And if they're convinced you have it, then they're going to want to make sure you are alive."

"I want to speak to the sheriff and get his opinion," Griffin said. "We'll keep this quiet, and I'll leave out the connection with your husband's death for now, but at some point it's going to come up."

Gabby nodded. "I just want to keep my daughter safe. That's all that matters."

Liam nodded. "And that's exactly what we're going to do."

"Why don't the two of you head back to the ranch now," Griffin said, sliding out of his seat. "And in the meantime, I'll see what I can do from this end."

"I know you're ready to get back to active duty, but do you know how much I'm enjoying having boots in the house?"

Liam glanced past his mom at the row of shoes lined up in the mudroom adjoining the kitchen, including his army boots, then smiled back at her. The house still smelled like cookies and hot chocolate like when he was a kid, and he was certain his mom hadn't aged a day. It had been the perfect place for four boys to grow up. The perfect childhood.

"Even though I'm anxious to go back," Liam said, dropping the dish towel onto the rack, "I've enjoyed every minute back on the ranch with you and Dad."

"A mother always knows that one day her children are going to fly the nest, but as proud of each one of you as I am, I can't help but wish every now and then that you had boring desk jobs that didn't include risking your lives."

He gave his mom a hug. "You raised us well and deserve some of the credit. Don't forget that."

"Oh, I take all of the credit." She laughed, then her gaze shifted to the staircase. "How is Gabby doing?"

"Okay, I think. I was just going to go check on her. I've been waiting, hoping she finally fell asleep. She's exhausted."

"Why don't you take her a few of these oatmeal cookies in case she hasn't fallen asleep yet." She grabbed a small plate from the cupboard, then started filling it with a few cookies from the cooling rack. "I made them for your father for after dinner, but he won't mind sharing. I don't think she ever ate lunch."

"As long as he won't mind sharing with me, too." Liam grabbed one and took a bite.

"Tell her I'll have dinner ready about six-thirty. Chili and corn bread." She shot him a wide grin. "Which means you'd better not spoil your dinner."

"Don't worry, I'll have room for both."

"You know, Liam…"

He waited for his mother to continue.

"She's the kind of girl I always pictured for you. She's pretty, smart and that baby of hers… Well, I'm a bit smitten. I'd forgotten how wonderful it was to have a baby in the house. It's been so long."

Liam frowned. "Let's not go there, Mom. Please."

"In case you forgot, I'm your mom and I can go anywhere I please."

He glanced at the bar stool. "Do I need to sit down for this conversation?"

"Funny. All I'm saying is that I'd like a grandchild or two, and don't think that's asking too much."

"In case *you've* forgotten, I'm the baby of the family with three older and very eligible brothers. Why don't you go talk to them?"

"Who are, unfortunately, at the moment all very single."

"That's not my fault."

"Of course not, but there's a beautiful young woman upstairs who thinks the world of you. And as for you…

You feel something toward her, don't you? There's this something in your eyes when you look at her."

"There's nothing in my eyes, Mom. She's my best friend's wife. I'm worried and plan to ensure nothing happens to her, but that's it."

"She *was* your best friend's wife. Second love can be just as beautiful if you give your heart a chance."

If he were honest, he wasn't sure why none of the O'Callaghan brothers had tied the knot. It wasn't as if they hadn't come close. Caden had been engaged a few years ago, and at one time Liam had thought Reid would get married, but so far none of them had made it to the altar. A fact their mother was always quick to point out.

"Liam…you okay?"

"Yeah." He leaned down and kissed his mom on the forehead before grabbing the plate of cookies. "I'm going to check on her and, in the meantime, forget we had this conversation."

"Do what you want, but remember I want to enjoy my grandchildren while I'm still young."

He chuckled as he headed up the stairs.

Gabby's door was open, and she was sitting next to the bed in an overstuffed chair reading. He leaned against the door frame. "Hey…sorry to bother you. Is Mia finally sleeping?"

"Hey…yeah. She must have been completely wound up to where she couldn't settle down, but she finally crashed about fifteen minutes ago."

"Sounds like she had a good time with my mom and dad."

"She did. Your parents are amazing with her."

"I'd say it's the other way around. She has them

wrapped around her finger. But you should take a nap as well. It's still early."

"I thought about it but I'm worried I wouldn't be able to sleep tonight."

He glanced down at the plate he was carrying. "Mom wanted me to bring you some of her homemade cookies. She's making chili for dinner, but we won't eat for a couple hours."

She folded her arms across her chest. "You and your family have done so much for me. I hope you know how grateful I am."

There were a couple bags he hadn't noticed at first lined up at the edge of the bed. Mia's diaper bag, Gabby's purse, the leather satchel. "Looks like you're going somewhere."

"Griffin told me my car had been checked over and it's drivable." She walked across the room. "I know you're not going to like this, but I've made a decision. Mia and I are leaving first thing in the morning."

"Wait a minute... Do you really think that's a good idea?"

"Talking with Griffin just confirmed how I've been feeling. Besides the fact that there are things I need from my house, you've done enough for me, and I can't ask you to fix this."

"In case you forgot, I'm already involved. And I have no intention of just walking away. We can always send someone to get whatever you need."

"I can't risk you and your family's lives. This isn't your battle."

He motioned for her to follow him out of the room, worried about waking the baby, then sat down in the sitting room in front of the large window overlooking the mountains. "I'm sorry, but your leaving isn't an option. Until we figure out what those guys are after, it's not safe for you to leave."

She sat down next to him on the edge of the seat. "I've got some money saved away. I can go—"

"Go where? Maybe this isn't any of my business, but you need to involve someone in this. You don't want the authorities to know about the connection to Will, and that I get, but don't push me away."

Her gaze dropped. "I can't stay."

"Gabby, stop. Please. You're not making any sense. I can't let you leave."

"Can't or won't? This isn't your battle to fight. I never should have involved you in this."

He tried to curb his frustration. "You're wrong, and you're being ridiculous."

Her eyes widened. "Ridiculous?"

"Will was my friend. I should have seen that something was going on, but I didn't. Don't you understand that I want resolution for this as much as you do?"

"It doesn't matter. I've made my decision."

"You're being stubborn. I know when Will died, you took on a heavy load. You were suddenly a single mom with bills to pay and a daughter to care for. But as strong as you are, you're not thinking straight. You can't live on the run. Where are you going to go?"

"I don't know. I don't want to involve my parents, but as long as I have a computer and an internet connection, I can work anywhere. I'll figure it out."

"Don't do this, Gabby."

She shook her head. "You don't understand. No matter how hard I tried to prepare myself, when those officers came to my door and told me that Will was dead, it was like my world ended. I felt that everything we'd dreamed of together was gone. And now, just when I finally feel as if I'm escaping the fog, someone's threatening my daughter. I can't just sit here and wait for things to be resolved."

He ran his hand down her arm, searching for the words to convince her she had to stay. "We're not just going to sit here. We're going to figure out who these guys are. And we're going to find out what Will died for."

Silence hung between them as she blinked back the tears.

"Please stay," he said. "I'm asking you to stay and let me help. You don't have to do this alone."

Her shoulders dropped as if she were starting to give in. "I feel like I've been doing this alone for a long time. Living on my own. Making my own decisions. Fixing my own problems."

"What about your church family? Have they been there for you?"

"They have. Especially at the beginning, but you know how it goes. Time passes. I'm no longer a couple, and it's harder to fit in now. People moved on. And I can't really blame them. They have their own lives to lead."

"I know Will struggled with his faith at times," Liam said. "He was strong, but you were always his anchor. Spiritually. Emotionally."

The tears started to fall, making him hate to see her hurt like this.

"I've tried not to let it happen," she said, "but when Will died, I felt so alone. I never blamed God, not really, but somehow in the process I just…stopped praying. Stopped feeling His presence. And while I've made progress, I feel like I'm getting pushed back into that place again where I don't want to go."

"Then don't, Gabby. Stay here with my family. You need to be surrounded by people who care about you. Not running. And what about Mia? If you want to protect her, you certainly don't need to be on your own."

She glanced out the window at the cloudless sky. "I'm sorry."

"For what?" he asked. "For feeling? For caring? Don't try to close yourself off."

"I just… I don't know how to do this."

"I know I can't understand what it's like to lose a spouse. But I lost a friend…and I still might have lost a career. I know what it's like to feel helpless and uncertain."

She grabbed a tissue from the coffee table next to her and blew her nose. "Maybe we do need each other."

"I think you're right." He smiled, trying to ignore the stirring of his heart, as he had ever since she'd shown up. "Don't make any decisions now. I promise everything will seem better tomorrow. Okay?"

She looked up at him with those big dark eyes of hers, pulling his heart toward a place he wasn't ready to go.

"Okay."

"Just promise me you'll stay here for now."

She reached up and grasped his hand, letting him

pull her up. Sunlight streamed across the shimmering aspen trees in the distance. "It's beautiful, isn't it?"

"Stunning."

"When I'm looking out there, I know God's here," she said. "I can feel His presence. I just have to find a way to completely trust Him."

He brushed her hair behind her shoulder. "Promise you won't go running off in the night?"

She nodded. "I promise."

SIX

Gabby watched Mia squeal as she grabbed the last piece of banana off the high-chair tray. "Do you want some more banana?"

Mia gave her one big nod. "Peez."

Gabby laughed.

Liam grabbed another banana from the counter, then crouched down in front of Mia. "Aren't you getting sleepy?"

She shook her head at him.

"Of course not."

"She took a long nap. Maybe too long," Gabby said.

Liam's father Jacob stepped into the room with a big grin on his face. "And perhaps she's a bit spoiled by my wife."

"You can blame me." Marci grabbed a cookie from the plate at the center of the table. "But since my darling boys have yet to give me grandbabies, I claim my right to enjoy Mia while she's here. As you can see, I've even kept in storage the high chair, crib and a few toys from when my boys were little, simply in anticipation of those grandbabies."

"I know my parents would agree with you. They love being grandparents," Gabby said.

Liam laughed. "Please don't get her started."

The back door opened. "Anyone home?"

"Griffin, Caden… I was hoping you boys would make it. There's chili on the stove if you're hungry."

"I'd love some, actually." Griffin glanced at Gabby. "How are you doing?"

"I'm good. Especially with all your mom's cooking."

"You really know how to win extra brownie points with my wife, though no one would argue with you." Jacob grabbed a couple more chairs for the brothers. "Why do you think I've gained forty pounds over the course of our marriage?"

Marci winked at him. "You're as fit as the day I met you, and twice as handsome."

"Just a bit more of me to love now, but talk about brownie points."

"You remember Caden, don't you, Gabby?" Liam pointed to his brother as he sat down in one of the chairs.

"Yes. It's good to see you again."

"It is," Caden said, "though from the little I've heard from Griffin, this hasn't exactly been a restful visit."

"No, it hasn't," Gabby said. "Any news?"

"There is, actually," Griffin said. "I've been in contact with the authorities in Denver."

"And…"

"They told me that Casada died instantly from the gunshot. And they found a second gun and a second bullet in the wall."

Gabby glanced at Griffin. "What does that mean?"

"They think Casada shot at the intruders but missed. And here's something else." He thanked his mom for the bowl of chili, then slid into the empty chair. "We were able to identify the men who ran you off the road."

"How did you do that?" Gabby asked.

"We have a new program in the county where we encourage residents and businesses to register any security systems that record public areas. It enables us to quickly access camera footage that might in turn give us information on crimes. There was a gas station camera that caught footage of them in the stolen vehicle."

"Who are they?"

"Kyle Thatcher and Silas Maldin. We don't know anything about Maldin at the moment, but Thatcher has been in and out of jail, always on small-time stuff. He was discharged from the army about three years ago. I'm still waiting for those records."

"Sounds like an all-around good guy," Liam said. "Have you found either of them?"

"Not yet, but we will." Griffin pulled up a photo on his phone, then set it in front of them. "Do either of them look familiar?"

"Wait a minute. Maybe." Gabby picked up the phone. A memory surfaced. "What's that on his neck?"

"It's a tattoo. That's Thatcher."

"That's the guy that pinned back my arms inside Casada's house. I'm sure of it. I couldn't remember any details when we talked to the police, but he had that same tattoo."

Griffin nodded. "That's good. Very good. Because that means we can definitely connect the two cases. We've got a BOLO out for him. We'll find him."

Liam grabbed another slice of corn bread and started buttering it. "There's got to be a connection between the army and the tracking device."

"Agreed," Griffin said.

"Gabby asked me to read through Will's letters," Liam said, "to see if there's something I might be able to find that she missed. I've started reading them again and taking notes. Everything that might be related to what he was looking into. If it's alright with Gabby, I'll email you my notes on what might be relevant."

Gabby nodded. "That's fine with me."

"I think that's a good idea," Griffin said. "And in the meantime, I'll do some more digging into Kyle Thatcher and his connection to all of this while we try to find out something about Maldin."

Their voices faded as they discussed the situation. She'd never imagined things could have progressed this far. A man dead. Someone threatening her and her daughter.

She suddenly felt hot. Memories she'd managed to suppress over the past few months engulfed her. Memories she didn't want to relive. The knock on the door to inform her Will was dead. His funeral. And then today, Casada's dead body on the kitchen floor.

Mia started fussing. Gabby handed her another piece of banana, but she couldn't think. Couldn't breathe. She needed some air.

She rested her hand on Marci's shoulder. "Would you mind watching Mia for a minute? I'll be right back."

"Of course. Are you okay?"

"Yeah. I'm fine."

She hurried outside onto the front porch, then immediately wished she'd thought to grab her coat. But she couldn't go back inside. Not yet. Instead, she braced her hands against the railing and stared out across the shadowy outlines of the ranch and the canopy of stars above her.

"I know You're there, God, and I really want to trust You."

She prayed out loud, hoping that would somehow make God hear her better. Which seemed foolish. If God could create the stars and the mountain ranges surrounding her, did she really doubt He could hear her small voice?

She bit back the tears. "I want my faith to be strong like it used to be. Strong enough that it's isn't choked out by fear and anxiety. But sometimes it's just so hard. Sometimes I just don't know how."

The screen door squeaked open.

"Hey…" Liam walked up beside her. "Are you okay? My family can get a bit rambunctious, which can be overwhelming if you're not used to it."

"It's not them. Really. And I'm the one who's sorry." She wiped away a tear and forced a smile. "I shouldn't have run out like that but hearing you all talking about Will… It all just dragged up a lot of memories I thought I was finally coming to peace with."

"I never meant to be insensitive." He grabbed a blanket from one of the chairs and set it around her shoulders. "None of us did."

"You're not. I promise."

She caught his profile in the soft light, surprised at how quickly he'd become an anchor in her life. He'd always been there for her, but from afar. Now he was here, with her. A place of calm and refuge in the middle of the storm. Something she'd been looking for without even knowing it was what she needed.

She lowered her gaze. "And you were right about something."

"What's that?"

"I've spent so much time taking care of Mia and myself on my own I've forgotten what it's like to have someone take care of me. You and your family have been amazing. I'm so grateful. Really. I want you to know that."

"Family's nice, and something I know I've taken for granted as well. Because you're not the only stubborn one in the bunch. After my accident, I hated having people help me with things I felt like I should be able to do. I fought and fought until one day I realized I needed those around me if I was going to make it. And that was okay."

She turned her attention back to the night sky. "It's a beautiful and clear tonight."

"Hard to believe there's a storm that's supposed to come through in a few hours. They're predicting snow by morning."

"I love the snow. My dad taught me to ski. It's funny, though, because now he's the one who wants to flee to Florida at the first sign of snow."

"Have you told them what's going on?"

She shook her head. "I need to, I know, but they worry about me. It took me weeks of convincing for them not to give up their winter in Florida. They're planning to be back in a few weeks for Christmas, but I guess I felt the need to prove I could do it on my own."

"You have nothing to prove. Nothing at all."

She turned back to him and caught his gaze. Her heart was racing, and her palms were sweating, but this time it wasn't from the anxiety of the situation. He was next to her, calming her fears, making her feel safe again. Making her feel as if she weren't alone anymore.

A noise at the end of the porch jerked her back to reality.

"Did you hear that?" she asked.

"Hear what?"

"I don't know. It sounded like there's something at the end of the house. If they're here…"

"We get quite a few wild animals that pass this way, but stay here. I'll go check it out."

She stood on the edge of the porch, the hairs on the back of her neck raised, from fear as much as from the cold. And added to that was the confusion of what she'd just felt with Liam next to her. But she couldn't go there. No matter how much she longed to feel safe again. Whatever feelings she thought she had weren't for the right reason. And she wouldn't do that to him. And on top of that she couldn't get involved with another soldier.

There was only one thing she needed to focus on right now and that was keeping Mia safe and finding a way to end this. Because as much as she trusted Liam, until the men who were behind this were in prison, she wasn't going to be able to stop searching for an answer to what was going on. Anything else was simply a distraction.

Another noise shifted her attention back toward the other side of the porch.

"It's just me," Liam said.

She frowned. "I can't shake this jumpiness. Did you find something?"

"No. There were no signs of anything out there."

It had probably been nothing more than a fox or raccoon that she'd heard. She was letting her imagination run wild.

"You're going to think I'm completely paranoid."

"After all that's happened?" He let out a low laugh. "Hardly. Don't worry about it. I'd always rather be safe than sorry. Why don't we go back in? It's late, and you never got that nap. I know you're exhausted."

She stifled a yawn and nodded. "Maybe I'm more tired than I thought." She rested her hand on his arm for a moment. "Liam...thank you. For everything."

Her stomach flipped like she was eighteen again and a boy had just paid her a compliment. She had to ignore whatever was going on between them. Liam had been Will's best friend, and this was simply her feeling vulnerable. Nothing more. As soon as they found out the truth, she'd go back to her own life and he'd go back to his.

"You okay?" he asked.

"Yes. I think I'll head to bed like you suggested. I know Mia needs to go to sleep as well."

He smiled down at her. "We'll all feel better in the morning. Trust me."

Gabby woke with a start. Sweat beaded off her forehead and her pillow was damp. She'd had a nightmare. Like the ones she'd had after Will had died. They left her feeling like the walls of her room were closing in around her, as if it were happening all over again. She grabbed her cell phone from the bedside table and checked the time. It was only three in the morning.

She pulled back the sheets and crossed the room to check on Mia. Moonlight filtered through the window's sheer curtain. Her daughter's tiny fingers were wrapped around her giraffe, a hint of a smile on her face. Perfect. Peaceful. That was how Gabby needed to keep things for her.

She dropped the intercom receiver in the pocket of her robe, then headed toward the kitchen. What did the Bible say about having the faith of a child? Mia was completely reliant on her for all of her needs. When was the last time Gabby had come to God with the faith of a child, giving up control and trusting in His promises?

Thank You for this sweet girl, God.

The words came automatically in the form of a prayer. She'd avoided praying for so long after her loss, and yet she'd missed that relationship she knew she needed. Liam was right. She had to find a way not to feel ashamed to ask for help and depend on others.

She grabbed a glass from the cupboard, filled it with water from the fridge, then took a sip. There was no way she should be hungry, but the plate of cookies sat on the counter and she took one.

Something crackled on the intercom. She reached for the receiver and caught someone's faint whisper. Panic swept through her as she dropped her glass into the sink and it shattered. She ran up the stairs, taking them two at a time and screamed as she stepped inside the room.

The bedroom window was open, the curtains floating in the breeze. Mia's crib was empty.

* * *

Liam heard a scream, then someone banging on his door. He glanced at the clock as he fought to pull himself out of the fog of sleep. It was just past three o'clock. The door opened, letting light from the hallway pour into the room. Gabby stood at the foot of his bed.

"Liam…hurry, please. It's Mia. Someone's taken her."

It only took a second for what Gabby said to register.

"Wait a minute… How's that possible?" He grabbed his cell phone from the side of the bed and headed out of the room with her, not fully awake.

"I went downstairs, heard something on the baby monitor and when I came back she was gone."

He ran into the room where Gabby and Mia had been sleeping. The window had been forced open, bringing a cold draft into the room.

"How long?"

"A minute at the most."

"Which means they couldn't have gotten far."

"That's not all." Gabby grabbed his sleeve and handed him something. "They left a note. I've got twenty-four hours to give them the evidence, or I won't see Mia again."

"That's not going to happen."

His parents appeared in the doorway. "What's going on?"

He headed back down the hallway, shouting out instructions to call Caden and the ranch hands to the house as he dialed Griffin's number.

"Mia's gone," he said as soon as Griffin answered.

"What—"

"I don't have any answers yet, but we need to get a search team together and put out an AMBER Alert. I figure they've only got a couple minutes lead, so I've called in Caden and the ranch hands."

"Did you see who it was?"

"No, but this has to be connected."

"I'm on my way now."

"What do you want us to do?" his mom said as soon as he'd hung up the phone.

"We're going to need extra warm layers, flashlights and the radios. The temperature's already started dropping."

He headed outside as Caden and the three ranch hands arrived.

"I checked the barn on the way here," Caden said, following him to the side of the house where the men had to have accessed Gabby's bedroom. "Two of the horses are gone."

"Did you see any tracks?"

"There were some heading toward town, but they got lost in the tire tracks."

Liam's frustration grew. "It's supposed to start snowing soon, but right now the ground is still hard. Tracking them in the dark isn't going to be easy."

"If they're moving by horse, there are only a couple options out of here," Caden said.

"Agreed. We need to split up." Liam nodded at his brother. "Take one of the ranch hands and head toward town. Have the other two saddle up a horse for me, then head toward Wayward Creek and scout out the immediate terrain. I'll head up the mountain on the off chance they went that direction."

"By yourself?" Caden asked.

"I'll be fine. I think Dad should stay here with Mom and Gabby."

Caden nodded. "I have to agree with that."

"I'm coming with you."

Liam glanced up at the edge of the porch where Gabby stood. "I need you to stay here with my mom and dad. Keep the coffee hot and be our communication center. It's cold out and there's a storm scheduled to hit in the next couple hours. I don't want you out there."

She marched down the stairs.

He let out a huff of air, knowing what she was thinking. Temperatures were dropping, and Mia was out there with a couple of abductors who could care less about what happened to her. They would find her, but he didn't want Gabby caught in the crosshairs as well.

"Gabby—"

She stepped in front of him, already bundled up. "I'm going with you."

"Forget it."

"Please. You can't make me stay here in this house without doing something, and there's no time to argue. Every minute we spend here is another minute they're ahead."

He hesitated, but if he were honest with himself, he knew he'd do the same thing if he were in her place.

"Do you ride?" he asked.

"Since I was ten. I can keep up."

He pulled on his boots and layered up, including the wool cap and gloves his mom handed him, hurrying as fast as he could. They'd been watching. He was sure of that now. And he'd thought it was some wild animal.

But heaping himself with guilt wasn't going to help him find Mia. They needed to get out there. Now.

He passed out the radios to everyone.

"How are we going to find them in the dark?" Gabby asked, pulling her wool cap down over her ears.

"It will be slower going, but they have their own disadvantages that will slow them down as well."

Like Mia.

His dad handed Gabby a pair of gloves. "Part of Liam's military training was combat tracking and counter tracking. He knows what he's doing."

His mom squeezed Gabby's shoulder. "And Caden's a former army ranger. If anyone can find her, my boys can."

Liam caught her gaze. "She's right. We will find her. There are only two ways out of here that would make any sense in the dark. The main road that leads to town and a well-worn trail that heads southeast through the forest. The terrain is more difficult, but definitely passable when there's no snow on the ground."

"What can I do?" his mom asked.

He turned and kissed his mom on the forehead. "Once they're done saddling the horses, have the ranch hands search the vicinity and see if they can pick up anything we miss. And have a big pot of coffee waiting when we get back."

He hurried to the barn with Gabby. Griffin and one of the ranch hands were already in the truck and heading out.

He quickly checked around the outside of the structure before heading inside. "Caden was right. There are horse tracks leading east toward town, but these guys are smart and will try to throw us off."

He quickly secured a saddle scabbard for his rifle on the side of the horse. The cold was already biting, but he couldn't worry about that now.

"You're riding out armed?" she asked.

"I have no plans of giving them any more advantages than they already have."

"It just never seems to end." She stood beside the second horse while the ranch hand got it ready for her. "This nightmare."

"I know you're scared, but we're going to find Mia. We're only a few minutes behind them and my brothers and I know this land better than anyone. They also have the disadvantage of it being dark. The four of us used to spend every minute we could exploring the ranch."

"But if they're trained soldiers as well—"

"We're going to find her."

He mounted his horse, praying at the same time that everything he was telling her was true. He couldn't even imagine how terrified she must be. But they were going to find the little girl. They had to.

"I know you don't know the terrain but keep up the best you can," he said, praying he wouldn't regret his decision to let her come. "We're going to have to move fast."

They headed south on the path, silence hovering between them. When he'd spent time training how to track the enemy, he never imagined having to track his best friend's daughter. But this was no different. If they were out there, he would find them. Which meant not only did he need to be aware of everything going on around

him—any footprints, disturbed soil, trampled grass—
he also needed to get into the head of the kidnappers.
Figure out what their plan was.

If he were them, this is how he would have left. The
easiest way out of here might be the road leading to
town, but it also would be the riskiest and the easiest
to get caught.

He glanced at Gabby, impressed with how she was
keeping up. As much as he wasn't happy about risking
her coming, he knew she was strong. He wasn't sure she
saw it in herself, but he did. She'd managed to stay calm
tonight. She hadn't gone into hysterics. Instead, she'd
demanded to be a part of the search. Maybe she'd break
down when this was all over, but for now she'd managed to find the inner strength that enabled her to cope.

"I'm pretty sure they went this way," he said. "There
are two sets of hoofprints."

"Where does this path go?"

"It's a pass that leads toward Mountain Springs."

"And between here and there?"

"Nothing more than the forest, and a cabin a friend
of mine owns."

He didn't want to tell her that the path would be covered in snow in the next few hours, making it harder
to pass. And there were other things that bothered him
since they'd left. He could out-track anyone he knew.
The army had ensured that with his training. But if
they were right about who had been hired, he was sure
they'd come with their own set of skills. And they had
to have equipment as well. The tracking device they'd
used on Gabby's car wasn't something they could have
picked up just anywhere.

He wasn't sure how they'd done it, but they must have planted another to find out exactly where Mia would be sleeping, and the exact moment Gabby would be gone. He was pretty sure they'd come through the window and not one of the other doors. It had been a plan well thought out and executed. Which was exactly what had Liam nervous. They weren't dealing with amateurs. Thatcher might have a shady past, but that didn't mean he wasn't well trained.

He heard something snap, then stopped, raising his hand for Gabby to be quiet.

Liam jumped down off his horse and listened for something out of place. He turned back around, staring out into the night toward where they'd come from. He heard it again—a subtle crunch.

Someone was behind them.

"Liam…"

"We're definitely on the trail of someone, but that's not all. We're also being tracked."

He scanned the darkness, trying to figure out what he'd missed. He'd been tracking two people. Where had the third come from? Or maybe that wasn't what was happening at all. Had one of the men looped around, trying to box them in? He searched the wooded forest, but the only thing he could see was tree limbs moving in the wind. The only light was from the moonlight, but as soon as the storm clouds came in, they wouldn't even have that.

He grabbed for his rifle from the scabbard, but it was too late. A gunshot ripped across the night. Gabby's horse bolted, throwing her to the ground.

SEVEN

Darkness closed in around her followed by an eruption of stars as Gabby hit the hard ground. Her mind fought to focus as she waited for the sound of another gunshot. Someone was out there. Close enough to fire shots at them. And Mia… She had to be with them, which terrified Gabby. She listened for the sounds of Mia crying, but all she could hear was the rush of wind around her. If Mia was somewhere nearby, she had to get up and find her.

"Gabby… Gabby talk to me."

She opened her eyes and stared up at Liam, who was framed in darkness with only a hint of moonlight allowing her to make out his features.

"Are you okay?" he asked.

"I think so."

"Move slowly, but you need to get up. We have to get out of here. Now."

She let him help her up, making sure as she moved that nothing was broken. For the first time all night, she was thankful for the cover of darkness. But why shoot at them? So far, the men had seemed to want her alive. Liam put his arm around her and helped her to her feet. She stared down the path ahead of them, but darkness made navigating the terrain almost impossible. If it wasn't for Liam and his training, they'd never have made it this far.

"Why did he shoot at us?"

Liam was guiding her down a smaller trail that deviated away from the main path, keeping his arms around her as they hurried through the icy darkness.

"Maybe he was trying to slow us down. I don't know."

She glanced around her as another realization hit her foggy mind. "Where are the horses?"

"They were spooked by the gunshot and ran. I managed to grab my rifle, but that's it."

"So what do we do now?"

"We're going to have to walk out of here."

She heard the anger in his voice. The cold felt like a knife through her lungs as she took in a deep breath, trying to settle her nerves. They'd been traveling on horseback for a couple hours, but now that it had started to snow, the terrain was going to be even tougher to cross. If they turned back to the ranch, it would take even longer. She had no idea what was out there. Only that trusting Liam was her last hope now.

The realization left her feeling vulnerable. Out of control. And she hated feeling out of control.

She glanced back through the eerily shadowed forest. "Do you think he's behind us?"

"He's out there, but I don't think he's coming after us."

"Which leaves us where?"

"There's a cabin south of here off the main path. The one I mentioned earlier that belongs to a friend. It will be a lot quicker to reach that than heading back to the ranch. The man who lives there should have a way for us to warm up."

She zipped her coat up a couple inches, then wrapped her scarf around her neck a second time. They pressed through the trees in silence. She forced herself to keep up with his pace, trying to follow in his footsteps so she made as little sound as possible. Night sounds echoed around her. She shivered, both from the cold and from the fear that had settled in her gut. They were out there. The men who had broken into her house… killed Casada…kidnapped her daughter.

Where are you, Mia? Mama will find you. I promise.

Her lungs were burning, and she didn't know if it was the altitude, the fall or both, but either way she needed to stop and catch her breath.

She stood in the middle of the trail and turned to Liam. "I just need a minute."

"Of course. How are you feeling? How's your head?"

"It's sore, but fine. I just need to catch my breath."

He led her to a flat rock on the side of the trail. "Rest here. I'm going to try and radio my brother."

An owl hooted in the distance. An ensemble of insects chirped, even in the cold.

"I can't get through." He knelt in front of her. "Tell me how you're really feeling. Do you feel nauseated or dizzy? You took quite a blow back there falling off that horse."

"I really do think I'm fine, though the back of my

head hurts. I'm pretty sure I'm going to end up with a lovely goose egg."

He shot her a smile. "Trying to compete with me, huh?"

"Funny, because I'd have been perfectly happy to have skipped this drama. Do you know where we are?"

"More or less. Not sticking to the main trail is going to make it harder, but this is a shortcut to the cabin."

"I'm slowing you down."

"You're fine, and besides…you're definitely much better company than my brothers used to be when we played hide-and-seek out here. We'd spend half our time arguing about who was the best tracker, or the best aim."

"Let me guess. You were the best tracker out of the four of you?"

"My brothers would never agree with that statement, but I was pretty good. Their problem was they couldn't go more than a minute without talking or making some kind of noise. I loved tracking, even back then."

She glanced toward the east where a hint of light was already breaking above the horizon. "It's going to be light soon."

"We will find them. There's nowhere they can escape. We'll figure out how to let my brothers know where we are. The cabin's not too far now."

She nodded, wanting to believe him, and yet whoever had taken Mia still had the advantage.

He caught her gaze in the soft glow of dawn. "You're shivering."

He sat down next to her and wrapped his arm around her waist, letting her burrow her head into his shoulder.

He took her gloved hands and rubbed them between his, trying to warm her up. She was so cold. They were dressed for the weather, but losing the horses put them at a huge disadvantage. Besides that, they had no access to water and food. They needed to get somewhere safe and warm, but at the moment all that mattered was finding Mia.

A branch creaked overhead while the wind whipped around them. Her head throbbed, but she couldn't focus on that. His warm breath tickled a small exposed place on her neck. And with his arms around her, she finally felt as though she were warming up.

"When I found out Will was dead, I felt as if my whole life was over," she said. "No matter how much you prepare for the possibility of something bad like that happening, you really can't know what it's going to be like until it happens. The grief and numbness that follows. The feeling that nothing will ever be okay again. But in the middle of everything was Mia. This part of Will that was still alive."

She took in a deep breath before continuing. "Then in my third trimester, suddenly I had something else to worry about. The doctor diagnosed me with preeclampsia. I had high blood pressure and my hands and feet were swollen. Once again, I was suddenly facing another crisis."

"You never told me that."

"There was nothing you could do. I didn't even know what to do except follow the doctor's orders. My parents were there for me. I was so scared something would go wrong and I would lose her."

"But you didn't."

"No. And when Mia was finally born, the doctor laid her on my chest and told me she was perfect. I suddenly felt that somehow things would be okay again. Not perfect. Not even happy-ever-after, but okay. It seemed impossible. I was a single mom, about to raise a child on my own, and to be honest, I was terrified and anything but prepared. But this beautiful baby had managed to take away some of the numbness."

"I'm sorry. I wish I could have been there."

"No. I don't want you to feel guilty at all. You came home fighting for your own life. You did exactly what you needed to do." She dropped her gaze. "But I feel like I'm there again. Hearing the doctor telling me the risks of what could happen. I can't lose her, Liam. I can't give them what they want—I don't even know what they think I have—so how are we going to end this? I don't know what to do."

"We're going to find her, but in order to do that we've got to keep going. We need to get to that cabin and get ahold of Griffin. Can you do that?"

She pulled away from him and nodded. "Yeah."

Because Mia was out there somewhere. There was no way she was going to give up.

They started walking again, pressing through the early morning glow of dawn toward the cabin. Snow was falling, but not hard enough that it was slowing them down. Even though Gabby was managing to keep up, Liam was worried about her. She'd proven to be strong over the past few days, but that fall had knocked the wind out of her—and possibly more. He'd continue to monitor her symptoms, but the reality was she needed to be checked out by a doctor, not trooping through the woods in the middle of the night.

He glanced at her silhouette in the soft light. He'd never really noticed how beautiful she was. Those big brown eyes, long hair and full lips... It shouldn't make him feel the way he did, but he couldn't deny it. This was more than just wanting to keep her safe. More than just wanting to ensure they found Mia.

He was falling for her.

Which seemed insane when he stopped and really thought about it. For one, she'd never fall for someone like him. She knew far too well the cost of being a military wife. How could he ask that of her when she'd already lost so much? Expect her to wait for him while he was deployed, never knowing if he'd come home. To deal with him leaving in the middle of the night for a mission he couldn't tell her about. To handle being separated for months on end...

It all sounded so brave and patriotic and even romantic, but what about the day-to-day realities of her having to be a single mom when he was gone. Assuming he was finally cleared for active duty, that was what he had to offer her and that was asking too much.

No, he couldn't—wouldn't—ask that of her.

He could see her breath forming a mist in the early morning air. The sun would rise above the horizon before long, hopefully warming up the temperatures, but they had to keep moving. Their best bet was to find a way to communicate and give Griffin a heads-up as to where the men were likely to emerge on the other side of the forest.

He forced his mind to shift gears and picked up their

conversation from the day before. "We started talking yesterday about your struggling to pray."

She hesitated before responding. "Since Will's death, I haven't been able to pray. I mean, really pray. Even if it just meant crying out to God in anger and fear and hope, believing He's really there."

"I think I understand. After the accident, I struggled with so much guilt. I'd watched my best friend die and couldn't stop it. For a while, I took it out as anger against God. Which really didn't make sense, but I didn't know how to cope with what I was feeling."

"What changed things for you?"

"I finally realized that there was something left in the middle of all the loss. That my faith was still there. Not intact, maybe, but there."

"And now?"

"I still struggle to accept what's happened, but I realize that God is there through the healing and doubts now, just like he'll be there in the midst of whatever the future brings. I'm not sure if my doctor is going to approve me for active duty. And without that, I'll end up with a medical discharge and back in civilian life. I'm not sure how I'll deal with that."

"So you don't want to leave the military?"

"It's what I know. Who I am. I honestly can't imagine doing anything else."

He spoke the words, knowing what they would mean to her. Knowing that his need to serve his country meant he could never win her heart.

"You warm enough?" he asked.

"Walking actually helps. Plus, I'm trying to imagine sitting in your house, watching a movie with a huge mug of hot chocolate and marshmallows."

"Ha! What kind of movie?"

"Nothing in particular. I'm guessing you like action. Maybe sci-fi."

"Yep, but they're not your favorite."

"No, but I do love a good apocalyptic movie. You know…end of the world meteor shower or devastating virus."

"Really…then we'll have to make it a date." He stopped, wondering how he'd just opened his big mouth again and said something stupid. "I'm sorry. I just meant, you know, I thought we could hang out some. Like we used to."

When Will was alive. Boy, he was getting good at saying the wrong things.

"I'd like that, actually." Her response surprised him. "Though I have to ask you one question, why aren't you married or at the least dating someone? You're smart, good-looking, funny…"

He glanced at her. "And…"

She laughed. "Seriously. You're a catch."

"I don't know. Saying I haven't found the right person sounds like a cliché, but it's true. And being deployed didn't help, either. Most women aren't looking for someone who's going to be gone a good chunk of the time. It tends to make them run the opposite direction toward the stable guy working a regular job who's always home for dinner."

"I suppose being a military wife takes a certain kind of person and some getting used to—on both sides— but if it's the right person, it's worth it."

"I was always amazed at how you and Will managed to balance your marriage with all his field training and deployments. What about you? Have you thought about dating again, or is it too soon?"

The pause left him regretting his question. "I think I'm going to have to apologize again."

"No...you don't. I just... I haven't really had time to think about it. You mentioned how being deployed didn't help a relationship, try throwing in a baby and a full-time job. Between work and taking care of her, I don't exactly have a lot of free time to go out on dates. Falling in love again sounds frivolous between changing diapers and working full-time."

"I can't see why that would be an issue. Mia's adorable. Just like her mom."

"You'd be surprised at how many guys start flirting until they notice you're carrying a diaper bag. Then they suddenly vanish out of your life. No. Most guys are not interested in a ready-made family. It's not exactly a Cinderella story."

His hand brushed against her arm as they maneuvered over a spot of uneven ground, making him pause. Why did she look completely kissable? A narrow sunbeam lit up her dark hair. He stopped walking then reached down and pushed back a loose strand from her face, fighting the unwanted feelings of longing that continued to surface. If he kissed her, everything would change. If he didn't, he'd never know what might have happened between them.

And maybe that was best. He was risking far too much by letting this scenario between them play out.

"You look so serious," she said. "What is it?"

"I'm not sure. Maybe it's just the sunrise and this golden halo over you from the sunlight. You're so beautiful."

"I've been out half the night in freezing temperatures, was thrown off a horse and—"

"Trust me." He smiled at her. "You still look beautiful."

"Liam…"

He tried to read her expression, but he couldn't.

"Liam…" She was staring at something behind him. "There's a mountain lion."

EIGHT

Gabby stared at the cat as Liam turned around to face it beside her. Its ears were perked up, head cocked and its gaze aimed right at them like a dart.

"Two rules." He grabbed her arm. "Don't panic. And don't run."

She wanted to laugh at the advice. Running wasn't an issue. She was pretty sure fear had her paralyzed. But panic. Oh, she was already there.

He held up his rifle and started shouting at the cat while waving his hands over his head. She followed his lead, trying to convince the cat—she assumed—that they weren't prey and definitely not this morning's breakfast.

It didn't move. Just stared at them, muscles tense and ready to pounce at any second.

"What do we do?" she asked.

"Keep yelling and slowly move backward."

She waved her arms and shouted at it, staying even with Liam as they took one step back and then another.

Seconds later, it crouched down farther, moving in slow motion as if it were ready at any moment to strike.

Her heart raced. She'd heard stories about mountain lion attacks. How they were rare, but still happened. And she wasn't sure which was more terrifying: the men tracking them with their weapons, or the mountain lion less than twenty yards in front of them. She grabbed for the remainders of faith she still held on to.

I'm so tired, God. I've got nothing more to give. I'm going to have to trust You to take over, because I can't stand up emotionally on my own anymore.

The cat kept staring at them. Thirty seconds later, it suddenly stalked off into the bush.

Gabby let out the lungful of air she'd been holding, her eyes still fixed on the spot where it had disappeared. Her heart wouldn't stop racing and adrenaline overload had her exhausted.

"You okay?" Liam asked.

She glanced at the spot where the cat had been, wondering if it was safe to keep moving or if it would return. "I don't know. My heart's pounding."

"Still, I'm impressed. For being normally so soft-spoken, your yell packs a lot of punch."

Her laugh helped deflate some of the stress that had built up inside her, but it only managed to barely soften the edges of this nightmare.

"The good thing is that they don't want an encounter any more than we do," he said. "You just have to convince them you'd make a terrible meal."

"Have you ever been that close to one?"

"Only once. Griffin and I were out hiking. I was thirteen, maybe fourteen. As soon as it disappeared into the bushes, I ran like lightning all the way home. I had nightmares after that for weeks."

She glanced at him. An up close encounter with the animal wasn't the only reason her heart was racing. He was looking at her again with that smile of his, making her realize she hadn't just imagined whatever was going on between them. It was a look that had somehow managed to break through the walls of her heart and leave her defenseless. What in the world had she been thinking, talking to him about dating? Then he'd wanted to kiss her—she was certain of it—catching her totally off guard. What would have happened if she hadn't spotted the mountain lion?

What would have happened if he'd kissed her?

"You think he'll come back?" she asked.

"I doubt it. Like I said, they don't want an encounter with us any more than we want one with them."

She tore her gaze away from him, because whatever she had felt didn't matter. That was a place she couldn't go. She forced herself to refocus. She wasn't ready to put her heart on the line. Not with Liam, and certainly not with another soldier. Not with anyone. It simply wasn't a place her heart could go, especially now of all times.

"How far are we from the cabin?"

He glanced up the trail. "Another mile at the most."

He pulled out his radio and tried to call again.

"Still no signal?"

"Nothing. But it won't be long now."

Despite the sun now hugging the horizon, the temperatures seemed to be dropping and snow was falling again. The wind had picked up and if it kept snowing, it was going to be even harder to maneuver over the terrain. But what choice did they have? With only two ways out, the cabin was closer than going back to the house.

She worked to push away the fear. Fear that Mia wouldn't survive the cold. Fear that her daughter was hungry and wet.

Fear that she wouldn't see her baby again.

Liam wrapped an arm around her as if he understood the emotions flooding through her, leaving her tingling from his touch. "Let's get to the cabin and rethink our plan."

She nodded, then started walking beside him, focusing on the stunning sunrise and her determination to find her daughter instead of his nearness.

You know I'm so tired of doing this alone, God. So tired of feeling like all I'm doing is surviving.

But that didn't mean Liam was the answer.

Or had He answered her prayers before she even asked? She pushed back at the question, wanting to suddenly run away from everything, to beg God to let her wake up back at the ranch in the bedroom with sweet Mia still sleeping in her crib and make all of this go away.

Just because Liam had always been someone she admired, didn't mean she was falling for him. Like Will, he'd volunteered to serve his country, risked his life so she and others could have freedom. She'd never make him leave that for her. But neither was she willing to go back to that life. Falling for him meant a future of deployments, moving and dangers. She knew the toll military life could take on a marriage. Leaving friends and family, giving certain life decisions over to the army, parenting alone, being apart...

She didn't want that again. If God was going to ever send her someone else to love, it would have to be someone who had a normal nine-to-five job.

A flash of color caught her eye about twenty yards to the left. She blinked twice then looked again. She was tired and had to be imagining things, but it was still there. A flash of bright orange in an otherwise gray and white terrain.

"Liam…"

"What is it?"

"I'm not sure, but it looks like Mia's giraffe."

She pulled away from him. She was so tired and cold. Maybe her eyes had simply been playing tricks with her.

A lake spanned out in front of them to the right. The sun shone down on its shiny surface, and it was surrounded by rows of tall spindly trees.

"Gabby, wait… Don't get too close to the edge. The water's frozen, but this time of year it can crack easily."

"I'm not going far. I just need to find out what's out there."

She pulled away from him and walked toward the edge, careful to stay on the ground and not too close to the water. She was a few feet away now. Panic settled in again. It was Mia's giraffe. There was no doubt about it now. But why had they come here? This far off the main trail? Had they known, like Liam, that this was a shortcut to the cabin? She listened for her daughter's cry in the wind. She had to be out here somewhere nearby.

She studied the horizon, looking for a flash of red from the blanket that had gone missing along with Mia.

She turned back to the stuffed animal. It was close now. Only a couple feet away. As she reached out and grabbed the orange giraffe, the ice split beneath her with a loud crack. She hadn't even known she was on the water, but by then it was too late. She heard another crack, screamed, then slid into the icy water.

"Gabby…"

Liam pulled her out onto the solid ground, away from the ice, thankful she hadn't completely fallen through, but even with the sun out, the temperatures were dropping and this was only going to make things worse.

Her lips had paled, and she was shaking. No. This couldn't be happening. Why hadn't he convinced her to stay back at the ranch? Why did she have to be so stubborn? But he couldn't think about that now. He needed to get her to the cabin. He managed to peel off her wet coat, then slipped his on her before shoving Mia's stuffed giraffe into his pocket.

He glanced back at the trail. Thankfully, they were close to the cabin now. Gus would have a fire going and something hot for her to drink. He managed to lift her over his shoulders and started walking. He'd known Gus since he was a little boy. He wasn't sure if the old man would have a cell phone, but he did remember Gus had a ham radio for emergencies.

His limbs felt frozen from the cold by the time he pounded on the cabin's wooden front door.

"Gus… Gus are you in there?"

The door swung open and Liam was met with the barrel of a shotgun. "Put your hands in the air where I can see them now."

Liam's gaze shifted to Gus's bearded face. "It's me. Liam."

"Liam?" Seconds later, the door swung all the way open, and Gus dropped his gun to his side. "What in the world happened?"

Liam didn't wait for an invitation. Instead, he strode into the one-room cabin with a bedroom loft and set Gabby on the thick shaggy rug in front of the fire place. "Sorry to barge in, but I need to warm her up."

"What are you doing out in this weather?"

"Long story, but the bottom line is that she fell in the lake."

"I'll grab something to help warm her up, then get the kettle going. You'll need to take off anything that's wet."

Liam took the pile of blankets Gus handed him, then hurried to get her dry. "Gabby...can you hear me? I need you to talk to me."

"It's so cold." Her teeth were chattering, but at least she was conscious. "And I'm so sleepy."

"I know, and I'm going to warm you up, but I want you to stay awake for now, okay?"

"Where's Mia's giraffe? It was there near the water. She has to be nearby."

"I have the giraffe and we're going to find Mia, but right now, I need to get you warm."

Gus rummaged around in the small kitchen on the other side of the room while the hot water heated up on his stove. "Does this have anything to do with the men that just burst into my cabin about half an hour ago?"

Liam glanced around the room. Nothing looked out of place and Gus seemed fine. At least they hadn't hurt him. "I need to hear exactly what happened as soon as I get her warmed up, but more than likely, yes. Was there a baby with them?"

"Yes. She looked fine. Snuggled up in a thick blanket, sound asleep. I gave them what they wanted, and they left."

"What did they want?"

"A radio, for starters, but with this storm, communication's pretty impossible. They were trying to get ahold of someone. Ended up taking some water and food and leaving after they'd warmed up."

A minute later, Gus handed him a steamy mug of tea.

Liam helped Gabby sit up, hoping to get as much of the hot drink into her body as possible. "I need you to take a few sips of this."

She pressed her hands against the mug, her fingers still shaking, but at least she swallowed some.

"Good girl." He set the mug on the mantel when she was done, then felt her pulse. It was already stronger than it had been twenty minutes ago. And her breathing seemed more even as well. This could have ended so differently. She'd be okay. He only wished he could say the same for Mia.

There's got to be a way to find her, God. Gabby's already lost so much. Please...please help me find these men.

"Who is she?"

Gus's question pulled him away from his prayer. Gabby had laid her head down on the stack of pillows, her cheeks now flushed from the warmth and her eyes closed again. He stood up and walked across the room.

"Her name's Gabby Kensington. The men that came

here have her daughter. I need to get ahold of my brother in Timber Falls and let him know where they are."

"That's actually what I've been trying to do." Gus headed for the desk in the corner of the room. "I didn't mention to the men that I've been tinkering with a new system that allows me to get on to the internet when wireless carrier signals are spotty. Even with the storm, I think I should be able to get through with my antenna. Keep an eye on her and get her to drink the rest of that tea when she wakes up. I'll keep working on getting a message to your brother."

"I also need your ATV," Liam said.

"Sorry, but they decided to split up. One of them took off in it with the baby while the other one left with the horses. They didn't talk much, but from what I gathered, they were heading for Mountain Springs and trying to get ahold of someone." Gus nodded toward the fireplace. "How do you know her?"

"She was married to my best friend, Will Kensington."

"The soldier who was killed back in the Sandbox?"

"Yes."

"I remember you talking about him. And telling me about his death."

"Liam?"

He turned back to the fireplace where Gabby was stirring again. "Hey...can you drink some more tea?"

She managed another couple sips before pushing the drink away.

"Do you feel any warmer?"

She nodded. "I think so, but what about Mia?"

"Gus is trying to contact Griffin right now. We think

they're headed to Mountain Springs, which is really the only way out of here. The only easy way, anyway." He brushed back a strand of her hair, knowing he had to tell her everything. "Gus saw Mia."

"What?" She struggled to sit up.

He rested his hand against her shoulder. "Stay still. They stopped here, then one of them took her on his four-wheeler."

"She was okay?"

He nodded. "I don't think they want to hurt her. They just want leverage."

"But I don't have what they want." She pulled up the blanket against her cheek, her eyes welling with tears. "I've got to get up. We need to find her."

"We will, but there's nothing you can do right now. Go back to sleep. Gus will get ahold of Griffin and let him know what's going on, then once the storm passes we can rethink our plan."

She snuggled back down beneath the blankets and closed her eyes, seemingly too tired to argue with him. He watched her breathe. Her heart rate and breathing were regular, and her lips were back to a normal color. But the incident had scared him. For the past year and a half, he'd done his duty checking on her. But he'd also done his best to keep his distance, because he'd carried guilt over not saving Will.

How had all of that suddenly changed? The sense of duty had vanished along with any motivation because of guilt. Now, she'd somehow managed to leave his heart in a tangled mess. He watched her sleep. She looked so calm and peaceful.

The heaviness of fatigue surrounded him as well.

All the worry had drained him and he couldn't keep his eyes open. The fire crackled next to him. Gabby's breathing stayed steady as her core temperature continued to rise. But he needed to stay awake. Needed to keep checking on her. As soon as the weather cleared up, he was going to leave her here and go after Mia. But for now, he was so tired.

Movement beside him jolted him awake.

Liam sat up with a start. "I'm sorry. I must have fallen asleep."

The old man dropped another log on the fire. "If you ask me, that's exactly what you needed. Besides that, there isn't much you can do. Snow's coming down pretty hard. It would be foolish to go out there right now."

"What about Griffin? Did you reach him?"

"The connection was bad, but I finally managed to get him a message. The authorities will be waiting for them."

"I need to go out there. I promised Gabby I'd find her daughter."

"I know this isn't easy, but going out into the storm will just put your life in danger. Wait until things clear up some." Gus glanced at Gabby. "That girl there, she's beautiful."

Liam chuckled. "Might be a bit young for you."

"I wasn't talking about for myself. I saw the way you look at her. Looks like you've lost your heart."

He frowned. Surely, how he felt wasn't that obvious.

"I'm just worried about her. But as friends. Nothing more."

"If you say so."

He had to, because falling for Gabby was too complicated. She'd never give her heart to another soldier, and he couldn't blame her. "She was married to my best friend. It wouldn't be fair to ask her to risk her heart again."

"So you do feel something toward her, you're just too stubborn to admit it."

"Gus…"

"I guess we all have secrets. Pieces of our past we'd like to forget." He hesitated, then pulled out a photo from the desk drawer. "This is my wife and daughter up at Garden of the Gods. We used to hike that loop every summer, even before Kelly could walk. I'd strap on one of those backpack contraptions, so I could carry her. We hiked all the trails. Up to Emerald Lake, the Fern Lake trailhead…"

Liam studied the photo of the three of them. "I never knew you were married."

"I don't tell most people about them. Always ends up making the other person uncomfortable and me… well…it's always easier not to remember. Easier for people to think I'm just a cranky old man who lives in a cabin by himself."

Liam handed him back the photo. "Can I ask what happened?"

"They died in a car wreck on seventy. That was thirty-five years ago."

"You never remarried?" Liam asked.

"Thought about it once. I guess you were right about one thing. Sometimes it's not easy to risk your heart again."

"Do you regret it?"

"I did for a while, but now I can't imagine anyone putting up with me."

"I wouldn't go that far."

Gus caught his gaze. "Just don't do anything you're going to regret one day. Or in your case, don't avoid taking a chance you maybe should take. Love doesn't come around too often, but when it does, you've got to grab onto it and hold on tight."

Liam shook his head. "Now you're starting to sound like my mother. She's always talking about her need for daughters-in-law and grandchildren."

"That's the way the good Lord made us. We love and raise them, then have to send them out of the nest into the world. Grandchildren, I suppose, help feed that loss."

Liam stared into the fire. He couldn't imagine what Gus must be thinking about. How he'd never had the chance to watch his daughter grow up. Never held those grandbabies.

"Liam… I've got a call coming through from your brother."

He went to stand by the Gus, praying for good news. "What have you got, Griffin?"

"We found the pair's abandoned car not far from the ranch and managed to trace it back to Silas Maldin."

"And Mia?" Liam asked.

"I'm sorry, but we still have no idea where she is."

NINE

Liam paced the cabin, trying to fight the restlessness, but the walls of the cabin felt as if they were closing in on him. He glanced at the door, then back at Gabby who was still sleeping next to the fire. Doing nothing wasn't exactly his strong point. His beliefs in both justice and loyalty were what had compelled him to join the military in the first place. And now he needed to do something—anything—to put an end to this.

Like he'd felt ever since the accident.

His jaw tensed at the reminder. Being taken off active duty had sent him to a place he never thought he'd be.

Will was dead, and he'd spent months recovering instead of fighting. Letting someone else wage the war while he was down had left him feeling useless, something he still fought on a daily basis. And according to the army, there were still no guarantees he was going back in.

He turned back to Gus. "I need to do something. I need to be tracking Thatcher down. He's out there somewhere and has to have Mia."

"That would be foolish. Your brother and the police are going to find her. Let them do their job. You need to wait out this storm and make sure Gabby's okay."

Liam glanced over at her again. Her cheeks were flushed, but at least her breathing was still regular. "And if she's not, or if they don't find Mia?"

"She'll be fine. She's strong." Gus stood up from his chair and stretched his back. "Listen, I just checked the weather. There's a break in the storm coming. Temperatures are going to rise a few degrees and hopefully make it easier to navigate the trails. But until then, you need to stay here."

"I know. I just…"

I need to stop this.

For a split second, he was there again. Moments after the IED went off. Moments before his best friend died. He shoved away the memories. The days and weeks after he was transported back to the US. Two surgeries to remove shrapnel and weeks of physical therapy to rehabilitate his leg. On top of all of that was the realization of how much had been lost that day. The guilt that he hadn't been able to stop it.

"You lost a lot over there," Gus said.

"You were in the military, weren't you?" Liam asked, needing to release his emotions.

"Eight years, including two deployments. It changed me. Both for better and worse."

"I keep thinking about what you said. Wondering if Gabby's someone I could see myself with one day."

"Only you can know that, but there's something about the way you look at her. That intense feeling I see in you to protect her. Maybe it's just who you are. Or maybe it's something more."

"It—the thought of us—seems so complicated."

"Why?"

"I'm not sure she'll want to follow me back into military life. She is strong, but that life can be hard. She's already paid the price and knows all too well what can happen. Is it fair to start something with her? To ask her to put her heart on the line again?"

"Have you thought about asking her how she feels? Maybe it's not as complicated as you think."

Liam let out a sharp sigh. "Why is it that love sometimes seems scarier than facing the enemy?" He turned back to Gus. "And I'm not sure I could even consider having a relationship with Gabby. I need someone willing to wait for me when I'm deployed. Someone willing to put up with months of being apart, and the risk of what can happen… It's too much to ask of her."

"Love has a way of making the sacrifices worth it."

But could he start something he wasn't sure she'd be able to finish in the end?

"Liam?"

He moved across the room at the sound of her voice. "Gabby… I'm right here."

He knelt down beside her and brushed a strand of hair out of her eyes. "Hey… I've been worried about you. How are you feeling?"

"It's so cold in here."

He took her hands that had been wrapped beneath the blanket. She was warmer, but there was still a chill to her touch.

I need her to be okay, God. Please. And Mia…

Why did all of this have to happen? He knew no matter what the outcome, things were never going to be the same for him again.

He reached for the tea Gus had heated, which was sitting on the table beside her. "You need to drink more of this. It will warm you. Can you try?"

She shook her head and started to rise. "I can't… I shouldn't be sleeping. We have to get back out there and find Mia."

"Hold on." He rested his hands on her shoulders and laid her back down onto the pillow. "I know how you feel, but we can't go anywhere. Not yet. You're still warming up and there's a storm."

He could hear the panic in her voice. "My baby's out there. I have to find her."

"Gabby, listen to me. The snow has picked up outside. There's supposed to be a break in the weather soon, but right now we can't go anywhere."

"But if she's out there—"

"They would have found shelter for her and them. They need her alive. I've spoken to Griffin. We know where they're headed and the police are mobilized. Griffin is going to let us know as soon as they find her, but they believe she's in town. And Gus saw her, remember? She's okay."

Gabby pulled the ransom note out of her pocket. The ink had run when she'd fallen into the water.

"She has to be close. They were here. We found her giraffe—"

"Why don't you let me make you an omelet," Gus said, interrupting their conversation. "I might not be the best cook on this side of the Rockies, but I went to town a couple days ago and have plenty of fresh eggs. You both need to eat."

Gabby shook her head. "I don't think I can."

"I know this is hard. Waiting always is, but Gus is right. You'll feel better if you eat something."

She nodded, then held out her hands in front of the fire. "I'll try. Is my jacket dry yet? I feel like I'm finally warming up, but I'm still cold."

He grabbed the jacket off the back of the chair to see if it had dried, then shook it out. Something clanged onto the floor. He reached down and picked up a tiny circuit.

"What's wrong?" she asked.

"We might have another problem."

Gabby moved to the hearth to get closer to the fire, not sure she'd ever warm up. "What's wrong?"

"You remember the tracking device they found on your car? The one that enabled them to follow you?"

Gabby nodded, trying not to let fear continue to work its way through her.

He sat down next to her. "I just found another one on your jacket."

"Wait a minute… They're still tracking me?" She ran her finger across the tiny black device. "How's that even possible?"

"I don't know."

Her brain tried to reach through the fog and pull together what had happened. They'd come back to the ranch and this was how they'd found her. How they'd been able to take Mia.

"This gave them the chance to follow me right back

to the ranch." Tears welled in her eyes. "They were able to know exactly where I was staying. All they had to do was watch and wait for an opportunity to take her."

But how had they managed to get the tracker in her jacket?

She stared at the chip in her palm. There was only one thing that made sense. "It had to happen at the house. At Casada's. What if they were there to search his house and leave the tracker on his car, or maybe even on his person, but when Casada was killed and we showed up, they took the opportunity to track me instead."

"Giving them a way to follow us and take Mia." Liam stood back up. "That makes sense. If it had been on you before, then they'd already have come out to the ranch. And since they couldn't track you any longer with your car or phone, this was their chance."

The heat from the fire baked her back, but she barely felt it. Instead, guilt swept through her. Guilt that she hadn't been able to keep her daughter safe. That had been her responsibility.

"Gabby." He knelt down in front of her. "This wasn't your fault."

"It doesn't really even matter whose fault it was. I chose to ask questions about Will's death, and in turn put my daughter's life at risk. And now..."

"This isn't your fault," he repeated.

"I hate to interrupt, but he's right," Gus spoke up from the kitchen where he was chopping vegetables for the omelet. "I learned a long time ago that blaming yourself for something you have no control over does little to change the circumstances. And it certainly isn't going to change anything now. What we have to do is find a way to get your daughter back and put an end to this."

"But how?" she asked.

Gus set his knife down and crossed the room. "Can I see it?"

Liam handed the chip to him.

"I used to work with electronics back when I was in the military. Granted, technology has changed over the past few decades, but a lot of the concepts are the same." He pulled out a small magnifying glass from his desk, then sat down in front of it.

"Can you disable it for starters?" Liam asked.

"I should be able to turn it off."

"Will that matter?" Gabby asked. "They have to know where we are by now."

"True, but at least if we leave, they won't be able to track us."

Gus held up the tracker in his palm. "Problem solved. I've disabled it, but I still wouldn't advise going back out there at this point. The snow's yet to let up."

"So we're supposed to just stay here?" Gabby asked.

"I've been battling the same thing," Liam said. "But their options are limited as well. They'd be foolish to be out there in this weather. We're held up inside because of the storm, and I have no doubt so are they."

With Mia.

"Let's focus on what we can do," Liam said.

"Which is?" Gabby asked.

"Try to figure out the end game. What do they want?"

"Evidence of corruption." Gabby said. "Will was

gathering evidence of a contractor who was defrauding the government."

"Why didn't Will go to one of his superiors?" Gus asked, now back in the kitchen working on breakfast.

She shook her head. "I don't know, except that he didn't know who to trust."

"You said you spoke to several of Will's superiors," Liam said.

"I did, and no one knew what I was talking about. Unless one of them was lying."

"But that Will wasn't sure who to go to seems significant."

She moved off the hearth away from the fire and back onto the stack of blankets, then pulled one around her. "What do you mean?"

"Will was afraid that it wasn't just the contractors involved, but someone in the military."

"That makes sense," Gus said.

Gabby ran through the implications of their assessment. It did make sense. Why else wouldn't Will have gone to someone? Only if he didn't know who to trust.

"So where do we go from here?" she asked.

Liam headed back to the desk. "Gus, you said your setup here has internet connection?"

"The storm might slow it down, but it should work. I've got a pretty powerful antenna and I was able to contact Griffin once already."

"I want to get an update from him, see if he's gotten his hands on those military records for Kyle Thatcher."

A minute later, Griffin's voice came over the line.

"Griffin...this is Liam. We're hoping for an update."

"I've been holding off calling you until we had something substantive."

"And Mia?"

"We're still looking. For her as well as Thatcher and Maldin."

"What about Thatcher's army records?"

"They were just sent over, but his file's pretty thin. Looks like he was discharged, then managed to get hired by a contractor and worked for them about two years. I can send you what I have, but it's not much."

"Anyone he stayed in contact with since leaving the military?" Liam asked.

"There's no way to know. Listen, as soon as this weather clears, we'll send an ATV to pick you up. In the meantime, I can send you the parts of his file that are unclassified, so you can see if you can make a connection to something Will said in his letters. We need to find these men. And Gabby, if you can hear this, we've got the entire county looking for your daughter. We're going to find her."

As soon as the file downloaded, she started scanning through the notes, looking for anything that connected with Will's letters.

"Falcon Enterprises... Wait a minute." She turned to Liam. "Do you have your notes on Will's letters on your phone?"

Liam grabbed his phone. "Yes."

"I remember him saying something about a falcon."

"So do I," he said, pulling up his notes.

"At the time, it didn't make sense, but now..." She turned to Gus. "Can you look something up on the internet?"

Gus set one of the omelets in front of her. "As you can see with that file, it's slow, but I can try."

She took a bite of the eggs, surprised at how hungry she was.

"Okay…". Gus said a couple minutes later. "Looks like the company is involved in facilities management for the military. That would include catering, cleaning, laundry, wastes, etc. The company was run by a… Daniel Graham."

"Was?" Liam asked.

"Says Graham was CEO of the company up until about eighteen months ago."

"Right before Will died," Gabby said. "Can you find anything about him after that date?"

"I'm Googling his name, but it's strange… I'm not finding anything. It's like he vanished."

"With government funds, I'd guess," Gabby said.

Gus looked up. "I suppose it's possible."

"If he was working with someone inside the military," Gabby said, "this might all be starting to make sense. Graham defrauds the government but has help from someone on the inside. Then at some point, he takes his money and disappears."

"Will discovers what's going on," Liam said, "but doesn't want to confront one of his superiors without having any solid evidence."

"What about whoever was involved inside the military?" Gabby asked.

"Maybe he found a way out," Liam said. "Or maybe he stashed the money and is waiting until he retires. But just when he thinks he's safe—Will's dead and no one else is suspicious—"

"I start asking questions."

"We're making a lot of assumptions," Liam said, "but they do add up."

Gabby pushed her empty plate away. "Could Thatcher and Maldin have done this on their own?"

"Maybe, but what would be their motivation? Will's letters definitely imply that there's someone on the inside."

"And they have to be the one who hired the men."

Liam shrugged, still not looking convinced. "As much as this makes sense, it really is all just conjecture. There still isn't any proof that Graham is involved."

Gabby moved to the window near the front door where she could watch the still falling snow. A wave of fatigue washed over her. She was so tired, but they couldn't stop yet. There was a piece of the puzzle that was missing, but even if they did figure out what was going on, that wouldn't necessarily be enough to find Mia.

All of a sudden, the sound of splitting wood ripped through the cabin as the door slammed open. A rush of cold air sliced into the room. Gabby lunged away but wasn't fast enough as someone grabbed her and pressed a gun to her temple.

TEN

Gabby sucked in a lungful of air as the intruder wrenched her away from the door and slammed it shut, while still pressing his gun against her head. She looked up, heart pounding, and saw the familiar tattoo on the man's neck. Kyle Thatcher. Why had he returned to the cabin?

Liam and Gus's loaded weapons pointed back at him.

"You're outnumbered," Liam said. "Let her go now."

"Forget it. Set your weapons on the table, or I will shoot her. Because I don't have anything to lose at this point."

Liam took a step forward but didn't drop his gun. "What do you want, Thatcher?"

Gabby caught the man's expression and realized he was thrown at the realization that Liam knew his name. But only for a split second.

"Do what I said," Thatcher said. "This is not a negotiation. Do it, or I will shoot her."

Liam glanced at Gus and nodded. "Okay. We're putting our weapons down, but you need to let her go. None of us are going anywhere."

Thatcher pushed her into a chair, then quickly unloaded their weapons, before putting the cartridges inside his coat pocket.

Gabby fought back a wave of fear, along with the tears that threatened to follow. She didn't care about what happened to them. Her only concern at the moment was finding Mia. "Where's my daughter?"

"She's safe. Don't worry about her."

"And I'm supposed to believe you?" She started to stand up, but he aimed his weapon at her.

"I said she's fine. Sit. Down. Now."

"Just tell me where she is." She bit the edge of her lip, determined not to cry.

"I said she's safe. That's all you need to know."

"You were at James Casada's house," Liam said. "And you're the one who fired on us in the woods, I'm guessing. The police know who you are. They know you ran Gabby off the road and killed Casada. They know you're involved in the kidnapping of Mia."

"I didn't mean to kill him, but all of this...this shouldn't have happened." Thatcher started pacing in front of her. "And Mia... We didn't have a choice."

Nausea swept through Gabby. "You always have a choice."

He turned around and faced her. "None of this would have happened if you would have done what you were told to begin with."

"Give you evidence? I don't have any evidence."

Liam took a step forward. "Who hired you? We know you didn't do this on your own."

"Stop asking so many questions. There's only one thing that matters right now. My partner made it down the mountains before I did, but now the police are swarming the town. I need another way out of here."

"No chance of that. Your partner took my ATV," Gus said. "Where is it?"

"And where is Mia?" Gabby asked.

"Shut up. I'm the one running this now. Not you."

"Then what do you want us to do?" Liam asked.

Thatcher searched the room. "You had to have let the cops know. How did you communicate with them?"

"Last I recall, you also stole my radio while you were here," Gus said.

Thatcher stormed back across the room, grabbed Gabby by the shoulder and jerked her off the chair. She fought back tears, more from fear than pain.

I don't know how to make this end, God. I know I keep coming to You when things go wrong, but things are going very, very wrong right now...

"Tell me now or I will start shooting."

"Fine." Gus moved to the other side of the room. "I have another system I built."

"What can it do?"

Gus's gaze dropped. "Works with IP infrastructures and connects to Wi-Fi."

"Sounds exactly like what I need."

"Who do you want to call?"

"A cell phone."

"It can do that." Gus headed for the desk. "Give me the number, and I'll set things up for you."

Thatcher nodded back at Gabby. "The two of you stay exactly where you are."

Once Gus had managed to connect the call, Thatcher said, "Colonel Peterson...this is Thatcher. Everything's about to blow up in my face, but I'm not going down alone."

Gabby glanced at Liam, wishing she could talk to him. She'd spoken to Colonel Peterson on the phone, looking for answers. But if he was connected to Thatcher, he could be their inside man.

The radio worked on speakers, allowing all of them to hear the conversation.

"Thatcher…what's going on?"

Thatcher frowned, clearly agitated. "I've got the evidence, but it's going to cost you. Two million dollars."

"Who are you with, Thatcher?"

"All you need to know is that I've just upped the stakes. I've got three hostages now. Plus the baby."

"Okay. Listen, I understand you're upset, but you're just making things worse for yourself."

"Say what you like, but you're out of time, and the stakes have just gone up. If you don't do what I say, I will start killing them. And your involvement in all of this will come out because I'm going to tell everyone."

"Thatcher, listen—"

"No. You listen to me. I want the money transferred. Two million into the account I gave you. No games. No excuses. You got me into this mess, and now you're going to get me out of it. Because if you don't get me my money, I will go to the police and tell them everything you've done."

"Thatcher…you know I don't have that kind of money."

"I've been doing my own digging and we both know you're lying. You've got two hours."

Thatcher hung up the call, then slammed the receiver against the floor before crushing it with his boot.

Gus lunged toward him. "What are you doing?"

"Sit down, old man. You think I'm going to let you give the police a heads-up before we leave."

"Tell me what's going on," Liam started moving toward him. "Maybe I can help you."

"I doubt it. Just sit down and shut up."

"Holding us hostage isn't going to help your case," Liam said. "You're in too deep. I can see that. But it doesn't have to get worse."

"As soon as he transfers the money, I'll be able to disappear."

Liam stopped about four feet from their captor. "Do you really think it will be that easy? He said he didn't have the money."

"He's lying. Colonel Peterson can come up with the money. He got in league with some shady contractor. Why do you think he wanted me to come after you? He's terrified someone's going to find out his secret."

"What is his secret?" Gabby asked.

"A few million government dollars in an off-shore account. The kind of secret that would get him court-martialed and sent to prison for a very long time."

Despite the warmth from the fire, a chill shot through her. "He was afraid I had evidence of what he'd done."

"You're finally catching on. Only his plan to scare you into handing over the evidence didn't exactly work."

"That's because I don't think there is any evidence."

Thatcher started pacing the floor. "This was all supposed to be simple. No one was supposed to get hurt.

Casada pulled his gun on me and tried to shoot me. I never meant to kill him."

"You broke into his house," Liam said. "Did you really think that was going to end well?"

Thatcher rubbed the back of his neck. "Stop asking so many questions. There's nothing more to say. As soon as he transfers the money, this will all be over."

"You'll still be a wanted man."

"Do you know how ironic this all is?" Gabby stood up, clenching her hands into fists at her sides. "If Colonel Peterson really is involved, he did all of this for nothing because I have no idea what evidence he's looking for. Don't you see? I don't have the evidence, because Will didn't leave me any. But now my husband is dead, Casada is dead… None of this had to happen."

"He didn't know that."

Gabby moved across the room, stopping in front of Thatcher. "Can I ask you a question?"

"What?"

"Did Peterson have my husband killed because he found out what he knew?"

"I'm sorry about your husband. I really am, but I don't have the answer to that."

"So what happens now?" Liam asked.

"I need to get out of here, and you know this terrain better than anyone." Thatcher grabbed his coat. "You two are going to be my ticket out of here."

"Wait a minute." Liam's jaw tensed. "If you hadn't noticed, there's still a storm out there. Leaving the cabin would be foolish."

Thatcher took a step toward him. "You get me out

of here safely, and I'll not only make sure nothing happens to your girlfriend here, I'll make sure she gets her daughter back. But if you try anything stupid, let's just say there won't be a happy reunion."

"And where are we supposed to go?" Liam worked to rein in his temper. "I do know this terrain. Know it enough to realize that the weather's not getting any better, and taking the horses—"

"Forget it. I've already made my decision. The horses have their winter shoes. We'll go through the canyon to Canyon Falls. The authorities won't be expecting us to go there."

Liam glanced at Gus. "They won't be expecting that because they know how foolish that would be. The terrain through the canyon is difficult enough during the summertime but now, even without ice, there's already snow in the high places—"

"He's right, Thatcher," Gus said. "That route is too dangerous this time of year. You need to end this. You're only going to make things worse. What if all three of you end up losing your lives?"

Thatcher clearly wasn't convinced. "We'll manage. The snow has stopped, so even in this weather it can't be more than what…an hour, two at the most, to go down the canyon. She and I will ride together bareback." He turned back to Liam. "That will help ensure you don't do anything stupid on our way out. I'll bet you're trained military. I saw how you tracked us back on the trail tonight. If anyone can get us out of here, you can. And whatever the risk… I'm willing to take it. They won't expect me to go there and it will be a lot easier to disappear once I'm off this mountain."

"I still don't think it's worth the risk," Liam said, needing a way to convince him. "You have a good defense. If Colonel Peterson did everything you said he did, then you can work out a deal with the DA—"

"You think I'm stupid?" He glanced out the window. "They only make deals like that on TV. Not in real life. They won't listen to me. My word—a soldier who was dishonorably discharged—against an army colonel? Who do you think will win? I already know how bad things are. If I stay, I'm going to be charged with murder."

"So what will you do if I can get you off this mountain? Leave the country?"

"That's *my* problem. I think two million dollars will get me wherever I want to go. Grab us something to eat and some water, then we're leaving. And make sure you dress warm enough." Thatcher glanced out the window. "It looks like the snow has finally stopped, so I want to leave now while there's a break in the weather."

Liam frowned, frustrated at being out of control. He weighed his limited options. He and Gus could try to take Thatcher down, but the man was clearly desperate, as well as agitated. Anything they attempted could quickly spiral out of control and get one of them seriously injured or shot. And at this point, it wasn't a risk he felt he could take.

But the other alternative meant facing the danger of going out into this weather through the canyon. This time of year, that was a real risk, not just an excuse he'd come up with. He'd seen the dangers firsthand when joining rescue teams sent to search for lost hikers. Storm slabs often formed over weak layers of snow and could turn into avalanches during periods of heavy snow, especially on slopes and gullies… Exactly the kind of terrain they'd be traversing. And if they ended up caught in a terrain trap, the chances of them getting out alive would be slim. He'd lived most of his life in these mountains and even trained with the army in Arctic conditions for nine months. But all of his knowledge only confirmed that they were making a huge mistake.

His biggest concern, though, was for Gabby.

"Let her stay," he said, slipping on his coat. "I give you my word that I'll do everything I can to get you safely to Canyon Falls, but a third person will simply slow the horses down—"

"Forget it. I make the rules, and I say she's coming. It's time to leave. You, old man, need to sit down in that chair." Thatcher pulled a couple zip ties from his coat pocket, then secured Gus to one of the chairs. "Don't get any ideas about playing hero and going for help."

Outside, the snow had stopped falling and the temperature had risen a few degrees, but none of that took away Liam's worry. A minute later, they took off at a slow, steady pace with him in the lead and Gabby and Thatcher behind him. He'd wanted a moment to talk with her alone. A moment to tell her he was going to do everything in his power to get them safely off this mountain. And what he couldn't do, he could only pray that God would help them end this.

The sun was slowly melting the snow that had covered the ground overnight. But that also left the possibility of sink holes and avalanches from above them. Still, Liam couldn't help but notice the beauty around him. White snow dusted the green trees and canyon walls. On any other day, he would have loved to show Gabby this part of the mountains. While dangerous to the unprepared hiker, the canyon that wound its way next to the river was not only secluded but held some of the most stunning views in the county. But they clearly weren't here to sightsee.

While the canyon narrowed significantly at several places, it would still be wide enough for the horses to get through. But it was the snow and potential ice, even with the warming temperatures, that had him worried. The horses would be able to adapt to the cold weather, but they could also easily fracture a leg. The risks in his mind were simply too great, but for the moment there was nothing he could do but keep moving, and pray they made it to Canyon Falls in one piece.

The sound of falling ice to his right shifted his attention. He pulled on the reins of his horse, then signaled for Thatcher to stop.

"Move back. Now."

Liam turned his horse around on the narrow trail.

"What's going on?"

A second later, a massive amount of snow crashed down the mountainside from above them like a raging river.

"Liam…"

He had to shout above the noise. "Stay where you are and we'll be okay."

He stroked the horse at the tip of its shoulders, working to keep it calm so it wouldn't bolt.

The eerie silence that followed seemed to swallow them. He studied the rise above, but for the moment, it seemed they were safe. Most of the snow had fallen on the other side of the trail, giving them just enough room to pass. He glanced at the familiar landmarks. Another fifteen minutes and they should be out of here.

Liam felt the tension in his neck begin to dissipate as they finally approached the mouth of the canyon. Sunlight streamed into the valley ahead of them, sparkling on the snow covering the open fields. Liam stopped his horse beneath the sheer red-rock cliffs rising up beside him and waited for them to catch up. "What happens now?"

"My phone should work here. I'll check and see if he's deposited the money."

"And my daughter?" Gabby asked. "You said you'd tell me where she is if Liam brought you here, and he did."

"As soon as I verify the money, I will."

"The trail leads to the edge of town. The horses are worn out and are going to need water and something to eat."

"There's no signal yet. We have to get closer to town so I can connect."

A minute later, Liam caught sight of an older man wearing one of the army's cold-weather jackets and walking toward them near the trailhead.

"Colonel Peterson?"

The colonel took a step forward. "Thatcher... I thought I'd find you here."

An uneasy feeling settled over Liam as they approached the man.

ELEVEN

Exhaustion swept through Gabby, heavier than the cold. All she wanted to do was find Mia and go home, but the realization of who was standing in front of them didn't make sense. If he'd been the one to hire Thatcher, showing up seemed foolish.

Thatcher slid down off the horse, leaving her alone on the back of the animal. "How did you find us?"

"I know you better than you think, Thatcher. I trained you, didn't I? My job was to anticipate your next move and always stay one step ahead of you. Mountain Springs was swarming with law enforcement. You're smart. I figured you'd use the canyon to try and escape, which would mean you would have to pass by here, and I was right."

Thatcher's hands shook as he pulled out his weapon and aimed it at the colonel. "That doesn't explain why you are here."

"I heard what happened on the news and called the authorities. Told them I might be able to talk some sense into you. So despite this nasty weather, I decided to make the drive. They said a man is dead and a baby has been kidnapped. I know you're in a lot of trouble. That's why I came. To help you."

Thatcher took a step forward, tension showing in his jaw. "You thought you needed to talk some sense into me? To help me? Who are you? My shrink?"

"Of course not. But I do think I can help."

Thatcher laughed. "You're lying. You're here to make sure I never get a chance to talk to the authorities. But whatever your plan is won't work. I've told these two the truth. They know everything. You might be able to explain why you shot and killed me, but not all of us. You'll never get away with that."

"You're wrong, Thatcher. I don't want to hurt you. And no one else needs to get hurt. That's why I'm here. Why I want you to listen to me."

"Why should I listen to you?"

"When you first enlisted, you had noble reasons for what you were doing. You ended up getting in with the wrong people and followed them. I know it wasn't your fault. Not entirely anyway. I always wished back then that you would have come to me. I might have been able to fix things.

"You want to fix things? Then tell them the truth." Thatcher gripped the gun with two hands. "Tell them that you're the one who got me into this mess, because I'm not going to prison the rest of my life for what happened. This is on you. Not me."

"Thatcher…listen to me. I know you're upset, and I understand. But you need to put the gun down before someone else gets hurt. And we can't let that happen, can we?"

Thatcher pressed his left palm against his temple.

"Why do you keep lying? Is that really what you want? It would be a lot easier to explain why you shot me if I was armed."

"Thatcher, you need to listen to him." Liam got off his horse. "We have to put an end to this now. No one else needs to get hurt."

"I've been talking to the authorities," the colonel said. "They're on their way right now. I just thought we could end this peacefully without anyone getting hurt. Without *you* getting hurt, Thatcher. I was worried what would happen if you didn't feel like anyone here was on your side. Afraid you might do something foolish like shoot someone."

Thatcher took a step toward the colonel. "Don't talk to me that way. Like I'm imagining things. All I did was what you told me to do. I did everything you asked. Broke into her house. Put a tracking device on her car…"

"I've tried to help you, Thatcher. Tried to make you listen to reason." The colonel pulled out his own weapon. "Put the gun down, Thatcher. You know everything you did was your choice, not mine. I'm not going to take responsibility for what happened, but I will help you. Just like I've always tried to do. But not this way."

"He's lying."

Thatcher caught Gabby's gaze. She could hear the panic in his voice but had no idea which one of them was telling the truth. And at the moment she didn't care. All she wanted was to find Mia.

"Everything he says is a lie," Thatcher continued. "He is the one who told me to go after you. To find the evidence Will had and make sure no one ever got it. You believe me, don't you?"

"But there is no evidence, is there, Thatcher?" The colonel kept speaking, his words barely above a whisper. "Because none of that is true. You did this on your own. Everyone knows that. You know that. I know that. The cops know that. It's time to stop and get the help you need."

Gabby got down from the horse, tired of the games. Tired of everything. Thatcher's story about the colonel had been completely believable. But the truth was, she didn't care about who was to blame. She just wanted her baby. And one, if not both, of these men knew where she was.

She walked up to Thatcher.

"Gabby, stay back."

She ignored Liam's warning. "I don't care who did what anymore. All I want is my baby. Where is Mia? You know where she is, Thatcher. You promised me she'd be okay if we did what you said. We came with you here."

Thatcher shook his head. "This wasn't supposed to end this way."

"Where is she, Thatcher?"

"Shut up." He pressed his hands against his ears.

"Thatcher…" Colonel Peterson took a step forward. "Tell her where the baby is. This can stop. All of it. We'll make sure you get the help you need when this is over."

"I don't need help." He was shouting now. The veins in his neck pulsed. "I told you to shut up. All of you. Mia was my leverage to get you to pay. My leverage to make sure you did everything you promised. You told me you'd send the money. Where is the money?"

"We can work this out, but first put the gun down, Thatcher. I just want help."

"It's a lie. You never wanted to help. Never intended to give me the money, did you? You only took advantage of me. Because I know you have it. Five-point-three million dollars. I didn't even ask for all of it. Just enough to allow me to disappear. Tell them that. Tell them you had to wait until you retired before you disappeared with the money."

"None of what you are saying is true, Thatcher, and you know it. All I ever wanted to do was help you, but you never wanted me to. And that is why I can't. There is no money. There never was. I'm sorry. This has to end. I can make sure you get the support you need. Why don't you let me?"

"You were never planning to help me. You lied about the money—"

"You're not listening. There is no money. This was all your imagination. Think about it. All your idea."

"No…no…" Thatcher fired his gun, but his shot missed.

The colonel's return shot hit Thatcher in the chest.

Thatcher dropped to the ground next to Gabby, blood spreading on his abdomen.

"No!" Gabby heard her own scream as she looked down at Thatcher. "Why did you do that? You didn't have to shoot him. He's knows how to find Mia."

Gabby knelt down beside Thatcher. They couldn't lose him. Not now. Not without knowing where her daughter was.

She yanked off her scarf and pressed it to where he'd been shot. This couldn't be happening. She had to find Mia. "Where is she? Tell me where Maldin took my daughter."

"She...she's safe."

"Tell me where they are...please."

He was rambling now. His face had paled. He was losing too much blood. "He took her to...to a hotel. Pass... I'm...sorry."

Gabby checked for a pulse. Panic ripped through her. He couldn't be dead. Not yet. He knew were Mia was and without him... What if they couldn't find Mia and Maldin?

She grabbed Thatcher's hand, trying to get him to talk to her.

Liam knelt down beside her, then squeezed her shoulder. "He's gone, Gabby, but we will still find her."

"He can't be. We don't know where Mia is." She didn't even try to stop the flow of tears this time. Exhaustion mingled with panic overtook her, sending her to a frightening place she didn't want to go. "We don't know where my baby is."

Liam pulled Gabby away from Thatcher's lifeless body, still trying to process how quickly things had spiraled out of control over the past couple days. And now he had no idea who was telling the truth. But for the moment, it didn't matter. His priority had to be keeping Gabby safe and finding Mia.

Gabby ran toward the colonel, her cheeks flushed as much from anger, he was certain, as from the cold.

She pounded her fists against his chest. "You didn't have to shoot him."

"He shot at me. What was I supposed to do?"

"You don't get it. He took my daughter. Knows where she is, but now—"

Liam pulled her back from the man. He understood her anger and believed it was even justified, but there were still too many unanswered questions to make a judgment.

"It's alright," the colonel said. "I understand. I can't even imagine how terrified you must be right now."

Liam took out his phone, praying Griffin would pick up quickly. "Gabby…what did he say?"

"Just that she's at a hotel. Through the pass, I think."

"Where?"

"I don't know. He didn't say."

Not being able to narrow down where he'd taken Mia was going to make the search more challenging, but starting in Mountain Springs seemed like the most logical step. He turned back to the Colonel. For the moment, they needed the man's help, which meant they had no choice but to trust him.

"Colonel Peterson, do you have a vehicle?"

"Yes. I drove here. My car's parked in a lot just around the corner—"

"Call 911 and get someone here. I'm sure the local authorities are going to need to talk to us about what happened, but we need to get to Mountain Springs."

Gabby stood in front of the colonel while Liam waited for Griffin to answer, her hands at her side, the muscles in her jaw tense. "This is your fault. He told us you put him up to this. That you hired him to search my house and scare me in order to get the evidence my husband had against you. And now, not only is Will dead but James Casada and Thatcher as well. And my daughter... I have no idea where she is."

The colonel shook his head. "I know how all of this looks, and I'm so sorry for everything you've had to go through, but I knew Private Thatcher. He struggled to assimilate into military life until he was discharged. Truth is, he never should have joined the military."

"Griffin...where are you?" Liam said, once his brother answered.

"On my way to Canyon Falls. We just got a lead from a Colonel Peterson that Thatcher is there, but I was about to ask you the same question."

"I'm just outside Canyon Falls. Have you found the other suspect?"

"No, but what about you? How did you get there?"

"Thatcher arrived at the cabin and forced me to go with him as his guide through the canyon. Gabby's here as well. But Thatcher..." He paused before continuing. "Thatcher's dead."

"Dead? How did that happen?"

"Colonel Peterson was waiting for us at the end of the canyon and he shot Thatcher. I was here and saw what happened. It was clearly self-defense. Thatcher pulled a gun on him and shot at him first, but..." He hesitated again.

"But what?"

Liam turned away and lowered his voice. "Let's just say I'm not sure the situation is really as black-and-white as it appears. But there's something more important right now. Mia's still out there somewhere and we need to find her. The second man is our only link right now. According to what Thatcher said before he died, we think Mia is in a hotel, probably in Mountain Springs, but we don't know which one."

"That narrows it down a bit, but there are at least two dozen hotels in town. We'll start canvassing them immediately. We've already set up roadblocks for every way out of town. Wherever he is, we will find him. It's just a matter of time."

"But you need to be careful. I'm worried about what the man might do. He's going to panic if he finds out Thatcher is dead. And if he decides to use Mia as leverage, we could have a hostage situation on our hands or worse."

"What about the local authorities?" Griffin asked.

Sirens blared as three police cars pulled up. The colonel put his weapon on the ground and raised his hands. "They've just arrived, so I'm going to go for now, but Gabby and I will meet you there as soon as we can. You're going to need all the manpower you can get to find her."

"First, let me talk to whoever's in charge at the scene."

"Put your hands in the air…all three of you."

Liam raised his hands above his head. "My brother, Deputy Griffin O'Callaghan with the sheriff's department in Timber Falls is on the phone and would like to talk to you."

One of the officers stepped forward. "Who are you?"

"Captain Liam O'Callaghan, sir, with the US Army. You can check my ID if you need to."

Liam looked at Gabby while they waited for the two

men to talk. Officers were already cordoning off the scene, so they could start their investigation.

"Are you okay?" he asked her.

"I just need to find Mia. That's all that matters right now."

He squeezed her fingers. "We're going to find her."

A minute later, the officer walked back to them. "Your brother's pretty convincing. I'm still going to need full statements from both of you, but in the meantime, I'll have my deputy drive you to Mountain Springs so you can help with the search. But you, sir..." He turned to Colonel Peterson. "You're going to have to come with us now so we can get a complete statement."

"Of course. I understand."

"And the horses?" Gabby asked.

"I'll have one of my officers take care of them."

An hour and a half later, they were canvassing hotels in Mountain Springs with two officers from the local police station. Liam still had a pile of questions, including why the colonel had suddenly appeared and, even more disturbing, had he really felt forced to shoot Thatcher. But only one thing really mattered right now, and that was finding Mia.

"How many hotels are left?" She glanced at him as they pulled into the parking lot of their third hotel.

"This is one of the last ones," Officer Thompson answered.

Her frown deepened. "This is like looking for a needle in the haystack. We don't even have any guarantees that they're still in Mountain Springs. And if Maldin saw the news...knows that Thatcher is dead, his next move is going to be to get as far away from here as possible. What if we're too late?"

He squeezed her hand, feeling her frustration. "She's got to be here. The authorities have set up roadblocks. Wherever this guy is, he's not going anywhere, and he knows it. Someone out there has seen her."

"What do you want us to do?"

"The two of you take this one. We'll take the one across the street."

"And after that?" Gabby asked.

"We're going to find her, Gabby. Whatever it takes."

They climbed out of the squad car and headed for the hotel lobby. Gabby's worry was justified. Pretty soon, they would have to expand the perimeter of the search.

Liam burst into the lobby of the hotel in front of Gabby and stepped up to the receptionist. "Have you seen either of these men? Possibly with a baby."

The clerk stared at the photo a few seconds, then shook her head, clearly not interested in getting involved. "Sorry. I don't think so."

"Please look at this again. This is my baby." Gabby leaned against the counter. "Are you sure?"

The woman glanced back at the photo a few more seconds. "Actually... I think I do recognize him, but I don't want any trouble here."

"He kidnapped the baby he was with," Liam said.

"Kidnapped?" The woman's face paled. "He told me his wife was sick and had just been admitted into the hospital. Made me feel so sorry for him. I can't believe he's wanted by the police."

"What room is he in?" Liam asked.

"He was in room 124."

Gabby rushed out of the lobby in front of Liam toward the row of rooms with parking-lot access while he called in their find to the authorities. He had no desire to confront an armed man on his own, but if he had to, he would.

The door to room 124 swung open as they approached.

"Mia?"

The little girl was sobbing in a crib in the back corner of the room. Maldin tried to shut the door, but Liam stopped it with his foot. Rushing across the room, Maldin dropped the ice bucket he'd been holding, grabbed Mia out of the crib and held up a gun. "Stay back. Both of you. Or I will hurt her."

TWELVE

Gabby caught the desperation in the man's voice. Mia whimpered in his arms. So close and yet she couldn't go to her without risking her daughter's life. Maldin was panicked. She could see it in his eyes. They couldn't count on the police to get here in time, which meant they needed to find a way to stop him before someone got hurt.

She grabbed onto Liam's coat. "We've got to get her out of here," she whispered.

"We will." He grabbed her hand, his focus trained on the man standing in front of them with a gun. "Silas Maldin... That's your name, isn't it?"

"How do you know that?"

"We saw Thatcher up at the cabin."

Sweat beaded on his forehead despite the cold temperatures. "Thatcher told me to wait here, then never showed up."

"Thatcher never should have done that, but this is over. I want you to give Mia to her mother, because if you hurt her, you're going to be in a lot more trouble and I don't think either of us wants to see that happen.

The police are already here and will be at your door any second now."

Mia was crying harder now, her cheeks flushed red as she squirmed in the man's arms. Gabby's fingers pinched Liam's arm.

"Please let me have her. She's hungry and tired."

"I don't want her to get hurt. I don't want anyone to get hurt, but in order for that to happen, you're going to have to do what I say."

"Then tell me what you want," Liam said.

"A way out of here. We never meant to hurt that man. The money they offered us was good, but we never meant to hurt anyone. Instead things got out of control. That man was shot in self-defense."

While you were burglarizing his home.

She bit back the sharp response on the tip of her tongue. Angering him further wasn't the answer, but what was? He wasn't going to take responsibility for what he'd done. In his eyes, he was the victim.

"That might be true, but we don't want that to happen again." Liam's voice was calm and steady. "Not only have you killed a man, you've kidnapped Mia."

"That was only for leverage. We never would have hurt her."

"Then let me help you find a way to put an end to this. I'll help you deal with the police, but give us the baby."

He shook his head. "I can't go back to prison."

"You can make a deal with the DA for a lesser sentence. Who hired you, for starters?"

Shadows breached the window, turning the man's attention to the front of the room.

"Who's out there?" he asked.

"I'm guessing the officers who've been looking for Mia."

"Tell them to get back or someone's going to get hurt."

Liam held up his hands. "I've got their direct number. I'll tell them."

Gabby studied Liam's expression for a moment while he talked with the police, then looked back at Mia. She was so close. A dozen steps away and crying, and yet there was nothing she could do.

We're so close to this being over, God, but I feel so hopeless.

Liam hung up his phone. "The officers are moving back, but we need to find a way to end this without anyone getting hurt."

Maldin leaned against the yellowed walls, trying to get Mia to stop crying. "Can you make her stop?"

"Just let me take her. Please."

"I can't do that. She's my leverage."

Liam squeezed Gabby's elbow, then took a step forward. "Let's figure a way out of this together. It is correct someone hired you, right?"

"Yes, but Thatcher never told me who. Told me it would make sure I didn't get into trouble if things went wrong. The less I knew the better. But now… I just know that I need to get out of here."

"Here's what I know," Liam said. "If you run, you're only going to make things worse. But if you end this now—give Mia back to her mom and give yourself up—you'll have more of a chance of making a deal. I promise."

"Forget it. One way or the other, I'm going to walk out of here free."

"Where do you want to go?" Liam asked.

"It doesn't matter, but here's my deal. I need unmarked cash. Enough to get me somewhere I can't be traced."

Mia continued to fuss, and Gabby could tell by Maldin's expression that he was getting irritated. Despite Liam's calming voice, she felt her own anxiety growing. Because at this point, was whatever he said going to be enough?

Gabby drew in a deep breath. "She's hungry. There's a vending machine around the corner. Let me get something for her. It will calm her down. Please…"

Liam pulled a dollar out of his pocket and handed it to her. "Let her go get something. I'll stay here with you."

Maldin hesitated, then nodded. "Don't do anything stupid. Get her something and come straight back."

"I will. I promise."

"And don't talk to anyone out there. Because if you do, you won't see either of them again." He glanced at his watch. "You've got ninety seconds starting now."

Gabby slipped out of the room, praying her legs wouldn't give way as she followed the sign and turned down a narrow hallway. Paint was chipping off the walls as if the place hadn't been repaired for years. But she barely saw anything. Griffin and his men were here somewhere, but clearly following the instructions to stay out of the way.

She slid the dollar into the vending machine, then pushed the button for a bag of cheese crackers, feeling the weight of the situation pressing against her chest like a vise. It might not be something she typically bought for Mia, but at least it should calm her down.

She jumped as ice clanked in the machine next to her, dumping a batch of frozen cubes.

Griffin stepped up next to her. "Did he let you go?"

"He gave me ninety seconds to buy something for Mia to eat," she said. "But I have to go back."

"Which gives me about thirty seconds. What's going on in there?"

"He's alone but motivated by fear. He wants out of this but is afraid of going back to prison. He wants cash to drive out of here."

"Where is he standing?"

"Toward the back of the room. He's got a handgun… a Glock…and he's holding Mia."

"Which definitely limits our options. We've got a SWAT team lined up. Try to get him to let you take Mia. Then get him by the window if you can, though with the three of you inside we won't take any unnecessary risks."

She caught Griffin's gaze and realized what he was saying. But as much as she didn't want anyone to get killed—including Maldin—she knew she'd fight to save her daughter.

"As a last resort only, I promise."

She nodded before heading back to the room, carrying the crackers and her hands held up. Mia was still fussing in Maldin's arms, her eyes red from crying. "Can I take her? Please? It's the only way she'll stop fussing."

He hesitated, then handed her to Gabby. Mia lunged

into her arms, then nestled her head on her mom's shoulder still sobbing. "Hey, my sweet girl. How are you doing? Mama missed you so much."

Mia pulled back and looked up at her, big tears running down her cheeks. Gabby opened the cheese crackers and gave her one.

"Sit down over there, because this isn't over." Maldin paced the worn carpet in front of her but away from the window. "I still need a way out of here."

Gabby glanced at Liam. It was clear Maldin had no clear plan and was simply winging it, but she also knew it wasn't going to take much for him to explode.

"Thank you," Liam said. "You made the right decision letting her go back to her mother."

"Maybe, but here's the plan," Maldin said. "I want you to call the police again. Tell them I want ten thousand dollars cash and a car. I'll take the two of them with me to make sure I'm not tailed. If my instructions are followed, I'll leave them somewhere safe. But that means no one comes after us. No cops."

"That can't happen, Maldin." Liam took a step forward. "But I'll make a deal with you."

"What kind of deal?"

"I'll go with you. I'll leave with you and guarantee that no cops follow you. I'll take you somewhere safe where you can disappear."

"There are roadblocks. I saw it on the news."

"I'll get you past them. I'll be your hostage. But let them go."

Gabby tried to swallow the lump that had formed in her throat. "Liam, no—"

He signaled her to be quiet. "I'll go with you, but that

means you let Gabby and her daughter go. They don't need to be involved in this any longer."

The man glanced at the window. "No games?"

"No games."

Gabby pulled Mia closer against her chest and sat down on the edge of the bed. There had to be another option. One that didn't involve either of them leaving with the man. Once he got wherever it was he wanted to go, he wouldn't need any of them. It was too big of a risk.

"Liam, you can't go with him."

"I want this over as much as you do. Trust me." He turned back to Maldin. "My brother's a deputy in Timber Falls. I can have him arrange your demands."

"Call him, but put it on speaker phone."

Liam placed the call, then held up his cell. "Griffin... I've made a deal with Maldin. He's going to let Gabby and Mia go, and in exchange, I'm going to drive him out of here. He's also demanding ten grand."

"Ten grand? That will take time to get together."

"You've got thirty minutes," Maldin said. "Pull all cops back at least three blocks and leave the money and something for lunch outside my door. If you follow me or try to do anything, I will kill your brother."

Thirty minutes later, Gabby felt her lungs constrict as she watched Maldin walk Liam out of the hotel room. The man stood behind Liam so there wasn't the possibility of the sniper taking him down from his position. Which meant there was no way out of this for Liam. Everything that had happened over the past couple days pressed in around Gabby. Mia was safe, and for that she was grateful, but this was far from over.

Griffin stepped into the room. "Are you both okay?"

"Yes, but you can't let Liam drive away with that guy. There has to be another way."

"I'm not sure we have a choice. When you're driven by fear, you don't make logical decisions. If we interfere at this point, someone's going to get hurt. And that someone's going to be Liam."

"Yes, but you can't just let him leave. Is there a way to track him?"

"We're counting on it. We'll be able to keep tabs on where they go through the GPS on the car and possibly through their cell phones as well. I've got a tech already working on it. And in the meantime, Liam's trained to handle situations like this. He's going to be okay."

Except he couldn't promise her that.

"And you think that will be enough to ensure Liam's safety?" Mia started fussing again. Gabby handed her another cracker. Liam had traded himself for her and her daughter. She owed him their lives. There had to be something she could do to help.

"Everything we could find about Maldin—which wasn't much—shows that he has a temper and is impulsive. So as much as I hate the call Liam made, there weren't many options. I don't think it would have taken much to set him off."

"But what happens when he's done with Liam? If he gets to where he thinks he's safe, then Liam is no longer insurance but a liability."

"We're following protocol as much as possible, but things don't always play out the way we want them to.

In a sense, Liam has become the negotiator, the setting has just changed. But Liam can handle this. He took the man seriously, showed empathy and gave him an option—"

"An option that could cost Liam his life."

Griffin sat down next to her. "I know this is hard, Gabby, but Liam knew what he was doing, and I can promise you, he doesn't want you to feel guilty for the situation he's in. None of this is your fault."

"None of this would have happened if I hadn't come to him."

"What do you think would have happened if you'd faced those men alone? You did the right thing, because no matter what you think, he feels responsible for you. And that kind of responsibility isn't something Liam takes lightly."

"But what if he's killed?"

"I have no plans of taking any chances with my brother's life. Which is the one reason I let them walk out of here without any physical force involved."

"He saved my daughter, but if anything happens to him... I just need to do something."

"I am going to need your help. I know you're exhausted, but we need to take a full statement on everything that's happened while it's fresh on your mind, then we'll get you and Mia out to the ranch where my parents are waiting. And in the meantime, I promise to keep you updated on what's going on." He stood up and signaled to one of the other officers. "We'll get him back."

She nodded. "I'll do everything I can to help, but what do you think Maldin plans to do?"

"Hopefully, as soon as they're far enough away

that Maldin feels it's safe to disappear, he'll let my brother go."

"And if he doesn't?"

Mia started fussing again. Gabby needed to get her to bed. And Mia wasn't the only one exhausted.

"Liam can handle a situation like this, Gabby. He's trained and he's smart."

"I know, it's just…" She pressed her lips together, unable to sort through the pile of emotions fluttering to the surface. She could taste the metallic flavor of blood where she'd bitten her lip. She grabbed Mia's giraffe and gave it to her. Right now, she needed to focus on her daughter, tell the detectives anything that might help put an end to all of this and let the authorities do their job.

But what if that wasn't enough to bring Liam back safely?

"We'll try to keep it short, so you can get her to bed."

"What will you do?"

"Make sure we keep our tail on him, for starters."

"I trust you. I trust Liam, but Maldin…he was involved in Casada's murder and now the stakes are rising. He's staking everything on getting away no matter how foolish his plan is, and he'll do anything to ensure he doesn't go back to prison." She grabbed Mia's blanket, then stood up. "There's something else you need to know. According to Kyle Thatcher, Colonel Peterson is the one who hired them."

Griffin stopped in the doorway. "What?"

"He's the one who hired Thatcher and Maldin. The one who's been behind all of this."

"Thatcher told you that?"

"Yes."

"The colonel told us Thatcher had accused him of a number of things, but so far there is no evidence that points to the fact that Thatcher was working for Peterson. In fact, everything we have so far indicates Thatcher and Maldin were working alone."

Gabby shook her head. "He told us everything in detail. Why would he have made all that up?"

"Clearly, he didn't want to go to jail. I'm not sure what his plan was, but I've seen it dozens of times. People in Thatcher's situation never take the blame for what they did. They always try to transfer it to someone else."

Gabby paused. Hadn't Maldin done the same thing? Pushed the blame for what had happened on to someone else? But Thatcher had been convincing with details and the timeline of what had happened. He knew things that made the colonel's involvement seem plausible.

"But what if he's telling the truth?" she asked.

"We will continue to investigate everything that happened, but so far there just isn't any evidence."

No evidence of his involvement seemed impossible. Unless Colonel Peterson really was telling the truth.

"Gabby, I promise we'll get to the bottom of this. But right now, we need to go. I'm concerned about Liam's safety as much as you are."

"I know. And I'm sorry. He's your brother. I know you care. I just feel as if I owe him so much."

My life. Mia's life...

Mia's head lay burrowed in Gabby's shoulder as she shut her eyes and her breathing deepened. The poor baby was exhausted. They were both exhausted.

"I'm going to drive you back to the ranch," Griffin

said. "I can take your statement from there. Just know we're doing everything we can to find him."

"I know."

Ten minutes later, she held back the tears as she put Mia into the car seat. She slid into the back seat next to the little girl and put on her seat belt. She felt numb and scared. Liam had saved her daughter's life. Now they just had to make sure they saved his.

Gabby took Mia's small hand and enclosed it in her own. Liam would be alright. She had to believe that.

She stared out the window, still holding Mia's hand. The snow had stopped after leaving several inches behind. But she barely noticed the view. What if she never saw Liam again? The thought of something happening to him hurt, but it shouldn't hurt this much. It shouldn't feel like her heart was shattering into a thousand pieces. He was just a friend. Someone who'd been close to Will and who had helped her out of obligation. Nothing more. And certainly not someone who'd managed to wedge his way into the recesses of her heart and made her wonder for the first time if loving someone again was even possible.

Was it?

Will had told her once if he didn't come home from deployment, he wanted her to fall in love again and get remarried. At the time, she'd fiercely rejected the idea and felt it would somehow be unfaithful to her husband. Instead, she'd imagined them growing old together. A houseful of kids. Summer vacations and skiing in the winter. Not losing him like this. But reality was never as nice and neat as a fairytale where the bad guys always lost and the prince and princess always lived happily-ever-after.

But what about second chances? What about picking up the messy baggage and trying to put the pieces together for something new? Was that even possible? Maybe. Eventually. But Liam… She couldn't fall for him.

Memories surrounded her. Every time Will had left for deployment or for another mission, she'd carried her phone with her everywhere she went, constantly checking to make sure the ringer volume was up and she hadn't missed a call.

Which was the problem. If she allowed something to happen with Liam, she'd be right back in the same place again. Liam was a soldier, dedicated to his country. That was who he was. Brave, loyal, heroic… It was what she loved about him, but when it came to her heart…that was another story. That wasn't going to happen again. Couldn't happen again. Because getting involved emotionally would be disastrous for her heart.

THIRTEEN

Liam pushed his way through Denver traffic, heading north as instructed. Maldin had insisted he drive but made it clear if he did anything to get someone's attention, he wouldn't hesitate to make him pay. And with the man's nerves clearly strung tight, Liam had decided to simply follow directions and wait for an opportunity when he could put an end to all of this without the risk of someone getting hurt. Besides, all that really mattered right now was that Gabby and Mia were safe. That had been his goal through all of this. He'd find a way to take the man down, but right now wasn't the time.

He glanced into his rearview mirror at the tan sedan four cars back. He'd spotted the tail when they'd left Mountain Springs and hoped Maldin hadn't noticed. But he couldn't be sure. The guy wasn't stupid.

What he didn't know was if Maldin actually had a backup plan in place, or if he was simply figuring things out as he went. The man had been on the phone on and off for the past thirty minutes, talking to someone about an apparent exit strategy, but Liam had no idea who he'd gone to for help. But assuming the man had no plan and no resources would be a mistake. He had a loaded gun and if given the right circumstances, there was no doubt in Liam's mind that the man would use it.

Maldin let out a huff of air, then dropped his phone into his lap. "I want you to take the next exit, then turn left at the light."

"I'll try, but the traffic's heavy." Liam turned on his blinker from the center lane, then started to merge into the exiting lane. "Where are we heading?"

"You don't need to worry about that right now."

Maldin glanced into his side window again and frowned. There was no doubt in Liam's mind anymore. The man had discovered the tail.

"Something wrong?"

"Don't be stupid. I told them no tails, and they've got someone behind us." He fingered the gun in his lap. "You will lose them, because I'd hate for your brother to find you dead in some ditch when all of this is over."

Liam took the exit ramp, then quickly made a left turn at the green light. He followed the man's instructions, weaving through the heavy traffic in an attempt to ditch their tail. A mile later, he glanced at his rearview mirror. The tan car was nowhere in sight.

"Keep heading north. We'll turn off in a few minutes."

Liam tightened his fingers around the steering wheel, wishing he were home right now eating dinner with his parents and Gabby. His mother had told him she was planning to make lasagna, one of his favorites. He'd been looking forward to spending time with Gabby. Instead, he didn't want to know what his mother was thinking right now. He knew she worried every time one of her boys found themselves in a dangerous situation, which happened more often than not in their lines of work. Maybe he hadn't told her enough how he felt.

But he knew she would understand his decision. Taking Gabby and Mia's place had been automatic. He'd have done the same for anyone. Or at least that's what he'd tried to convince himself of. He was still sorting through his feelings toward Gabby. Feelings he probably wouldn't be able to fully process until all of this was over. And when it was over, they'd both go their separate ways, but he'd still feel responsible for her. There was no doubt about that. But he also couldn't ignore that there was something more.

Maldin's threats to take Gabby and Mia had shown Liam how terrified he was of losing them. There was nothing really noble or brave about his decision. It was simply how he'd been trained and who he was. And a reminder of how he wanted them in his life.

He glanced over at Maldin as he followed the now narrow road northwest. He wasn't sure building a rapport with the man sitting next to him was possible, but it was worth a try. The more he could understand Maldin's motivation and even possibly figure out what his plan was the better.

"Thank you for letting them go," Liam said.

"Are you the baby's father?"

He glanced at the man, surprised at his question. "No."

"Then why do you care what happens to her?"

"She was my best friend's daughter."

"Something happened to him?"

"He was killed."

His answer was ignored. Gaining Maldin's sympathy wasn't working. The man clearly had no desire to talk with him.

He decided to try a more direct approach. "Where are we heading?"

"Another fifty miles or so. I've got a friend with access to an airstrip. I'll let you go once we're there, as long as you don't try anything in the meantime."

"You know you don't have to follow through with this," he said. "The sooner you turn yourself in, the fewer charges you'll be facing. Being a fugitive isn't easy."

"Turn myself in? Forget it. I don't have anything to lose at this point."

Liam shifted in his seat, frustrated. Because he did.

The thought surprised him. The past year had taken a toll on him emotionally. Months of physical therapy had meant hard work mixed in with occasional bouts of depression. And he still had no idea if he was going to be able to go back to active duty. The decision had been taken completely out of his hands and weighed heavily on him, leaving him feeling out of control. Like he'd lost everything he'd worked for in one moment.

The moment that had killed his best friend.

Except for the occasional command, silence hovered between them until Maldin directed him to turn off down a narrow gravel road lined with trees. The headlights caught a deer running out in front of them in the cover of dusk, pulling Liam back to the present. He slammed on his brakes and skidded on the gravel, barely missing the animal. The car slid to a stop, but his heart kept racing.

"What are you doing?" Maldin braced his hands against the dash. "Trying to get us both killed?"

"Hardly."

Maldin banged on the console between them. "Keep going. We're running out of time."

Time for what, he wasn't sure. He focused his attention back on the road. Darkness began to settle in around them, forcing him to drop his speed. On top of that, he wasn't sure where they were. No other cars. No cabins. Wherever they were going was isolated. There were a handful of private airstrips, and if Maldin had the right connections, it would be the easiest way out of here. Though where the man would go, Liam had no idea.

"We're here. Stop the car, then get out."

Liam checked the odometer, then turned off the car. Maldin snatched the keys out of his hand. They'd driven just over twenty miles from the turnoff. He stepped out of the car. The temperatures were dropping again, and a dusting of snow already covered the ground.

"Where are we going?"

"You're not going anywhere. Get out."

"You're leaving me here? We're twenty miles from the main road."

"What did you expect? I could shoot you, too, but instead I think I'll let you walk out of here. There are no cell phone towers nearby and very little if any traffic. But it's the best I can do."

"So I'm guessing there isn't a cabin or somewhere I can stay till morning?"

"That's not my problem."

The question probably sounded ridiculous. He was a hostage, not a guest. Maldin had made that clear.

Liam shivered as he looked around, wishing he had his heavy coat that had gotten left at the hotel. Unlike his parents' ranch, he didn't know the terrain. While Maldin might have let him go, this wasn't over. If he didn't find shelter, he wouldn't make it through the night.

Gabby sat in the O'Callaghan living room, telling Griffin everything she could remember about the past twelve hours. But relaying the details about Thatcher and their conversation in Gus's cabin and the moments surrounding the man's death felt more as if she were reciting scenes from a movie. Certainly not from her own life. The knot of fear in her gut tightened, reminding her that this was all too real. And until they found Liam, she wasn't going to be able to put all of this behind her.

Griffin's phone rang, giving her a brief respite from steady stream of emotion that had come with the retelling of what had happen. He checked the caller ID, then stood up.

"Give me a sec… I need to take this call."

"Of course."

She glanced down at Mia, who had finally gone to sleep and was now breathing softly in her lap. At least one thing had gone right today. Mia was finally safe.

Griffin walked back into the room a few moments later and stopped in front of her. "We have a problem."

"What's wrong?"

"Apparently Maldin had a jamming device on him,

and my team lost visual contact. They have no idea where Liam is."

"Wait a minute…" A rush of adrenalin ripped through her as she stood up. "Isn't there a way to—I don't know—disarm it?"

"There is, but it's not easy. Maldin must have figured out he had a tail and made sure Liam ditched the officers."

Gabby pressed her fingers against her temple. "What happens now? There's got to be another way to track them. A phone…the car…city surveillance cameras… something."

"There's a statewide search on the vehicle. He won't be able to get far. But we also have to ensure that law enforcement doesn't engage Maldin."

Which meant finding Liam had just gotten more complicated. Without having any idea what Maldin's plan was—or even if he had a plan—they could have potentially gone anywhere. It was about thirteen hours to the Canadian border and less than that to the Mexican border. Depending on his connections and how much he was willing to risk, there were also airstrips and bus terminals scattered across the state.

But there was one lingering question that scared Gabby more than anything else. When Maldin got to wherever he was going and didn't need Liam anymore… what was going to happen?

She tried to shake off the growing layer of fear as she entered the ranch house. Marci met her and Mia at the door with a big hug, then ushered them straight to the kitchen that smelled like garlic and onions. Her stomach growled, reminding her it had been hours since she'd eaten. Maybe she was hungry after all.

"I knew you'd find her." Marci squeezed Mia's hand. "I know you must be so relieved. Griffin's been keeping us updated and we've been praying nonstop."

"I am relieved, but Liam's still out there."

A shadow crossed Marci's face. "They're going to find him. He was trained to handle situations like this. He'll be fine."

Gabby nodded. She knew Liam was trained to handle a crisis, but as relieved as she was to have Mia back, his situation dented her relief. Because this wasn't over. Liam was out there somewhere, and if the colonel was involved—like she was still convinced he was—this was far from over.

What if he came after her again?

"How is she?" Marci asked.

Gabby glanced down at Mia who was awake but nestled quietly against her chest. "They had someone check her out at the station, and she was just a little dehydrated. And clingy."

"I don't blame her." Marci kissed Mia on the forehead. "Can I get you some lasagna? There's plenty."

"I didn't think I was hungry, but it smells wonderful. I think I can eat a small helping."

A minute later, Marci set a plate of the pasta in front of Gabby along with a slice of garlic bread. "If you want to put Mia in the high chair, I can get her something as well."

"Thank you." She set Mia in the high chair, hoping the little girl would be able to stay awake long enough to eat something. "You've done so much for Mia and me. And I'm sorry for dragging your family into this. I know you have to be scared—"

"Don't even go there. Griffin told me you were feeling guilty over what happened. Don't. I know my son well enough to realize that everything he did, he did because that's who he is. And no matter how much I worry about him, I know he'd make the same decision again in a heartbeat. He won't have any regrets, which means I can't, either. What I can do is pray, something I've been doing a lot of lately."

Marci set a few bits of finger food on the tray in front of Mia, then watched her daughter perk up.

"That has to be hard," Gabby said. "Knowing they're all out there willing to take risks that most people would run from."

Marcy caught her gaze. "You know what that's like."

She nodded, then took a bite of her bread.

"I remember the first time Liam told me he was going to be a soldier. He wanted to be just like his grandfather. It was at that point I realized my boy was a warrior. And really, I guess all my boys are warriors in their own way. For justice and duty. I'm proud of them, but that doesn't mean it's been easy. A mom's job is to love and support her children but taking worry out of the mixture feels pretty impossible most days. Today especially."

Gabby set down her spoon and shook her head. "How do you do it then? Get through another day of worrying."

She might not have any claims on Liam or his heart, but that didn't take away her own worry for him.

Marci filled a mug of coffee for herself, then came

and sat down next to Gabby. "I've learned that the only thing I can really do is trust them into God's hands. There are no guarantees in life whether they're deployed or working right here in Timber Falls. God created Liam to be a soldier. That's who he is. And in the end, I have to trust God's plan for his life. I don't always succeed, but I try to shove the worry aside and concentrate on the moments I have with him. It's the only way I've found to get through life. For now, they're out there looking for him and I have to believe they'll find him. My advice for you right now would be to finish eating, then get some sleep. And I'm praying that all of this will be over by morning."

Gabby set her fork down. "Thank you."

"Did you get enough to eat?"

"I did. Thank you."

"Why don't you go upstairs and take a shower before you go to sleep? I'll get Mia cleaned up and watch her for you."

Gabby glanced at Mia, whose eyes were starting to close. But she still hesitated, unsure if she was ready to leave her daughter, even for a short time.

"She'll be fine," Marci said. "Poor girl's exhausted, and I know you are, too. I'll go rock her in the living room, then you can both get some sleep."

Twenty minutes later, she was thankful she'd washed off the grime from the past day.

She'd just slipped into a fresh pair of flannel pajamas Marci had left for her and now went to find Mia already asleep. She took the sleeping girl from Marci and nestled the child against her shoulder.

"Will you promise me one thing?" Gabby asked Marci.

"Of course."

"If there's an update on Liam… I don't care what time it is…will you let me know?"

"You bet. And Gabby…" Marci hesitated in the doorway. "I'm probably completely overstepping my bounds for saying this, but I've waited a long time for my boys to find themselves good wives. Sometimes I wonder if I'll actually live to see the day I have grandchildren." She let out a low laugh. "I just hope Liam finds someone like you one day."

A moment later, Gabby closed the door behind her, then carefully laid Mia in the crib next to her bed. She didn't want to read into Marci's words. The woman hadn't said that she wanted Liam to marry her specifically, but the implication had been there.

None of that mattered. Not tonight.

She moved to the window, pulled back the heavy curtains, then checked the lock. It had started snowing again, and moonlight reflected off the white ground. Liam had saved her and Mia because that was who he was. A hero, in her eyes. One who'd chosen to take her place in the face of danger. Which was why she needed to compartmentalize what her heart was feeling. His actions didn't speak to his feelings toward her, but to something greater. His sense of duty and honor. But for some reason, she was having a hard time separating the two. Tonight, though, had proven once again why she couldn't fall for him. His willingness to face danger head-on made it far too big a risk for her heart.

She'd loved and lost once before, and she had no desire to do it again.

Mia stirred, and Gabby picked her up again and started singing to her. She needed confirmation that Mia was safe. Needed to feel her baby sleeping against her chest. Needed to breathe in the familiar scent of baby lotion and powder while trying not to think about how close she'd come to losing her little girl. And how that reality still terrified her.

And Liam… No matter what her heart said, she couldn't lose him, either.

God, I've pushed You away for so long. Coming back to You only when I need something seems wrong, but I need You. Not just today, but every day. And I need Liam to be okay.

She stood at the window with Mia until she knew she couldn't stay awake any longer. Marci had promised her again to update her if anything happened. In the meantime, she'd just have to trust, and try—as hard as it was—to let go of the fear and panic. Because for now there was nothing she could do. She'd just have to trust that God would protect him and bring him home safely tomorrow.

She laid Mia down on the bed next to the giraffe that Gus had washed and dried—almost as good as new. She only wished she knew how long it would be until *she* felt as good as new. Letting out a deep sigh, she closed her eyes and prayed for sleep.

FOURTEEN

The frigid wind swept through Liam as he weighed his options. While he was grateful Maldin hadn't shot him, a bullet wasn't the only threat he'd faced today. He was already shivering, and it wasn't going to be long until the beginning stages of hypothermia started to set in.

Memories of his time in the field while on active duty surfaced—ruck marches, rehydrated meals and long nights of training in remote locations. But tonight he couldn't let the cold flowing through his body gain any ground. He picked up his pace down the narrow, tree-lined road and started working on a plan. It wasn't likely that he'd run into another car out here in the middle of nowhere, which meant that for now, he was on his own. Darkness had already settled in around him, dropping the temperatures further, but at least the sky had cleared and it wasn't snowing any more.

He jogged in the direction of the main road, mentally going through his limited options. He could hunker down, build a basic emergency shelter, and try to get a fire going for warmth while waiting for someone to find him, but there was only one obvious solution in his mind. He felt for the receiver he'd dropped into his pocket after finding it on Thatcher's body. His plan was simple. He'd managed to plant the tracking device they'd found on Gabby in Maldin's jacket during the man's escape to the car. Combined with the receiver, the authorities should be able locate Maldin. But in order to stop him, Liam needed help deactivating the jammer he was certain Maldin was still using, and he had to get the receiver to someone who could read it before the man got into the air. Which meant he was running out of time.

Headlights appeared on the horizon, temporarily shifting Liam's attention. He picked up his pace, lifting up a prayer at the same time, that whoever was behind the wheel would help him. A minute later, he stepped out into the middle of the road and waved down the vehicle until it came to a stop.

"Sir—" the driver stepped out of the car "—it's a pretty cold night to be out here. Are you okay?"

Liam let out a long sigh of relief. "I am now. I'm Captain Liam O'Callaghan, and I need your help."

At three forty-five in the morning, Liam stood in the doorway of the room where Gabby slept, hesitant to wake her. His mother had insisted she wanted him to let her know he was okay, but he also knew she needed her sleep. The past few days had taken a toll on them, both mentally and physically. Watching her sleep reminded him of how grateful he was that she was alive and safe. Things could have ended so differently.

The soft glow from an outside security light shone through the window and across Gabby's face. Mia lay on the bed next to her, her curls splayed across her cheek. He knocked softly on the open door, then crossed the hardwood floor and sat down on the edge of the bed.

"Gabby?" He gently shook her shoulder.

"Liam…" She sat up, eyes wide open as she looked at him. "You're here. What happened?"

"My mom said you wanted me to wake you up. And honestly… I couldn't wait until morning to see you and make sure you're really okay."

"We're fine. Both of us." She touched his cheek briefly, then pulled away. "But you… You're the one I've been worried about. What happened? How did you get away from him?"

"I'll tell you about everything in the morning, because honestly it's been a long night." The little sleep he'd gotten over the last couple nights was beginning to affect him. "But Maldin had me drive him to an airstrip where he'd managed to get a ride from a pilot friend of his. He left me to walk twenty miles back to the main road, thinking he'd be long gone by the time I found help."

"It's freezing out there, dark and you didn't even have your coat—"

"I know, but a local astronomy group was headed out to the airstrip to do some stargazing. Told me they were there because it's the best time of year. Something about when the temperature drops and the humidity in the air turns to ice crystals, you end up with a more transparent sky and better views. But I told them it was no coincidence."

She shook her head. "I never stopped praying. And I'm not the only one."

"I know."

"What time is it?"

"Just before four." He glanced toward the windows. "Sun's going to be up in a couple of hours—"

"And you need sleep."

"Agreed." He studied her face in the soft light, wishing she didn't affect his heart the way she now did. But everything that had happened over the past couple days had proven to him it was something he couldn't ignore. It wasn't simply going to go away. "I might not see anyone again till noon. Mom's promised to fix us all a big brunch once I'm up."

"I'd like that."

Mia stirred next to Gabby.

"I don't want to wake her up."

"You're fine." Gabby picked up the giraffe that had rolled to the edge of the bed and put it back in Mia's arms. "She's still sound asleep. It's like she's already forgotten what happened. But it's going to be a long time before I forget."

"She's resilient. Just like her mama."

"What about Maldin?" Gabby asked.

"The authorities just arrested him. Which means it's all over now."

She shook her head. "How did they end up tracking him?"

"After the colonel shot Thatcher, I searched his pockets and found the receiver he'd used to track us. I was counting on the fact that Maldin would dump me somewhere, because I still had the tracker they planted on you."

"So you turned it on and planted it on him?"

"Not a bad plan if I do say so myself. Especially after they were able to deactivate his jammer."

She swung her feet over the edge of the bed and caught his gaze. "You could have told me about your plan. Given me a hint that you were going to be okay, because I was so worried." She didn't even try to fight the tears. "I was so afraid he was going to kill you. You saved my daughter and I will be forever grateful, but I didn't want to lose you. And I thought…"

He squeezed her hand. "I wanted to tell you, but there was no way."

"I know, I just…" She pressed her lips together. "I'm glad you're okay."

"We're all okay. And that's all that matters."

"You say it's over, but what about Colonel Peterson? Do we know the truth about him?"

"I asked Griffin on the way here. They've been digging into his background. According to Maldin, he never was told who they were working for. And despite what Thatcher said, there is still no evidence that Peterson was ever involved."

Her gaze shifted to the floor.

"You don't agree?" he asked.

"I still have questions. What reason did Thatcher have to make up a story like that? It doesn't make sense. He was scared. I'm just not convinced yet that he was lying. But we might never know, because he's dead."

"I agree, but even I can't deny that Peterson killed him in self-defense."

"So that's it? It's over?" she asked.

"Not yet. Griffin is convinced—as am I—that there is still someone on the inside involved."

"Like Peterson?"

"If it is Peterson, the authorities will find out the truth." He studied their entwined fingers, fighting against his heart's longing to kiss her. "Peterson also asked if he could talk to us tomorrow...well, today. Apparently, he wants to explain his side of this."

"Sounds noble of him. Making sure we don't have any unanswered questions left."

He caught the sarcasm in her voice. "I'm still not sold on his innocence, either, but at the least we need to listen to the man."

"I agree. And I'm ready to put an end to all of this, but if there's any chance—any chance at all—he's involved—"

"For now, we both need to sleep. Things will look clearer in the morning, and we'll feel better."

She nodded, then looked up at him. "Liam...thank you. You knew the risks in what you did, and yet you still went with him. You put your life on the line and saved Mia and me. I'll never be able to repay you, but thank you."

"There's no way I'd let anything happen to the two of you. But we're all safe. That's all that really matters right now."

He kissed her on the forehead, then left the room. There were other things he wanted to say to her. Questions he wanted to ask her, like was she feeling the same things he was. Because everything at this moment seemed to be filled with uncertainties. His career, his future and now somehow Gabby stepped into his life and made those issues not seem to matter as much as they used to. It was as if being with her was the final piece of the puzzle he was looking for in his life. The piece that made everything right again.

But falling for her still seemed so unexpected. And until he knew how she felt…

He stepped into his room and shut the door behind him. He sat down on the bed and pulled off his boots. He was exhausted, which meant that now wasn't the time to process how he felt. There would be time for that in the days and weeks to come. Because if she felt even a fraction of what he did, he knew he was going to have to take things slow. She'd loved and lost, and he was pretty sure her heart wasn't ready to jump into another relationship. Especially with all the risks involved in loving a soldier.

He'd find a way to let her know how he felt while at the same time ensuring her that there was no rush. Because he was willing to wait for her until she was ready to open her heart again.

"Gabby…"

Gabby looked up from her half-empty plate of eggs, bacon and biscuits the next morning to where Liam sat next to her at the kitchen table. "Sorry. My mind's a million miles away."

"I can tell," Liam said. "You've barely spoken a dozen words since we sat down."

"I'm sorry."

"Don't be. I just want to make sure you're okay."

She smiled at him, still tired despite sleeping until Mia woke her up at nine o'clock.

Mia banged on the tray of the high chair on the other side of her, sending a Cheerio into the air and landing on the floor. Gabby grabbed her daughter's chubby fist and kissed it. "We're not going to be invited back if you keep making messes."

Mia just grinned, then shoved a piece of strawberry into her mouth.

Marci topped up their coffees and laughed. "I had four boys, remember. This is nothing."

"You deserve a medal," Gabby said.

"I'd say they turned out pretty good, which is better than any medal in my book."

"Sounds like Griffin just drove up with the colonel." Liam nodded toward the front door. "You ready for this?"

"I don't know." She glanced out the window, unable to deny that Colonel Peterson was the source of her anxiety. "I just saw the man shoot someone. I don't know if I'm ever going to be able to erase that from my mind."

"I know this is hard, but I think he will be able to answer some of our questions."

She caught his gaze. "You think he'll also be able to convince us he's not involved in this?"

"That's what I'm hoping."

Griffin stepped into the kitchen alone. "Good morning. I hope the two of you were able to get some sleep."

Liam stood up from the table. "It was a short night, but at least I'm home."

"I agree. Are you both ready to talk to the colonel? He needs to head back to the base right after this."

"You both go on in there," Marci said. "I'll get Mia cleaned up."

Gabby started for the living room, then stopped.

"Griffin… I'm hoping you're still planning to do a thorough investigation into what happened."

"I can assure you that our investigation is far from over."

"I know, and I'm sorry. Everything that has happened has shaken me up."

"Which is completely understandable."

"Can I ask him questions?" she asked.

"Whatever you want."

The colonel stood in the middle of the living room with his hands clasped behind his back. A fragment of guilt surfaced. What right did she have to question his loyalty to his country?

"Captain O'Callaghan… Mrs. Kensington…" The colonel took a step forward. "I appreciate you both meeting with me, though I'm sorry it has to be under these circumstances. And I'm so sorry for everything you've had to go through." He turned to Gabby. "I honestly can't imagine how terrifying it was to have your daughter taken so soon after losing your husband. I was thrilled to hear she's safe."

"Thank you. I appreciate your concern."

"Your husband was a hero and died a hero. Don't ever forget that his service to our country was not in vain."

"I won't. Thank you."

"You have to understand that Thatcher was never stable. I tried to help him on several occasions, but he was never able to be the soldier your husband was and maybe that's why he did what he did. He was disillusioned and honestly needed help, which is why I'm not really surprised at what happened. I just wish he could have received that help, because things never should have ended the way they did."

"I agree, sir," Liam said.

"Do you have any questions for me?" the man asked.

Gabby pressed her lips together before speaking. "There are some things that are still bothering me. Thatcher told us he did the things he did because you hired him. Hired him to search my house, and ultimately to scare me into giving you evidence my husband had about your involvement with a military contractor who managed to defraud our government."

Colonel Peterson clasped his hands behind him. "That's quite an accusation, but I can understand, considering the circumstances, why you might believe the things he said."

"While I hate to imagine that's true," she continued, "I don't understand his motivation to do something like this on his own."

"Unfortunately, we never will, but the bottom line is that there isn't any evidence, if I understand correctly."

She shook her head. "No, there isn't."

"Which seems to me that he was disillusioned about something. I'm just very sorry you and your baby ended up in the crosshairs of this situation. My only words of consolation to you are that Thatcher—and the man he was working with—are no longer a threat to either of you."

Gabby nodded. "And for that I am grateful. But I do have a couple more questions if you don't mind."

"Of course."

"Why did you seem to go along with him on the phone? If there really wasn't any money—"

"There were hostages' lives involved. You, Captain O'Callaghan… I decided I didn't want to anger him any more than he already was. And if I could find a way to buy more time, then the authorities would be able to step in and stop this. Arguing with him wasn't going to work because I knew he wouldn't listen. But the money he wanted was nothing more than an illusion. I'll be retiring on my army pension and nothing else. I can guarantee you that."

She nodded, wanting to believe his explanation, but she still wasn't fully convinced. "Do you have any idea why Kyle Thatcher did what he did?"

"I've been talking to the deputy here, trying to answer that very question. It is possible that your husband crossed paths with Thatcher at some point. There might have even been a confrontation between the two. Accusations against Thatcher about his involvement in government theft. If he heard you were asking questions about your husband's death and he was involved, Thatcher would have wanted to stop the truth from coming out."

"So he decided to ensure that didn't happen."

"That would be my explanation." He reached out and shook Liam's hand and then hers. "I need to head back to the base, and I'm sure you both need to rest. Again, I truly am sorry for your loss and all that the two of you have had to go through over the past few days. And I'm glad your daughter is safe."

"Thank you, Colonel. I appreciate it."

"I hope that having the chance to talk in a more neutral location will help all of us put this behind us."

Gabby watched them walk out the front door to the

car, then sat down on the edge of the couch. The realization of how close she'd come to losing Mia settled over her afresh. Maybe everyone was right. Maybe she just needed to be grateful her daughter was safe and put it all behind her.

Liam sat down next to her. "What are you thinking?"

"I need to put all this behind me. I realize that. And while Thatcher was apparently a very good actor—or maybe very disillusioned—everything the colonel said made sense. Seemed believable. To think that Thatcher was just saying all those things in hopes of framing the colonel…" She felt a shiver slide through her despite the gas fireplace crackling in the corner of the room. She shook her head. "I want to believe him."

"But you don't?"

She shook her head.

"I know none of it seems to make sense," Liam said. "Especially after hearing Thatcher, but there's nothing we can do. Griffin and the other deputies will do a thorough investigation to make sure they didn't miss something. But honestly, I think all we can do at this point is be thankful it's over, Gabby. It's time to let things go. Time to put all of this behind us."

"Do you think Will's suspicions were wrong?" She blinked back the tears. "He seemed so certain."

"I don't know. We might never know, and as hard as that is, we're going to have to find a way to live with it."

"What if I can't?" The familiar doubts had begun to resurface. "When the colonel walked away from Thatcher's body, it was as if he were relieved because he'd silenced the man. And the way he looked at me…

It wasn't like a man filled with regret. Instead, it was like all the loose ends had finally come together."

"Thatcher was the only witness who has said that the colonel was behind this. If there is no evidence, no proof of what he did, there's nothing more that can be done."

She looked up and caught his gaze. "But we're witnesses, aren't we? Thatcher told us what happened. Why would he have made all that up. It doesn't make sense. Nothing makes sense about the whole situation. And remember, this nightmare started after I found Will's letters and started calling around asking questions, and the colonel was one of the men I spoke with."

"But without any evidence to the contrary, I just don't know what else we can do."

"Sorry to interrupt." Marci carried a squirming Mia into the living room. "I think someone wants her mama."

Gabby took Mia into her arms and kissed her on the top of her head.

Oh, sweet baby, I came so close to losing you.

The thought surrounded her like a crushing weight and brought with it a cache of unwanted memories. The knock on her door when Will had died… The blur of his funeral… The realization she was on her own… Mia's empty crib here at the ranch…

Liam took her hand, as if he sensed what she was feeling. She felt the rush of adrenaline at his touch and knew she was losing her heart to him.

But that was something she couldn't afford. Her heart couldn't handle losing anyone else she loved, because even if she wanted to explore what was happening between them, he'd leave her for deployment and one day...one day he wouldn't come back.

FIFTEEN

Gabby sank onto the couch in the small sitting area outside the guest room and let out a soft sigh. As tired as she'd been, Mia had finally managed to go down for her nap. Hopefully, she'd sleep long enough that she wouldn't be grouchy the rest of the day. Otherwise, Gabby would probably be in for a long night.

She closed her eyes, relishing the momentary quiet surrounding her. She'd hoped to find time to get caught up with some of her work this afternoon, but between her fatigue and her inability to focus, she'd instead decided she needed to send out a letter to her clients affected. She wouldn't give specifics; just tell them the temporary delay was due to a personal emergency in her family.

No one would believe the truth.

"Gabby?" Liam came up the stairs and stopped in front of her. "Hey… Mom wanted me to ask you what your favorite pie is."

"My favorite pie?" Gabby let out a low laugh. "You do realize if I stay here much longer, I'm going to end up gaining at least five pounds. Maybe more."

He sat down in the chair across from her. "While enjoying every minute of it, I hope."

"Oh, I'll admit she's a far better cook than I am, and yes, I'm enjoying her food. Way too much."

"What's your answer?"

She shot him a smile. "Cherry, but she doesn't have to make a pie. Seriously."

"Is Mia asleep?"

"I had my doubts for a while if she would ever fall asleep, but yes, though she'll probably be up again soon. At least I was able to get a little work done. Actually, I was able to postpone work for another day or two."

"Good." He glanced to where Mia was sleeping. "How is she?"

"More resilient than I am." Gabby pulled her legs up under her. "She still seems a bit clingy, but really, you'd never know she'd been through anything. All she wanted to do was play before she finally crashed."

"And you? How are you feeling?"

"Like I'm coming out of some dark tunnel. I still can't shake the fact that I almost lost her, Liam."

"I want you to know that what you're feeling is a hundred percent normal." He leaned toward her and rested his elbows against his thighs. "Someone took your daughter from you. It's okay to be mad, sad and even to grieve. Because you've not only had to deal with Mia's kidnapping, you've been forced to relive Will's death. And that in itself is an emotional rollercoaster I'm sure you would have preferred to avoid."

She caught his gaze, surprised not for the first time how his presence managed to act like a balm on her heart. "Sounds like you know a thing or two about loss."

"I'd say we both do."

She bit the edge of her lip, suddenly feeling self-conscious. "Thank you."

"For what?"

"For returning my call. For coming to my rescue. For being there when I thought my world was about to end. I can't stop thinking about what could have happened. You risked your life for Mia and me, and I... I was so afraid I was going to lose you."

"But you didn't."

"I know."

He moved next to her on the couch and pulled her into his arms. She felt herself relaxing as she laid her head against his shoulder. His arms around her felt strong. Steady...safe... And yet, this wasn't a place she could lose herself. She would be leaving soon, and she had no intention of leaving a piece of her heart behind. Loving and losing again wasn't a place she intended to go.

She pulled back from his embrace, wishing he didn't have that mesmerizing effect on her. "I have something I need to ask of you, but it's a pretty big favor."

"Anything."

"I know I'm probably the only one, but I can't get rid of the nagging feeling that Colonel Peterson was involved in all of this."

"To be honest, I can't shake that feeling, either. Do you have an idea?"

"Maybe. Will's footlocker is back at my town house, and I'd like to go through it one last time. I wondered if you'd help me. I need to let this go, but I also need to make sure—one final time—that I didn't miss anything."

"Going through Will's things can't be easy for you, and on top of that, you're going to have to deal with your house that was trashed. Are you sure you want to do this so soon? You've been through so much the past few days, and this only brings with it more reminders—"

"It took me about a year before I could even open it. I'd say that was progress. But yeah… I know I need to let it go, but I just… I guess I'm still looking for my own answers. Even if it's just figuring out what Thatcher's motivation was."

"With him dead, I'm not sure we can, Gabby."

"I know. But it still doesn't make sense. We can't even prove that he knew Will. But then why target me? None of this seemed random. I know it's a long drive, and I'm asking a lot—"

"I don't mind at all." He smiled at her. "And besides, the pie will be here waiting for us when we get back."

It was half past five by the time they made it to her town house. She pulled out the chest, then started laying out all of Will's things on the coffee table in her living room, trying to ignore the rest of the house. She'd have to deal with the mess later. For now, she simply had to find a way to put all of this to rest once and for all.

Everything was there—his uniforms, the letters she'd written him. His camera with photos he'd taken… She sat cross-legged on the floor and started searching through it all methodically, looking for that one clue she was still convinced he'd left. She stopped at a photo of Will and Liam wearing fatigues and grinning at the camera and showed it to Liam.

"We ended up playing an impromptu game of football that day. It was a nice change from the grueling sweeps and field assignments."

"You were always a good friend to him. He loved you like a brother."

"The feeling was mutual."

She set down the photo and started through another pile of letters. Liam was right. It was time for her to let go of all this. There was nothing here and nothing was going to change or give her the answer she wanted. Nothing would help prove that Thatcher had been telling the truth.

"You okay?"

She dropped the letter onto the pile, then sat back against the couch. "It's hard. Like saying goodbye again. And I suppose I'm wishing now I'd brought Mia with me. I know she's fine, but I can't stop worrying."

"She is fine. And as much as I wanted to find something, too, I just don't think the evidence is here. Or at least anything that's connected to the colonel."

"So, Thatcher did all of this on his own to find whatever evidence Will might have and save himself. When things went bad, he tried to blame it on the colonel."

"That's what it looks like to me."

"Okay." She stood up and stretched her back that had knotted up. "Then I think it's time to stop. Whatever I'm wanting to find just isn't here. The colonel was right after all. There isn't any evidence, which means for all of the unanswered questions... I guess we'll never know."

"I did have one other thought." Liam set the field notebook he'd been reading through back into the trunk. "What about his phone or his email account? Did you talk to people he might have contacted before he died? Someone he might have told about his suspicions."

"I read through his email account and looked through his phone after they gave it to me," she said, following his lead and starting to put things away. "The only people he really spoke to were me, his parents and a few friends. There was nothing in there that stood out to me."

"Clearly, he was careful."

"Maybe he was too careful."

"Did he have any other email accounts?" Liam asked.

"Another account. You know… I can't believe I never thought of that, because he did." She grabbed her computer out of her bag, surprised she hadn't remembered, but certain it would simply be another dead end. "It was one he didn't use often. He told me at one point he had no idea why he even kept it because it was only full of junk mail."

"I confess, I have one of those."

She opened the computer and went to the online website. "He used my laptop some when he was home, so I shouldn't need a password."

His account popped up, along with a long list of unopened messages in his in-box. She shoved aside the painful reminder. There was one email in the draft box.

She opened up the drafts, then clicked on the email and started reading it.

"Anything important?" Liam asked.

Her heart pounded. "Liam… I think I just found what we're looking for."

Liam sat down next to her on the couch. "What is it?"

"An email with photos and documents attached." She started opening the attachments. "Liam, this has to be it. It's dated the day before he was killed. He was getting ready to send all of it to me."

"What does his letter say?" Liam asked.

"You need to read it yourself."

He took the computer from her and started reading through the email that brought with it the stark reminder that Will was gone.

Gabby, I can't believe I'm even writing this email. I'll leave it in the draft box for now. You're the only one who knows about this email account, so I'm praying you will check it if anything happens to me. I plan to talk to Liam, but I'm worried. Until I can ensure I've gotten proof of everyone involved, I don't want to put anyone's life at risk. I've been as subtle as I can digging for information, but I think they know.

I'm attaching all the evidence I have gathered so far, which includes a paper trail connecting Peterson to Graham. Honestly, I'm still numb from what I've discovered. I never would have imagined Colonel Peterson could be involved in something like this. He might have lost three wives to the army, but his biggest mistake was going into business with Daniel Graham. Finding hard evidence has been almost impossible—the man knows how to hide his tracks—but I've attached files that should be enough evidence to prove his involvement.

If something does happen to me before I turn this in, go to Liam and show him what I have. He'll know who to go to. I know I mentioned at least once that James Casada might have answers, but I haven't been able to get ahold of him yet.

Gabby…never forget how much I love you and the baby. There's nothing more I want than for us to be together as a family. But if that doesn't happen, I want you to move forward with your life and find the happiness again that I found with you.

"Gabby…" The lights in the house flickered. He glanced at the ceiling lamp, hoping the bad weather wouldn't affect the power in the area. "I know how personal this is…"

"I'll be okay." She pressed her lips together as if trying at the same time to hold herself together. "I just wish I'd found this sooner. Wish Will would have gone to someone he could have trusted and turned this over to them."

"According to the date on this email, he didn't have a chance. He died later that day."

Her eyes glistened with tears. "Do you think the colonel was behind the IED that killed him?"

"We might never find out, but it seems like too much of a coincidence to dismiss it."

She nodded. "I agree."

"You were right all along. Thatcher was telling the truth. Colonel Peterson was behind all of this."

"And he almost got away with it."

Nausea swept through him, knowing how close they had come to letting the man get away with murder. He started going through the documents Liam had left behind, the picture of what had happened suddenly becoming clear.

"It looks like after all these months Peterson believed he had gotten away with everything. Will, the one person who had questioned what was going on, was dead, and the money from Graham was safe in an offshore account."

Gabby glanced at Liam. "But then I started asking questions."

"Which scared him. According to what I'm seeing so far, Peterson is only three months from retirement, which has to be why he panicked when he received your call. He knew if he was going to get away with it, he needed to make sure you didn't have any evidence of his involvement."

"He tried to squelch any concerns I had on the phone, but when he found out I'd spoken to another one of Will's commanding officers, he knew it wasn't going to be enough."

"So he decided to hire Kyle Thatcher to make sure you didn't ask any more questions."

"Thatcher probably wasn't the best choice. An old recruit of his whose moral compass wasn't far off from Peterson's. He might not have planned to kill Casada, but when he did, he panicked."

A shiver ran through her. Everything was finally coming together.

"Peterson first has him scare you by bugging your phone and threatening you," Liam said. "Next he has

Thatcher search your house for evidence. When he doesn't find anything, Peterson tells him to keep following you in order to find out what you have."

Gabby nodded. "With my phone bugged, he would have known I was going to see Casada. They had to find out what Casada might know before we got there, but when Casada found them searching his home, shots were fired—"

"It changed the game," Liam said.

"Thatcher realized they were in trouble and, on top of that, he decided he wasn't going to prison for the colonel. He knew—or dug around and found out—that the colonel had money stashed away. A lot of it. And he decided that was going to be his ticket out. Taking Mia was meant to get back at the colonel for money. He was going to frame Peterson and the whole scheme would blow up in the colonel's face."

"I need to call my brother." Liam grabbed his phone from the edge of the coffee table, then stopped on hearing a creak on the kitchen floor.

Someone else was in the house.

SIXTEEN

Gabby froze as Liam shoved her phone into her hand. This was no coincidence. No burglar. She heard the familiar creak of the flooring in the kitchen and tried to fight off the wave of panic. Someone had broken into the house. And she knew exactly who it was.

"Call 911." Liam's voice was barely above a whisper. "But first get out of the house through the front door. Go to a neighbor's."

"Liam—"

"Go. Now." The lights flickered again. "I'll be right behind you."

She stumbled to her feet, feeling numb. They'd just found Will's evidence proving that the colonel had been behind this, and immediately someone had broken into her house. That had to mean someone was watching her. Listening. But how?

She unlocked the front door, trying to ignore the flood of questions. Had Peterson somehow bugged her house? Heard what they'd found and now planned to stop them in order to save himself?

"Step away from the door."

Gabby froze, then turned around slowly at the booming voice. Peterson stood at the edge of the living room, no longer a decorated soldier but a man who'd sold out his country. A man who was willing to do anything—including murder—to save his own skin. How had that happened to him? What had made him cross the line? She focused on the gun he held pointed at her. The answer to those questions didn't matter at the moment. All she knew was that she'd seen him murder a man in cold blood, and she knew he wouldn't hesitate to do it again.

"What do you want?" Liam asked.

"For you to shut up." He held out his hand toward her. "Give me the phone, slowly. Then sit down on the couch. Both of you."

She handed it to him before moving to sit down next to Liam. "You bugged my house."

"Obviously a good decision looking back." He set her phone down on the coffee table, then grabbed the laptop. "Just what I was hoping. The email hasn't been sent. He wouldn't give up, your husband. Always poking into things that weren't his business. Asking too many questions. Like the two of you."

Gabby's heart pounded. "Did you kill him?"

"Does it matter?"

"It does."

"Not directly. It was more like David and Bathsheba. You remember that story, don't you? In order for David to cover his sins, the king sent Uriah out in front where the fighting was the fiercest. The rest was inevitable."

"You meant for our entire unit to die that day," Liam said.

"One of the consequences of war."

"You won't get away with any of this," Liam said. "Because if I remember correctly, David paid for his sins in the end. And so will you. We know the truth now."

"That's where you're wrong, though I am going to have to ensure you don't tell anyone."

Gabby felt a shiver run up her spine. "You're going to kill us."

"Unfortunately for you, I don't have another option. I'm just trying to figure out the least messy way."

She glanced around the living room, desperate for a way out. At least she'd decided at the last minute not to bring Mia with her. But leaving her baby to grow up an orphan... No. That wasn't an option, either. There had to be a way to stop this man once and for all.

"You're fooling yourself if you really think you can get away with this," Liam said. "My brother knows where we are, and how long do you think it will take them before they put two and two together and realize what's going on?"

"Long enough for me to clean all this up." He pushed Delete, then slammed the computer shut. "I've been careful to make sure nothing can come back to me. If it wasn't for that email, you never would have been able to tie me to any of this. And if there happens to be an unfortunate accident tonight—"

"An accident?" she asked.

"The weather's pretty bad out there. Do you know how easy it is for a car to spin out of control and run off the road? An accident like that could snuff out the lives of whoever was in the car in an instant."

The power flickered again, then went off and darkness flooded the house. Gabby heard a scuffle then a shot rang out, shattering the lamp beside her.

"Gabby, get out of here!"

She dove behind the couch, then heard a sharp crack followed by a groan as the men fought in the darkness on the other side of the room. Liam might be in good shape, but Peterson had at least thirty pounds on him. And in the dark… No. No matter what Liam said, she couldn't leave him. She needed to find the phone. Needed to find a way to give Liam the advantage.

She felt for the coffee table, ran her fingers across the top of it, then grabbed the phone. A second later, she swiped the screen for the flashlight and turned it on. Peterson was swinging his fist at Liam.

"Liam, watch out!"

Liam ducked at the sound of Gabby's command, barely missing being struck by Peterson's right hook. The unexpected cover of darkness had given him a moment's advantage, allowing him to lunge at the man, but now, with the light from the phone, he could engage in a more targeted attack. He dove at Peterson like a linebacker for a second time, hoping to make up for the older man's bulk by being quicker.

Peterson stumbled backward at the assault, unable to keep his footing as Liam tackled him to the ground, knocking the gun out of his hand in the process. The older man tried to grab for the weapon, but Liam was quicker and managed to pin down the man's arm.

Peterson swung at him with his free hand, clipping Liam's cheekbone, then tried to come at him again.

"Don't move." Gabby stood over them with Peterson's gun pointed at the man. "Because like you, I will shoot if I have to."

The lights flickered back on as Peterson tried to get up, but Liam shoved his boot onto the man's shoulder. "I wouldn't move if I were you. From what I hear, she's a pretty good shot."

"He came prepared with zip ties." Gabby nodded at the floor.

As Gabby held the gun, Liam grabbed the zip ties that had fallen out of the man's pocket. He quickly tied the man's hands behind him, then moved to secure his feet, irritated at Gabby for not running, but grateful for her help. Except for the shiner he was probably going to have, thankfully neither of them had been badly hurt in the ordeal.

Her hands shook as she handed him the gun she'd been holding.

"Call 911 and get us some help. I'm going to call my brother."

She nodded.

"Griffin…" Liam said as soon as his brother picked up, his attention still on Peterson. "We found Will's evidence. Colonel Peterson lied about everything."

"Where are you?"

"At Gabby's townhouse. We came to look through Will's locker when Peterson showed up—"

"What? Are you okay?"

"I've got a shiner and probably a couple bruised ribs, but you should see the other guy." Liam let out a low laugh, feeling the need to break the tension hanging in the air. "But seriously, we're both okay."

"Are the local police there?"

"On their way. Gabby just called 911, and as for Peterson, well…" Liam glanced at the former soldier as sirens whined in the distance. "He's certainly not going anywhere."

Twenty minutes later, Liam was answering the police's questions, something that was beginning to feel oddly routine. Which was fine by him—as long as this was the last time.

Gabby was sitting on the edge of the couch, shoulders slumped and hands folded in her lap, when he finished giving his statement to the officer. All he could think about was getting her out of here and away from all of this. Because what she'd gone through the past forty-eight hours would have crushed even the strongest person.

She looked up at him, her eyes dark. "They wouldn't let me clean up the house. Said it was a crime scene now and CSI still had to finish processing everything."

"I know, but we don't have to stay." He stepped up next to her. "The detective in charge just gave us the go ahead to leave. They will make sure everything is secure when they are finished."

"I need to get back to Mia. I'm glad she wasn't with us, but this mess…"

"You can deal with this in a couple days. And you won't have to do it alone."

Things could be replaced. Their lives couldn't.

"Thank you." She grabbed her phone and stood up. "I'm ready."

"Are you sure you're okay?" he asked.

"Just feeling very shaken."

He studied her face as they walked out the front door. "By the way…you are a good shot, aren't you?"

She shook her head. "I'm a terrible shot, actually."

"Really?" He let out a low chuckle. "I'm glad I didn't know that earlier. But thank you. You saved my life. Picking up both the phone and gun was fast thinking, and on top of that, I managed to miss that first right hook."

"You'll have a bruise from the second." She took his hand. "But I'd say it was the other way around, actually. You saved my life."

"We'll call it even then. What I do know for sure is that I think we can finally put all this behind us."

What he wasn't sure about was how he was going to put his feelings for her behind him.

SEVENTEEN

Two days later, Gabby had just finished putting the dishes into the dishwasher when a car pulled up in front of the house.

"I appreciate your help." Marci stepped into the kitchen with three more glasses. "Griffin's here. Liam told me he wanted to give you both an update in person."

Marci set the glasses on the top rack, then turned to Gabby. "Remember that the truth often works like a salve. It helps heal. And on top of that, more often than not, God manages to redeem situations that seem unredeemable. That's what I'm praying for in this situation."

"Thank you."

Mia threw one of her toys and started fussing from where she was sitting in her high chair.

Marci shook her head. "Don't worry about Mia. I think you have to have realized by now how much I'm enjoying her. Griffin is going to want to talk to you."

Gabby thanked Marci, then kissed Mia on the forehead before heading to the living room. The waiting had been the hardest part. They'd been able to recover

Will's email, but after handing over all the evidence, there was nothing else they could do but wait. That, and pray those involved would soon be behind bars.

Liam walked into the room right behind her. "You have good news, we hope?"

Griffin took off his coat, then sat down on the edge of the couch. "I have to admit that even I'm surprised how quickly all of this has gone down, but once we were able to verify Will's evidence, we put together formal charges. And we ended up taking them by surprise. Just over an hour ago, authorities in Las Vegas picked up Daniel Graham and arrested him for his collaboration with the colonel in this mess. Apparently, he'd come back into the country for his daughter's wedding and she posted photos on Facebook and even tagged her father. Not a very smart move.

"The investigation isn't finished, but I'm pretty confident that they will both be going away for a very long time. Which means you're safe. Both of you."

Gabby let out a soft sigh of relief. "Thank you. For everything. All of you. I just never imagined that my desire to find out the truth would affect so many people."

"You did everything right. Though there is one other thing." Griffin caught her gaze and she felt the worry niggling through her again. "I know this must feel like you're having to relive everything all over again, and for that I am very sorry. But you need to know something else. Because of the information you gave us, the army will be further investigating Will's death to see if Colonel Peterson needs to be charged with your husband's murder."

She pressed her fingers against her mouth and tried

to fight down the wave of nausea. She might have already suspected what he was telling her, but hearing Griffin say it out loud made it all too real.

"I want you to know," Griffin said, "as trite as it might sound at this point, your country acknowledges and truly appreciates the sacrifice you, as well as Will, made."

Gabby nodded. "Thank you. I appreciate it."

Griffin stood. "I need to head back to the station, but I felt as if I needed to tell both of you in person. There are still a lot of loose ends that need to be tied up, but that's where we are for now."

Liam walked his brother to the front door. "I know you'll keep us updated."

"I will." Griffin grabbed his coat. "Tell Mom I'll try to make it for dinner tomorrow night."

Gabby stayed on the couch, still trying to process everything Griffin had told them. Part of her felt relieved that the truth was finally out. But the other part of her still felt numb. She wasn't sure if she wanted to go bury herself away in her room or scream. How was one supposed to react to what had happened over the past few days? Maybe there was no script for the right way to feel in a situation like this.

Liam sat back down next to her. "Do you want to talk?"

"Honestly, I don't know what I need right now."

"How about a walk? The sunset's beautiful."

She nodded, feeling suddenly claustrophobic in the house. "I'd like that."

"It's not too cold, is it?"

"I'll just grab my coat and be fine. There's another

layer of snow that has covered all the mountains in the background. I could never tire of the view."

He waited for her to put on her coat and beanie, then opened the front door for her. Outside the wind had died down, making the cold more bearable, but it was the view that almost made her forget the chill.

"I just wanted to make sure you were okay," Liam started, walking beside her down the gravel road. "I know all of this has to be a lot to take in. And even with all the pieces coming together, it has to be hard on you."

She nodded, wishing she could untangle her feelings toward him. But she'd save that for another day. "To be honest, my head is still reeling a bit. I feel like I came so close to losing everything that was important to me. On top of that, knowing they're going to reopen the investigation into Will's death feels like having a scab ripped off. It's like I'm having to relive everything that happened. But your mom said something earlier that stuck. God is somehow managing to bring closure for me and redeeming a situation I never thought possible. As crazy as it seems, I truly believe that this is going to go a long way toward my healing."

"I'm glad to hear that. You're a strong woman, Gabby. But no matter how strong you are, you still need give yourself time to grieve through all of this."

"I know you're right. But I also want you to know that I appreciate everything you've done for Mia and me. You went way, way beyond the call of duty, risked your life for us." She stopped and looked up at him. "Somehow thanking you really doesn't seem adequate."

"There is one other thing I wanted to tell you."

"What's that?"

"In the middle of all of this I just heard from my commander. The doctor has cleared me, and they're finally putting me back on active duty."

"That's great news." She smiled, truly happy for him. "When do you leave?"

"There's still paperwork that has to be finished up, but I'm supposed to report for duty at Fort Carson in Colorado Springs in two weeks."

"That's wonderful. You'll be close to your family."

He glanced down at the ground, suddenly avoiding her gaze. "I'd like you to stay awhile longer if you'd want to. It would be good for you. Allow you to rest. My mother would love to spend more time with Mia and I… I'd love to spend more time with both of you before I have to report back."

She felt her breath catch at his words, realizing he wasn't asking her to stay as a friend. Things had changed between them, but she still didn't know how to interpret her own heart. If she said yes, she had a feeling that things would never be the same between them again. That there would be no going back. But her heart wasn't ready. Not now, maybe not ever. And it wouldn't be fair to him to give him hope when she knew that risking her heart loving another solider wasn't a place she wanted to go. And neither would she ever do anything to stand between the job she knew he loved and his service to his country.

"You know I'd love to stay…"

"Why do I feel as if there is a big *but* coming?"

"When your mother found out that Saturday is Mia's birthday, she insisted we stay till then. She's so excited about it, and to be honest…so am I. But after that, I'm leaving. I need to start over somewhere fresh. Make new friends and put this part of my life behind me. I've been talking with my parents. There's an open apartment in their complex in Florida. They're considering staying year-round but want to be closer to Mia. And it will be good for her to grow up close to them as well."

"What about your heart? What does it say, Gabby? I don't think I'm the only one who's felt something happen between us. I just… I don't want you and Mia to go without knowing if there's something there."

She turned away, avoiding his gaze. The sunset had bathed the valley in stunning pink and gold. But she wasn't ready to listen to her heart. Because while it might be begging her to stay, she knew that she couldn't. Liam was the part of her life she needed closure from. To stay here—to see what might continue to develop between them—how was that going to let her put her past behind her?

"I'm sorry." She pushed away the battling thoughts and shook her head. "I don't think I can."

"Just consider it. You say you need to start over…" He took her hand and laced their fingers together. "What if you started over with me?"

Liam caught the confusion in Gabby's eyes and immediately regretted his words. He hadn't planned to say what had just come out of his mouth. At least not today. He'd pushed her too far, too soon. And on top of that, this was the day they were reopening the investigation on Will's murder. But for some reason, he couldn't stop his heart from fighting to be heard. He'd never know how she felt if he didn't try. And he wasn't ready to walk away. His brother Reid had lost his fian-cée because he hadn't fought for her. Liam wasn't going to let the same thing happen with Gabby.

"I'm sorry." He caught her gaze, praying he hadn't totally pushed her away. "My timing's all wrong, and honestly, I never meant for this to happen. Somehow, in the middle of all of this, I started falling in love with you, and now I don't know how to just walk away and pretend it didn't happen."

"I know, and I'm sorry. I just can't." Gabby took a step back, the confusion on her face clear. "We can't. Life is going to go back to normal soon, but you'll al-ways be a protector. Someone who will risk everything to make things right. It's what you do as a soldier. It's what you did with Mia and me. But that's not love. And in the end, I'll always be a reminder of what happened on the day Will died. I don't know if it's possible to separate the two, but I do know that's not a reason to love someone."

He fought the urge to pull her into his arms and kiss her like he'd wanted to for the past few days. Maybe he was crazy, but he knew if she could find a way to get past the fear, she had feelings for him as well.

"In the middle of everything that happened," he said, "I realized how afraid I was of losing you and Mia. And I don't want that to happen, Gabby. I don't want to just walk away. I don't want you to walk away. I want you in my life—both of you. Not because of Will. Not be-cause I need to fix you or save you. Because I love you."

"I just don't think I can." Her eyes filled with tears. "There is too much baggage between us."

"If you don't feel what I'm feeling, then I'll walk

away and never bring this up again. But if you are feeling anything at all toward me, don't close your heart off because you're scared of letting me in. Please. It's not because I feel sorry for you or am trying to make up for what you lost. I'll give you time…wait for you… whatever you need."

"I'm sorry." She pressed the back of her hand against her mouth, tears glistening in her eyes. "We'll stay until the party's over tomorrow, but then Mia and I are leaving."

Liam watched her walk away from him and felt his heart shatter. He waited until the screen door slammed shut behind her, then headed for the barn. That wasn't the reaction he'd expected. He'd somehow convinced himself that she felt the same way he did. Clearly, he was wrong. But losing her now? How was he supposed to watch her walk out of his life?

Or had he simply lost it?

He headed toward the barn where the horses were grazing outside nearby. Once inside, he grabbed a metal pitchfork. Physical labor had always helped him figure things out. Maybe he should have tried it before he made a fool of himself. Maybe she was right, and there was too much emotional baggage between them.

What had he been thinking?

He'd never been the impulsive type. He was never quick on decisions—more methodical and precise, unless the situation called for a swift result. And his methods had always worked well for him. But now… he wasn't even sure how this had happened. He'd never seen Gabby as a romantic interest, but clearly all of that had changed. At least it had for him.

Liam turned around as his brother Reid stepped into the barn, but didn't stop working. The last thing he wanted right now was a conversation with one of his brothers. "Just finished a shift?"

"Yeah. I wanted to make sure you were okay. Plus, I promised Dad I'd come help repair some of the fencing along the west end."

"I know he'll appreciate that."

Reid leaned against the door frame. "I don't remember you ever mucking out stalls unless Dad made you. Growing up, you preferred to do just about anything else."

"I needed to blow off some steam."

"What's going on?"

Liam frowned. Dodging questions wasn't going to work. Reid was the one brother who could always read him. "Let's just say I put my foot in my mouth and more than likely ended up ruining everything between Gabby and me."

"How did you do that?"

"I told Gabby I've fallen in love with her." He paused, waiting for a reaction. "You don't look surprised."

"I'm assuming she didn't react the way you wanted her to."

"I thought she might feel the same way, but I was wrong."

"She said that?"

Liam leaned against the shovel. "She told me she didn't think a relationship between us was a good idea."

"Give her some time. She's been through a lot. Mom told me how she looks at you."

"Like the best friend of her husband?" He spat out the words.

"Not exactly. More like a woman who's fallen hard for someone and isn't sure how to deal with it."

"Mom's biased."

"Maybe. But even if she hasn't fallen for you, she doesn't live far. The two of you need to spend time together outside everything that's just happened."

Liam leaned the pitchfork against the stall wall. "It's more complicated than that. She's leaving for Florida to be closer to her parents."

Reid hesitated at the information. "Then what's stopping you from hopping on an airplane and going to see her?"

"I just got my orders from my commander."

"Really?" Reid let out a low whistle. "They're letting you stay in?"

"Yeah. Doctor finally says I'm deployment ready. I'm heading to Fort Carson in two weeks."

"Congratulations. Does she know that?"

"Yes. But I don't know what I was thinking. Asking her to put her heart on the line for another soldier. I'm pretty sure that's the root of all of this, and if I'm honest with myself, she doesn't deserve that. I've got four more years to serve, but for the first time in my life, I'm realizing I don't want to do this by myself. And I guess I had this idea of making a family with her and thought she might feel the same."

"Did you tell her all of that?"

"Some of it."

"Like I said. Give her some time. The last few days

have dredged up Will's death. Plus, she almost lost her daughter. It's a lot to deal with."

Liam pulled off his gloves and headed out of the stall. "Maybe, but I have a feeling I'm out of time."

"There are always options. We could have Mom invite her back up here for the holidays. Mom's hard to say no to and it would give both of you more time—"

"Thanks, but I'm not going to push her on this, and I don't need Mom as a matchmaker. I told her if she didn't feel the same way I do, I'd respect that decision, and I meant it."

"Wow… I'm sorry." Reid frowned. "I know what it's like to lose someone you love."

Liam caught the hurt in his brother's eyes, even after all these years. The woman Reid had been in love with had left him, and so far, he'd never managed to find anyone he could love the way he'd loved her.

"Sorry," Liam said.

"So am I, but I have learned something. Loving and losing…they're all a part of life. Sometimes you get your heart broken, but sometimes love lasts a lifetime."

"That's pretty profound. Almost like there's someone new in your life that you haven't told us about."

"Let's just say I've been better at giving out advice than taking it myself. I always regretted the fact that I didn't fight for Claire. Because if I had to do it all over again, trust me, I would have. Love is worth the risk, even if it doesn't work out in the end." Reid let out a low laugh. "Or at least that's what I'm still trying to convince myself of."

Liam started back to the house where his mom was reading to Mia on the veranda. He heard Mia squeal and felt his heart constrict. He wasn't supposed to feel this way for a child that wasn't his own. Wasn't supposed to have fallen in love with her mother, but somehow he had. And letting Gabby walk away? Well, he had no idea how to do that.

Gabby watched from the kitchen window the next day as Liam swung Mia around in circles on the front porch while she giggled. Her little sweetheart. The one thing that had kept her going these past months. But now...now there was someone else who made her heart want to live fully again, and she didn't know how to deal with it. She'd managed to avoid being alone with Liam yesterday, which with most of his family around hadn't been difficult. But she'd sensed his presence around her no matter where he was.

And she wasn't sure she could fight it anymore.

She let out a soft sigh. She wasn't sure exactly when or how it had happened, but Liam O'Callaghan had managed to stir the places in her heart she'd thought were dead. Her capability to trust again. To love. To imagine that there could actually be joy after loss.

Stepping outside onto the porch, her heart melted when Mia noticed her. She walked toward Liam and kissed Mia on the side of her neck, relishing in her response as her daughter lunged into her arms.

"You're going to spoil her." She glanced at Liam. "Both you and your mother."

"I have a feeling my mother would say that it never hurt a child to receive too much love."

"I'm not complaining. She's really taken to the both of you."

Mia squirmed out of her arms, then grabbed on to Gabby's fingers so she could walk.

A second later, Mia let go.

"Mia?"

She wobbled across the porch on her own.

"Liam…" Gabby grabbed his hand. "She just took her first steps."

Mia grinned from ear to ear, clearly proud of herself before grabbing on to a potted plant for balance.

Marci stepped onto the porch. "Did she just walk?"

Gabby laughed. "She did."

"Your little girl's growing up," Liam said.

Mia teetered for a moment, then tipped the plant over, scattering dirt across the porch as she plopped down on her bottom.

"Mia!"

Marci laughed. "She's fine. I'll get her inside and get her cleaned up. Why don't the two of you sit out here and enjoy the sunshine for a few minutes. Lunch won't be for another thirty minutes, and I heard the temperature's about to drop with more snow on the way."

Gabby watched as Liam's mom took Mia into the house, leaving the two of them alone. She shifted her gaze to the horizon as a wave of self-consciousness washed over her. They needed to talk and now was as good a time as any.

"Do you mind?" he asked.

She shoved her hands into her pockets and nodded. "I'd like a walk."

She had so much to say to him, and no idea how to start.

"I have to admit," Liam said. "I've never spent a lot

of time around kids, but that little girl's pretty much stolen my heart."

Gabby laughed. "Mine, too. From the first day she entered this world. Though, I still can't believe she's turning one. Doesn't seem possible."

They stood beside each other in silence for a few moments, giving Gabby time to take in the now-familiar snowcapped mountains that rose up in the distance beyond the ranch. Giving her time to wonder how she'd managed to lose her heart. But she had.

"I feel as if I owe you a huge apology," Liam said. "I realized that I overstepped my bounds when we spoke last, but honestly, Gabby, I don't regret it. I told you I would walk away if that's what you wanted, but I meant what I said. Mia's not the only one who's stolen my heart. You have."

"Liam—"

"Wait." He turned to her. "Before you start throwing out excuses at me, just hear me out one last time. And I promise it will be the last time. But as hard as I know this must be for you, I think you feel something for me as well."

She smiled, trying not to chuckle at his serious expression. He was so focused on convincing her that he didn't even realize she already agreed.

He took her hand, not giving her a chance to respond. "I meant what I said when I told you why I'd never married. It was because I'd never found the right person. And I never would have imagined it could be you. On top of that, for this past year, all I've wanted to do was run from you and the memoires you brought. But then, somehow, you made me smile again and wonder what it would be like to have a family. And while we both know being married to a soldier isn't easy, you're the one I want to come home to. You and Mia."

She looked up and caught his gaze, her heart about to burst. "Can I talk now?"

"Of course, I just… I can't let you go without a fight. And I want you to understand—"

"Liam." She laughed, then pressed her palm against his cheek. "I wasn't going to argue with you. I hardly slept last night, wrestling with my own heart. And I realized you're right."

"What?" He dropped his hands to his side.

"I've been so caught up in surviving and doing things on my own that I honestly hadn't thought about ever falling in love again. And then, when my heart started to feel once more, it terrified me, and I only pushed you away. Part of it was the idea of being a military wife again. I know the benefits, but I also know how lonely and scary it can be. And how much can be lost. Honestly, it still scares me." She shook her head. "But somehow you made me remember it's worth it if you can be with the person you love. I want to take things slowly—need to take things slowly—but I've realized that I want to be the one you come home to."

He stared at her, his jaw slack as if he were trying to take in what she'd just said.

She smiled up at him. "Isn't that what you wanted to hear?"

"Yes, but… I guess I'm just having a hard time believing I'm not dreaming."

"Maybe this will help convince you." She stepped up to him and kissed him on the lips.

A moment later, Liam wrapped his arms around her and pulled her tighter against him, deepening their kiss until she finally pulled away, breathless.

"Convinced you're not dreaming?" she asked.

His smile widened. "You might have to convince me some more, but what do we tell my family?"

She glanced back at the front door and laughed. "Oh, I have a feeling they already know."

EPILOGUE

Eight months later, Gabby stood at the edge of the reception area with the mountains rising up in front of them, set off by wispy clouds across the pink sky ablaze from the setting sun. It was the perfect evening for an outdoor June wedding. They'd kept everything simple, just like she'd wanted. A private ceremony on the ranch with their parents, his brothers and a handful of close friends. Lanterns had been strung above them, and a live string quartet played in the background while the guests mingled.

Everything had turned out perfect.

"I can't tell you how happy we both are for you." Gabby's mother gave her a hug, then took a step back and caught her daughter's gaze. "I know you've been faced with a lot of difficult things these past couple years, but to see you smiling right now means more to me than you'll ever know."

She matched her mother's smile. "I think I do know, Mom."

Her father squeezed her hand. "We're very proud of you. And extremely happy for you."

While she might never be completely the same because of loss, Liam had come into her life and managed to put back together the broken pieces of her heart.

Liam stepped up beside her and her parents. "Would you mind excusing us for a moment? I need to speak with my wife."

Her breath caught as she looked up at him in his military dress blues. "I like the sound of that... Your wife."

Liam grabbed her hand and pulled her away from the guests, before drawing her into his arms and kissing her.

"Sometimes it felt like this day would never come, but it's been perfect."

She let out a soft laugh and wrapped her arms around his neck. "It was perfect. Though I have to admit, I think Mia stole the show today."

"What did you expect? She takes after her mother."

Gabby reached up and kissed him again, feeling her heart swell at his nearness. "Flattery will get you everywhere, you know."

She'd noted the changes that had taken place over the past eight months in both of them. Peterson's conviction had helped erase the anxiety his criminal actions had left. No longer did she have to worry about her safety or Mia's. But the greater change had been how God had gifted her with a renewed sense of lasting peace she'd never expected. She never thought she'd ever be ready to step into the shoes of a military wife again, and while she couldn't deny moments of anxiety, with it had come a chance to enjoy each day spent with Liam.

"This time last year I had no idea what direction my life would take." Liam smiled down at her. "The army was considering discharging me, and as for falling in love...well...it wasn't even in the picture. Especially with you."

"Any regrets, Mr. O'Callaghan?" she asked.

"None at all, Mrs. O'Callaghan."

He leaned down and kissed her, this time lingering longer and sending her heart racing.

"I supposed we should go back to our guests," she said.

"As long as I can have you all to myself for the next ten days, I supposed I can share you for another hour."

Gabby hesitated. "Do you think our parents will survive keeping up with Mia for that long?"

"Please don't tell me you're having second thoughts of leaving her for our honeymoon."

"I'll miss her, but not a chance."

"Good, because I can promise you that they're going to love every minute of it. And I'm going to love every moment alone with my wife."

He took her hand and started back to where their guests were eating wedding cake and dancing beneath the stars. But the only person she could see was Liam. Her heart seemed to still for a moment. The seasons of life had brought their own share of pain, but today was a reminder of love, hope and of God's gift of second chances.

* * * * *

Ever since she found the Nancy Drew books with the pink covers in her country school library, **Sharon Dunn** has loved mystery and suspense. Most of her books take place in Montana, where she lives with three nearly grown children and a hyper border collie. She lost her beloved husband of twenty-seven years to cancer in 2014. When she isn't writing, she loves to hike surrounded by God's beauty.

Books by Sharon Dunn

Love Inspired Suspense

Broken Trust
Zero Visibility
Montana Standoff
Top Secret Identity
Wilderness Target
Cold Case Justice
Mistaken Target
Fatal Vendetta
Big Sky Showdown
Hidden Away
In Too Deep
Wilderness Secrets
Mountain Captive
Undercover Threat
Alaskan Christmas Target

Visit the Author Profile page
at Harlequin.com for more titles.

NIGHT PREY

Sharon Dunn

He will cover you with his feathers,
and under his wings you will find refuge;
his faithfulness will be your shield and rampart.
—*Psalms* 91:4

A special thanks to Becky and Kyla for showing me around the local raptor rescue center and to all the dedicated people across the country who rescue and care for these awe-inspiring birds.

ONE

"What are you doing on this land?" The male voice pelted Jenna Murphy's back like a hard rain.

She dropped the empty pet carrier and raised her hands slowly, not wanting to spook whoever had called out to her. Most of the locals knew her, but a lot of strangers were moving in and buying ranches. If she had stumbled on an overzealous landowner with a rifle, the situation could get sticky. Her skills lay in soothing birds, not people.

"Please, I can explain." She struggled to get the words out, already winded from running up and down hills.

"Explain away." The silky smooth quality of the voice behind her did nothing to diminish the threatening tone.

Chances were, she was trespassing. When she got focused on something, she tended to space out everything else. Whose land had she wandered onto anyway? She'd been too busy trying to catch an injured hawk to notice if she had crossed boundaries. She had started her chase out on the King Ranch.

A glance at the mountain range to her left helped her orient herself. She was still on Norman and Etta King's ranch. Both of them were getting up in age. Maybe they had hired some help. The man's voice had a distant familiarity to it. If he wasn't barking orders, she might be able to place it.

His voice softened. "I didn't mean to scare you. You can put your hands down and turn around."

Jenna pivoted. She studied the man in front of her. He didn't have a gun. Instead he held a tool that was used for digging fence posts. His forehead glistened and the front of his shirt was stained with sweat. So the Kings *had* hired help...or had they? She looked closer.

"Keith? Is that you?"

Twelve years of her life fell away. He had changed quite a bit, but there was enough of the old Keith Roland for her to know this was her childhood friend and the Kings' grandson. The gray eyes that appeared blue in intense light were the same. "It's Jenna Murphy," she added when he didn't respond. "We used to play together when you spent summers with your grandparents, remember?"

The man standing in front of her bore little resemblance to the boy she had rafted the river with. Together, they had built a tree house that attracted a neighborhood of kids, summer after summer. His features were the same, though his muscular frame was a sharp contrast from the skinny kid she remembered. Keith's wavy brown hair now fell past his ears. The long-sleeved shirt he wore was a little out of place considering what a hot summer day it was. The almond shaped eyes still held the same gentleness, but something about this man seemed…haunted.

Keith blinked as if she had stunned him. He shook his head and furrowed his brow. "Sorry."

Did he really not remember her? Jenna's spirits sank. Funny, he had been such an important part of her childhood, the highlight of her summer. Yet, she hadn't even been a blip on his radar. Maybe she had just been the scraggly little tagalong kid to him. Somehow, she couldn't believe that. She touched her palm to her chest. "You almost gave me a heart attack when you shouted at me like that."

"I didn't mean to frighten you." His voice held a warm quality. "We had a trespasser yesterday, too. I was concerned Gramps's place had become Grand Central Station."

Jenna laughed. Now she understood why he had been so quick to confront her. "That was probably me you saw. I'm the director of the Birds of Prey Rescue Center up Hillcrest Road." When she got a call on an injured bird, there usually wasn't time to inform landowners. All the locals knew if they saw her on their land, she was probably just taking care of a bird. She always dressed in bright colors, so she could be spotted from a distance.

"So that was you I saw tromping around yesterday when I was mending fence. Do you make a habit of trespassing?"

"The bird I rescued yesterday was an eagle with buckshot in her wing." Finding that bird flapping its flightless wings had broken her heart. Hopefully, she had gotten to the bird quickly enough to prevent infection but only time would tell. And now, she had an injured hawk to catch in the same area. It was unsettling to have two injuries occur so quickly. If someone was hurting her birds on purpose, she would get to the bottom of it. "I don't suppose you know anything about people using shotguns on eagles around here?"

Keith shook his head. "Gramps has a rifle, not a shotgun." He narrowed his eyes. "He wouldn't shoot at a bird anyway."

He seemed protective of his grandfather. She hadn't intended to accuse. "That means you have trespassers."

"Trespassers?" He rubbed the five o'clock shadow on his jaw. "You mean other than you, Jenna Murphy?" His tone lightened; all the suspicion she had heard earlier was gone.

Jenna's breath caught. Something in the way he had said her name made her think he remembered her more than he was letting on. But why had he tried to hide it? Was her perception of their friendship so much different than his? True, he had been two years older than her, but she had felt such a special bond with him until that disastrous summer when he had changed so much.

The last time she had seen Keith, he had been seventeen and deeply troubled. That was the summer his visit had ended abruptly with an arrest for drunk driving. Etta and Norman King had been heartbroken about sending their grandson away, but the arrest had been the final straw. Keith's drinking had led to wrecking farm equipment, nearly running over his grandfather and stealing from his grandparents. They had had no choice. His wildness had put everyone at risk. Jenna shook off the memories and returned her focus to the task at hand.

"That eagle went down on your grandfather's property. Any idea who might be doing something like that?"

He drew his eyebrows together and his voice intensified. "No, but I will find out who it is. It's not right to do that to my grandparents."

Jenna turned her attention to the pet carrier she had dropped. "If you don't mind, I have an injured hawk to catch." She scanned the shorter trees and the undergrowth. No sign of the bird. The wounded hawk couldn't get airborne, but had managed to bounce for miles as she'd tried to chase him down. A flightless bird didn't stand much of a chance of survival. She had to find him before nightfall.

Jenna picked up the carrier and stalked a few feet away. She turned back around. "Good running into you, Keith Roland. I didn't think I'd ever see you again."

He lifted a chin in acknowledgment of her comment but offered nothing in return, no explanation of what he was doing in town or how long he planned to stay. He must have mended his relationship with his grandparents, but when? What had he been doing for the last twelve years?

Shortly after the summer Keith left, Etta King had run into Jenna in town. She'd shown Jenna a picture of a clean-cut soldier, Keith. Etta had expressed hope that enlistment in the marines would "straighten that boy out." Jenna didn't run into Etta very much, and talking about Keith was painful for both of them. She had no idea if the military had been good for Keith or not.

She strode a few feet up the hill.

"Do you need some help finding that bird, Jenna Murphy?" Keith shouted after her.

For someone who didn't remember her, he seemed to like saying her name.

A gust of wind wafted down the mountain, causing the limbs of the evergreens to creak. The breeze caught Jenna's long brown hair and plastered it against her face. She shoved the wayward strands behind her ears. "That would be nice."

After staking the post hole digger in the ground, he walked toward her with large even strides.

The wind settled. Something crashed in the forest, breaking branches. The injured hawk? No, it sounded like something bigger. Heavier. More dangerous. Jenna caught a flash of movement up the hill.

A noise she had never heard before shattered the silence. A sort of explosive snap pounded against her eardrums.

Keith's eyes grew wide. He leaped toward her. "Get down." He wrapped an arm around her, pulling her to the ground.

Her palms hit the hard earth; vibrations of pain surged up her arms. "What is going on?" She scrambled to get to her feet; he yanked her again down to the ground.

His arm went across her back like an iron bar. "We're being shot at. Stay down."

"Shot at?" Jenna shook her head in disbelief. Why would someone be shooting at them? Could it have anything to do with the injured birds?

Still on his stomach, Keith scanned the landscape around them.

A second popping explosion stirred up a poof of dirt five feet in front of them, confirming Keith's words.

Jenna's heart revved into overdrive. Her mouth went dry. "I've never been shot at before."

He put his lips close to her ear. "I have. I know what to do. Those rocks up there will give us some cover." He rose to a crouch, pulling her with him by grabbing the back of her shirt. "Stay low."

Jenna's mind reeled; she fought for a deep breath. What was happening? Why would anyone want to shoot at them?

Keith wrapped his arm around her waist. "You have to keep moving."

The strength of his voice in her ear freed her from the paralysis of panic. At least somebody knew how to respond.

Her heart pounded wildly. Keith dragged her up the mountain.

Another shot shattered the air around her. She screamed. She stumbled.

Keith pulled her to her feet. "Stay with me, Jenna."

She gasped for breath as he nearly carried her the remaining feet to the outcropping of boulders. Keith guided her in between two large rocks. The massive rocks allowed them both to crouch unseen and safe for the moment. Jenna pressed her back against the hard surface while Keith faced her.

Her pulse drummed in her ears. A tingling chill spread over her skin. She placed a hand on her somersaulting stomach. She could have died.

He touched a warm hand to her cheek. "You all right?"

Every muscle in her body trembled. "No. I'm definitely not all right. Maybe you get shot at all the time, but I don't."

"Jenna, look at me and take a breath." He clamped his hands on her shoulders.

She shook her head, unable to focus. Her thoughts moved in a hundred directions at once.

His palms pressed against her cheeks forcing her to look at him. "You're safe here. You are out of the line of fire. Do you understand?"

The warmth of his touch and the steadiness of his gaze calmed her. She stared into the deep gray of his eyes. She nodded. Not only did he have experience with being shot at, obviously he had dealt with someone falling apart, too. As he had said, he knew what to do.

The forest fell silent. Keith scooted away from her and scanned the sky above them.

"Why...why would someone be shooting at us?" Her throat was parched. An intense craving for a cup of cool water overwhelmed her.

"I don't know, but they didn't do a very good job of it. Either they are really bad shots or they weren't aiming to kill. Maybe they are trying to scare us away." He leaned forward to see beyond the protection of the rocks.

"Be careful." She grabbed his arm, feeling the hardness of muscle beneath fabric.

"I don't see anything out there." He settled back, pulling his knees up to his chest. "We'll wait a while."

Their feet intertwined in the small space. Pebbles

pricked the skin on Jenna's hand as she rested her palm on the ground.

"I wonder what the trespassers are doing on Gramps's land."

"You mean besides shooting at us...and shooting at eagles and maybe hawks, as well?" A shudder ran through her body. She pressed her feet harder into the ground in an effort to get beyond the trauma of what had happened. They would have to report this to the sheriff when they got out of here. *If* they got out of here.

Minutes ticked by. Her heart rate returned to normal. Searching for something to take her mind off the gunshots, she studied the man in front of her, looking for signs of the boy who had been her summertime friend. The scar over his left eyebrow was new. She wondered what other scars he carried. Had they made him want to forget his past? Maybe for him the pain of what had happened when he was seventeen overshadowed any of the positive memories. She had chosen to remember the good things about those summers.

"So where did you learn how to dodge bullets like that?"

Keith shifted his feet and looked away from her. "It's the second lesson they teach you in the marines."

"What is the first?"

"How to shoot them."

The vagueness of his answer and the icy tone indicated that he didn't want her probing. She stared down the hillside where she had left the cage intended for the hawk. With any luck, the bird hadn't gotten too far away.

Keith combed his fingers through his hair. "You think the people that just shot at us shot at your eagle?"

Jenna shrugged. "One eagle doesn't mean there is a pattern. I don't know what is going on with this hawk." She sucked in a breath as concern about the eagle ate at her stomach. Her vet friend had helped her dig out the buckshot. The female eagle, who she had named Greta, was on antibiotics. Hopefully, she would make it. But at least she was getting treatment. The hawk was still there on its own.

He rubbed at a spot of dirt on his worn jeans. "You take care of birds?"

"Just raptors, birds of prey. We rehab them and release them back into their habitat. I landed the job after I finished my degree in wildlife management."

He studied her for a moment. The corners of his mouth turned up. "You always did attract wild things."

Warmth pooled around her heart. "So you do remember me?"

"I remember you liked wild things. You were the only girl in town who thought feral cats made good pets."

Jenna lifted her chin. "All they need is love and for their food to be in the same place every day."

Keith laughed. A familiar twinkle returned to his eyes.

A connection sparked between them, and she leaned closer. "Is it all coming back now?" she teased.

The change in mood was short-lived. A veil descended over his eyes, and he pulled away from her. "You look different, that's all."

"People grow up. They change." How much had he

changed over the years? Was he still battling the same demons that had driven him to drink at seventeen?

"Been quiet for a while. Maybe it's safe for us to head back down the mountain, huh?" He leaned out, glancing from side to side.

Her heartbeat sped up as fear returned at the thought of leaving their safe haven. Her stomach clenched as she wrestled with her choice. Part of her just wanted to leave, but she knew a flightless bird didn't stand a chance. He would starve or be eaten if she didn't catch him. If only Keith would stay with her. It wouldn't be so frightening if she wasn't alone.

A shrill cry pierced the forest.

"The hawk," she whispered.

Keith pushed himself to his feet. He studied her for a moment. "So how hard is it to catch a wild bird?"

Relief spread through her. He had all but read her mind. "Not hard at all if I have help," she gushed. Shielding herself behind the boulder, she eased to her feet. "But we need to catch him soon. He might be able to survive on bugs for a while but some creature is bound to decide he looks like a delicious main course before nightfall."

"I can't leave you out here considering what just happened." He rolled his eyes theatrically. "So I guess that means I have to help you."

She scooted toward him and smiled. "I guess so."

Keith stared at the petite, slim woman standing in front of him, her dimple showing as she smiled. One thing for sure hadn't changed about Jenna Murphy. She was as cheerfully determined as ever when it came to rescuing wild animals. "We need to be cautious."

Anxiety flashed over her features, but then she squared her shoulders as if summoning courage. "I know. Let's go get the cage. With two of us, he shouldn't take any time at all. We can surround him."

Keith squinted, studying the mountain and forest. The shots had come from uphill. He suspected a long range rifle had been used. The knowledge that the shooter was far away didn't make him any less vigilant.

A slight breeze bent the boughs of the pines. He didn't detect any movement that might be human. "Okay, but be ready to drop to the ground if you hear anything." He could handle being shot at, but the thought of anything happening to Jenna didn't sit well with him.

Jenna ran down the hill and picked up the cage. Keith trailed behind her, assessing the landscape for any movement or sound that was out of place. He stayed close, so if he had to, he could pull her to the ground quickly. Her reflexes weren't as fine-tuned as his, which meant he'd have to be doubly vigilant to protect her. And he *would* protect her.

Of course, he remembered her. Over the years, she had come to mind more than once, but he had always pushed those memories down to some hidden place, not wanting to visit the bittersweet emotions that came with remembering.

Seeing her again had shocked him. Jenna was a bright girl who could have done anything with her life. He had always assumed she would move away from the small town of Hope Creek. He never thought he would see her again. Memories threatened to swamp him now, but he refused to let himself get distracted.

Keith remained tuned in to the forest, watching the trees and listening.

Out of breath, she came up to him. "The last time I saw the little guy he was headed in that direction." She pointed to a stand of lodgepole pine.

"What's the game plan here?"

Jenna pulled a cloth from her back pocket. "If we can get a covering on his head, it will calm him. Then I can get him in the cage for transport to the center." She untied the silk scarf around her neck. "You'll have to use this."

He nodded. "Let's get this done so you and the bird can get somewhere safe. And then maybe next time you can forego the trespassing."

"I have to make the birds my priority. There is not always time to inform the landowner. Everyone around here knows me." Strength had returned to her voice.

Keith clenched his jaw. When Jenna got an idea in her head, she was like a pit bull. She just wouldn't let go. "We need to be careful up here from now on, Jenna, even if it was just teenagers being stupid with guns this time." He hoped that's all it was. That was bad enough. His grandparents were older and vulnerable. He didn't like the idea of some town kid taking advantage of that.

"I'll be careful, but this is serious. Someone shot at that eagle on your grandparents' land. That is against the law." Her voice, fused with emotion, broke. "I don't like it when people hurt the birds. I won't know what's going on with that hawk until I can get a look at him. What if someone has been shooting at him, too?" She turned and stalked up the hill.

The scent of Jenna's perfume lingered on the scarf she had given him. He held it for a moment before putting it in his front pocket as he followed her uphill. It would be so easy to get caught up in the whirlwind of Jenna Murphy trying to save all the wild animals. Twelve years ago, the house where Jenna and her father had lived had been a menagerie of the songbirds her father took care of and all the unwanted and injured animals Jenna had adopted. He smiled at the memory.

She stopped and turned to face him. "If you don't want me tromping on your grandfather's land, you can come with me each time." Her tone was playful.

Heat swept up Keith's face. She was standing so close. "I've got a lot of work to do for my grandfather." His heart hammered in his chest. Did she have any idea what kind of effect she had on him, even after twelve years?

Jenna pivoted. "I saw movement over there." She craned her neck. "That's the hawk." With the cage banging against her thigh, she darted toward the trees.

Keith followed behind. She stopped abruptly on the edge of a clearing. He peered over her shoulder and saw a medium-size bird with gray-brown feathers. Jenna stepped back and slipped behind a tree, pulling Keith with her. He towered over her by at least ten inches. She stood on tiptoe and pulled his head toward her to whisper in his ear.

"He hasn't seen us. If you circle around to the other side, we have double the chance of getting him. Wait for a moment when you have a clean shot to throw the cloth on his head, and I'll do the same. Whoever gets to him first, the other person needs to move in quickly."

His heartbeat sped up when she stood this close. Her

breath made his ear hot. Twelve years ago, he had just begun to see her as a young woman and not a buddy. The feelings that had barely blossomed before she rejected him were still as strong as ever.

After squeezing her shoulder to indicate he understood, he slipped into the evergreens, careful not to step on any underbrush. He knew plenty about moving silently through the woods. He had trained for cold weather combat and then they sent him to the desert. Sometimes, the military didn't make any sense. He walked until he estimated that he was positioned opposite Jenna. He edged closer toward the clearing, still using the trees for cover.

A gust of wind blew through the trees. The hawk hopped off a log to the ground. The bird cocked his head and flapped his wings before settling. Almost indiscernible movement on the other side of the clearing told him where Jenna was. The bird fluttered as though alarmed and turned so he was facing Keith. Jenna materialized in the clearing and tossed the cloth over the bird. In a flurry of movement, Keith dove in. His vision filled with feathers and a sharp object pierced his hand. He swallowed a groan of pain.

When he oriented himself, Jenna had secured the cloth on the bird's head with a piece of leather. Her fingers wrapped around the animal's feet.

Blood oozed from the cut on his hand as the pain radiated up his arm. He followed Jenna to where she had set the cage.

Jenna made soothing sounds as she slipped the now still bird into the cage and secured the door. Her voice was like a lullaby. She turned to face Keith. A gasp escaped her lips as she grabbed his hand. "You're bleeding."

He pulled away, tugging the cuff of his shirt so it covered his wrist. "It's all right. I can take care of it." He didn't want her looking at his arms.

"I should have warned you—their talons are like knives."

"So I discovered." Keith held out his uninjured hand for the cage. "I can take that."

They hiked toward Jenna's Subaru with the sun low on the horizon and the sky just starting to turn gray and pink. His old Dodge truck was farther down the road.

"Thanks for helping me," Jenna said. "I always thought we worked together pretty well."

Flashes of memory, of kayaking and rock climbing with Jenna, surfaced. They had had fun together. "We didn't work. We played."

"Still, we were a good team."

Keith studied Jenna's wide brown eyes. Being with her opened too many doors to the past and the painful memory of her turning her back on him when he had needed her most.

A muffled mechanical sound caused them both to stop in their tracks. In the distance, just beyond the rocks where they had taken cover, a helicopter rose into view. The machine angled to one side moving away from them.

Jenna's expression indicated fear. "Tell me your grandfather has recently purchased a helicopter."

Keith shook his head.

Jenna's fingers dug into his upper arm. Her voice trembled. "Do you still believe this is just foolish kids with firearms?"

TWO

Jenna placed some live grasshoppers in the rescued hawk's cage. Though the sense of panic had subsided, she still felt stirred up by what had happened. She tried to calm her nerves by focusing on doing routine things around the rescue center. She could deal with anything a wild bird did, but being shot at was an entirely different story. The hawk picked hungrily at the food. Except for the occasional beating of wings, the rescue center was quiet this time of night. All the volunteers and the one other staff person had gone home.

Outside, she heard Keith's truck start up. Their encounter with the helicopter and being used for target practice had left her feeling vulnerable. When Keith had seen how shaken she was, he'd offered to follow her in his truck to the rescue center.

She had phoned Sheriff Douglas and told him about the helicopter and being shot at on the King Ranch on the drive home. Even then, as she retold the events to the sheriff, it had been a comfort to look in the rearview mirror and see Keith following her.

She didn't know what to think about Keith Roland.

He seemed like a different person from the one he'd been that last summer, but the memory of his destructive teenage behavior made her cautious. And there was no denying he was more distant now. She thought of how he had jerked away when she'd tried to pull back the cuff on his shirt to check the wound from the hawk's talons. But he still was able to make her feel safe. She wouldn't have had the courage to get the hawk without his help.

She grabbed a torn sheet and safety pins from a bottom shelf where medical supplies were stored. As she pinned the sheet onto the cage, the beating of wings and scratching sounds slowed and then stopped altogether. She'd done an initial exam but couldn't find a reason why the rescued hawk couldn't fly. It had been a relief not to find any sign that this bird had been shot. Both dark and pale mottling on the bird's breast and flanks indicated that he was a fairly immature Swainson's hawk. She had a theory about this bird. Flying was part instinct and part learned skill.

In the morning when her assistant Cassidy came in, they'd be able to do an X-ray to make sure there was no physiological reason the bird was flightless. Cassidy was on call 24/7, but Jenna had decided that the bird had been traumatized enough for one day. The X-ray would go better once the bird was hydrated and had his strength back. And Jenna would do a better job after a good night's rest let her shake off the last of her jitters. Maybe by morning the sheriff would call with a perfectly logical explanation for the gunshots and helicopter…and even if he didn't, it would be easier to feel brave in the daylight. For now, she'd just finish up things at the center and head home—hoping that her hands would stop trembling somewhere along the way.

Jenna checked on the bald eagle she had found yesterday, Greta. They had done an X-ray to make sure they'd gotten all the buckshot but that didn't mean the bird was out of the woods yet. Infection from the wound was still a concern. The eagle didn't react when Jenna looked in on her. She was still weak.

Jenna skirted the area that housed the cages filled with smaller birds and stepped into the office. An owl sat on a perch by her desk. She made clicking noises at Freddy, who responded by stepping side to side on his perch. Freddy was one of the center's permanent residents, who served as an ambassador bird when Jenna did her presentations to schools and groups. Only the birds who would die if released in the wild got to stay at the center on a long-term basis. Freddy had fallen out of his nest and been rescued by a boy. The bird had imprinted on humans. As an owlet, Freddy thought he was a person. He was capable of flight but probably wouldn't last long in the wild.

Jenna filed through the stack of papers on her desk. There was still work to do, but she could do some of it from her house, located just behind the center. She grabbed the camera from a drawer. She had a bunch of photos she needed to transfer to her laptop for the center's newsletter. Once she had everything she needed to take home with her, she stepped out the back door into the cool evening of late summer. The flight barn to her right and a separate building up the hill that housed the other ambassador birds were silhouetted against the night sky, and she smiled at the sight of them. She loved the world she'd built for herself and her birds—and she wouldn't let anyone harm it.

Her feet padded on the stone path to her house. The cool breeze caressed her skin, and a handful of stars spread out above her. God had done some nice artwork tonight. Late summer in Montana was her favorite time of year. The center stayed busy, and the weather was perfect. Jenna opened the door and stepped inside her living room. She left the door open to allow the evening breeze to air out the stuffy house.

After retrieving the computer cord for her camera from a kitchen drawer, she shifted a stack of magazines and bills she had piled on her coffee table and flipped open her laptop. The wallpaper on her desktop was of an eagle perched on a tree. Now that people had been shot at, the sheriff seemed more concerned.

He had been dismissive yesterday when she had called him about the eagle. He had theorized that the bird had been in the wrong place at the wrong time and had been shot by accident. She had reported the incident to the game warden, as well, who had expressed a little more concern. She didn't expect everyone to be as upset about injured birds as she was, but shooting at eagles was illegal even if they weren't on the endangered species list anymore. Jenna shuddered. She cared about the birds, but after what had happened today, going out into the forest alone would be no easy task.

She wasn't going to let herself get hopeful. In her experience, poachers were almost impossible to catch unless they were discovered with the dead animal or there were witnesses. Because Greta had been injured with a shotgun, there was no bullet to trace.

Knowing Sheriff Douglas, his looking into the events on the King Ranch would probably not happen until the next afternoon. Finding out who had shot the eagle was probably even lower on his priority list, and she doubted he was giving any weight to her theory that the two shootings might be related—that someone could be targeting the birds.

A crashing noise emanated from inside the rescue center. Jenna jumped to her feet. What on earth was going on? She ran through the open door and raced up the stone path. The sound had come from the side where the birds were housed. Jenna pushed open the back door, and gasped.

The sheets had been torn off all five of the cages. A golden eagle fluttered and bashed itself against the wooden bars. A red-tailed hawk let out its distinctive cry, like a baby's scream. Medical equipment and the X-ray table had been pushed over. Two small Kestrel hawks flew wildly around the room, making high pitched noises that indicated agitation.

Jenna stepped toward one of the cages, then knelt and picked up the torn fabric that had covered it. Twisting the cloth, she turned a quick half circle. Fear spread through her. It looked like someone had gone through and randomly tossed off the cage covers to stir up the birds. It didn't look like any of the birds had been hurt, but they *had* been spooked, and so had she.

She shook her head as her mind raced. Who would do such a thing? And why? And most frightening of all—was the person still there?

The sharp slap of one object slamming against another startled her. It had come from the office. Her heart pounded. Someone was in the next room. She wished she could call for help—she had the sudden memory of Keith from before, sheltering and protecting her—but her house had the only land line. They used cell phones for the center, and her cell was in the Subaru.

Grabbing a pair of surgical scissors for a weapon, she pushed open the door that separated the birds' cages from the office area. She scanned the room. Freddy's perch had been knocked over. That must have been the noise she heard. Freddy might have been alarmed and pushed it over himself...or someone could have knocked it over. Her eyes darted from the top of a low file cabinet to her desk, Freddy's other favorite places to perch.

"Freddy?"

Her stomach twisted into a knot. If someone had hurt or stolen that little bird... She checked several more places before finding Freddy backed into a corner behind an empty bucket. Poor little guy. After settling Freddy again on his perch, she surveyed the rest of the room. Her breath caught. The front door was slightly ajar. Someone had been in the office, too. She raced across the room, slammed the door shut and dead bolted it. Then she grabbed the keys off a hook and exited the rear door, careful to lock it behind her. Was the intruder still around? She was going to have to call the sheriff right now. Her feet pounded the stone walkway. She glanced from side to side. She'd have to check on the birds in the other buildings and clear up the mess the vandals had made later.

By the time she burst through the open door to her house, her legs were wobbly. Her sweating hand fumbled with the lock, and then she turned her attention to the phone. She had just heard the dial tone when she noticed her laptop had been turned around. She walked over to the coffee table and stared at the screen. The photograph of a bird had been replaced by a message.

STAY OFF THE KING RANCH OR THE BIRDS IN THE CENTER WILL DIE, ONE BY ONE.

Keith lifted the cover off the painting he had been working on and dipped his brush in a shade of blue he thought would capture the intensity of the Montana sky. He clicked on a light and positioned it so it shone on the canvas. This attic room in Gramps's house, which he had set up as his living space, was hardly an ideal artist's studio. It had small windows. At this hour, there wasn't any natural light at all. Lack of ventilation made the space hot in the evening. But even with all its flaws, he liked the place for the quiet it provided.

In the corner of the sparsely furnished space, a German shepherd rested on a bed. With only a little brown on his nose and at the ends of his paws, Jet was an appropriate name for the therapy dog the V.A. had provided.

Keith took in a deep breath. It had to be past midnight. He slept on an erratic schedule and when he couldn't sleep, he painted. Originally, his physical therapist had prescribed painting as a way of getting his dexterity back, but the hobby had proven to be useful for working out emotions, as well.

Seeing Jenna again had stirred him up. Had it been a mistake to come back here? After the death of his mother, it had seemed as though God was leading him back to the ranch to heal things between him and his grandparents since they were his only living relatives. Now he wasn't so sure.

Grandma and Gramps had long ago turned off the evening news and gone to bed. They had adjusted to their night owl in the attic. The arrangement seemed to be working out well. The attic had a separate entrance with outside stairs, so he could come and go without bothering them. He helped out as much as they would let him. In the two weeks since he had been here, he and Gramps had mended some fence and repaired the dilapidated barn. He had tiled an entryway for his grandmother and weeded her garden. It felt good to make amends for what had happened twelve years ago, and they had welcomed him back with open arms.

The summer he had his first drink, a fellow kayaker who had been like a father to him had drowned on a run that Keith had decided not to go on at the last minute. Keith had spent a week in turmoil wondering if he would have been able to save his friend if he'd been there. At seventeen, he hadn't known why he'd started drinking. Only when he was in treatment did he realize the alcohol numbed the guilt and confusion. His brush swirled across the canvas. In the left-hand corner, he'd painted an eagle in flight. He'd done that before he had ever run into Jenna Murphy. Jenna with the bright brown eyes. Jenna who had been a skinny-legged ten-year-old the first time he had seen her sitting in the park reading a book. Jenna who had become a beautiful woman.

He angled away from the easel and massaged his chest where it had grown tight. He had kept all those

memories behind some closed door. Whenever he allowed the good memories in, the bad ones were bound
to follow.

The last time he had seen her, she had been fifteen,
standing with her back pressed against the door of her
house. The silence of the summer night had surrounded
them as she looked up at him. That night, he'd come
to her house for a reason. He hadn't expected her cold
response.

"Keith, I heard about what you have been doing…
about the drinking."

"I haven't had anything to drink for a week." She
had refused to be a part of his drinking life, so they
hadn't seen each other for two weeks. The time apart
made him realize how much she meant to him. His
grandparents' lectures hadn't stopped his craving for
alcohol, but he'd quit for Jenna…if she'd help him. He
didn't want to lose her.

"I know about all the bad things you did. Everyone
is talking." Her voice held a desperate pleading quality. "You're my friend, but we—we can't stay friends
if you're going to act this way."

"I'm trying to change here, Jenna. I have changed."
He pressed the heels of his hands against his forehead.
"I know this summer has been a mistake."

Her lips pressed together, disbelief evident in her
features, like she didn't have any faith in him. Didn't
she know who he really was?

"Jenna, I've realized something. That's why I came
here tonight. To talk to you. To tell you I don't want to
be just your friend." He leaned toward her, close enough
to be enveloped by her floral perfume. "Please."

She studied him for a long moment. She turned her head away. "You need to go. You're scaring me." Her voice fused with fear.

He had seen his life as being at a crossroads that night. He was looking for a safe harbor to escape the destructive storm he had created. Her friendship had always been a stabilizing force in his life. After two weeks apart, he had thought maybe he knew what she meant to him. He had gone there with plans to kiss her for the first time, to let her see how important she was, how badly he needed her help. Apparently, the friendship had just been about fun to her. She hadn't been willing to listen to him or weather the challenge he faced. Her rejection had propelled him back to his drinking buddies.

Though he had been angry at the time, he took responsibility for the arrest that had happened later that night. Looking back, he was glad it had happened. It had been a wake-up call. When his legal entanglements had been addressed, he enlisted. By the time he was finished with boot camp, he had gotten help and sobered up.

But the way Jenna had abruptly and completely cut him out of her life was what he could not get past. She hadn't come to see him in jail and wouldn't come to the phone when he'd called to say goodbye, as if all five summers together were washed away by one month of bad choices. She didn't stick around long enough to see that he had changed.

The image of her turning her head to one side was as vivid as if it had happened yesterday. Keith clenched his jaw. He squeezed out more blue paint on the palette. His brush made broad, intense strokes across the canvas.

If Jenna hadn't cut him out of her life, things would have been different. They would have stayed in touch. She would have known he'd gotten his act together shortly after that night.

Though the death of his friend had triggered his drinking, the emptiness of never having known his father had laid the foundation. If AA had taught him anything, he knew he couldn't blame Jenna for his life choices. But still, he had been vulnerable with her, revealed his true feelings. And he had been rejected. He would never put himself in a place where she could hurt him like that again.

He had dated other women in the twelve years since he'd left Hope Creek in disgrace. Some had broken up with him and he had ended other relationships, but nothing had hurt as much as her turning away from him that night.

He flexed his fingers to try to work out the ache in them. Even though he had stripped down to his T-shirt, the attic space was still hot. He collapsed in a chair and stared at the work he had done so far. It was an okay landscape, but nothing that threatened Charlie Russell's reputation.

Apparently sensing Keith's distress, Jet rose from the bed and padded over to his owner. He rested his head on Keith's leg, licked his chops and let out a sympathetic whine. Keith stroked Jet's smooth, soft head, the movement drawing his attention to his wrist.

He ran his fingers along the braided scar that started there and moved up the inside of his arm to the crook of his elbow. He had an identical scar on the other arm, only not as far up. Scars on his chest, as well, showed where the power of the blast had embedded debris.

His life had changed in an instant by a roadside bomb. Both arms had been blown apart by the explosion. The speed at which they had moved him off the battlefield and a skillful surgeon had saved his life and his arms. He had lost some strength and dexterity and the scars would be there forever. But he thanked God every day that he was alive.

He didn't realize it at the time, but God had brought a father replacement into his life in the form of a caring drill sergeant, who helped him find his sobriety while still in boot camp. But it wasn't until his tour in Iraq and the accident that his understanding of God had changed. When he was in rehab staring at a hospital ceiling, he had found the faith that his grandparents had modeled summer after summer. Like his grandfather, he didn't talk much about his faith, though he felt it deeply.

Keith wiped the sweat from his brow and stared at the eagle soaring in the immense painted sky. Despite his attempts to forget, he did remember Jenna; and now every detail of their summers together came at him like a flood. He hadn't thought he would ever see her again. He had assumed she would leave for college and never come back. There was nothing to keep her in this dinky town. Her mom had died when she was two and though she'd been close to her father, the man had always encouraged her to follow her dreams.

He had come back to Hope Creek for two reasons: to make amends to his grandparents for the damage he had done when he was seventeen, and for the solitude. Iraq had been more than he had bargained for. He needed time to sort through his life and find his bearings again. Jenna hadn't been on the agenda. How was it possible that with all that had happened, the dormant attraction could be revived just by seeing her?

Keith rose to his feet and picked up his brush. Maybe he should just paint over that eagle. He stood back to examine his work. No, the bird looked right flying up there in the huge sky. He dipped the tip of his brush in the blue and mixed it with white.

Someone rapped gently on the outside door. Who on earth would be knocking at this hour? Keith's chest tightened. Maybe there had been an emergency with Gramps or Grandma.

He grabbed his long-sleeved shirt and raced over to the door.

When the door swung open, Keith's jaw dropped, and he took a step back. "Jenna. What are you doing here?"

THREE

Keith's reaction to the sight of her was a lot calmer than she had expected, considering the hour. He seemed surprised, but not displeased to see her. Even though he was barefoot, it didn't look like he had been sleeping. Streaks of paint decorated the thighs of his faded jeans. His brow glistened with sweat, yet he wore a long-sleeved shirt.

"Someone broke into the center...and into my house. They left this note on the computer." The trembling in her hands made the sheet waver.

Keith took the piece of paper she'd printed out.

"I know it's late, but I thought you should see that." Jenna's legs were still wobbly, and her stomach had tied itself into knots. Right now, it didn't feel like she would ever eat again.

Keith read the note. His expression hardened. "Did you tell the sheriff?"

"Both him and his deputy are over there right now. They let me go after I answered their questions. They could see I was upset, and they asked me if there was anyone who..."

He reached out and brushed a hand over her cheek. "You don't look so good. Do you want to come inside?"

Like breath on a window, the warmth of Keith's touch faded slowly. He was the first person she'd thought of when the fear over the vandalism had overwhelmed her. Even if the incident didn't involve the King Ranch, she would have craved his calming influence. As though a day hadn't passed, she had slipped into the old patterns of their relationship.

Though she was curious about where he lived, it was enough of an imposition to show up at this hour. "I don't need to come inside. Sorry to bother you this late. I just thought you should know, since it concerns your grandparents' place."

He relaxed his posture and leaned against the door frame. "How did you know I was up here?"

"It was the only part of the house with lights on." Her hand fluttered to her neck, where her pulse was racing. She hadn't calmed down even after the drive over. Whoever had broken into the raptor center and her house had succeeded in their attempt to scare her by threatening to harm the birds at the center. She was furious at the threat, but she was also scared. Very, very scared.

Keith ran his hands through his wavy brown hair, then slapped the note with his hand. "Don't tell my grandparents." Strength returned to his voice, and he lifted his head. "Grandma and Gramps shouldn't have to deal with something like this."

"Good thing you are here to help." The protective stance he had taken toward his grandparents was admirable. She found herself wishing he had been at the center earlier. He would have known what to do with the intruder. Maybe if Keith had stayed awhile to visit, there wouldn't have been a break-in at all. Though she tried not to, mental images of birds fluttering wildly and the note on her laptop made her legs wobbly all over again.

Keith stepped toward her. "You look kind of pale. Are you sure you don't want to come in and sit down?"

Jenna stepped across the threshold. "It's kinda hot in here."

"Not much ventilation," he said.

She moved back outside and turned on the tiny landing. "I think the cool night air would be the best thing for me." She was surprised that after all these years, he was still keenly tuned in to her emotional state. Surprised and flattered.

They had learned to read each other while rock climbing the last summer they were together. As climbers, they had always gone out in a group, but Jenna had proved to be his best climbing partner. Keith had been mentored by an older climber the year before. The next summer, their last summer together, he had taught Jenna. Because their lives depended on it, they had become adept at knowing not only what their climbing partner would do physically while hanging from a cliff face, but how their emotional states affected them. She wondered what he was reading from her now. She felt so anxious and confused, she didn't know what to do. But his presence was making it better.

She stared up at the sky. Pulsating stars and wispy clouds accented the black dome above her. Strength returned to her limbs. She wasn't shaking anymore.

Keith rested his back against the railing, lacing his

hands together over his lean stomach. He looked up. "It is peaceful out here, isn't it?"

"Always calms me down." She took in a deep breath of fresh night air. "Better than therapy." She bent her head, tracing the dark outline of the jagged mountains and flat buttes against the lighter shade of sky. Off in the distance, a light blipped and disappeared. She pushed herself off the railing. "What was that?"

Keith leaned toward her. "What?"

"Over there by those buttes. I think I saw a light." She squinted and took a step toward the opposite railing, cupping her hands over the rough wood of the two-by-four. "I'm pretty sure I saw something. Do you have a pair of binoculars?"

"I can find some." Keith stepped into the huge room, opened a couple of bureau drawers and lifted a coat and sweater as Jenna peered inside. Artificial light gave the space a warm glow. The place was free of clutter. Keith seemed to desire a bare bones existence. A black German shepherd settled in the corner.

She took a step inside. "I didn't know you had a dog." The shepherd lifted his head but remained in the bed.

Keith opened a cupboard. A dorm-size refrigerator and double burner resting on counter space indicated that the area functioned as a mini kitchen. "That's my buddy, Jet."

Jenna took another step inside. Two paintings, both landscapes, caught her eye. They were places she knew well, a river and a mountaintop no more than a few miles away. Was Keith aware that he was painting their childhood haunts?

"Found them." Keith pulled a pair of binoculars from a lower cupboard.

She retreated to the balcony and turned her attention back to the area where she had spotted the light. Nothing caught her eye. Still, she couldn't shake the feeling that something or someone was out there.

Keith's bare feet padded lightly on the wood floor. Once outside, he handed her the binoculars.

She leaned toward him and pulled the binoculars up to her face. She adjusted focus and scanned the landscape filled with shadows. "I saw what looked like a glowing light."

Keith surveyed the tiny landing and then looked up. "Maybe if we get higher." He tested the railing by shaking it. "I'll climb first and then pull you up."

He jumped on the railing and flipped himself on the roof with the deftness of an Olympic gymnast. He turned and stared down at her. "Your turn."

Already, her heart was racing. As a young girl she had had a fear of heights. Keith had helped her overcome that, but she was out of practice. The old fears were back. She handed him the binoculars first and then crawled on the railing. "This brings back some memories."

"We never climbed houses." There was something guarded about the statement.

"Just rock cliffs, right?" Her life would have gone on a completely different trajectory if she hadn't met Keith when she was ten. Like her father, who was the town's librarian, she'd spent most of her time with her face buried in a book. She had always loved nature, but Keith's desire to teach her to kayak and climb had awakened her sense of adventure. If it hadn't been for him, she probably would have ended up working in a lab somewhere instead of running the rescue center. And she definitely wouldn't be here, about to climb on the roof of a house, looking for answers to a mystery.

"You're going to have to stand on that railing," he coaxed.

"I know." Her hands were sweating.

Keith pushed himself to the edge of the roof. "My hand is right here."

She eased to her feet, finding her balance by resting a hand on the wall. Whether showing her how to rock climb or build a campfire, he'd been a patient teacher. Jenna lifted her head and locked into Keith's gaze. She reached for him. He gripped her wrist. The warmth of his touch permeated her skin to the marrow. "I'm dizzy."

"I'm right here. Other hand. Let go of the wall, Jenna," he soothed.

He pulled her up and into his arms in one easy movement. She scooted toward him and away from the edge of the roof. Her hand rested on his chest. Beneath the softness of the cotton shirt, his heart pounded out a raging beat. She bent her head, out of breath. "I never did learn to like heights." The truth was that when she was hanging from a mountain, if it had been anyone else beside Keith holding the rope, she probably wouldn't have been able to climb.

"You always did just fine." His voice warmed.

His face was close enough for her to hear the soft intake and exhale of air. She could smell his soapy cleanness. She'd kept Keith Roland frozen in time. All these years, he'd been the boy who was her summertime buddy. But he wasn't a boy anymore. His transition into manhood had been marked by such tragedy that she'd held on to the part of him that had been so wonderful, the boy part of him. Here in front of her, holding her, was the man she couldn't make heads or tails of.

He scooted away, and the coolness of the night enveloped her. "Let's see if we can spot anything from here," he said, clearing his throat.

Jenna pulled her knees up to her chest. Then she studied the outline of the mountains. Again, a light flickered and disappeared. She pointed and grabbed his arm. "Right about there."

He lifted the binoculars, craning his neck slowly.

"See anything?"

He shook his head. "Maybe if we stand."

"On the roof?"

He laughed, and there was something of the adventurous boy in the laughter. "Come on, you know I can talk you into almost anything."

"That was when I was twelve. This is not a mountain. We don't have any ropes to catch our fall. *You* stand up."

He nodded. "Suit yourself." He handed her the binoculars and eased himself to his feet. His hand reached down, brushing the top of her head while he continued to look straight ahead. She grabbed his hand at the wrist and placed the binoculars in them.

He wobbled as he lifted them to his face but maintained his balance. Jenna held her breath. She tilted her head.

"I see them," he said a moment later. "Lights...moving." After putting the strap around his neck, he let the binoculars fall against his chest.

"What could it be?"

"People on my grandfather's land." His voice intensified. "It's hard to tell exactly where they are at this distance. Gramps and I used to ride all over the place on dirt bikes, but it's been a while since then. I don't know the trails as well as I used to."

"I've gotten pretty good at reading the landscape from having to rescue birds in the weirdest places."

"That would involve you having to stand up," he teased.

She took in a breath. "I can do it."

"That's my brave girl."

Her heart lurched. That was what he used to say to her when she made the decision to do something, even if it scared her.

He extended a hand to her and she rose to her feet. She leaned against him to steady herself. She could see the front edge of the roof from here. Even before she straightened her legs, the night sky was spinning around her. She dug her fingers into his arm. He braced her by placing his arm around her waist.

"Steady," he whispered in her ear.

His hair brushed against her cheek. "Ready now?" She nodded, and he brought the binoculars up to her eyes. The view through the lens was not spinning. Pulsating circles of light floated phantomlike across the landscape. She could discern another larger stationary glow. "Somebody is definitely out there."

"But where are they exactly? Gramps's place is thousands of acres."

She moved the binoculars across the view in front of her. The outline of the mountains revealed the shape of a wizard's hat and a formation that everyone called the Angel's Wings. "They have got to be close to Leveridge Canyon."

"I remember that area. Should we call the sheriff, tell him where to go?"

Jenna shook her head. "The sheriff's still looking for fingerprints at my place. It would take him a while to get over here. We should go out there now before they leave. What if what is going on out there now is connected to the shooting and the note?"

He rubbed his hands on his jeans, angling his head away from her.

"Someone is trespassing on your grandfather's land. We can find out who is doing this and turn them in," she persisted. If they caught whoever was doing this, they wouldn't be able to harm the birds at the center.

The thought of any kind of confrontation terrified her, though. She needed Keith's help. Why was he hesitating? The events of the afternoon showed that he could handle himself just fine, better than she could. "Please Keith, I can't do this alone."

He crossed his arms and stared out at some unknown object as though he were mulling over options. He turned toward her. "I don't want you going out there by yourself. It could be dangerous."

"Thank you."

He shook his head and let his arms fall to his side. "I'll see if I can find a map that might help us pinpoint where they are. The dirt bikes are fueled and ready to go in the garage."

In less than fifteen minutes, they had climbed down from the roof and run to the garage. Jenna placed the bike helmet on her head. She watched him buckle a gun belt around his waist. Considering what had happened this afternoon, the gun was a reasonable precaution. Still, her heartbeat quickened as she slipped on her bike gloves. What were they riding out to?

Jenna turned the petcock on the fuel tank, choked the engine, flipped out the kickstart.

Without a word, Keith sauntered over to her bike while she stepped aside. He jumped down on the kick start. The engine revved to life. She had never been able to get a bike started on the first try.

While Keith started his own bike, Jenna swung a leg over the worn seat. She twisted the throttle to a high idle.

Keith burst out of the barn on his bike. Jenna clicked on her headlight and sped out after him. He waited for her on the road. The hum and *putt putt* sound of the bike motor surrounded her as she caught up with him, and they headed toward the dark horizon.

FOUR

The helmet enveloped Keith's head, pressing on his ears and creating an insulated sensation. He glanced back, taking note of the soft glow of Jenna's headlight. Despite the rough terrain, she kept up pretty well. Part of him wished he could leave her behind and check out the danger on his own. He didn't want to put her at risk. But he doubted she'd let him go without her, and he wasn't about to let her go into the canyon by herself. Even after all these years, he felt the need to protect her.

Still, the pinprick to his heart, the memory of her rejection, had made him hesitate. When he had held her in his arms on the roof, her hand on his chest had seared through him. It had taken every ounce of strength he had to pull away.

At seventeen, he had just begun to see Jenna as a young woman. He had been clumsy and unsure of himself. His attraction for her came out through roughhousing and verbal jousts. When they were on the roof, her touch had been like breath on a glowing ember. He clenched his jaw. He revved the throttle on the bike and lurched forward. So what if the feelings were still there, stronger than ever? That didn't mean he had to do anything about the attraction and be hurt by her all over again.

The road narrowed. The bike bounced over the rocks. Up ahead, he could see the dark shadows of the granite boulders that formed the opening to Leveridge Canyon. He stopped the bike and flipped up his visor. The smooth hum of Jenna's bike growing closer filled the night air. The crescent moon hung just above the flat-topped buttes in the distance.

Jenna came beside him, geared down the dirt bike and flipped up her visor.

Keith pointed. "If we go this way, we can get pretty far into the canyon before we have to hike in."

She nodded. "Sounds good," she shouted as she revved up the bike motor. She flipped down her visor and sped off, kicking up dirt.

He closed the distance between them and rode beside her. She nodded in his direction and then sped a little ahead. Finally, she brought the bike to a stop and dismounted. Keith caught up with her, stopped his bike and pushed the kick stand down.

Jenna pulled off her helmet, gathered up her long hair and twisted it into some kind of knot that held it off her face. He had never quite figured out how she did that. Moonlight washed over her tanned skin accentuating the melting curves of her neck.

She hung the helmet on the handlebars.

Keith turned away. His forearms had begun to hurt from shifting gears and managing the bike over uneven terrain. "You probably ride all the time." He massaged the area above his wrist. Frustration shot through him.

He just wanted to be able to do the things he used to do and not have to be reminded of his injury.

"Bikes do come in handy for work sometimes. Only when I try to start one, it takes three or four tries. It was nice to have help this time."

He detected a tone of gratitude in her voice.

She turned off the headlight on her motorcycle and took in a deep breath. "Tell me we have a flashlight."

"Why? You scared of the dark?" he teased as he clicked off his headlight.

"I'm not scared. You're the big chicken," she said.

He picked up on the strain in her voice. They were joking because they were both nervous about what they might find in the canyon.

Sitting in the darkness, he said a quick prayer that he would be able to keep Jenna safe. His calm returned.

He loved the remote parts of the ranch far away from houses and any artificial light. The intensity of the darkness had always caused his heart to beat faster. Tonight, the surrounding vastness reminded him of how huge God was. He was just a speck in the universe and God loved him anyway.

"I'm not afraid, are you?" she challenged and then laughed at their game. Her boots scraped the hard rock. She moved so she was standing next to him. Her shoulder brushed against his, sending a charge of electricity up his arm. "It's like a game of chicken, right?" she whispered.

They stood for a moment, shoulders pressed together. The game helped lighten the tension over what they might be facing in the canyon. Keith focused on the gentle inhale and exhale of Jenna's breathing.

He leaned forward and felt along the handlebars until he touched the canvas tool bag, then reached in. His fingers wrapped around the cold metal cylinder of the flashlight. He clicked on the light and shone it in her direction being careful not to shine it directly in her eyes.

"Should we get going?" She turned and headed into the canyon.

Once she wasn't looking at him, he touched the gun on his hip. He had every confidence all his training meant he could deal with whatever they faced, but could Jenna? Once again, he thought that maybe he should have told her to go back home. But he knew he wouldn't have been able to talk her out of coming. Her determination to end the threat against her birds was strong. That somebody thought his grandparents' land was open for public use was wearing on him, too. The sooner they got to the bottom of this, the better.

He increased his pace and caught up with Jenna. He tuned into the sounds around him, ready to respond to any threat.

He shone the flashlight ahead of her. "Careful, you don't want to fall."

"I'll be fine," she said.

They hiked over the rocky ground as the canyon walls closed in on them.

She stopped and grabbed his wrist. "You hear that?" She spoke in a harsh whisper.

Keith turned his head and listened. A faint mechanical thrum, like a bee buzzing under a glass jar, pressed on his ears. He shone the light. Only the granite walls of the canyon came into view.

Jenna rested a hand on his shoulder. "We must be close. I say we keep going."

He picked up on a hint of fear in her voice. "Let me stay in front." He trudged forward, and she followed behind him. The noise faded in and out, but always sounded far away. The canyon walls, though, had a way of creating echoes that played tricks with sound.

The smolder of wood burning thickened the air and filled his nostrils. They were close.

The distance between the walls of the canyon increased as they stepped into an open flat spot with no vegetation.

He shone the flashlight which revealed motorcycle and four-wheeler tracks. "What happened here?"

"Trespassers, big-time." Anger coursed through Keith. The nerve of people disrespecting his grandparents like this.

Jenna grabbed his hand and aimed the flashlight toward the source of the smoke. "It looks like the campfire was just put out." She walked over to it and kicked at the rocks that formed a circle.

Keith edged toward Jenna. "We could hear the sound of their bikes on the way up the canyon. They are probably still pretty close."

Even though he couldn't hear anything now, an inner instinct told him they were not safe. The air felt stirred up.

He shone the light around the edges of the camp. Only blackness. A coyote howled in the distance. Jenna gripped his arm. Keith aimed the flashlight a few feet from the fire, revealing empty beer bottles. He wanted to believe that it was just teenagers having a party, but something felt more sinister here.

"Where do you suppose they went?"

He stepped away from the fire. The tire tracks went around in circles like someone was joyriding.

She continued to hold his arm as they stepped toward the surrounding forest. Some of the tracks led out of the camp to the east and others went in the opposite direction. "They split up," she said.

Or maybe not. It was hard to tell. The tire impressions were distorted by darkness and uneven ground. The riders had crisscrossed over each other's paths a dozen times.

As if she had read his mind, Jenna said, "I count two four-wheelers and two, maybe three dirt bikes."

"At least." It was a big group, anyway. He turned his attention in the other direction. Maybe another three or four riders had gone that way. What were they after? What had brought them here?

Jenna gripped his arm even tighter. "That's a lot of people," she said.

Whether they were teenagers or not, the thought of someone tromping around his grandfather's ranch and shooting at him and Jenna infuriated him. Had Gramps's land been targeted because he was older and less able to fight back?

Jenna tensed. "They're coming back." Panic filled her voice.

The mechanical clang of a bike motor echoed through the canyon. "I can't tell where it's coming from." Keith angled his torso to one side and then pivoted in the opposite direction.

The noise grew louder, then softer, then increased in volume again.

"This way." He wrapped an arm around her shoulder and stepped toward a stand of trees. After Jenna slipped behind a tree, he clicked off the flashlight and settled beside her on the ground.

The roar of the bike intensified. A second motor was added to the mix. He brushed a hand over the gun in his holster. Jenna pressed close to him.

They crouched with the darkness surrounding them. Jenna's clothes rustled as she shifted on the ground. She stiffened when the bike noise got louder and then relaxed when the clatter of the motors faded.

"I think they are gone," she said as she melted against him.

"Maybe." He couldn't hear anything, either, but he wasn't convinced the danger was over.

He clicked on the flashlight to have a quick look. Jenna uttered a sound as though she were about to say something. But then her fingers gripped his upper arm.

The roar of a four-wheeler was on top of them with the suddenness of an explosion.

Jenna stood up halfway, and Keith pulled her down as he clicked off the light. "You'll be seen."

In an instant, a four-wheeler was in the camp, followed by a second one, blocking the path Keith and Jenna had taken into the canyon. As the noise assaulted his ears, adrenaline surged through him. They couldn't leave the way they had come. Jenna clung to him, wrapping her arm through his.

The riders wore helmets, making it impossible to tell who they were. One of the four-wheelers turned in their direction, catching them in the headlights. They'd been spotted. Keith turned, pulling Jenna deeper into the trees.

The rider turned off his engine and dismounted from the bike. He stalked toward the trees where they had taken cover.

Keith searched his memory for the layout of this part of the ranch as they ran through the forest. Behind them, one of the four-wheelers faded in the distance.

They scrambled through the darkness. A branch whacked against his forehead. He shone the light briefly to find the path with the least hazards and then turned it off.

Jenna tugged on his shirt. "This way." She sucked in air and struggled to speak. "We can circle back around to the other side of the canyon."

Behind them, branches broke and cracked. They were being chased.

Still holding on to Jenna, he plunged into the inky darkness. They worked their way down a rocky incline away from the trees. Keith glanced behind them where a light bobbed.

Out of breath, he whispered in her ear. "We need cover." He directed her back toward the forest.

After ten minutes, he stopped, leaning over and resting his hands on his knees. He took in heaving gusts of air. Jenna leaned against a tree, tilting her head. He slowed his own breathing so he could listen. Maybe they had lost their pursuer. He couldn't hear anyone behind them, but better safe than sorry.

He signaled for them to keep going. She fell in step behind him, resting her hand on the middle of his back to keep track of him in the dark. Their pace slowed, which allowed them to be more quiet. The forest thinned. Keith turned on the light. The landscape ahead looked familiar. They weren't far from the bikes.

Jenna came alongside. Her breathing had evened out.

They made their way across the rocky landscape. Keith kept his ears tuned to the area around them. Their feet caused an occasional stone to roll and crash against another.

Jenna planted her feet. "Where are the bikes?"

Keith clicked on the light and swept across the area where the bikes should be. The bikes were there, but they had been knocked over. He ran to the first bike and lifted it off the ground. After four tries, it started.

He helped Jenna get her bike up, but repeated attempts at starting didn't even produce a choking sound. Keith lifted his head. The rider who left must have come down here to sabotage their bikes. It was a trap, meant to delay them. And it was working.

Jenna pointed from the control cluster across the handlebars. "It looks...looks like they pulled out these wires." She tried to ignore the rising panic.

"They must have run out of time before they could do that to mine."

"So they...they just pushed yours over."

The trauma of what they had been through was getting to her. Keith leaned close. "You doing okay?"

Jenna tilted her head to look into his eyes. His attentiveness helped her shake off the impending panic. "I'll make it. None of this seems to have ruffled your feathers."

"I've had more practice."

"You mean with the military?"

He angled away from her, picking up his helmet off the ground. "There is no electricity getting to the starter on that bike. You'll have to ride with me."

Just like that, he changed the subject. There were walls between them now that hadn't been there when they were kids. He seemed guarded about sharing any part of himself. What had he been doing for the last twelve years?

Keith got onto the functioning dirt bike and scooted forward, making room for her. Jenna put on her helmet and swung her leg over the bike. She sat up straight and placed her palms delicately on Keith's sides. Being this close to him made her feel even more light-headed and breathless than being chased down the canyon.

Keith flipped up his visor and turned his head toward her. "You can move closer. I don't bite."

"I'm okay." The smoldering tone of his voice made her heart race. At the same time, a fear seeped into her consciousness. She really didn't know anything about him, who he had become. The memory of the night of his arrest charged through her with full force. He had come to her for help. She had been afraid then, too, afraid that his turn toward delinquency would destroy her new and fragile faith. Her friends at church had told her to stay away from him. He could talk her into almost anything. She did not want to be pulled into that world. Not when she already knew how badly it could hurt.

The bike jerked across the uneven path heading up an incline. Jenna slipped back on the seat, nearly falling off. She wrapped her arms around Keith's waist to stay on. His gloved hand patted hers. They lurched down the mountain until the path grew smoother.

He pulled onto a dirt road and increased his speed. Jenna glanced behind her. She couldn't see any headlights, but that didn't mean they weren't being followed. She held on even tighter to Keith, pressing against his back. Keith angled the bike into a curve. Despite the fact that he was a risk taker, she was sure he knew his limits. In all their cross-country treks as kids, he had never wrecked a bike. True, he was a daredevil, always had been, but there was something measured and calculating in every daring thing he did. She was safe on this bike. The only thing that had ever scared her about Keith had been the drinking.

Keith's wavy hair stuck out from beneath the helmet. She was tempted to touch the soft curls. She rested her chin against his shoulder as her eyelids grew heavy. The muffled rumble of the dirt bike motor surrounded her. Her arms relaxed. She closed her eyes and rested, still aware of the movement of the bike. When Keith leaned into a curve, she leaned with him.

He brought the bike to a stop by the farmhouse. The sky had turned from black to gray. Still enveloped in the insulating bubble the ride had created, Jenna sat up straighter. She pulled her arms free of Keith, slipped off the bike and flipped up the visor. Cool morning air surrounded her.

Keith flipped up his visor. "One of us is going to have to call the sheriff."

"I can do that. He's probably not at the center anymore." Their encounter in the canyon and being chased loomed in her mind, but the ride, being close to Keith, had made her less fearful.

Keith slipped off his helmet and ruffled his wild hair. "I don't know what to think about all this. I just know we have to put a stop to it."

"If we *can* put a stop to it." Her anxiety returned.

He stepped off the bike. "If all that has been happening is connected, it's too elaborate to be just teenagers."

She couldn't think about this right now. It was all too much. "I have to get back to the center." She wasn't looking forward to dealing with the aftermath of the break-in and the sheriff scouring for evidence. It had been a long night. Maybe she could catch a nap before she had to start another day. She shoved the helmet toward his stomach. "Thanks for the ride."

"At least that part of the night was okay, huh?"

Jenna looked into Keith's almond-shaped gray eyes. She found herself wanting to get to know him better, which meant that even after all the years and all that had transpired, she still liked him.

"Jenna?" His eyes searched hers. The intensity of his gaze electrified the air between them. He turned his chin toward his shoulder, shifted the helmet in his hand and said, "That was a good ride."

Somehow she had a feeling that was not what he had intended to say. "I'll tell the sheriff what we found. I don't know if it has anything to do with the shooting, the helicopter and the threat on my computer or not."

"I think it does." He lingered, kicking the dirt with his motorcycle boot. "I'll let you know if I find out anything."

"Let me give you my cell number." Even before she

had finished her sentence, she knew she was looking for an excuse to see him again. She had to stop this. She couldn't hope for even a friendship with someone who was all closed doors and guarded secrets.

"I'll get a pen." He bolted up the stairs to his place, but stopped halfway.

Jenna drew her attention to where he was looking. She halted at the base of the stairs. Her breath caught in her throat. A red smear across Norman and Etta's door spelled out the word. STOP.

A chill seeped through her skin as Jenna struggled to form the words. "Is that…is that blood?"

FIVE

Sheriff Douglas raised an eyebrow when he saw Keith enter the station. No surprise there. Christopher Douglas had been a young deputy twelve years ago when Keith had caused so much trouble. Keith couldn't erase the prejudice some people in town had against him. In a way, he understood it. All he could do was show them that through his actions he had changed. But whether the sheriff believed that or not, Keith needed him to take this seriously.

The blood on the door had been the final straw for Jenna. Even though she put on a strong facade, he could tell she was rattled. Keith had decided to drive Jenna to the sheriff's office. No doubt, the men they had seen in the canyon had left the bloody warning. This was escalating fast, which only made his desire to get to the bottom of it even stronger.

The sheriff rolled his chair a few inches away from his desk. "Hello there, Jenna…and Keith."

Keith held out a hand. "Sheriff."

"Is this about the trouble up at Norman and Etta's place yesterday?" The sheriff's chair squeaked when he moved it back and stood up to shake Keith's hand. "I'm headed out that way later today. Or did you want to talk about the break-in at the center, Jenna?"

"I'm afraid that things have gotten worse rather than better." Keith filled the sheriff in on what they had seen in the canyon, and what had awaited them back at the house. He held up a baggie that contained a cloth with some of the blood on it. "Not only did we find evidence of trespassing, this was used to write a warning across my grandparents' door."

The sheriff tugged on his mustache before picking up the baggie. He opened it, took out the cloth and sniffed. "I'll have my deputy take a look at the door when we go out."

"Actually, we scrubbed it clean. I didn't want to upset my grandparents any more than I had to. We thought the blood sample would be enough."

"You won't be able to file vandalism charges. All the same, this might be helpful." The sheriff rested the bloody cloth in the plastic bag in his open palm. "I'll send it up to the state crime lab. Gonna take a while to process it. Nobody has reported a shooting. No one came into the emergency room."

"I was thinking it was from an animal...not a person. Maybe an eagle." Jenna shuddered. Keith placed a supportive hand on her back.

"Could be." Sheriff Douglas set the blood sample down on his desk.

"Did you find anything at my place last night?" Jenna asked.

The sheriff laced his thick fingers together. "My deputy and I went all over the center and your house. Place is like a crime scene nightmare. Lots of fingerprints and lots of footprints. We dusted your laptop and only found one set of prints, which is probably yours."

Jenna crossed her arms. "So that was an exercise in futility." Her voice swelled with frustration.

The sheriff held up a hand as if to stop her escalating emotion. "One thing concerned me. The way you described things happening made me think one person couldn't move that fast from your office to your house. My deputy and I reenacted what you said happened. We think one person distracted you with the mess in the center while somebody else was leaving the note on your computer."

Jenna's face blanched. Fear flashed across her features. "Two people." The pulse in her neck became visible. "In my house. And in the center."

Keith leaned toward her. If it was that easy to break in, Jenna was not safe at the center. "Do you have a security system?"

She rested her palm against her forehead. "We're a nonprofit. It's on our wish list right after more cages and medicine." Her voice trembled.

This was upsetting her. He had to get her out of here. He spoke to the sheriff. "We'll stay in touch. I'll inform my grandparents you are coming out there. You don't need to tell them about the door, but they need to know about the trespassers. Call us if you find anything." He put light pressure on her back and guided her toward the door.

Once outside, Jenna crumpled as though she had been punched in the stomach. "I was okay last night, but now..." Her hand fluttered to her neck and she laughed nervously. "It...it just kind of hit me all of a sudden. A least two people were in my house, touching my stuff and disturbing the birds at the center." Her voice faltered.

Keith hadn't seen the layout of the whole rescue center, but she was vulnerable there living by herself if she didn't have a security system. "I suppose a watchdog is out of the question."

"You mean your dog. He'd freak out the birds." She combed her hands through her long hair, something she always did when she was anxious.

Her face still didn't have any color. He had to get her mind off this. "Look, neither one of us has had any sleep or food. I can solve one of those problems. What say I buy you breakfast?"

Jenna took in a deep breath and visibly relaxed. "Hunger might be part of what's making me feel so shaky. My stomach is growling." She pointed up the street. "Nora's Corner is open at this hour."

They walked the nearly empty street past the library. Even though the windows of the library were dark, Jenna's shoulder jerked when she looked in that direction. Her jawline tensed.

"Your father still work there?"

"Last I heard." Her words were clipped.

"So I take it you don't see him very much?"

"Can we please leave my father out of any discussion?"

Keith opened the café door for Jenna, who gave him a dark look. "I see him when I need to see him."

The café hadn't changed much in twelve years. The blue checked curtains looked new. If memory served, they used to be yellow. The Formica tables and vinyl covered chairs were the same, just a little more worn. The scent of bacon and maple syrup hung in the air. A plus-size blonde waitress looked up from the newspaper she was reading at the counter.

"Take a seat anywhere. Be with you in just a minute." The waitress grabbed the coffee pot and refreshed the cup of the only other customer, an old man wearing a baseball hat hunched over the counter.

Pots and pans banged and something sizzled on the grill in the half-visible kitchen. Country music spilled from a radio.

Jenna chose a table by the window. She glowered at him when he took a seat opposite her.

The waitress set two menus down on the table. "The blueberry pancakes are especially good today." She drew out her pad from the front of her apron. "They come with your choice of bacon or sausage."

"That sounds good. With sausage." Keith pushed the menu toward the waitress.

Jenna's lips flattened and her forehead creased. She opened the menu. "I think I would like to see what else is available." The waitress nodded and slipped away to give her more time. Jenna held up the menu, clearly using it as a barrier against him. Why was she so angry that he'd asked about her father?

If Jenna had chosen to stay around Hope Creek when she could have gone anywhere in the world, it must be because she still desired some kind of contact with her father. There was nothing else that would have kept her in town other than the need to be close to Richard Murphy, who had raised Jenna alone.

Jenna had been a free spirit, running around town in the early morning hours and late into the evening. At noon on the dot, though, she dropped everything she was doing and raced to the library to eat lunch with her father. Keith had gone with her a few times. He had envied the lively conversation between father and daughter as they discussed whatever book they were reading together. What had happened to spoil that? He wanted to know, but she obviously didn't want to tell him.

"What looks good to you?" he asked, hoping to change the subject.

Jenna didn't respond. She lifted the menu even higher so it covered all of her face. He reached across the table and slowly pulled the menu down. The wounded look in her eyes nearly knocked him from his chair. He'd struck a nerve. He needed to back off about her father.

He offered her a faint smile. "If I remember correctly, you liked cold pizza for breakfast."

She hunched her shoulders. "I don't think that is on the menu."

"Guess you'll have to settle for French toast."

"My second favorite thing." A faint smile brightened her face, revealing the dimples. She put the menu down and leaned toward him. "You remembered."

He was starting to think there was very little he had forgotten about her. He'd buried the details about her in some deep place, but her preferences in food, what she'd said and done on each adventure, the way she tilted her head to one side when she was thinking, it was all there. During the school year when he lived with his mom, he had had girlfriends. There had been women after he had enlisted. But he would be hard-pressed to recall much about them beyond their names.

The color had returned to her cheeks. Her long brown hair fell softly around her heart-shaped face. He rested his elbows on the table and leaned toward her.

The waitress returned. "Have you folks decided?"

She looked up from the menu. "I think I will be daring and have the blueberry pancakes."

"With sausage?"

"Bacon," she said.

He raised a teasing eyebrow. "Always got to be different, don't you, Jenna Murphy?"

Jenna's heart fluttered at how easy it was for them to fall into their familiar banter. A lot of things were easy with Keith. The waitress walked away from the table.

Keith tossed a sugar packet at her and she zinged it back across the table. "So you think the sheriff will figure out what is going on up there?"

"He'll do his best." The tension eased from Jenna's muscles when she realized Keith wasn't going to bring up the subject of her father again. "What do you think it is about, all those men and motorcycles and four-wheelers? Maybe some kind of smuggling?"

Keith shrugged. "A lot of drugs come into Montana from Canada."

The waitress brought their meals along with the pot of tea they had ordered. Jenna hadn't realized how hungry she was until she took the first bite of pancakes slathered with maple syrup. Her mouth watered. Both of them ate quickly.

Keith shoved the final piece of sausage in his mouth. "Come on, it's been a long night for both of us."

Jenna checked her watch. "The center will be opening in an hour." She'd just have to go without sleep.

Keith opened the truck door for Jenna, and she slipped into the passenger seat. He eased onto the two-lane road looking straight ahead. She studied his profile. The prominent nose and the angled cheekbones had always made him appealing, but now there was something weathered and wise in his demeanor that hadn't ever been there before.

He turned to look at her. "What?"

Her cheeks warmed. He'd caught her staring. "Nothing, just keep your eyes on the road, all right, buddy?" She said with feigned bossiness. His gray eyes held a depth and a knowing that was different. She turned away and stared out the window as the fields and forests clipped by.

She was glad he had dropped the questions about her father.

Except to make sure he was alive, she hadn't spoken to her father since the emergency room trip a year ago. It had been an awakening for her and the letting go of a secret that she had kept for so many years.

Her father drank. When she lived at home, the drinking began at night after he got home from work while he took care of his birds, so Jenna stayed away. In the morning, he hated himself for drinking so much, so Jenna left the house early to avoid his bad mood. Lunch at the library had given her a brief window of solace. She had her warm and intelligent father back. If the library wasn't too busy, they would sit in the soft chairs by the window, their feet touching while they both read. From time to time, one of them would read a passage out loud that they found funny or original.

As a kid, she had kept the secret without ever asking herself why. Maybe she had wanted to maintain her father's respectability. Embarrassment had been a factor. She'd feared too that the authorities might step in and separate her from her only parent.

She had started to see what a normal life was like when she moved away to college and didn't have to deal with her father's craziness every day. Then she had come back home, and the trip to the emergency room had been the final straw that told her things needed to change.

The emergency room people probably weren't gossips, but they had seen the damage Richard Murphy had done to himself over the years. That someone else knew the secret had given her the strength to find help for herself, to confront her father and tell him that she couldn't handle it anymore. Fine if he wanted to keep drinking, but it hurt too much to watch him slowly kill himself. Richard Murphy was never angry or abusive when he drank, he was just sad.

Keith pulled onto the gravel lane that led to the center. He focused on the road, arms relaxed as he drove. Guilt had risen up in her when he had asked her about her father. Maybe it wasn't right to limit contact. She had wanted to tell Keith, to explain, but she hadn't been able to. Sharing this part of herself was still new and never easy. It was even harder with Keith, since her fear of him becoming an alcoholic like her father was what had caused her to turn away from him all those years ago.

Her eyelids felt heavy. She rested her head against the window. He brushed a hand over her hair with a touch as delicate as butterfly wings. Even though the road was gravel, Keith drove so the car didn't jostle very much. The fog of sleepiness filled her brain.

She felt the car come to a stop and heard Keith talking to Cassidy through the open window, but the heaviness of fatigue made her awareness fade in and out.

Her car door opened.

"Come on, sleepyhead."

Her eyes burst open. His face was inches from hers. Keith smelled like the air after a cleansing rain. They were at her house.

"Keith, I have work to do." Her voice lacked commitment.

"I've already taken care of that." He held an arm out for her. "You're not going to be much good to anyone anyway until you have had a couple hours sleep."

She stepped toward him. He supported her by wrapping an arm around her waist. "You haven't had any sleep, either. You don't seem tired. Is that some kind of military trick?"

His body tensed. "Something like that."

More vague answers. They were both keeping secrets.

He led her down the stone path. When they got to her door, he held up a key. "I got it from Cassidy. She is the only other person that has a key, right?"

"Some of the volunteers have keys to the center, but not to my house."

"You might want to collect those…considering."

Jenna shivered, considering that someone had promised to hurt her birds and was capable of breaking in. "All the volunteers are good people."

"That might be true, but you don't know who they know, who has access to their keys." He unlocked her door and pushed it open.

She trudged in. Her limbs felt weighted. "Okay, I am just going to take a nap and then I will get up. Can you tell Cassidy to come and get me if we have any calls to go out on? I don't want her to have to handle those alone."

"It's been taken care of, Jenna." The warm tone of his words comforted her.

She turned to look at him. Even in the ragged cotton shirt and the paint-stained jeans, he was good-looking. Not to mention strong and capable. If he said everything was taken care of, she'd believe him. "Thank you."

"I'll lock the door behind me and give the key back to Cassidy." He gazed at her. A softness entered his eyes. "Okay?" His voice had gotten husky with emotion.

So much was going unsaid between them.

The look on his face caused a zing of electricity through her. "Okay." She fought to keep the rising emotion out of her own voice. Almost immediately an ache entered her heart where a single look from Keith had made her feel alive.

Jenna opened the door to her bedroom. She could hear Keith walking across the floor and fumbling with the lock as she took off her shoes and lifted her fluffy comforter. She slipped into bed with her clothes still on.

She liked the idea of renewing a friendship with

Keith, but it couldn't go beyond that. It didn't matter how nice Keith was. It didn't matter that even after all these years, they seemed to mesh so easily.

Jenna adjusted the pillow under her head as the soft comfort of down molded around her. She knew enough from the psychology rule book and her own dating history that she was attracted to men who in one way or another had the same destructive behavior as her father.

The night he had come to her door twelve years ago, she had wanted to keep her father's secret from Keith. She had been following the advice of friends to cut him out of her life. And, on some unconscious level, she must have known that Keith would only hurt her like her father had.

Keith did seem different, but he had a bad track record. She couldn't take the risk to her heart.

SIX

Jenna awoke with a start. Had the noise she heard been a part of her dreams or an actual sound? She slipped from beneath the warmth of the comforter, planted her feet on the carpet and rose out of bed. When she pulled back the curtain, it was still light out. She checked her watch, nearly five o'clock. She had slept a full eight hours. Cassidy would have gone home by now. Jenna stepped into her loafers.

She felt a sense of urgency she didn't understand. She needed to check on the birds.

She grabbed her keys off the counter and headed out the door. Her first stop was the flight barn. The barn was designed to help rehabbed birds practice flying in a safe environment. It was over a hundred yards long with perches scattered around the front of the barn. The flight barn was their newest building, only a year old, courtesy of rancher Peter Hickman's generous fundraising. Jenna suspected that Peter had chosen to help the center as a way of becoming a part of the community that was slow to accept outsiders, but in any case, his annual fundraiser was an answer to prayer.

When she pushed on the sliding door to the flight barn, a golden eagle flew by her. The flapping of wings so close always caused her heart to race faster. The golden drifted to the ground at the far end of the barn, the brown feathers catching the light and revealing the gold sheen that was the reason for the eagle's name. Two other birds, a red-tailed hawk and another golden, walked on the ledges around the windows, occasionally fluttering their wings and doing short, quick flights.

She loved these birds, but she knew that in a way, her choosing to pour her energy into saving the raptors was a form of rebellion against her father. Her father had loved the less volatile songbirds, the domesticated ones and the wild, injured ones people brought to him to take care of. She'd gone for the fiercer, stronger birds, less prey to the kind of weakness her father had shown.

All the birds in the flight barn were present and accounted for. Still, something in her felt unsettled. She headed up the hill toward the main building of the center. Maybe her uneasy feelings were just guilt over having slept so long when she should have been working.

She unlocked the back door of the center and walked over to a white board where they kept a record of activity. All the chores, cage cleaning, feeding and medicine had been checked off. Cassidy had gone out on one call. Her note on the board said "unable to locate the hawk." A note with Jenna's name on it was pinned to the wall beside the board. Jenna pressed open the piece of paper.

Everything went really smoothly today. Your friend stayed and helped take up the slack so you could sleep. He even went out on the call with

me. Nice guy. Call Peter Hickman about the up-
coming fundraiser. Mrs. Ephron said there is a
bear carcass on her property that is attracting a
lot of scavenger birds. She wants us to come and
take the birds away, like that is part of our job description. Why doesn't she just get rid of the carcass? You might want to go out there and calm
her down. You know how she is.

Cassidy

Jenna smiled as she folded the note. Last spring, Mrs.
Ephron had repeatedly called them because she was
convinced that eagles were carrying her kittens away.
But the smile faded as Jenna realized that was the second call in a week they had gotten about bear carcasses
and nuisance birds. The first one had been on the property right next to Mrs. Ephron. Maybe the bears were
getting into some kind of poison that was killing them.
The game warden might want to look at the carcass.

She put the note in her pocket, grateful for Cassidy's
recap of the day. She knew she could trust the other
woman's report. Cassidy was more than a coworker.
She was a good friend. After the drama with her father had happened a year ago, Cassidy was the one that
picked up on her distraction despite her efforts at hiding
it. Cassidy had taken her to her first Al-Anon meeting.

Jenna turned away from the white board and looked
around the center. All the birds were settled behind their
curtains. Cassidy was right. Keith was a nice guy. At
least what she had seen of him. She had a feeling though
that Keith was like an iceberg. What she saw of him
was only the smallest part.

Jenna double-checked to make sure the lock on the back door was secure before entering the office area. Freddy was resting in his cage. It was still too early in the day for him. Nighttime was his high activity time. The center's one and only desktop computer was turned off. She phoned the game warden about the bear carcasses and left a message. Then there was just one more stop to make.

She opened the front door and stepped out into the softening light of the summer evening. Her calves strained as she made her way up the hill to where the ambassador birds were housed.

She breathed a sigh of relief when she saw the padlock on the building was still in place. She filed through her keys and unlocked the door. The building was no more than an uninsulated barn divided into six sections, each stall was set up to house an education bird. In the winter, when it got below zero, the birds were often brought inside to keep them warm, but the current late-summer temperatures shouldn't be a problem for them.

The first two stalls on either side were empty. In the third stall, Jenna passed a rough-legged hawk with a wing that had been deformed at birth. She checked on the bald eagle whose beak had been shot off. An engineer at a nearby college had helped create a prosthetic beak so the animal could eat. The opposite stall contained an osprey that was blind in one eye.

An unusual amount of light seemed to be coming from the final stall where Georgina the turkey vulture resided. Jenna's heart skipped a beat as her rib cage tightened. She took the final step that allowed for a view of Georgina.

Her hand jerked to her mouth as her heartbeat sped up. At the back of the stall, someone had sawed a hole, reached in and taken Georgina.

Jenna sucked in a breath of air and shook her head trying to fight off the encroaching devastation. What good did locks do when the buildings were so flimsy?

She darted out of the barn and ran around to where the building had been cut into. Poor Georgina. Vultures were not known as the eye candy of the raptor world, but unlike so many of the birds, Georgina liked people. She walked up to volunteers and picked at their shoelaces when they brought her food in. Would she have even struggled when someone came in after her? Jenna ran her fingers along the jagged cut before studying the area around her. If a person crouched and used a hand saw, he wouldn't have been visible from the rest of the center. This barn was far enough away from the other buildings that during the day when there was a lot activity and people, the culprit wouldn't have been heard, either. She usually checked on the birds at the end of the day before locking up, but maybe the volunteers hadn't done that.

When she stood up, the rock path from her house to the main building was visible down the hill as was much of the center, but not the parking lot. It would have been easier to break into the flight barn, but it was too close to her house. Where had the thief taken Georgina? She glanced up the hill. That would be quite a hike holding a turkey vulture.

She raced down the hill, back toward her house. By the time she got to the door, she was out of breath. She fumbled with the lock and swung the door open. Jenna grabbed the phone and dialed the sheriff.

The deputy answered. Jenna explained what had happened.

The deputy said he would be right out and then asked her what a turkey vulture looked like.

"I'll find a picture." Jenna hung up, skirted to her laptop and opened up her photo file. They took pictures of all the ambassador birds for promotional purposes. She clipped through the photos until she found one of Georgina, turned on her printer and clicked the print command.

Jenna stood up and placed her hands on her hips. Despair seeped through her. Even though this was a sparsely populated county with low crime, the rest of the world probably wasn't as bent out of shape about a missing bird as she was.What else could she do? Jump in the car and search the countryside for Georgina? Put up "have you seen my bird" posters? Demand that the sheriff get search warrants for all the surrounding houses? Jenna slipped down into a chair and placed her face in her hands. Who was she kidding? That bird was gone.

Message received loud and clear. The culprits had made good on their threat. She would quit looking around on the King Ranch. She couldn't risk more harm coming to the birds in the center. She hung her head. She would just have to let it go.

"What are you doing?" Keith snapped out when he saw that after all the talk about security, she had left the door wide open.

She jumped in her chair and whirled, knocking over

the stack of papers she had piled on the other chair before she shot to her feet. "What are you shouting at me for, and what are you doing barging in here?"

"Anyone could have walked in here." He gestured toward the open door. "What were you thinking?"

Jenna opened her mouth as if to speak, but instead she shook her head.

All day since he had left the center, he had thought about her, worried about her. While he baled hay for his grandfather, he wondered if she was okay. He hadn't intended for his concern to come out in anger. But when he had seen the open door, with the threats still weighing heavily on his mind, his heart had pounded against his rib cage. His first thought was that something had happened to Jenna. His second was that he should have been here to protect her.

Jenna shook her head. Disbelief clouded her features. She seemed unable to form a response. She crumpled to the floor and picked up the papers she had knocked over. She directed her comment toward the carpet, not looking up at him. "You nearly gave me a heart attack."

"I'm sorry, it's just when I saw the open door I was afraid something bad had happened to you." He turned and closed the door.

"Well, you're not wrong. Something bad did happen." She slapped a magazine back on the coffee table. "Someone cut a hole in the barn and took my turkey vulture." Agitation colored her words.

"Oh, Jenna." He rushed to her where she kneeled on the floor. "I'm sorry about the bird."

Jenna stared at the ceiling. "What am I supposed to do? This place is hardly high security. Am I supposed to get the volunteers to walk the grounds twenty-four hours a day?" Her voice broke. "Who would take a stupid turkey vulture anyway? They are the ugliest things on earth."

Jenna's eyes were glazed with tears. Keith squeezed her forearm. Her voice had trembled with fear and sadness. This was about more than the loss of the bird. She felt violated, vulnerable.

Keith swallowed hard to quell the ire he felt for whoever had done this to her. He brushed his hand over her soft hair. He waited until he could speak without showing his anger. "Please consider keeping Jet here. He's a good watchdog."

She pulled back from him, seeming unaware of his request. "This has to have happened because of that threat. I'll just do like they say and stop looking around on your grandfather's ranch. You and the sheriff can figure it out."

He doubted that would stop the vandalism. These guys were ruthless and determined to hurt her. "Jet can just stay in your house." That way at least she would be safe. Though she had not been threatened directly, the boldness of an intruder coming onto this property in broad daylight made him wonder if the level of violence might escalate. "He's a quiet guy—he's only going to bark when there is a good reason to."

She gathered more papers off the floor. "I'll be okay."

"Wouldn't it be better to have the birds a little ruffled rather than have something happen to them?"

"I appreciate the offer, but it just won't work." She slammed a magazine on top of another.

Keith tried to loosen the tightness through his chest

by taking a deep breath. He couldn't just leave her here alone unprotected. "Maybe we can get the sheriff to patrol by here."

"Maybe." Lost in thought, Jenna traced her collarbone with a narrow finger. "The deputy will be here in a minute." She blew out a huff of air. "I'm sure this will provide a good laugh for them. Silly Jenna and her kidnapped bird."

"I don't think they will treat it like a joke. Too much has happened. It's got to be connected. Someone who would go to these extremes has something to hide." Anger flared anew in his muscles. The only way to end this—the threats and the fear and the trespassing on Gramps's land—was to catch the people who were doing it.

"Thanks for your vote of confidence." She slumped in a chair. "Why were you stopping by here, anyway?"

"Craig Smith bought a bull from Gramps. I told him I would deliver it."

A faint smile lit up Jenna's heart-shaped face. "This is a little out of the way from Craig Smith's ranch."

Heat rushed to his face over her realizing he'd come here to check on her.

There was a soft rapping at the door. Keith strode across the carpet and opened it. The deputy stood at attention. His face was flushed as if he had been running. Jenna came up behind Keith.

The deputy rubbed his Adam's apple. "I found your bird." His tone indicated that it wasn't good news.

Jenna gasped. "Where?"

"On the road up here. It was…uh…hung in a tree. Whoever did it wanted the bird to be seen from the road. I don't need to see a picture. I could tell it was a vulture."

A faint moan escaped Jenna's lips.

Keith rubbed Jenna's arm. Already, her gaze indicated that she was staring at some unseen thing in the distance. He knew that look. He'd seen it in the eyes of a hundred fellow soldiers when he'd worked as a combat medic. The loss of a bird didn't compare to combat, but the emotional meltdown could be the same. He had to get her out of here, get her mind off all of this.

"Deputy, can I talk to you for a minute?"

The deputy nodded.

Keith ushered the young man outside. "You are going to look around and see if you can figure out who did this, right?"

The deputy ran his hand over his buzz cut. "Sure. I doubt I'll find anything, though. Sheriff and I went over the place pretty thoroughly last night. Probably the same guys, huh?"

Keith nodded. "The crimes these people are willing to commit just keep getting worse. I'm concerned about Jenna's safety."

"Understandable. I can stay until I get off shift or get another call. After that, the sheriff can patrol a couple of times tonight."

"That will help." Jenna was so protective of the birds at the center. For sure, she wouldn't leave them and stay at the farmhouse with his grandparents or go to a friend's house. He'd have to figure something else out.

The deputy nodded. "Guess I'll go have another look around."

Jenna came to the door and leaned against the frame.

"The barn where the vulture was taken is up the hill." A veil seemed to have fallen over her eyes. She lifted her chin to show that she was doing okay, but he saw the quiver in her lips.

"Jenna, how about you and I go for a drive? The deputy can stay and keep an eye on things for a while."

The stricken look on Jenna's face concerned him. How much more would she have to take?

SEVEN

With a heavy heart, Jenna crawled up into the high seat of the old truck. Keith wasn't driving his old blue Dodge. This was a bigger truck, better suited for hauling the trailer with the bull. Jet whimpered and scooted toward the middle of the seat to make room for her.

The door on the driver's side creaked when Keith opened it and positioned himself behind the wheel. The entire truck bounced as he settled in the seat. He tried to shut the door, but it wouldn't catch. He shook it, trying to line it up with the truck's frame. "These old farm vehicles." He opened the door and slammed it again.

Keith started the truck and turned it around in the parking lot. Hindered by the weight of the trailer with the bull, the vehicle lurched forward.

Jenna was barely aware of their bumpy progress. The shaky feeling that had invaded her limbs when she first saw the hole in Georgina's stall had subsided, but her temples still throbbed. A sense of rage over what happened made it hard for her to think.

Whoever was doing this was smart. The culprit knew

that law enforcement wouldn't get overly excited about dead birds, but that it would shut her down.

As if sensing her anger, Jet licked her hand. She rubbed the dog's head and released a slow stream of air. She felt so helpless. What could she do?

The countryside had a warm glow. Flat fields abundant with crops rolled on for miles. The field changed from the green of alfalfa to golden barley: high enough for harvest and populating both sides of the road. Gossamer clouds, that looked like they had been brushstroked on the sky, blended into a soft pink at the horizon. All of it made a beautiful picture, but she was in no mood to appreciate it.

What choice did she have? If she backed off, her birds could be safer, but others, like Keith and his grandparents, could be at risk. *Something* was going on at King Ranch, and Keith and Jenna must be getting close to finding out what it was if someone would go as far as they had.

Jenna placed a hand on the dashboard when Keith drove over a bumpy part of the road. "You don't think they will leave me and the birds alone now, do you?"

Keith's shoulders stiffened and he straightened his back. "It's not a chance I would take. They might retaliate for something the sheriff finds out, whether it comes from you or not."

Jenna massaged her temples. Keith might be right about the culprits hurting her if the sheriff kept looking around. Maybe all this was revenge for alerting the sheriff in the first place. "I'm sure they took Georgina because of what we saw in the canyon. We were getting pretty close to something we weren't supposed to know about."

"But what?" Keith adjusted his hand on the steering wheel. "Hiding the fact that a bunch of guys on four-wheelers trespassed to build a fire and go joyriding wouldn't be worth that kind of effort."

Jenna clenched her teeth. This was nerve-racking.

Jet whimpered.

Keith glanced at her. "You sure you don't want Jet at the center?"

"He seems really attached to you." She stroked the dog's head. "Wouldn't you miss him?"

Like a flare blazing across the night sky, Jenna detected an intense flash of emotion on Keith's face. "He's good for people." His face turned to stone again.

She longed for him to let her in. There was a big chunk of his life he was unwilling to share. "He's been good for you. That's what you meant, right?"

Keith set his jaw. "I like his company."

Warmth pooled around her heart. Keith's offer to loan her Jet had been more of a sacrifice than she had realized. "What made you decide to get a dog?"

"The military gave him to me after I was discharged." His fingers flexed nervously on the steering wheel. "You don't get out of Iraq working as a combat medic without some consequences." He offered her a furtive glance and then focused on his driving.

The hardening of his expression told her that he didn't want to tell her anything more, but she appreciated the little bit he had been willing to share.

Jenna crossed her arms and tilted her head. "It was only one eagle. Maybe I should just let it go."

Keith smiled as he turned the huge steering wheel. "I know you, Jenna. You have a strong sense of justice. There is more going on than just an eagle being shot at. You can't let it go."

"It bothers you, too."

Keith rubbed the stubble on his cheek. "Let's not think about it right now. Both of us getting worked up over it won't change a thing."

Keith let up on the accelerator. In the distance, farm outbuildings came into view. A barn leaning to one side and in need of paint rested beside a newer metal building. Farther up the hill, a trailer house and a small shed were positioned. Trucks, a car and a large combine populated the area between the buildings.

The truck swayed as they made their way up the rutty dirt road. The entire vehicle creaked and continued to shake a few seconds after Keith brought it to a stop and killed the motor. "Believe it or not, Gramps keeps the engine in this thing in tiptop shape."

Jenna nodded. "I believe you." She had been around ranchers long enough to know that the successful ones cared more about having equipment run good rather than look good. She patted the duct-taped dashboard. "It's a good truck."

Keith bent his head as a faint smile crossed his face.

A forty-something man emerged from the trailer. The fedora he wore looked out of place with the western cut shirt and cowboy boots. Craig Smith had only been running the ranch for a few years since his uncle had died, so Jenna really didn't know much about him. He had grown up in a town about fifty miles from here.

Jenna had worked with him briefly to deal with

some abandoned baby owls he had found in his barn
last spring. He had been helpful in transporting the
owls. She'd given him a tour of the center, and he had
written her a small support check. He had pulled her
Subaru out of a snow bank last winter. That had been
the extent of their interaction. He seemed like a nice
guy, if a bit of a loner. Far as she knew, Craig had never
been married and had no children.

Keith leaped out of the truck and sauntered over to
Craig. He stuffed his buckskin work gloves in the back
pocket of his jeans. Craig pointed to a corral by the
barn, probably where he wanted the bull. The two men
spoke for a minute before Keith sauntered back to the
passenger side of the car and hooked his fingers on the
rolled down window.

"I've just got to back up the trailer and unload him.
It won't take but a minute."

Craig came up behind him. "Coffee is on inside, if
you want some."

"Thanks." Jenna jumped out of the truck. Jet stayed
in the cab.

Keith was already backing up the truck and trailer
when she stepped into Craig's double-wide. The living
space was tidy, but obviously no woman lived here.
No knickknacks populated the shelves. The windows
didn't have any curtains. The canisters on the counter
consisted of recycled coffee cans and mismatched plastic and ceramic containers. Several decks of cards and
poker chips cluttered the rest of the counter.

Jenna hadn't meant to snoop, but the "past due"
stamp on two unfolded bills caught her attention. She
turned away. Craig's finances were none of her busi-

ness. They were probably no different than any other rancher's. For most ranchers, breaking even was considered a good year. People didn't pursue this profession to get rich. It seemed a little odd that he'd be investing in a bull if money was tight, but it was really none of her concern, so she put it out of her mind.

She retrieved a coffee cup from the dish rack, poured a cup and stirred in sugar. The coffee was smooth, no acid aftertaste.

Still holding her cup of coffee, Jenna stepped on the porch. Over by the metal building, Craig used hand signals to help Keith position the trailer holding the bull. Jet's head was visible in the cab of the truck as it slipped out of view. Keith killed the engine and jumped from the cab, disappearing behind the metal building. She heard the screeching of the metal gate on the trailer opening and the two men shouting. A moment later, a muscular black Angus bull romped to the edge of the corral.

Keith emerged from behind the building. He stopped to lean on the metal fence, obviously admiring the bull. The late-in-the-day sun gave his brown hair a golden glow. He turned toward her, smiling. Ranching work seemed to come naturally to him. She wondered how long he planned on staying around to help his grandparents.

Jenna gripped her coffee cup a little tighter. Why was she even thinking about how long he'd be staying? She would enjoy the summer with him...as a friend. Any other thought of him she needed to banish from her head.

Keith let Jet out of the truck and tossed a ball for him.

Keith's laughter and cajoling along with Jet's barking floated up the hill.

Jenna took another sip of coffee and though she tried to enjoy the serenity of her surroundings, anxiety plagued her. Craig emerged from behind the metal building and strode toward the double-wide. When he was close enough for Jenna to hear, he said, "Got to get my checkbook."

"Thanks for the coffee." Jenna lifted the cup. "It was good."

"It's my specialty. I'm not much for cooking, but a good cup of coffee will wash down the worst meal."

"You have a real nice place here."

Craig wiped the sweat from his brow. "Thanks, but I inherited a lot more debt than I did land. Kind of hard to stay afloat." He grinned. "I need to win the lottery." He slipped inside the trailer and returned a moment later. He rested the open checkbook on the two-by-four railing.

Jenna looked off to the east. The outline of Angel's Wing Mountain told her which way the King Ranch was in relationship to Craig's place. If she remembered correctly, they shared a boundary. Maybe all this trouble extended beyond the King Ranch.

"Norman and Etta are having some issues with trespassers. You ever catch anyone on your land?" Even as she asked the question, fear crept back into her awareness. Just asking questions couldn't hurt. She'd pass the information on to the sheriff.

Craig shook his head. "No. Course, this place is huge. There are remote parts of it I haven't seen."

She set her coffee cup on the railing. "I don't suppose you have noticed a helicopter flying around."

Craig closed his checkbook and put it in his breast pocket. "I've seen a couple. People use them to check cows in the high country."

True, a helicopter wasn't unheard of, though they were still pretty uncommon. "Do you know anyone who owns a helicopter?"

He studied her for a moment before shaking his head. "No, can't say as I do."

His probing gaze made Jenna uncomfortable. She ran her finger around the rim of the coffee cup. He probably wondered why she was asking so many questions.

Craig's mentioning the vastness of the ranches needled at her. A person wouldn't have to store a helicopter where it could be found. These ranches had all sorts of places a helicopter could be hidden. Her memory of the helicopter was vivid, but asking the sheriff to search landing pads and barns for it would probably be futile.

Craig rested his elbows on the railing. "Be nice if one of my neighbors did have a helicopter. I rent both a chopper and pilot out of Billings when I need one."

Keith strode up to the porch with Jet trailing behind him. He still had on his buckskin work gloves and his forehead glistened with sweat. His demeanor seemed renewed and exuberant.

Craig handed him the check. "Say hello to Norm for me."

Keith held up the check. "Gramps will appreciate you paying on time."

"Like we agreed. Half now. Half when I get the money from the grain."

Keith nodded, then turned toward Jenna. "Ready to go?"

They walked back down the hill to the truck. After helping Jet up, Jenna climbed in. Keith pushed on the gear shift, and the truck lumbered forward. The black dog panted beside her as the big truck inched along the road, shaking from side to side.

She rested against the worn seat. Her nerves felt a little more settled. "Thank you for taking me away from the center. It helped."

"No problem."

"I bet your grandparents appreciate having you around to help. Is this a long-term thing?" She couldn't help herself. She had to know.

Keith shook his head. "Just 'til the end of the summer."

So that was that. Keith had only come for a visit. Jenna stared out at the passing landscape and tried to ignore the twinge of disappointment.

"I can come by tomorrow and get that hole boarded up for you," Keith offered.

"I'm sure you have lots to do at the ranch." His kindness touched her. "One of the volunteers can do it."

"Have you taken the keys away from the volunteers like I suggested?"

"My volunteers are all good people." Feeling defensive, her back muscles tensed. "Whoever did this didn't need a key, anyway." She did not want to believe that anyone who worked at the center would have anything to do with this.

"The person that took that bird had a working knowledge of the layout of the center."

"A lot of people come and go at the center." All the calm she had felt dissipated. "Those volunteers love the birds as much as I do." Even as she protested, she knew Keith was right. Anyone could have broken in.

She couldn't trust anyone.

Keith softened his tone. "I'm sure they are good people." His intent hadn't been to upset Jenna. He just wanted her to be safe. The whole thing enraged him. Other than the warning across his grandparents' door, he'd been left alone. What kind of a lowlife would go after a vulnerable woman living alone?

"Besides, it's the birds that are being targeted…not me."

"I hope that remains the case." He didn't want to make her afraid, but she needed to be realistic about the danger.

When he pulled into the center's parking lot, the deputy's car was gone.

Jenna's hand touched her cheek as she voiced the same thought that ran through his head. "The deputy must have gotten called out for something."

"The sheriff is going to patrol by here a couple times." Frustration coiled inside him. A few drive-bys wouldn't be enough to assure him that she would be okay. "I just wish you had a better security system."

"We're doing our big fundraiser ball at Peter Hickman's in two days." She pushed open the door and hopped down. "Purchasing some sort of alarm system just moved to the top of my wish list."

"Make sure you lock your door and don't go out until Cassidy gets here in the morning."

"Keith, I'm not twelve years old. I have to check on the birds in the night." She raised an eyebrow as if to challenge any objection he might give her. "See ya." She closed the door of the truck.

Jenna waved as she walked past the windshield. Keith watched as she checked the front door on the center to make sure it was locked before heading to the stone path.

Uneasiness spread through Keith as he watched Jenna heading down the hill to her house. Would she be okay tonight?

Jenna's long hair waved in the breeze like a delicate silk scarf. He waited until she unlocked the door and was safely inside before he pulled out of the lot and drove back home.

Etta King was standing in the front yard when he pulled up to the farmhouse. She yanked off her garden gloves after setting a trowel on a stump by the door. "Got some lasagna in the oven if you're hungry, Keith."

"That sounds good, Grandma." Despite years of hard work and harsh winters, Etta King projected a youthful energy with her rosy cheeks and perfect posture. Her long silver-white hair was twisted up on top of her head.

He glanced at their front door. He and Jenna had scrubbed so thoroughly that no trace of the warning written in blood remained. He had told them about the trespassers; they needed to know that much.

"You been out helping that Jenna Murphy today?" Etta's blue eyes had a vibrant sparkle to them.

Keith hesitated. He didn't want to alarm his grandparents, but they needed to be aware of what was going on. "Yes, she had some trouble over at the rescue center. There was a break-in and today someone killed one of the birds."

Etta covered her mouth with one hand and shook her head. "That poor girl. I'll keep her in my prayers." Etta stared off in the distance. "Who would do such a thing? Used to be, you knew who your neighbors were around here."

Her voice trailed off and he knew she was thinking about the trespassers as well as what had happened to Jenna. He rested a hand on her thin shoulder. "I am going to get to the bottom of this, Grandma."

She managed a smile. "I know you will." They walked into the kitchen together.

Italian spices swirled in the humidity from the oven's heat. His mouth watered. No one could make lasagna like Grandma.

"I always did like Jenna. Don't seem to run into her much anymore. She was such a sweetheart when she was a teenager."

Remorse spread through him. "Not like me, huh?"

Etta faced her grandson. "What is past is past, Keith." She cupped a hand on each of his shoulders. She was so short that she had to stand on tiptoe. "You are not that troubled boy anymore, and we are glad to have you here."

He couldn't undo the past; he could only make amends. Sometimes though, the guilt ate at him.

Norman King appeared in the doorway. "What cha got cookin' in there, Mother? Smells like an Italian diner."

Etta bustled over to the oven. "Got some garlic bread

and salad made with lettuce from the garden and home-made vinaigrette to go with the lasagna."

Norman rubbed his gnarled hands together. He wiggled his bushy eyebrows at Keith. "Sounds good, doesn't it, son?"

Keith smiled. He was twenty-nine. He'd faced death and worse. And his grandparents still talked to him like he was a kid. There was something endearing about that.

His grandfather shuffled over to the table. Keith pulled Craig's check for the bull out of his back pocket and handed it to Norman. The old man moved a lot slower than he had twelve years ago. The years had passed too quickly. Keith had been too wounded to accept the love they offered all those years ago. He was happy to accept it now, but chances were his future job would take him out of state. He only hoped to be able to visit them for many more years.

Etta set the steaming casserole dish on the table. "Keith's been helping Jenna Murphy over at the bird place she runs."

Norman plumped down in a chair and stuffed a fabric napkin into his collar. "I always did like that girl."

"She goes to that church over on Beacon Street now, but I see her once a year when all the churches get together for the annual garage sale. Such a sweetie." She held out her hand to Keith. "Hand me your plate, dear."

Keith shifted in his chair. If he didn't know better, he'd say that his grandparents were matchmaking. "I'm just here until the end of summer."

Etta piled the lasagna on Keith's plate and then sat

down, lacing her fingers together. "I'm only saying how nice she is."

They bowed their heads and said grace.

Norman scooted his chair closer to the table. "Been thinking about fixing up some fence in the northern quarter."

"I can give you a hand with that." Keith grabbed a piece of garlic bread. He had vowed to make sure that anytime his grandfather went to the remote parts of the ranch, he would go, too. He didn't want to think about what would happen if his grandfather stumbled on the trespassers.

They discussed the repairs that needed to be done on the tractor before harvest time and other things. After dinner, Keith spent some time watching television with them before heading up to his place.

He fell into his bed and slept for a few hours. When he awoke, it was still dark outside. He had yet to sleep a full eight hours since his discharge. He lifted the thin blanket and sauntered over to his easel. A canyon with a silver and blue river roaring through it was starting to come to life on the canvas. He and Jenna had rafted this river together.

He squeezed out some white on his palette. They had just been kids having fun back then. Rock climbing and rafting were a lot different than a relationship. As easy as it was to be with her, it didn't make sense to start anything now.

He was still alert after painting for several hours. He opened his Bible and read for a while. Jenna's weary, anxious look from earlier kept flashing through his mind. That uneasy feeling that snaked around his rib cage returned. He wasn't going to sleep anymore tonight.

"Come on, Jet. Let's go make ourselves useful."

He padded softly down the stairs. The lights were out in his grandparents' place so he was as quiet as possible as he started up the old Dodge. The headlights cut a swath of illumination as he rumbled down the road. He was sure everything was fine—Jenna was right when she said the birds had been targeted, not her—but he knew he wouldn't feel easy again until he saw that she was safe with his own two eyes.

He pulled into the dark parking lot and retrieved his cell phone. He'd probably be waking her, but that would be better than scaring her by making her think he was an intruder. He was surprised when she picked up after the first ring.

"Hello." She didn't sound like she had been sleeping.

"Jenna, it's me, Keith."

"I know, I saw the caller ID." A second of silence filled the line. "Besides, I know your voice."

"I'm in the center parking lot." When he leaned his head sideways, he saw that her living room lights were on. "I thought I would watch the place for a couple of hours."

Jenna sighed audibly. "Thank you. I haven't been able to sleep a wink. Every noise makes me jump. But what are you doing up?"

Thinking about you.

"I keep kind of strange hours." He scooted across the seat. She was visible in the living room window. "It's a holdover from Iraq. I sleep lightly and in short intervals."

She turned facing the window so she was looking directly at his truck. "That sounds like a lot to deal with."

"Sometimes it is." The compassion he heard in her voice made him want to share more, but maybe this wasn't the time. He shifted on the seat so he could see her better. She waved from the window. Light washed over her, making her hair appear glittery and her expression bright.

After saying goodbye, Keith hung up and grabbed a flashlight from his glove compartment. He walked the grounds with Jet padding silently behind him. The stillness of the night surrounded him. He patrolled for several minutes and then returned to the truck. Unless someone hiked in from the hills, the only access to the center was on the road behind him. He'd be able to see headlights way before they got to the center. He rolled down the window to catch any out-of-place noises.

Jenna's living room light clicked off.

Maybe now at least one of them would get some sleep.

EIGHT

Though Jenna could not discern words, Cassidy's voice sounded frantic. Distortion on the line made it hard for Jenna to understand her assistant.

Pressing the phone harder against her ear, Jenna paced through the raptor center. "What did you say?"

"I said I'm pretty sure I just saw a bird, an eagle, shot out of the sky."

Ice froze in Jenna's veins. "Where...where are you?" She sank into a chair as the numbness invaded her limbs.

"Gleason's Road just west of the center, but the bird was off in the distance." Static broke up her words. "It will take a while to figure out where it went down."

"I'll come out and help you. Do you mind waiting?"

"I can start looking."

"No." Jenna's heart squeezed tight. "Don't start searching for it alone." She didn't want to alarm her friend but given what had happened the last few days, if the shooter was still around, Cassidy might be in danger. "Stay close to your car and just wait for me, okay?"

"Okay," Cassidy said. "You think this has something to do with the vandalism?"

"We can't take that chance." Cassidy knew most of the details of everything that had happened.

Jenna grabbed her purse and headed out to her Subaru. Keith stood in the parking lot holding a cardboard box. For a guy who never slept, he looked pretty good. The teal shirt he wore gave his eyes a bluish hue. The five o'clock shadow and ruffled hair made him look rugged but not unkempt.

"Back already?"

When she had awakened this morning, his truck was gone. His coming to keep vigil over the center was just what she had needed to finally get some sleep.

He lifted the box toward her. "I was in town and I found this motion sensitive light at the pawnshop. It's not a whole security system, but it will help. I can install it."

His thoughtfulness warmed her heart, but panic over what might have happened to the eagle and concern for Cassidy overtook her good feelings. She ran her fingers through her long hair. "Thank you. You can just leave it inside with one of the volunteers."

"What's wrong?" Keith stepped closer, his eyes searching. "You seem upset."

She never could hide her emotions from him. "Cassidy thinks she saw an eagle being shot. I'm going out to see if we can find where the bird went down."

"I'll go with you." He placed the box beside the door and turned to face her.

"We'll take my car." She had no desire to argue with him about joining her. She had no idea what she and Cassidy might be facing. Having Keith along sounded like a good idea.

Keith opened the passenger-side door and pulled out the dry-cleaning bag she had hung over the seat.

"That's my dress for the fundraiser tomorrow night. Just toss it in the back."

Jenna drove a little too fast over the gravel road. Her heart raced as she fought to keep panicked thoughts at bay. If this bird had been shot, it meant the eagles were being targeted. The first eagle hadn't just been an isolated incident.

Jenna sailed over a bump and the car caught air. The impulse to get there and get there fast made it hard for her to slow down.

Keith cleared his throat, but didn't say anything. She noticed he gripped the handle of the door.

She took in a cleansing breath and let up on the accelerator.

Jenna rounded a hill. Cassidy's white truck was visible in the early evening light. She must have been looking for Jenna in the rearview mirror because she had opened the door and stepped out by the time Jenna brought the car to a stop.

Cassidy walked over to them while they got out of the car. Her blond hair was pulled back from a face etched with worry.

Jenna stood beside her friend. "Where did you see the bird?"

A flat area with clumps of grass stretched out from the road and went on for a mile or so. Forest to the east and west and buttes to the south bordered the flat area.

The sky took up three quarters of the view. "I was driving home when I spotted the eagle soaring." Cassidy pointed up midway in the sky. "I stopped the car to get out and watch him. They are so beautiful when they fly, so carefree."

The sight of a soaring raptor had always filled Jenna's heart with admiration, too.

"And then," Cassidy continued as she drew the path of the bird across the sky, "I heard a sound. I can't say for sure that it was a gunshot. But...he wobbled and spiraled downward."

"Do you think he landed in the flat area?" Keith paced away from the road, studying the area around him.

Cassidy nodded. "I got out my binoculars and started looking." She touched her fingers to her lips. "I couldn't see any kind of movement on the ground." Sorrow permeated her voice.

It was a lot of territory to cover, but the probability of finding the bird was far greater than if he had gone down in the trees. "The three of us can do a grid search."

Jenna's gaze scanned the open area. If someone had shot a bird, where would they have hidden? The trees provided cover. If they lay on their stomach, the rolling hills that jutted up against the buttes would be a good place to hide. She shivered. Was the shooter still out there?

It didn't make sense to call the sheriff unless they found something. She had been seeing way more of Sheriff Douglas in the last few days than she did all year. If the eagle had been shot, it was a crime, and they would have to report it, but first they needed to find the eagle.

"I can only give a rough estimate of where I think

I saw it go down." Cassidy's shoulders jerked. "I was looking away when it registered in my brain what might have happened."

"So maybe he was just diving?" Anxiety made Jenna's stomach churn. She did not want to find a dead eagle.

"Maybe." Cassidy didn't sound too hopeful. "He was moving across the sky and then he was gone."

Jenna ran to her car and grabbed two pairs of binoculars. She handed one to Keith. He must have picked up on her fear because he leaned close and whispered, "It's gonna be okay."

The small assurance bolstered her resolve. "How far out do you think we need to walk?"

Cassidy retrieved her binoculars from the bumper of her truck. "It was closer to the buttes than the road. I'd say we need to hike almost all the way out there."

"Okay, let's spread out."

Cassidy placed her hands on her hips. "About thirty yards apart should do it. If we can't find him, we can't find him."

Of course, Jenna knew Cassidy wouldn't give up as easily as her words implied. Neither would she. They would stay out here until dark if they had to.

Jenna paced out toward the buttes, examining the ground in front of her and to each side. She ran a little faster, still scanning the hard earth for the distinctive white feathers, knowing that the eagle could be hidden by the tufts of grass and rock.

Once she reached the base of the rolling hills, she jogged out ten yards toward the trees and then turned and faced the road and parked cars. When she looked up, Cassidy's blond hair was easy enough to spot. Jenna worked her way closer to the road and then whirled around to do another trek back to the buttes.

More determined than ever, she continued to search. Some of the tension in her muscles subsided when she saw Keith working his way east. The light had begun to dim, making it harder to see him.

Jenna headed back toward the buttes again. Her feet pounded out a rhythm. She stopped to study the ground. The eagle's coloring was designed to help him blend into his surroundings. Years of bird spotting, though, had trained her eyes to separate wild animal from wilderness.

She stepped forward. Her heart stopped. Ten yards in front of her was a lump that didn't look like grass. She took two big strides and then ran. Instantly, she dropped to her knees. Sorrow flooded through her as wind rustled the feathers of the dead bird. She reached out a hand to touch its head. The mature bald eagle had had at least a six-foot wing span. It must have been beautiful in flight.

Her hand trailed down to the bloody breast feathers.

She heard pounding footsteps and then Keith knelt beside her. He gasped in air from running.

She touched the bloody spot. "That is a bullet hole, isn't it?"

His voice was gentle. "Yes. It's a clean shot." He turned, looking at the area that surrounded them. "If Cassidy never saw the shooter, he must have had a high-powered rifle with a good sight on it."

"We have proof now that someone's doing this on purpose. The sheriff doesn't seem to be able to make much progress. This is clearly poaching. We can bring the game warden in on this." Jenna clenched her teeth, trying to hold back the rising tide of fury.

"Somebody is sure gutsy." Keith rose to his feet. "Do you know who owns this land?"

"It's government land." Jenna rocked back and forth. She couldn't get a deep breath because of the tightness in her chest. "I don't know who is leasing it. Mrs. Ephron's acre of land isn't far from here."

"Gramps's place is behind us." He pivoted. "It's all happening in the same area."

Jenna heard Cassidy's hurried footsteps.

Cassidy dropped down beside her friend. Her breath caught. A faint moan escaped her lips.

"I'll have to wait here until the game warden comes," Jenna said. "No doubt this bird was a trophy to someone and they might come back for it. She had a feeling Cassidy had interrupted the hunt. The tail feathers and the talons all had monetary value—maybe that was why they were being hunted.

"I can wait with you," Cassidy offered.

"You go on home. I'll stay here with her," Keith said.

As she stared at the dead bird, its feathers ruffled by the breeze, Keith's voice sounded so far away.

Cassidy wrapped her arm around Jenna and squeezed her shoulder. She could barely feel Cassidy's touch. It was as if she were experiencing everything underwater.

"I'll call the warden before I leave," Cassidy said.

Jenna uttered a "thank you" though her voice did not sound like her own.

Keith leaned close to Jenna. He touched her face at the jawline and gently turned her head away from the bird. "Don't torture yourself by looking." The devastation on her face floored him.

"I'm going to get to the bottom of this." Anger colored her words. "I'll do everything I can to make sure the warden finds this guy."

He could only hope that the warden and not Jenna found the shooter first. The resolve he heard in her voice told him nothing would deter her. He couldn't blame her for her anger. But the thought of Jenna confronting someone brutal and arrogant with no respect for life made Keith's heart clench in fear.

Jenna sat back on the ground. Keith scooted up toward her. On the road, Cassidy waved at them before getting into her truck.

Jenna dug her heels into the earth. "This bird was killed with a bullet from a rifle, not a shotgun. Bullets can be traced."

Keith's gaze darted from one high place on the landscape to another. They were exposed if they stayed out here. "Why don't we wait over by the car?"

"We can't move the bird. It's just like a regular crime scene."

Keith rose to his feet, spotted a stick a few feet away and walked over to it. "We can mark the spot and watch from the road." He pushed the stick in the ground next to the dead eagle. "Hand me your scarf."

Jenna untied the scarf from around her neck. It fluttered in the breeze as she handed it to him. Keith knotted it firmly to the stick to enable them to sight it from the road.

They walked back to the car and settled on the bumper. Jenna crossed her arms and kicked at the dirt. The wind caught her long hair and it brushed over his cheek. He'd do anything to take her anguish away. "This game warden is pretty good?"

"I don't know. He's new. I don't think we have even had a poaching case since he got the job." Frustration undergirded her words.

Keith pushed off the bumper and stalked forward a few steps. "Maybe you should let the warden do his job." The harder Jenna pushed, the more he feared for her safety.

"I will, but I am not going to stop trying to figure out who is behind this." She shifted slightly on the bumper. "I just hope I can keep the birds at the center safe. Peter's fundraiser should give us enough to buy a security system. That will help a lot."

"Who is this Peter guy, anyway? You keep talking about him." Jenna spoke so warmly of him; Keith's curiosity was piqued.

Jenna drew back as though she had been caught off guard. "He's the center's biggest supporter. Last year his fundraiser allowed us to build the flight barn. You should come to the ball. It's a lot of fun."

A fundraiser that could finance a whole security system made his motion sensitive light look like nothing. Keith rubbed the back of his neck where it had grown tense. "It's a formal thing, huh?" The thought of wearing a tie made him itch.

"The women like to go all-out, but dressed up for a Montana guy means you wear clean jeans and you scrape the mud off your boots."

The sparkle had returned to Jenna's round brown

eyes and her dimple showed when she smiled. Talking about the birds did that for her.

"You are welcome to come to the event," she said.

Formal events really weren't his thing, but he didn't want to hurt her feelings.

Up the road, a dust cloud indicated that the game warden was on his way. The warden pulled over to the side of the road and opened the door. He was a weathered-looking man with white hair and a silver white beard. Though he had a start on a pot belly, his stride indicated strength.

"Keith, this is Leland Furness. Leland, this is Keith Roland, Norman King's grandson."

Leland offered Keith a handshake with a solid grip.

"Been seeing a lot of you in the last couple of days, Jenna." Leland pulled a toothpick out of his shirt pocket and rolled it around in his mouth.

"Did you check on the bear carcass on Mrs. Ephron's land?"

"Yep." Leland crossed his arms over his chest. "Carcass was pretty well consumed, hard to say what killed it. Took what samples we could."

Jenna filled the warden in on the details about the eagle and pointed to the area Keith had marked. "Do you need us to stay and help out?"

Leland shook his head. "It's a one person job. 'Bout suppertime. I'm sure you two are getting hungry."

They talked for a while longer. As Leland filled them in on what he would do, Jenna's confidence seemed to return.

Jenna thanked Leland before she and Keith got in her car and headed back to the center.

When they pulled into the center, Jenna seemed to sense his reluctance to leave her by herself. She turned to him and said, "Thank you for coming over and doing patrol last night. I see the need for extra security now. I think I am going to ask one of the volunteers to stay with me tonight. She's older and single and loves the birds as much as I do. We'll take turns checking on the birds."

He liked that she was taking steps to stay safer, but Jenna and an older lady wouldn't be much of a match for an intruder. "Can't Cassidy stay with you?"

"She's married, Keith. I am sure she wants to be with her husband."

"I still might swing by if I can't sleep."

"It should be okay. No one bothered the center last night. They must think I backed off." She took in a ragged breath. "Maybe that is why they felt so free to get back to shooting at eagles."

If the culprits found out she had called the game warden, they might come back and do more damage, she mused.

Jenna slammed her head against the back of the seat and stared at the ceiling. "What can I do? It's obvious now that the eagles are being targeted."

It bothered him that the bad guys seemed to have the upper hand. "Cassidy didn't say anything about seeing a helicopter. I wonder how that fits in."

Jenna shook her head. "When we saw the helicopter, it was midday. The trespassers and this shooting happened in the evening and late at night." After reaching back to grab her dress in the dry-cleaning bag, Jenna opened her door.

Keith got out as well and sauntered over to his truck.

She picked up the box containing the motion sensitive light. "Thanks, this was really thoughtful."

Keith said good-night and jumped into the cab of his truck. He rumbled down the road back to the ranch. The game warden had seemed hopeful about matching the bullet to a gun just like Jenna had said. But that would mean they would have to have at least one suspect and a reason to search his home for a rifle. So far, the culprits had remained invisible. The warden had said, too, that he could search the area for spent shells to find where the shooter had been. Maybe what he would be able to piece together would put an end to this. Keith wanted to believe that, but he still wasn't sure.

The whole time they were waiting for the game warden, Keith had that strange sensation that they were being watched. Maybe whoever had shot the bird was waiting for the chance to get his trophy. Once the game warden showed up and took the eagle, that chance had been thwarted. Certainly, that wouldn't sit easy with the shooter. But what would he do to retaliate?

Would he escalate to hurting people…like Jenna?

NINE

Keith raised the ax above his head and brought it down on the piece of wood. As he stared at the pile of wood he had chopped, a sense of satisfaction filled him. His grandparents would be cozy warm in the winter thanks to his efforts. He had had a productive day helping his grandfather. Though his arms ached some, he could feel strength returning. All in all, a good day. Or rather, it would have been if he could've stopped himself from worrying about Jenna. He knew he was overreacting. Certainly, she would have called if something had gone wrong.

Etta came and stood in the door. He knew that look on her face. The crevice between the eyebrows indicated she was anxious about something.

Keith straightened and wiped the sweat from his brow. "What is it, Grandma?"

"Didn't you say you talked to the game warden yesterday?"

Keith nodded.

Etta touched her fingers to her face. "There was a story just on the news. He was in some kind of crazy car accident. The poor man will be laid up in the hospital for weeks."

The ax felt weighted in Keith's hand as a rising sense of panic filled him. He doubted the car wreck had been an accident. Someone wanted to put the warden out of commission for a while. He pulled his cell phone off his belt and dialed Jenna's number.

His grandmother stepped toward him. "Who are you trying to call, dear?"

"Jenna...I'm just...worried about her." He squeezed the phone a little tighter. "But she is not answering."

"She's probably up at that big shindig at Peter Hickman's house. Norm doesn't feel up to going, so we are staying home. Half the town is going to be there, though."

Half the town. That meant that someone who wanted to put Jenna out of commission might be there, too.

The satin skirt of Jenna's gown rustled as she took a sip of her punch. For the third time, she looked toward the door of Peter Hickman's house, thinking she would see Keith. Apparently he had decided not to come to the fundraiser.

Cassidy bustled up to Jenna holding a small plate piled with hors d'oeuvres. She pointed to a cracker with a dollop of white stuff and green onions on it. "These are really good."

Jenna took the cracker and nibbled. The smoothness of the cream cheese mingled with spices, making her mouth water.

Cassidy tugged at the waistline of her dress. "Good turn out, huh?"

"Yes, most of the town is here." Many of the volunteers had come, but she also saw a lot of people she didn't recognize. They must be friends of Peter's. Craig Smith stood in a corner leaning close to another man in a cowboy hat.

Again, Jenna caught herself glancing at the door. The fundraiser was fun. Why then did it feel incomplete without Keith?

Cassidy leaned toward her. "I haven't seen Peter yet, have you?" She adjusted a clip in her blond hair.

Jenna shook her head. Peter's house was huge and partygoers were spread throughout it. The room they were in was open with large wooden floor-to-ceiling beams and a slate floor. A bubbling fountain served as the centerpiece. The room stretched out into a balcony where more people gathered.

A man with brassy red hair peered at them through the doorway that led to a ballroom where country music and party chatter spilled out.

"Oops, there is my hubby, better go." Cassidy placed the plate of food in Jenna's hand. "Are your feet glued to the floor?"

"No." Jenna took another bite of cracker. She set the plate on a little table. She needed to stop nervous nibbling.

"Enjoy yourself, mingle, remind people that we need donations year-round." Cassidy scooted away, hooking her arm in her husband's and disappearing into the ballroom.

Craig Smith raised his voice; his face scrunched up into a grimace as he left the man he had been talking to. He stalked past Jenna.

"How is that new bull working out?" she asked.

He stared at Jenna for a moment as though he were trying to place her. "Fine," Craig barked and headed into the ballroom.

Jenna sauntered toward the balcony where several couples had their heads bent close together. She set her drink on the railing. A cool evening breeze wafted up to her. Peter had built his house in a high spot so most of the valley was visible. Close by, she could see Peter's barn and corral that held two horses. Beyond that were the mountain peaks of the King Ranch. The water tower on Craig Smith's place was visible, as well. But despite the lovely view, she still had the urge to turn back around and see if Keith had arrived.

She leaned on the railing and closed her eyes. She really had to let go of the idea of more than a friendship with Keith. His friendship was wonderful—more than enough for her. She had been so touched by his coming to watch over the center in the middle of the night and getting her the motion sensitive light. It was just nice to know that you were in someone's thoughts.

"Just the woman I want to see."

Jenna turned to face Peter Hickman. He was a short, broad-shouldered man with a thinning hairline. Despite his lack of stature, his physique indicated that he did a great deal of physical activity. He had moved to Hope Creek for the camping, climbing and hunting opportunities, hobbies that he had made into a business. Peter owned a corporation that made heavy-duty gear for all kinds of outdoor activities from hiking to camping.

"Peter, I was wondering where you were."

"Sorry, I had some unexpected business calls." He touched his thinning hair at the temple.

"Looks like most of the town showed up this year. The turnout is even bigger than last year," Jenna said.

"You'll be glad to know we have added up the donations. I think you will be pleased with the total. I'm sure more will trickle in—some people's consciences don't get pricked until after the party. We'll make the announcement in the ballroom in a few minutes."

"I'll be ready to receive the check." Jenna took a sip of her punch. "I'm hoping to get a security system."

"Oh?" Peter leaned closer. "I thought you said something about a new X-ray machine and medical supplies."

"Priorities changed." Even talking about this made her stomach tighten. As a major sponsor of the center, Peter had the right to know the full story of what was going on, but she couldn't quite bring herself to talk about it. Not tonight. "We have had some...vandalism issues."

Jenna turned back toward the railing, and Peter sidled up beside her so they were both looking out on the property.

"That's too bad. I hope the birds weren't harmed."

"We lost one of our education birds." She struggled to keep the sadness out of her voice. "Georgina."

"The turkey vulture?"

She was delighted to hear he remembered. She had given him the tour of the place over a year ago. "Yes."

"Georgina had her charm, didn't she?"

Jenna lifted her head and laughed. "There are few people who would say that about a turkey vulture."

"And you are one of them, Jenna." Peter's voice

warmed. "The work you do with these birds is important." He checked his watch. "It's about time." He held up his arm for her to take. "Shall we?"

Jenna turned. Her breath caught. Keith stood in front of her.

Keith tugged nervously at the collar of his stark white button down shirt. He had shaved and trimmed his hair. He patted his very clean jeans. "Dressed up for Montana, right?" Not that he felt dressed up, compared to the guy Jenna was with, who was wearing a suit and tie.

"You look nice," Jenna said after clearing her throat. She seemed startled to see him. Had she given up on him coming?

"You must be Peter Hickman. I'm Keith Roland, a friend of Jenna's." Keith held out his right hand on purpose so Peter would have to let go of Jenna's arm.

When he had seen Peter and Jenna together on the balcony standing near each other, he'd felt a spark of envy. They were leaning close together, and Jenna had laughed at something Peter said.

Jenna's affection for Peter must be because he cared about the birds. Peter had to be pushing fifty. All the same, Keith found himself wanting to be the one next to her, engulfed in her laughter and the sweet scent of perfume.

Jenna whirled back toward the railing and grabbed a plastic cup filled with punch, which she gulped.

"Why don't I give you and your friend a minute?" Peter suggested. "You'll hear me make the announcement over the PA. I'll talk for a while before you have to come up to accept the check and do your talk." Peter excused himself, leaving Jenna and Keith alone.

Jenna gripped her empty plastic cup. "You made it."

Her cheeks were flushed. She'd piled her hair on top of her head, revealing her long neck. The rich burgundy color of her dress made her tanned skin appear smooth and warm.

His fingers skimmed her bare arm. "You look nice." He pulled the plastic cup, which she had nearly crushed, from her other hand. His gaze went from her full, round eyes to her lips.

"What made you decide to come?"

It would be better to tell her about the game warden later. This was her special night. "How could I not come? Everybody in town is here." He just wanted her to be safe tonight.

Peter's voice, amplified by a microphone, filled the whole house. People migrated from the balcony toward Peter.

"We should go into the ballroom," Jenna said.

He followed behind Jenna, scanning the room which was full of people. Crowds provided ample opportunity to do harm and remain anonymous. Keeping an ear tuned to the people around him, he stayed close to Jenna.

"I need to go up there." Jenna pushed her way through the crowd and stood to the side while Peter continued to talk. A cage covered in a cloth rested on a table beside Jenna. She slipped a heavy glove from the table onto her hand. While Peter talked, Jenna opened the cage door and coaxed a smaller breed hawk onto her gloved hand.

Peter announced the amount of money the event had raised for the center and the crowd clapped. He introduced Jenna as the director of the center. She stood beside Peter while they bantered about the bird she had brought with her and the work the center did. Jenna's body language toward Peter was friendly, but nothing more.

Still, the sudden surge of jealousy had surprised him.

Jenna finished her talk, the audience applauded and Peter encouraged people to enjoy themselves. Peter and Jenna pressed their heads close together and spoke for a moment.

"Hello, my friend." A cold hand cupped Keith's shoulder.

"Craig. How are things with you?"

"Good. Your grandfather raises fine Angus bulls. At least that part of ranchin' is working out."

Though Craig tried to keep the tone of the conversation friendly, his voice held an undertone of agitation and he kept glancing around the room.

Keith made small talk a while longer and then disengaged himself from the conversation. He looked at the front of the room where he thought he'd find Jenna, but he couldn't spot her.

He glanced around the room. Craig had melted into the crowd. He studied each face, not recognizing anyone.

Keith pushed through the crowd toward where Jenna had been. The cage with the bird had been taken. There must be a back door she slipped out of. Mentally, he berated himself for not keeping an eye on her. She didn't know about the warden. She didn't know she wasn't safe.

* * *

Jenna placed the bird in the back of the Subaru and closed the hatch. Her stomach was still somersaulting. Speaking in public did that to her. She didn't want to go back and face the crowd until she calmed down. Instead, she walked down the path to Peter's barn and corral. Horses didn't interest her as much as birds, but she knew Peter was proud of his new stable and she had promised to see it before she left. Now was as good a time as any.

From the time Keith had stepped in the room, she had felt like she had been caught up in a whirlwind. She'd been lying to herself. She couldn't just be friends with him.

He had changed. While she was giving her talk she had seen a waiter offer Keith a drink from a tray twice, and he had refused each time. She didn't have to be afraid of that anymore. Still, she felt a hesitation she didn't understand. Where was his faith at? He never talked about God.

Jenna leaned against the metal corral. One of the horses trotted toward her and nuzzled her hand. She touched his velvet nose.

Peter had said he had more horses in the barn. She opened the small door and closed it behind her. She breathed in the heady aroma of hay and manure. The room was nearly dark. She fumbled on the wall for a light switch beside the door. When she couldn't find it, she ran her hand over the wall. The aged wood of the barn prickled her fingertips.

Jenna squinted. She couldn't see much beyond shadows. From the outside, the barn appeared huge. Though the sound came from very far away, a horse stomped and snorted.

The loft above her creaked. She heard a thud that sounded like a footstep. She swept along the wall searching for a switch.

Something tickled her face. A spider, maybe? She shuddered and brushed at her cheek. When she tilted her head, a string hanging from an incandescent light bulb came into view. No light switch required. She pulled on the string.

The tiny bulb illuminated only a small area, the low end of the barn where Peter kept bags of feed. She could make out the ascending roofline. It looked like the middle of the barn functioned as some sort of indoor arena. The horses must be on the other side of the barn in the darkness.

Jenna crossed her arms over her chest. Grappling through the dark, looking for a light switch, was not her idea of a good time. She didn't want to see the horses that badly. Her stomach had settled. Might as well get back to the party.

She pivoted to leave. The sound of wood scraping against wood reached her ears. A repetitive thundering beat dominated the space before she had taken her first step. When she turned, she was looking up the nostrils of a horse that had to be at least eighteen hands high. The horse stomped its front hoof and snorted. Someone really wasn't in the mood for visitors.

Jenna walked backward toward the door. Adrenaline kicked in; her heart pounded against her ribs. The horse continued to paw the ground with its hoof. She swiveled around to open the door and slammed against a hard muscular chest.

A strong arm grabbed her around the waist and pulled her through the door. Still holding her, Keith leaned forward and yanked the door shut.

"You all right?"

She nodded. Keith could feel her rib cage contracting and expanding as she tried to get her breath.

Her hand rested on his bicep. "That horse gave me a scare."

He gazed down at her. "What were you doing in there?" She hadn't broken free of his grasp. He liked the way she felt in his arms.

"I...was...just going for a walk. I needed to calm my nerves. Peter mentioned he had some beautiful horses in his barn." Her lips parted. Did she want him to kiss her? The softening of her expression stirred up old feelings.

She locked into his gaze. He leaned toward her.

She eased free of his arms. Her hand brushed over his scarred wrist. "Why did you come out here?"

Keith stepped back. He had probably read the signals wrong. She hadn't wanted to kiss him. "I was worried about you. You haven't seen the news?"

She shook her head. "I've been getting ready for the fundraiser all day."

"The game warden was in a car accident. I don't know all the details, but he is going to be in the hospital for a while."

Her jaw dropped. "Which means he won't be able to look into the shooting."

"Too coincidental, don't you think?"

"But it is possible that it is a coincidence." She sounded like she was trying to convince herself.

He reached a hand toward her. "You really need to be careful. Don't take matters into your own hands."

With each word, she seemed to be retreating emotionally. Maybe it was just the leftover adrenaline from her encounter with the horse or the news about the car accident, but she seemed agitated. And her irritation was directed toward him.

"I have to do my job. I don't enjoy feeling like my hands are tied."

"I understand, but we can't ignore what has happened to the warden."

"I should get back to the house." She stalked away from him, her long dress rustling as she made her way.

Keith touched his wrist where her fingers had trailed so lightly, feeling the rough texture of the scars beneath the cotton. Seeing her look so beautiful had put him off balance. He'd been swept up in the moment. Of course, she didn't want to kiss him. And he had no interest in being hurt by her again.

TEN

Jenna eased her Subaru up the mountain road. An owl in a carrier rested in the back. A knot had formed at the base of her neck, and it wasn't just because of the hazardous driving. She was on the King Ranch again, this time with permission. She'd phoned Norman and Etta's home number and was grateful when Etta answered. Hearing Keith's voice would have been too much for her heart. They hadn't spoken since they'd gone their separate ways at the fundraiser the previous night.

Gripping the wheel, she stretched her neck side to side in an effort to release the tension.

The best survival strategy for the birds was to release them as close to where they had been found. The owl had been found in the spring on the King Ranch, so that was where she was going, even though the driving conditions were less than ideal. This road was always rutty and could be called a road only if the term was applied loosely. Rain from earlier in the day had added extra slickness.

What had happened to the game warden weighed heavily on her. But Cassidy had called in sick. Jenna had no choice but to go to the King Ranch alone. All of this was so frustrating. She needed to do her job. These people didn't have a camera in the sky. They couldn't tell where she was all the time. Still, it would have been nice to feel comfortable asking Keith to come along.

She brought the car to a stop and pushed her door open. Her feet were clumped with mud by the time she opened the hatchback. She relished the stillness of early evening and drank in the clean air. Since this bird was an owl, the best time for his release was close to dark.

Jenna pulled the carrier toward the edge of the car. She'd have to hike in to get the bird to a good release area. She knew that there was a meadow up ahead surrounded by pine trees, good owl habitat.

She grabbed her vest from the backseat, slipped into it and picked up the carrier. Releasing the birds was her favorite part of working at the center. It meant she had done her job right, one more of God's creation would thrive.

Work was a lot easier to think about than Keith. He had almost kissed her last night…and she had wanted to feel his lips against hers. A flash of fear had caused her to step back. Both of them were keeping secrets. How could a relationship move forward if he wouldn't share his past with her? And every time she thought about telling Keith about her father, shame dominated her emotions. She felt foolish for having kept the secret so long.

She hiked toward a stand of trees that would lead into the clearing. The silence of being so far away from civilization surrounded her and every thought became a prayer of thanks.

As she walked, the symphony of the forest played. It was a composition she couldn't hear unless she listened very closely. The sway and creak of the trees provided the melody, her feet pounded out a rhythm and even the uncluttered air contributed an indiscernible but necessary part to the whole.

Her thoughts returned to Keith. From all she could see, he was not drinking anymore. Yet there seemed to be parts of his life he kept a tight lid on. She had no idea where his faith was at or what had taken place that led to him coming back to the ranch.

Oh, God, tell me what I should do.

She took in a deep breath. Like a glass breaking, a clanging and whirring noise shattered the silence. A second later, lights flashed and rose slowly upward. The helicopter. Jenna dropped to the ground. Even though she lay flat on her stomach, this open area left her exposed and vulnerable. Inside the carrier, the owl's wings beat against the plastic.

The helicopter was close enough that she could make out the outline of the pilot's head though she couldn't discern any details in features. Another man perched in the open door holding a gun.

The copter hovered, then angled in her direction. The windows of the helicopter looked like giant bug eyes staring at her. She pressed harder into the ground. No matter what she did, the bright colors she always wore meant she would never blend in with her surroundings. Maybe dimming evening light would work in her favor.

The helicopter turned to face her. The cacophony of blades and motor drowned out all other noise. Her heart hammered against her rib cage and the adrenaline kicked in. She fought the urge to get up and run for the cover of the trees. A brightly covered moving object was a lot more noticeable than a motionless one. If she held still, she might get lucky, and the pilot and his gun-toting friend would be focused on the sky, not the ground.

The helicopter surged toward her. She took in a sharp, quick breath and pressed her cheek against the grass. Without even thinking, she had placed a protective hand on the carrier. Her other hand dug into the soft earth. The helicopter flew directly over her. Once it was on top of her, the noise made her feel like she had been pulled under by an ocean wave, losing all control of what happened next, at the mercy of the tug of the waves. She remained motionless, not even daring to take a breath, fearing that she had been spotted, fearing that it would turn back merely trying to get a better angle on her, fearing that its armed occupant would take aim at her and she would be able to do nothing.

At first the whirring of the blades remained strong, but then it slowly grew more distant, started to fade as the volume of the forest turned back up again. Even after she could no longer hear the whop, whop, whop of the helicopter, she remained immobile, her stomach pressed into the earth.

Still shaken, Jenna rose to her feet. Off in the distance, she could see the glowing light of the helicopter, though she could not hear it anymore. As it had done before, the machine descended and disappeared for several minutes and then rose straight up.

Whoever was in that helicopter was dropping some-

thing off or picking something up at various locations.
She had to find out what it was.

Jenna turned her attention toward the trees the helicopter had risen out of. She picked up the carrier and returned the traumatized bird to the back of the car, then double-checked to make sure she had her flashlight and her pocket knife. Even though logic told her these would not be viable weapons, they made her feel safer.

The helicopter had done its second drop at least three miles from where she was, as the crow flies. Chances were they weren't coming back. Still, taking precautions always worked to dispel fear. Having the knife calmed her jittering nerves. She felt a twinge of pain. If Keith had been here with her, she wouldn't have been afraid at all. He knew how to handle this kind of thing.

Jenna closed up the car and jogged out to where she'd seen the helicopter rise. It was the same place she had planned on releasing the bird. A large open area surrounded by a circle of trees. The soft earth revealed where the helicopter had come down. The feet of the helicopter had left deep impressions in the mud.

In the time since she had started her hike, the sky had turned from blue to gray. She turned on her flashlight and surveyed the area around the helicopter markings. She walked a full circle, finally locating a footprint. The helicopter's weight probably would have left an impression even if the ground wasn't soft. The footprints, though, were not as discernible. Where the ground was harder, they seemed to disappear altogether. By getting low to the ground and shining her flashlight, she was able to follow the path of the runner into the trees. Jenna stepped into the forest. Deadfall and accumulated pine needles made the ground soft, and the tracks were cleaner.

She shone her flashlight around a fallen log. Why would someone jump off a helicopter and run into the forest? Maybe they weren't dropping something off, maybe they were picking something up. If something had been left behind, she would find out what it was.

She took a few more steps forward, leaning so she could shine the light low on the ground. She spotted an impression in the muddy earth. The waffle pattern of tread from a boot materialized as she studied the forest floor. She ran her fingers over the tiny bumps and then shone the light in the direction the footprint pointed.

The footprint led toward a healthy evergreen that was separated from the other trees because of its hugeness. If someone was going to hide something, this tree would be a good marker. Jenna searched all around the tree and then shone her light upward. Nothing.

Disappointment spread through her. Maybe something had been stashed here and taken away. Then she noticed one of the branches was longer than the others, like an arrow pointing. She followed the direction of the arrow to a log.

Closer inspection of the log revealed that it had been cut along the top and hollowed out. Jenna lifted the cover off the log. She drew out a note with numbers on it, a canister with a set of keys in it and a pistol.

Jenna looked around. Even though she knew the helicopter was gone, finding the gun made her edgy. Thoughts of Keith bombarded her mind. This would have been less scary with him.

The sheriff would want to see these items, maybe

even come up here. Her hand shook as she drew out the pistol. Guns made her nervous.

A tree creaked somewhere in the forest.

Jenna slipped the canister and the index card into a pocket of her vest. She held the gun at her side. Maybe there were fingerprints on these things. She headed back to her car, treading through the forest and out into the clearing. In the dim of evening, her car took on a dull shine differentiating it from everything else that was a natural part of the forest. Jenna placed the items on a piece of cloth and then put them into a box she had.

She should tell Etta and Norman King about this. She lifted her phone off her belt, but paused remembering that Keith didn't want to alarm his grandparents any-more than he had to. That meant talking to Keith first. She dialed his cell number.

"Hello."

"Keith, it's me, Jenna."

A moment of silence filled the line before he responded. "Hey, what's going on?" His voice sounded distant and guarded.

With some effort, Jenna managed a business-like tone. "I saw the helicopter on the ranch, and I found something hidden in a hollowed-out log about a mile from the double buttes. I thought you should know."

"Is the helicopter still there? Are you okay?" Concern colored his words.

"Yes, I'm fine, and no, the helicopter is long gone." A shiver ran down her spine. His concern was not un-founded. When they had been shot at before, it had probably been to scare them away from another cache that was being dropped. She'd been very lucky this time.

"What did you find?" His voice sounded shaky.

"Are you driving?"

"I just got done with a meeting in town. I'm headed back to Gramps's place. What did you find?"

"A gun, a metal canister with keys in it and a note with numbers written on it. I can't make heads or tails of it. Do you want to see it before I take it in to the sheriff?"

"I'll meet you up there."

"You might have trouble finding me. I am not even sure how far up the road I am. I can come down to you. Where are you?"

"I'm almost to the crossroads. How soon can you get here?"

"I've got to release a bird and then I can get right down there, probably in less than half an hour," she said.

"I can wait at the crossroads for you."

"Sounds good."

Jenna hung up. She pulled out the note card and looked at it closer. Most of the numbers didn't make any sense. One sequence of numbers, 20-8, might stand for August 20, tomorrow's date. Keith might know what the other numbers meant.

Jenna pushed the box farther in her car and straightened her spine. More shadows were evident in the trees as the sun slipped down in the sky. Her heart skipped a beat; a chill climbed up her back. She turned, taking mental snapshots of each section of the trees. Her heart fluttered. This whole thing had stirred her up; made her feel like the forest was no longer a place where she could find serenity. She'd be glad to get down the road and out of here.

Jenna grabbed the owl's carrier again. A repeated thudding caused her to turn halfway. She caught a glimpse of face before an object slammed against her shoulder. Then, as she crumpled to the ground, a flash of metal revealed a car hidden in the trees.

She saw feet. The box with the items she'd found in the log being lifted out of the car. She stirred, digging her fingers into the cold muddy earth. She had to stop him. She tried to pull herself to her feet.

A second blow caused her world to go black.

Keith tapped his fingers on the steering wheel. Two intersecting roads stretched out before him. Only a wooden sign indicated that one road led to the King Ranch and the other to Craig Smith's place.

From the passenger seat where he sat, Jet craned his neck, resting his nose against his chest.

Keith checked his watch. "It's been half an hour." He let out a burst of air.

As if picking up on his anxiety, Jet whimpered and licked his chops.

She could have just been delayed with releasing the bird. Keith grabbed his cell and dialed her number. By the third ring, unease entered his awareness. He'd noticed that she usually kept the phone on her belt. After the fifth ring, urgency replaced concern.

Jet whimpered again.

"I agree, my friend." He rubbed Jet's head. "Let's go find her."

Somehow, he had a feeling that she wasn't on her way down the mountain. Anger at himself caused his muscles to tense. His hurt over last night had made him hesitate. He should have just headed up there when she called. So what if it was hard to find someone on that road. The last time they had encountered the helicopter, it had been right after they were shot at.

Keith started the engine of his truck and sped in the direction of the two buttes. There was only one road she could be on, but it was a long road. Finding her would be an approximation at best. Three times, he tried her cell phone. Tension suctioned around his rib cage.

Jet licked Keith's hand as if to offer comfort.

Keith stopped his truck at the first place he thought Jenna might release a bird. He jumped out of his truck and called her name. He hiked a couple hundred yards. No sign of her car. He'd have to keep working his way up the mountain.

By the time he was seated again behind the wheel, his heart was pounding a mile a minute. He could not bring himself to believe that something bad had happened to her…not now. Allowing that thought to come into his head would cause him to shut down completely.

When he had been in Iraq, his job as a combat medic required him to separate himself emotionally from the violence around him. He learned to process later. It was the only way a soldier could stay alive.

Where Jenna was concerned that was hard to do. Even more so now that he had found out something about her. Jenna's rejection from the night before had left him feeling vulnerable, so he had located an AA meeting in town. Richard Murphy, Jenna's father, had been at the meeting.

Richard had shared with the group that he'd been sober for eleven months—beginning about a month after Jenna had stopped talking to him. Richard had left quickly after the meeting, only taking time to shake Keith's hand and tell him that he remembered him from years ago, but even their brief interaction had been enough to tell him volumes about why Jenna no longer spoke to her father—and why she'd turned away from him years before. If Richard Murphy had been drinking for all these years, that night twelve years ago made sense to him. His heart swelled with sympathy for Jenna. Of course his drinking scared her.

He took the anonymous in AA seriously. Without Richard's permission, he couldn't tell Jenna what he knew. The pain from last night's rejection had not gone away. His reaction to her voice earlier tonight told him that, but he saw Jenna in a new light now.

The truck wound up the rutty road, lurching over the bumps. The sky was dark gray the second time he got out to shout her name. Only the nighttime silence answered back. A mix of panic and despair spread through him. He had to find her.

He moved up the mountain at a slower pace, stopping frequently to study the landscape on either side of the road.

A car bumper entered the cones of illumination created by his headlights. Keith hit the accelerator and brought his truck alongside the vehicle. He jumped out of his truck. The car was a Subaru like Jenna's. He shone the flashlight into the windows. The contents of the car told him he had found Jenna's car. The doors and the hatchback on the car were shut but not locked. All four tires had been slashed.

He shouted her name, anxiety straining his voice.

He stalked around the car making a wider and wider circle. Jet followed close behind. Keith reached down and ruffled Jet's head.

Keith opened the passenger-side door of Jenna's car and searched for something that might contain Jenna's scent. He located a sweater under the back of the driver's seat. Keith brought the sweater to his nose. Yes, that was the sweet lilac scent of Jenna.

Jet was not a trained search and rescue dog, but it was worth a shot. He placed the sweater under Jet's nose. "Go find her, boy."

Jet jerked up his head and barked but remained close to Keith. "Go find her." He placed the sweater under Jet's nose again and then pointed. "Where is Jenna? Go get her."

This time, the dog ran in the direction Keith pointed. The same thing he did when Keith was tossing the ball for him. Keith shook off the creeping sense of hopelessness. Jet was a smart dog. It might work.

He continued to widen his search circle, working his way out toward the trees, swinging his flashlight across the ground. Had someone taken Jenna?

Again, he had to swipe the idea from his brain. He was no good to anybody if he played the "what if" game. Logically, he knew that if she was around here and conscious, she would have answered by now...unless she was tied up...or worse.

Keith swung the flashlight over the tall grass. Nothing. He would search for her all night and into the next day if he had to. He was not going to give up easily.

Jet barked twice. Keith lifted his head. The trees were more shadow than discernible evergreens. Jet bounded out of the trees, danced back and forth and then disappeared into the forest again.

Keith jogged in the direction Jet had gone. The dog's excitement could have been over a squirrel, but he had to check it out. As he got closer to the trees, he noticed an area where the ground was pressed flat as if something had been dragged over it. An icy cold washed over him.

His hesitation had put Jenna at risk. He would never let that happen again.

He ran faster. Keith saw a flash of bright pink. His light bobbed in his hand as he drew closer. He collapsed to his knees next to where Jenna lay on the ground, her legs twisted under her in an unnatural position.

Jet came back out of the trees. He licked Keith's face.

"Jet, go sit." The dog set back on his haunches, but his back legs quivered with anxiety.

Keith touched Jenna's face. Still warm. The throb of a pulse pushed back on his fingers when his hand trailed down her neck.

He shone the light directly on her face. She moaned. Dried blood crusted on her forehead. He gathered her head in his arms to try to find the source of the bleeding. Fresh blood streamed down her temple.

He tore the sleeves from his shirt and pressed one of them against her temple. It darkened with blood. He placed the flashlight in his teeth and angled her head. She had been hit, hard enough to knock her out. Rage coursed through him for what had happened to her.

Keith tied the two sleeves together and wrapped the makeshift bandage around her head. The bandage darkened. He pressed his face close to her lips. Her breathing was shallow, but still there. Keith lifted Jenna's eyelids, angling the light so it wouldn't shine directly in her eyes. It didn't look like her pupils were dilated. She hadn't jerked back when he shone the light in her face, so she was conscious but unresponsive. Keith stroked her forehead. Even though the color had left her cheeks she was as beautiful as ever. "Jenna, can you hear me?"

Come on, Jenna, answer me.

ELEVEN

A voice from very far away drifted into Jenna's awareness. What was going on? She felt like she was swimming through gelatin. The voice drew her upward. A deep bass voice whispered prayers. Was she dreaming?

"Please, God, let her be all right."

Warm fingers touched her cheek. With great effort, she opened her eyes. Keith gazed down at her with gentle gray eyes.

"Hey, there."

He had placed her sweater underneath her head. He'd taken such care with her. His prayer warmed her even more. Any man who would pray like that when there was no one but God to hear must have a deep faith. She tried to piece together what had happened. The moon above her told her that she was outside, but her brain felt fuzzy. What was the last thing she remembered?

She lifted her head, catching a glimpse of Jet who lay a few feet away.

Keith jerked. "No, don't do that."

Pain shot through her head. She moaned and lay back down. The throbbing lessened if she held very still.

Jet whimpered and licked her hand.

"You got hit pretty hard."

"Hit?" Ah, yes, now she remembered. "He must have come up here to get the stuff in that cache. The helicopter is for dropping the stuff." She winced and touched her shoulder.

"He hit you there, too." His touch on her shoulder was soft, but his voice was indignant at what had happened.

Jenna nodded. "I don't think it's bleeding, just bruised."

"Did you get a look at him?"

She couldn't think straight. "Kind of?" She searched her memory. She had seen him just for a moment. When she tried to picture his face, she drew a blank. Her temple pulsated.

"Don't worry about it now." His hand cupped her cheek. "I didn't want to move you in case there was additional injury. Can you feel your toes?"

She smiled. Now he was worrying too much. "Yes." His fussing over her was kind of sweet.

"Your legs were twisted funny. That's why I asked."

"He must have dragged me over here." She lifted her hands, touching the bandage. Just one more way Keith had taken care of her.

Keith nodded. "I should have just come up here right away. Anytime that helicopter shows up, it's bad news." His mouth grew into a tight line.

"I'm the one that said to meet me at the crossroads." She grabbed his arm. "I'm just glad you came." Her hand brushed over rough skin. He wasn't wearing long sleeves.

He jerked back, jumped to his feet and turned away from her.

"What happened to your arms?" She stared at his back.

"They're...scars." He placed his hands on his hips. "It happened in Iraq. When my whole life blew up in my face."

Somehow she had a feeling the scars were less about him being self-conscious and more about how they were a reminder of his life getting off course. No wonder he couldn't talk about the past. Despite the undulating pain, she lifted her head. Her heart swelled with empathy. "I have lots of scars, too. Most of which I got when we were out having our adventures." She struggled to keep her tone light, teasing.

"This is different, Jenna." He was still turned away from her.

"You got those in sacrifice to others...didn't you?" Her voice grew thick with sorrow for what he must have gone through. And she had thought the worst of him for covering his arms.

He bent his head, rubbing his forehead.

"I got my scars being stupid. Remember this one?" She sat up. The throbbing in her head made her eyes water. She lifted her pant leg. "I think this one happened when we were hiking. I collided with that sharp tree branch, remember?"

Keith remained with his back to her.

She rolled up her sleeve, brushing her hands over the area above her thumb. "I think this one happened when we built the tree house. I never was very good with a hammer."

"Jenna, it's not the same."

"I know." With substantial effort, she pushed herself to her feet. She wobbled and planted her feet. She stepped unsteadily toward him. When she placed her open hand on his back, he didn't pull away. "Yours mean something."

"I got off a lot easier than a lot of other guys. I'm still walking around."

The heat from his back seared through her hand. What had this man been through? Guilt washed over her for all the suspicions she had harbored about him.

He hung his head. "What bothers me is that I have a memory of what my arms used to look like." He turned slowly to face her. "That I used to be able to do things without pain."

She rested her open hand on the hard muscle of his bicep. Maybe his self-consciousness hinted at a deeper scar. Her fingers skated his arm to the crook of his elbow. With a soft touch, she traced his scar down his forearm to his wrist. With her other hand, she touched the other scar. "This doesn't bother me." She tilted her head. "It doesn't bother me at all."

Jenna's clear warm eyes held him in place. He searched for some indication that she was lying, just to make him feel better. The last thing he wanted was her pity. Her expression and the magnetic pull of her eyes communicated sincerity. Her fingers fluttered over his scars as light as wind. Her complete acceptance of him despite physical flaws caused him to let his defenses down. Her touch sent a charge of electricity straight through his skin to the marrow of his bones. With the back of his fingers, he traced the outline of her jaw.

He leaned closer, wanting more than anything to kiss her. But the memory of last night haunted him. He hesitated.

Jenna let out a gasp and stepped closer to him. Her hand rested against his chest. She locked him in her gaze. In her eyes, he saw that she would not hurt him... not like before.

He bent his head, brushing his lips over hers and then pressing harder. His hand trailed down her neck as she melted against him.

He pulled away. "I think I have wanted to do that for twelve years."

"Twelve years?"

"Never mind."

"I know what you are talking about. That night, right before your arrest. I was a brand-new Christian. My faith was fragile—everyone was telling me you were bad news. And the way you'd been acting all summer... You scared me."

He doubted that was the whole reason. "I see that now." He understood more than he could say. She had been so afraid that night twelve years ago because his behavior reminded her of her father. What was keeping her from sharing about her father now?

He longed to ask her more about her father...to say what he knew, but that would have to wait. How long had her father had a drinking problem? His heart swelled with sympathy. What a heavy load for a kid to carry.

He touched his hand to his chest where his heart

raged against his rib cage. Some scars were where everyone could see them and others were invisible. The unseen wounds had driven many of his choices. He saw now that he could trust Jenna.

"We should probably get back down the mountain, get you to the doctor and call the police," he said.

Jenna's eyes grew wide. "The owl. Was the carrier still beside the car?"

How quickly her thoughts turned to the birds. He shook his head. "I think so."

She was already halfway across the field. Keith sauntered behind her, still basking inside the warm glow of the kiss.

Jenna had opened the hatch of her car. She collapsed on the edge. "My head really hurts."

Keith rushed over to her. "Jenna, we need to get you checked out at the hospital."

He noticed trembling in the hand she brought up to rub the back of her neck. "I know that, but this bird has been through enough. I've brought him all the way up here." She gazed at him. "Can you help me? It won't take but a minute."

She wasn't going to leave unless they released this bird. Keith shrugged. "Sure. What do I have to do?"

Jenna burst to her feet, but swayed.

He grabbed her arms to provide support as she sat back down. "Maybe it's a good thing your car was disabled. For sure, I don't want you driving until we have you checked out."

Jenna furled her forehead. "That guy messed with my car." Irritation colored her words.

Keith pointed to the tires, and Jenna let out a groan.

She tilted her head back but stopped midway, pressing her palm against the back of her head.

"You really need to take it easy." He brushed a hand over her silky hair. "I can probably find some replacement tires at the ranch. Gramps has plenty. Let's get you to a doctor."

"First, the bird." She crossed her arms, her mouth drawn into a tight line. She was not going to give up without a fight. He had to admire her tenacity.

"I'll take care of this. You sit right there. A head injury is nothing to mess around with. One day you're fine, and the next you can't remember how to find your way home."

"You know this from experience?"

"Yeah, I have seen it happen to some guys I was stationed with." He kneeled on the ground. "You've got to trust me on this one. I can let this bird out on my own."

"Okay," she relented.

"Just tell me what to do."

Jenna craned her neck from side to side. "It's not really hard. You just want him to have as little human contact as possible. Open the door and tilt the cage. He should be ready to come out. Sometimes, they don't take flight right away. As soon as he is out, back away as quietly as you can."

Keith reached beside the car, grabbed the carrier; his bare arm brushed against hers. She seemed to almost lean into his touch, a nice assurance that the scars really meant nothing to her. The back of his hand brushed over the smooth surface of her arm. "Goose pimples."

She rubbed her own arms and tilted her head as he straightened. "I know. I need to put that sweater on."

Without a word, he set the carrier down, retrieved the sweater and wrapped it around her shoulders. "Better?"

She nodded. Again, his gaze fell to her lips. He really wanted to kiss her again, to hold her longer. To make sure the first kiss had been real. Maybe later. He drew back, turning his attention toward the carrier.

"I know it's dark, but you can't use a flashlight."

"Not an issue for me. I am used to tromping around in the dark."

"Something to do with your time in Iraq?"

Before, a wall would have gone up when she probed, but now he found himself wanting to share some of the details of his life. Some doors still had to remain closed. Even he couldn't revisit them, not yet. But for now... "Yeah, I'll tell you about it sometime."

"I'd like that."

Jenna watched as Keith stalked out to the open field. Her skin still tingled from his touch. The light-headedness wasn't simply from the head injury.

As he drew farther away, she could just make out his silhouette. The moon provided only a soft wash of light. He stopped and leaned over the carrier to unlatch the door. He tilted the cage. She saw a flash of white.

Jenna drew her knees up to her chest. The owl had not moved since its initial escape. Inside her head, she coached the bird.

Come on, little guy, take flight. You can do it.

Keith stood still, as well. Jenna touched her fingers to her lips. Though the kiss had been wonderful, it had left her feeling vulnerable. What happened now? At college, she had dated other men, but it had never gone beyond a few dates. Some of the men had been nice, solid Christian men. Some had only reminded her what a landmine relationships could be for her because she seemed to have radar for men like her father. With all those men, nothing had sparked inside her, even with the nice guys. Over the years, Keith had occasionally fluttered across her memory, especially in the summer. What if none of those other relationships got off the ground because she had met her soul mate when she was ten?

The thought made her heart beat faster as the strange mixture of excitement and fear flowed through her. Keith seemed open to sharing the parts of his life he had guarded before. That meant she had to let him into hers. Her back stiffened. Could she do that?

Keith took a few steps away from the bird. Jenna squinted, trying to separate the owl from the field. Owls do not make noise when they fly, one of God's special gifts that allows them to sneak up silently on prey. It did make it difficult, though, to tell if the bird had taken off. She waited for some flash of white in the moonlight. The standard policy was not to leave a bird until it showed it was capable of sustained flight.

Jenna rose to her feet. Keith increased his pace as he stepped farther away from where he had left the bird. He came up beside her.

"Did he take off?"

"Not yet." Keith stood close; the knuckles of his hand brushed against hers. His hand probed over her palm as he intertwined his fingers with hers. Her pulse surged. Delight at his touch and uncertainty about the future fought a war inside her.

She could barely discern the image of the bird taking flight. She pulled her hand away to point. "There, there he goes." The elation and feeling of victory flooded through her. This is why she loved this job. She turned to face Keith. His features were not discernible in the darkness.

"Kind of a good feeling, huh?" His voice was low and husky.

His kiss had turned her world upside down. She found herself longing to be in his arms again. Her head undulated, reminding her of her injury. She took a step back.

"Boy, do I wish I had an aspirin." She would be able to think clearer and sort through things when her head didn't feel like it was about to explode. Then maybe she would know what to do about Keith Roland.

TWELVE

Keith eased the truck down the rutty dirt road.

Jenna sat close to him while Jet occupied the spot next to the window. The dog angled toward Jenna and licked her face.

Her laughter was like a soothing balm. "Do you think he's mad because I took his spot in the truck?"

"He'll get over it." Keith chuckled. The road flattened out, and they came to a more open area as they neared the crossroads.

Jenna yawned and rested her head against the back of the seat. "I am pretty tired. It's getting late. I'll call the sheriff tomorrow and tell him about what happened."

"Have you forgotten we need to have a doctor look at your head?" He was suddenly aware of his own fatigue. Maybe he would finally sleep well.

"I'm feeling a lot better."

"Jenna, don't argue with me."

Keith turned his attention to the dark road in front of him as it changed from dirt to pavement. In his peripheral vision, he saw movement right before metal crushed against metal. The truck was pushed sideways.

Jenna screamed.

Another vehicle with no headlights had come out of nowhere and crashed into the driver's-side door. Jet yelped.

The sound of squealing tires and a roaring engine surrounded them and then faded.

Jenna wrapped her arms around the barking dog, making soothing sounds. "What was that about?" Her voice intensified with fear.

Keith's heart raced. "I'll give you one guess." The truck had stalled out. He turned the key while the engine chugged but didn't spark to life. "If we can get this thing started, we are going into town tonight to tell the sheriff."

Jenna gazed all around them. "And…what if…we can't get it started?"

She was thinking the same thing he was, that someone was still out there, waiting for the chance to bash into them again.

He turned the key once more. The two vehicles hadn't hit the engine. "We'll get it started." The engine turned over and hummed to life. He let out the breath he had been holding. He reached over and touched Jenna's cheek. "It's going to be okay."

He couldn't take the look of terror off her face, he could only get her to a safe place. He pressed on the accelerator.

Jet went into high alert stance, standing on all fours and barking. Keith increased his speed. Jenna's hand rested on his shoulder as she leaned into him. Jet turned on the seat, barking out the back window.

The old Dodge wasn't exactly a race car; its top speed

was sixty. All the same, Keith pushed the accelerator to the floor. The lights of the town came into view.

"Almost there." He kept his voice level.

Jenna nodded, but didn't say anything.

Jet whimpered and settled back down.

"We'll go to the emergency room first."

He drove through town, past a dark bank building and general store. When he pulled into the parking lot of the tiny hospital, there were only two other cars in the lot.

Keith pressed against his door, but it didn't budge. "This side is smashed in. I'm going to have to get out on your side."

"They damaged it so much the door won't open?" Though she was making a valiant effort, her anxiety was obvious.

He brushed a hand over her cheek. "You're safe here." Did he believe that himself? These people were relentless.

They scooted across the seat. Jet jumped out, pacing back and forth on the asphalt. Jenna got out next. She stayed close to the truck while Keith placed his feet on the pavement. Keith commanded Jet to get back in. He shut the truck door. Jet's face was barely discernible in the dark cab.

Jenna had grown quiet. It wasn't just her physical state he was worried about at this point. She was pretty shaken.

She hurried her pace and walked a few feet in front of him.

With a wary glance around the parking lot, he caught up with her and pushed open the glass doors of the ER.

"I'm so glad you are here." Her voice was faint.

A nurse bustled from behind a high counter and gathered Jenna into her arms. "Oh my goodness, Miss Murphy, what happened?"

"Long story," Jenna said.

The nurse addressed Keith. "You wait right here and Dr. Benson will have a look at her."

His makeshift bandages had come off her head, revealing the gash across her forehead.

Keith paced the hallway of the emergency room. If memory served, the rural hospital had only ten or so beds. If the doctor had any concerns about Jenna's condition, they would have to drive into Billings. A task he would be glad to do. She seemed okay…physically, anyway.

The nurse came back momentarily and settled behind the counter. "You've had quite a night."

Keith winced, suddenly aware of a pain in his shoulder.

"Are you okay?" She shot to her feet.

He must have banged against the door in the crash. "I'm fine."

The nurse stared at his scars. He pulled his arm back, but she grabbed his wrist. "I worked at a V.A. hospital when I was younger." Her voice was filled with compassion. "You don't need to hide those from me."

She was an older woman with salt and pepper hair and a sweet smile.

A lump formed in his throat. "Thank you."

She winked at him and then sat back down at her desk. "I am sure your girlfriend is going to be okay."

He didn't correct her on the girlfriend thing. Actually, he kind of liked the idea of it. He tensed. His plan had been to leave at the end of the summer. He stopped and leaned a hand against the beige wall. He hadn't thought about the implication of the kiss when it happened. The desire to kiss her had been so strong. The fallout from it might be that he would end up hurting Jenna.

If the kiss had meant as much to him as it had to her, maybe he could change his plans.

"Do you have a newspaper?" he asked the nurse.

She pointed with her pen. "Yesterday's is over there with the old issues of *Field and Stream.*"

Keith sat down and scanned the help wanted ads. Pretty scarce pickings where jobs were concerned, even if he decided to commute to a larger city. He tossed the newspaper back on the little table as frustration burned through him. This was total fantasy. What could he offer Jenna besides instability at this point in his life? He wanted to be with her. To take care of her. But he couldn't do that yet.

He rotated his sore shoulder. Pain shot down his arm.

"The doctor can look at that, if you want," the nurse said as she rose to her feet to clip a chart on a wall.

"I'm all right." Probably just some bruising.

He settled into an uncomfortable chair, resting his eyes.

Twenty minutes later, Jenna emerged from an exam room followed by the doctor, a middle-aged man in a brown cardigan.

"I am okay," she said. "I'm just going to have a bad headache for a couple of days."

The doctor pushed his glasses up his face. "A mild

concussion. I don't think we are dealing with any long-term problems. She knows what to watch for. She needs to rest and no strenuous activity until the headache goes away."

After Jenna handed the paperwork to the nurse, Keith pushed the glass door open and held it so Jenna could step outside. It was dark. Most of the windows of the downtown businesses were dark.

"Are you up to telling the sheriff about what you found and what happened while we are in town?" Keith studied her for a moment. She looked better already.

"I'm up to it. The sheriff stays at his office pretty late. Let's go over there now."

The sheriff's office was in a side entrance to the courthouse. Sheriff Douglas sat behind a desk. A second desk was unoccupied. The sheriff hunched over a piece of paper. His left hand twisted unnaturally above the document as he wrote. He raised his head and tugged at his mustache. "Just the people I want to see."

"Really?" Keith stepped into the office behind Jenna.

"That blood sample from your door came back from the state lab. The good news is it's not human blood. Lab said it was consistent with canine blood."

"Canine blood? You mean a dog?" Jenna asked.

"Could be a dog, could be a coyote, could be a wolf. No one has reported the loss of a beloved pet. I've notified the game warden. He should be out of the hospital by the end of the week. If it was a wolf, it was shot out of season. Wolf hunts are very controlled and require a special permit."

Keith stepped forward. "Jenna found a stash of items just west of the two buttes."

Jenna summarized what had happened and ended by saying, "I only got a quick look at the guy, but his face wasn't familiar. Either he just moved to town or he is not from around here. I keep thinking, though, that I have seen him somewhere before."

The deputy came in from a back room and poured himself a cup of coffee.

"Was there anything distinct about him?" The sheriff rose from his desk while the deputy carried his coffee over to the second desk and sat down.

Keith placed his hand on the middle of Jenna's back. Jenna was a strong woman, but she had been through a lot in the last few hours. "It's all right if you need time to think about it."

"I'm okay." Jenna stepped forward. "My head started to clear when I was lying in the emergency room. He was pretty ordinary. Brown hair and kind of big nose." Jenna touched her own face as though she were trying to form the image in her mind. Then she put her hand on her chest. "The only unique thing about him was that he was wearing a necklace that looked like a piece of carved ivory."

"Anything else?" The sheriff picked up his coffee cup.

She shifted her weight. "This is kind of weird, but right before things went black, I smelled a strange smell. Not aftershave but a more earthy organic smell, really strong like—"

"Patchouli." The deputy scooted his chair back from his desk.

"Yes, that is what it was. I haven't smelled that scent since high school."

"I think I know who you are talking about." The deputy pointed a stapler at Jenna. "Saw him a few nights ago at the Oasis bar. It's not an ivory necklace, it's a shark's tooth. He and four or five friends who weren't from around here were playing a lively poker game with some locals. They kept calling him Eddie. He was the only sober one in the bunch by the time the night was over. I stepped outside to make sure he was the one doing the driving. His vehicle was a candy apple red SUV, really distinct."

"We can call over to the Oasis and find out if he paid with a credit card. That would tell us his last name," the sheriff added.

"That is something, then," said Jenna. Her voice sounded faint. She squeezed her eyes shut and then opened them wider than usual as if she were trying to stay awake. The stress of everything and lack of sleep was probably starting to wear on her.

"Sheriff, if you want, later today, we can ride up to where it happened. I have to get Jenna's car anyway," Keith suggested.

The sheriff nodded.

Keith escorted Jenna out of the sheriff's office. They stepped onto the sidewalk. Jenna stopped for a moment.

"What are you thinking about?" Keith asked.

"I was thinking about how we have had an unusual number of calls about bear carcasses. We get the calls because the turkey vultures show up for dinner. It's always just a partial carcass. The claws are missing, sometimes the head, sometimes the hide. I just assumed another wild animal had already helped itself."

"I think I follow you—eagles, wolves and bears. All illegal to hunt this time of year."

"Eagles you are never supposed to shoot," she said. "One or even two people couldn't do all that poaching. The vandalism at my place was done by at least two people. It was a large group up in Leveridge Canyon that night."

"So this isn't about smuggling. We are talking about a group of guys who hunt illegally, mostly at night."

Jenna rubbed her forehead. "I wish I could remember the numbers on that index card. I know there was one that I thought might be a date."

"Maybe you don't need to remember. What if we assume it was some sort of code? Maybe a longitude and latitude that told them where to meet. The cache provided a weapon and keys to a vehicle—probably a four-wheeler or a motorcycle—that they picked up at a different location."

Jenna stopped and stared up at the sky. "We need to find this Eddie guy. Someone has to be organizing this. What if he is the one?" She touched the bump on her head. "The sheriff can charge him with assault and then ask him—" Her words trailed off.

She tensed as she peered up the street. Her father had parked his car and was making his way to his house carrying a stack of books. He stopped for a moment, aware that he was being watched.

Jenna waved. A look of sadness crossed his features and Richard nodded in response.

Keith studied Jenna for a moment. He read sorrow in her expression. "Aren't you going to talk to him?"

"A wave is enough."

"You guys don't have your noontime get-together anymore?"

"I'm a grown-up now, Keith." Irritation had entered her voice. "I don't need to discuss *Treasure Island* with my father."

From what he could tell, they didn't discuss anything. Richard's words at the meeting floated back into his head. The one thing Richard wanted more than anything was to restore his relationship with his daughter. He had a feeling that was what Jenna wanted, too. She didn't know that he had stopped drinking.

Keith knew enough not to push. This had to happen on Jenna's timeline. "Maybe someday, you'll walk over there and knock on that door."

"You think it's that easy?" Her words took on a defensive tone. "Things with my father had gotten really unhealthy. I needed to set some boundaries." Jenna's cheeks turned red.

"I can respect that."

Jenna twisted her hands together. Her tone softened. "It's just too hard."

"I understand." The anxiety he saw in her expression tore at his gut. But he would not manipulate the situation. This had to be Jenna's decision.

Richard passed by a window. Jenna took in a breath.

"I spent a lot of my life focusing on what I didn't have, a dad. I couldn't see that I had cool grandparents who loved me. I always thought what you and your father had was pretty special."

"My dad is special. He can be…wonderful." She pressed her lips together then turned to face him. "Keith, you just don't know the whole story."

"Try me." Was she ready to share?

She stared at the ground for a long moment, then tilted her head and blurted out, "My father has a drinking problem. Last year, it got so bad that he ended up in the emergency room." Her voice cracked. "I will not watch my father commit slow suicide. I have to keep myself healthy and not get caught up in his craziness. It hurts too much."

"What if he stopped drinking?"

"That has happened a bazillion times. He always goes back to it. I can't live through that cycle of becoming hopeful only to have that hope crushed again. If that makes me the world's worst daughter, then so be it."

"I would never think that about you. I can see how much you love your dad. And sometimes love means being tough."

She studied him for a moment. Her expression registered surprise, as if she hadn't expected him to say what he had said. Her eyes glazed. "That's what makes it so hard. If he was just a big fat jerk, I could walk away. I would have moved somewhere else after college."

He laced his fingers in hers.

"I do care about him." Strength returned to her voice.

"You'll know when the time is right."

"I think it is today." She squeezed his hand tighter. "Will you be the one to knock on the door?"

"Sure."

He led her across the street, and as he walked, each step was a prayer that he hadn't been out of line and made her feel pushed to do this. Time apart from someone with a drinking problem could be a positive thing for everyone involved, especially if it led to reconciliation. It had taken him twelve years to come back to his grandparents. He prayed that the outcome would be good for Jenna too. Her hand tensed in his when he lifted his free hand to knock on the door.

They waited for what seemed like an eternity. Footsteps crescendoed toward the door. Jenna squared her shoulders and straightened her spine.

The door swung open.

THIRTEEN

Her father's eyes widened when he opened the door.

Jenna planted her feet and fought the urge to run away. Her heart hammered in her chest. As if sensing her anxiety, Keith leaned closer to her.

The memory of the last time her father was in the hospital hit her like a punch to the stomach. As he lay beneath the blue hospital blanket, his skin had been almost yellow. Even in his sleep, his hands had been palsied. The words of the nurse on duty floated back into her head. "If your father doesn't stop drinking, he'll be dead in six months. He's done so much damage to his body already."

The warning echoed through her brain as she studied her father standing in the doorway. In the past year, Richard's skin had lost its sallow quality. He looked like he was getting a little sun. His eyes were bright and clear.

He said her name. "Jenna." He offered Keith a nod of recognition.

His voice pierced through her. Like an intense gust of wind, all the years of pain and secrecy hit her full force. If it hadn't been for Keith standing beside her, she would have turned around and walked away.

Keith cleared his throat. "Mr. Murphy, we thought we would come over and say hello."

Jenna almost laughed at the understatement. The need to laugh rose from nervousness. Keith spoke to her dad like they were old friends, which didn't make any sense. Maybe they had passed each other on the street and exchanged small talk, but she doubted they'd done any more than that. Keith hadn't been back in town that long.

Richard angled to one side. "You can do more than say hello."

They stepped inside. Bird cages containing finches and shelves of books filled the living room. The worn leather chair with the stack of novels beside it was still situated so the sun would warm it in the early morning. Her father had kept her papasan chair where she used to curl up to read. The plaid throw she covered herself with in the winter was flung over the chair as if he expected her to come home at any time.

The grandfather clock ticked away the seconds, punctuated with the chirping of the birds. The smooth voice of Frank Sinatra spilled from the radio in the kitchen. Her dad had always liked the Rat Pack crooners.

Jenna pointed toward one of the cages. "You've got a robin?" All the other birds were the domesticated species he had always had.

"Yes, that little girl who lives off Madison Street brought him to me. He got caught in some mesh that was put over a cherry tree to keep the birds from eating them."

She pointed to a cage that held a turtle dove. "Where is Maurice?"

Richard walked the few feet to the cage, opened the door and let the bird step onto his hand.

He brought the turtle dove over to Jenna. Her father cooed at the gray white bird. "I am afraid Maurice didn't make it through the winter." He tilted his hand.

Without thinking, Jenna lifted her arm, allowing the bird to transfer to her hand. "So Maureen is all by herself now." The thought of the turtle dove losing her life-long partner caused a sadness to swell in her heart. The sorrow was so intense; she knew it wasn't just about the death of the bird. The bird fluttered its wings. Jenna's throat constricted.

Her father stood close.

"You look good, Dad." She had not intended to whittle away the time with small talk, but what really needed to be said was so difficult. Everything they were saying was coming out in code.

Her father took a step back and blurted, "I haven't had a drink in almost a year."

Jenna glanced toward Keith. "How did you know?"

Keith looked at Richard, who nodded. "I have been sober for twelve years, but every once in a while, I still need a meeting."

Had her father really joined AA? And stayed sober for a year? This was different than the other times. At most, his past sobriety lasted a week. A small seed of hope budded inside Jenna. She looked back at her father. "Why didn't you tell me?"

"I figured you would come to me when you were ready." Richard held his hand out for the dove. "I didn't want to hurt you again. I saw that look in your eyes in the hospital."

There had been harsh words between them. Guilt had fueled much of her anger that night. If she had not kept his addiction a secret, thinking she was somehow protecting her father for so many years, maybe it wouldn't have gone this far. After a year apart, she understood that the responsibility to change was her father's.

The time apart had been good for both of them. All the anger she had wrestled with a year ago had dissipated.

He returned the bird to her cage. "Things are going so much better now." A sparkle flashed through his eyes and he raised his finger. "I want to show you something." He left the room, feet padding softly on the carpet.

Jenna mouthed a *thank you* toward Keith. Whatever the future held for them, Keith's gentle urging had led her to discover the change in her father.

Richard returned holding a stack of typed pages. "I'm writing again. My novel."

Her father hadn't written in years. When she was little, he had talked of writing a book. He would work on it in fits and starts and then Jenna would find the pages in the trash can or the kindling box. After that, she would catch her father flipping through photo albums, staring at pictures of her mother, usually with a drink in his hand.

"I even have a publisher who is interested."

"Daddy, that is wonderful." All of this was differ-

ent. He wasn't trying to quit on his own. He was going
to meetings. He was taking it seriously. And he'd done
it for her. The tiny seed of hope inside her budded and
pushed through the fragile earth.

"Some afternoon when you have time, I would love
for us to talk through what I have written." He gripped
the manuscript as excitement entered his voice.

"I'm not an editor or anything." Her father's enthusiasm made her smile.

"But you are a reader. You know a good story. I value
your opinion."

The clock struck midnight. "You have to get to bed,
don't you?"

Richard set the manuscript on a table. He grabbed
her hand but then pulled away as though he had been
too impulsive.

She took his hand in hers and squeezed it. "I will
come by the next time I am in town."

"I'll make a big pot of tea."

Her father sounded hopeful, too. Maybe things could
be repaired. That night in the ER, she had let go of her
father, left him to die. She had felt guilt over that decision, guilt that came out in anger. In retrospect, they
had been like two drowning people trying to save each
other. Now they had a life preserver between them.

Richard held out a hand for Keith to shake. Keith
pulled the older man into a back-slapping hug.

As they stepped outside, Jenna knew she had to be
realistic. This time was different, but she still needed to
be cautious about imagining a life with a sober father.
She looked at Keith. He really was a different person.

The wild seventeen-year-old kid who had broken

her heart and frightened her so much was gone. They crossed the street angling toward Keith's truck.

Jenna opened the passenger side door. "So did you totally give up on rock climbing when you left twelve years ago?"

Keith got into the cab and stuck the key in the ignition. "Pretty much, but I'd start it up again with you."

His smile sent shock waves through her. "You're the only person I trust to belay me."

Keith cranked the gear shift and hit his signal before pulling out into the street.

"I don't think I even have any gear still." She had gotten rid of everything that reminded her of Keith. She hadn't been climbing in twelve years. "I'd have to buy some."

His face glowed with affection. "We're both a little out of practice. I'm just starting to get some strength back in my arms."

Keith drove Jenna back to her house with the promise of bringing her car by later before he went out with his grandfather to spot cattle. Even though her head still hurt, Jenna felt lightness in her step.

She was okay with the kiss from Keith. She wasn't keeping secrets from him anymore. She was at a place of new beginning with her father. As she wandered to her house to get some sleep, Jenna found herself hoping for more kisses from Keith.

Keith turned slowly and stared down the path at his grandfather. The old man kept up pretty well. Keith remembered being a teenager and hiking this mountain with Gramps. Then, he was the one who had been challenged by his grandfather's huge strides.

Norman King peered out from beneath the rim of his weathered cowboy hat. "Don't go stopping on my account. We're burning daylight." Keith lifted his head and laughed, knowing they had hours before sunset.

Keith took the final few strides to the summit. They were nearly to the top of Cascade Mountain, the highest point on the ranch which provided a panoramic view of the valley. If they couldn't spot the unaccounted for cows from here, the cows were really lost, and they'd have to hire out a search plane or helicopter.

Summer on a ranch was mostly about upkeep and repair. The cows were turned loose to forage for themselves on the abundant grass. Once the weather grew colder, the cows would be brought in and fed hay until they were ready to sell and ship to the Midwest for fattening in November. February and March were the busiest months because the cows they kept would be calving. Depending on where he found a job, he hoped to at least get back to help Gramps with the calving.

Keith took in a deep breath of thin mountain air. A marine friend had called him with a lead on an EMT position in Denver. The job would provide some additional support while he went to college on the G.I. bill. The summer had done the healing he had hoped for. Leaving had always been the plan. What he hadn't anticipated was a renewal of his feelings for Jenna. He still wasn't sure what to do about that. She loved working at the center and things had been patched up with her dad. For sure, she wouldn't be open to moving. Long distance relationships usually fell apart.

Keith put the binoculars to his face, searching for the moving black dots that were the missing Angus. When he had enlisted and been deployed, his ability to identify objects at a distance had turned out to be an asset in the desert. Because most people were used to being surrounded by buildings, their eyes were trained to see only short distances.

"Spot anything?" His grandfather came and stood beside him, huffing for air.

"Not yet." He handed over the binoculars to the older man. "You want to take a turn, eagle eyes?"

Norman lifted the binoculars, peering at one spot, turning twenty degrees and studying another area on the landscape. "Two of them at twelve o'clock." With a look of triumph, he handed the binoculars to Keith.

Keith focused the binoculars on the place where his grandfather had just looked. He stared until two distinct black dots separated out from their surroundings. "Well, how do you like those apples."

"The old man still has it, huh?" Norman slapped his grandson on the back. "Think they'll be okay down there?"

"They will be all right. There is a water hole over there."

"Small one. Might be dried up. We'll have to check it." His grandfather grew serious. "Keith, we sure have liked having you here this summer."

Keith pulled the binoculars away from his eyes. "You have no idea what it has meant to me."

Norman stroked his chin. "I can still wrestle a calf to the ground as fast as a man half my age." His bushy eyebrows shot up. "You know that."

"Sure."

"But just because I can doesn't mean I should. Etta would like to spend some time down in Arizona with her sister. The winters get kind of hard and long for her."

"Wouldn't you go a little crazy with nothing to do but sit in the sun?" He couldn't picture his grandfather in a Hawaiian shirt and white shoes and black tube socks.

"This isn't about me. It's about Etta. She's lived through all these winters without complaint."

His willingness to sacrifice for his wife was a testament to why their marriage had lasted so long. Keith had a feeling where the conversation was leading. "That would mean you would need someone to watch the ranch for you over the winter."

"Not watch. Run, yearlong. You're my only grandkid. After I'm gone to heaven, this place would be yours."

A lump formed in Keith's throat. "Gramps."

"That Peter Hickman has offered to buy it, but I don't like the idea of selling it off to a stranger. I want to be able to come back to the place and help out. I'd rather put it in more trustworthy hands." He cupped his hands on Keith's shoulder and squeezed it tight. "I know that wasn't what you planned. Take some time to think about it."

Keith's mind spun with what the offer meant. He couldn't imagine any better way to make a living. Ranching brought him a contentment he wasn't sure he could find anywhere else. Only one part of the picture was unclear. Jenna. They had both been operating on the assumption that he would be leaving at the end of summer. How would she feel about him if she knew he was going to stay around?

"Yes, I do need some time to think about it."

"We still have three unaccounted for heifers." Norman handed him the binoculars. "Earn your keep."

Keith turned toward the east, studying the lay of the land without the binoculars. In the distance, he could see Craig Smith's water tower and the road leading into Craig's property. "Where's the boundary for your property again?" Not that cows paid attention to any boundaries. Much of the ranch was unfenced. If the cows had wandered onto Craig's land and were eating his grass, it was Craig's responsibility to call and let them know.

Norman leaned close to Keith and pointed along a river and some lower hills. The vastness of the ranch had always taken Keith's breath away. He drew up the binoculars and scanned along the border between the two ranches.

A flash of red caught his eye. At this distance, it was hard to see what kind of car it was, but as far as he knew nobody but Eddie, the guy who hit Jenna on the head, drove a candy apple red SUV. The car was headed toward Craig's property. A car had to slow to about twenty miles an hour over that road. It would be at least fifteen minutes before Eddie arrived at his destination. Another car came into view from around a corner. Keith lifted the binoculars to his eyes.

A bubble of panic formed in his stomach. Jenna's car was closing in on the red car. What was she doing? They had no idea what they were facing with this Eddie guy. Other than that he'd already shown himself capable of assault.

"Come on, Gramps. We need to get down off this

mountain." Keith explained what he had seen and the reason he was worried.

Norman rose from the rock where he had been resting. "We better get going, then."

The road down the mountain was winding and slow. Jenna would maybe get to Craig's place ten to twenty minutes before Keith could get there. He said a prayer for her safety. He strode down the mountain, mindful that he needed to allow his grandfather time.

Already his heart hammered in his chest. What was she doing trying to handle this on her own?

They arrived at his grandfather's truck. Keith's Dodge was still in the shop being fixed. Keith climbed into the driver's side and turned the key in the ignition. The engine purred to life. As the road evened out, he pushed the speed up to forty. Time seemed to stretch out. He wanted to go faster, but he would be no good to anyone if he put the truck in a ditch.

Jenna was smart, but if she thought Eddie had anything to do with the death of her eagles, she might throw caution to the wind.

Keith turned toward his grandfather. "Can you get cell reception?"

His grandfather pulled his cell phone out. "Yep. Looks like it's coming in good."

"Call the sheriff, fill him in and tell him to meet us at Craig Smith's place. And then try Jenna's cell."

After Norman completed the call to the sheriff, Keith recited Jenna's cell number.

His grandfather put the phone to his ear. Keith could hear the phone ringing over and over. Tension wrapped around his rib cage. When she was out in the field, she carried the phone on her belt. She should answer right away.

Come on, Jenna, pick up.

Norman pulled the phone away from his ear and shook his head.

FOURTEEN

Jenna's Subaru hit a bump, causing all her equipment to shake and rattle, but the car stayed on course. The new tires Keith had put on had nice traction. She watched the speedometer needle press past thirty. She had to get to Craig Smith's place fast.

She'd been headed back from a call about a bird stuck in a chimney when she'd seen the red SUV. The car had to belong to the Eddie guy who had knocked her unconscious and slashed her tires. Fortunately, the bird she had gone out to rescue had freed itself and flown away, so she didn't have to worry about jostling a bird in a carrier at these high speeds.

She had no intention of letting Eddie see her. Their last encounter had not gone well. There was a good possibility that Eddie didn't realize she could identify him, but it wasn't a chance she wanted to take. She really wasn't in the mood for another headache.

All she needed to do was make sure Eddie didn't leave and fall off the face of the earth. If she could get to Craig's first, she could talk Craig into detaining him.

She stared at her phone. As soon as she had her reception back, she'd call the sheriff.

She pressed the accelerator. Craig would have a phone she could use.

She'd have to risk a possible car accident if she was going to get there before Eddie. The front wheels hit a patch of gravel which acted like a bucket of marbles sending her car into a swerve. Her heart raced even faster as she muscled it back onto the road.

How much time did she have? If she couldn't beat the red SUV to the ranch, she would just have to block the road with her car and hope she could reach the sheriff and get him out here before Eddie left. A much riskier solution.

She turned onto the road that led to Craig's ranch. No sign of the red vehicle in front of her and nothing in the rearview mirror, either. Strange.

Concerned, she slowed her car. At the very least, she should see a dust cloud created by his SUV. She checked her phone again—still no service.

The water tower on Craig Smith's ranch came into view. She increased her speed until a flash of red in a ravine caused her to slow down. She pulled the Subaru over to a shoulder and braked. Jenna pushed open the door and trotted down the road. She shaded her eyes from the noonday sun and stared into the ravine.

Nestled in the junipers and boulders was the red car with its tail end pointed uphill. The car had left ruts where it had swerved off the road. She couldn't see Eddie anywhere. Fearing that he may be hurt and unable to move, she made her way down the hill, moving as fast as the steep incline allowed.

She slowed. What if this was some kind of trap Eddie had set for her? Maybe he had seen her car. She assessed the area all around her. Except for the boulders and junipers at the bottom of the ravine, the landscape didn't provide very many hiding places.

She walked faster again. She'd have to take that chance. She couldn't leave a hurt man alone in a car regardless of what he had done.

She trailed a hand along the side of the SUV. The front end of it had smashed against a rock, crumpling the hood. She drew her gaze to the driver's-side window. Eddie's head rested against it. He must be unconscious. She tried the door. It had been smashed in such a way that it wouldn't open.

Jenna raced around to the passenger side door. It was bent, as well. She darted to the back of the SUV, opened the hatch and crawled through. She scrambled toward the driver's seat, leary of what she might find.

"Eddie." He didn't stir. She leaned over the front seat. Fresh blood had stained the fabric. A pile of twenty dollar bills had spilled from an envelope and scattered. A coffee cup with the initials E.H. on it surrounded by a strange symbol sat broken on the floor of the car.

Eddie still didn't respond. Her fingers shook as she lifted them to his neck. No pulse. Paralysis set in as Jenna struggled for breath, encased in her own rapid heartbeat.

Eddie was dead.

She shook her head, fighting not to give in to the inertia that the panic caused.

She pulled Eddie's body away from the window. His

shirt was soaked in blood. What could he have hit in a car crash that would make him bleed like that?

Her eye wandered to the smashed windshield. Uneven concentric circles of crushed glass radiated out from a bullet-sized center.

Jenna backed out of the car as fear spread through her. Eddie had been shot. A million questions raged through her head, but it was hard to think clearly when she realized she had blood on her sleeves.

The breaking of branches and the crushing of undergrowth sent a new charge of terror through her. She stepped away from the car, her heart racing. The noise grew closer, louder. She was a sitting duck here.

Jenna leaped behind a boulder just as a cow emerged from the brush. The heifer wandered past her and back into the trees. Jenna whooshed out a breath and bent over.

She scrambled up the hill, falling twice and scraping her knee. Her shorts were ripped and she had blood on her leg. Her sleeves were stained with Eddie's blood. Unable to get a deep breath, she leaned against her car.

She pulled her phone out. Still no signal. She'd have to drive to Craig's place and call from there. Her hands were shaking uncontrollably. She lifted her head, staring at the high mountain and buttes that surrounded her. Maybe the shooter hadn't been close at all. What if Eddie had been shot with a long-range rifle from a high place just like the eagle? The thought that the killer might have been farther away gave her no comfort—with a rifle that powerful, she was still an easy target.

She couldn't think straight. She struggled to link one thought to the next one. It felt like her whole body was trembling from shock. Jenna took in a deep, prayer-filled breath and washed the images from her mind. All she had to do was think of the next thing she needed to do and then the next thing after that. She could do that.

She needed to calm down, so she could get in the car and drive to Craig's place and call the sheriff. She slipped into her vehicle and flexed her fingers on the steering wheel. She still felt like she was being shaken from the inside. She had just straightened her back when she glanced in the rearview mirror where a cloud of dust was visible. Someone was coming up the road.

Keith's breath caught in his throat when he saw Jenna's blue Subaru pulled off the road. He sped up the truck and turned off onto the first available shoulder. He jumped out and ran the short distance to her car.

The driver's-side door opened and Jenna stepped out. There was a look of wildness in her eyes. She was in shock.

She pointed down the mountain. "Eddie...Eddie's been shot."

That didn't make any sense. They'd been operating on the assumption that Eddie was the one behind all of this. "Are you sure?"

"There is a bullet hole through the windshield." Her voice trembled with distress as she pulled away from him and ran a hand through her long hair.

First things first. He needed to keep Jenna from descending any further into shock. "Let's get you lying down." Gramps had already brought the truck closer.

Norman King met them halfway. "Jenna, what has happened?"

"She's going into shock," Keith said. "Can you grab that blanket out of the cab, Gramps? She can lie down in the truck bed."

The older man ran ahead, grabbed the blanket and brought the tailgate down.

When they got to the back of the truck, Jenna pulled away. "I don't need to lie down."

Keith cupped her face in his hands. "Listen to me— you are in shock. We need to get blood back to your vital organs. Okay?"

"You're the medic." A little bit of resistance colored her tone.

He led her to the rear of the truck and helped her crawl in. She lay back; the look of trust in her eyes floored him. Something deeper than friendship was growing between them, a bond that could weather a struggle. He pushed a toolbox across the metal of the bed. "I'm going to elevate your feet." He hooked his hands under her ankles. He touched the bloody knee. "Got a boo-boo there, huh?"

"Is that medical jargon?" She laughed. "I did that one." She glanced again at the blood on her sleeve, which made her shake her head and close her eyes. "But that isn't my blood."

His hand brushed over her temple, pushing her hair away from her face. "Don't think about it, Jenna."

She turned her head to the side.

"I found this in her car." Norman handed him a coat. Keith took the coat and laid it over Jenna. It tore him apart to see her so emotionally distraught. If only he had gotten here sooner. "Take some deep breaths."

Jenna locked onto Keith's gaze and breathed in and out.

She visibly calmed. He spoke to his grandfather who was resting his elbows on the side of the truck bed. "Keep an eye on her. I'll be right back."

Keith glanced up and down the road. A man on a tractor was coming from the direction of Craig's ranch, but still no sign of the sheriff.

Keith trotted back toward the accident site. He studied the damage to the windshield of Eddie's vehicle. It did look like a bullet had gone through the glass. He peered inside the car. Eddie was slumped against the steering wheel. The glove compartment had been thrown open in the crash. Maybe that was where that money had come from. A broken coffee cup with a strange symbol and the initials E.H. on it indicated that the car may have rolled or at least hit something with substantial impact before coming to rest against the rock.

When Keith returned, Jenna was sitting in the truck talking to his grandfather. Craig had parked his tractor a ways down the road and was walking toward them. The tractor looked new. Hadn't Craig said he was strapped for cash?

Keith grabbed the first aid kit from his truck.

Craig came beside the truck. "What's going on here?"

"Was a guy from out of town named Eddie coming to see you?"

Craig's expression darkened. "Why?"

Keith sauntered toward Jenna and his grandfather.

Craig followed, stopping when he saw the wrecked car at the bottom of the ravine. His mouth dropped open.

"Is that his car?"

"He had…an accident." Keith elected not to tell Craig all the details.

"Is he—" Craig was visibly shaken.

Keith nodded. "At this point, the road leads directly to your ranch. There is no place to turn off and go anywhere else. Was he coming to see you?"

"I have never met the guy." Craig's tone was clouded with defensiveness.

Keith was pretty sure Craig was lying. He opened the first aid kit, pulling out disinfectant and a Band-Aid.

Craig took a step back. "Look, I got work to do."

"Sheriff will be here in a minute. This happened on your land. He might want to talk to you."

Craig drew his mouth tight. "If he wants to talk to me, I will be waiting at my place." Craig strode to his tractor.

Keith shook his head. Something was up with Craig. Why would he bring the tractor out if he was just going to turn it around and take it back to his place…unless he wanted it to look like he had casually happened upon the accident?

Keith held up the Band-Aid for Jenna to see. "For your boo-boo." Once Craig was out of earshot, Keith said, "He said he never met Eddie, but I don't know."

Jenna scooted to the edge of the tailgate. "He seemed nervous. I think I remember where I saw Eddie before. He was talking to Craig at the fundraiser."

"Really?" Keith squeezed out some disinfectant onto Jenna's knee.

"Yeah, they were having a heated discussion."

"Wonder what was going on?" Keith gently placed the bandage over her knee. "Better?"

Her smile shot a burst of heat through him. "Much," she said. She glanced toward the ravine. "It all feels... so surreal."

Combat hadn't made him immune to the impact of death, but he was probably better equipped to handle it than the average person. He brushed Jenna's soft cheek with the back of his hand. "It's never easy."

She closed her eyes as if gathering strength from his touch.

After opening her eyes, she jumped off the tailgate and grabbed her coat. "I thought finding Eddie would answer questions, not create more."

The sheriff's car came into view.

"We don't know for sure if Eddie was shot. Let's wait and see what the sheriff can find out."

Jenna crossed her arms. "Maybe we had it wrong. What if Eddie was just one of the hunters?" She stared up the road where Craig's tractor was still visible. "Someone else must be organizing all of this."

It did make sense that a local, someone who knew the area, would be the one dropping the caches and set-ting things up. He was probably charging the hunters a lot of money. Maybe Keith had not allowed that thought into his awareness because somehow it made it easier if it was an outsider who was doing all this. He hadn't wanted to believe that one of his neighbors was a criminal of this magnitude.

Jenna placed her hands on her hips and stared down

the ravine. "The sheriff is going to have to get a tow truck out here."

Jenna seemed to have recovered from the shock of finding the body. "Are you doing okay?"

She rubbed her bare arm and let out a shaky sigh. "As much as I can be." She shivered. "I'll be all right. I just need a little time."

Keith wrapped a protective arm around Jenna. If Eddie had been shot these crimes had gone to a new and frightening level.

The sheriff stopped his car and walked toward them.

Jenna brought her car to a stop outside her father's house. A flutter of anticipation zinged through her. She grabbed the stack of books she had already read that she thought her father might like. It was Sunday. The library was closed. She knew she would catch her father at home after she finished church.

The events from yesterday still weighed heavily on her. The sheriff had confirmed that Eddie, whose last name was Helms, had been shot, but the shooter was still at large. Yet worship had left her feeling renewed and the thought of reconnecting with her father lightened her step.

Jenna pushed open the car door and stepped onto the sidewalk. She rapped gently at the door. The windows were open, and she could hear birds chirping and music playing. She knocked again, a little louder. She hadn't called ahead to let him know she was coming.

Maybe he was writing with his headphones on and couldn't hear her. She turned the doorknob and stepped inside.

"Dad?"

No one was in the living room. She followed the sound of the music into the kitchen. The laptop was open on the counter. Jenna felt a little twinge of panic. What if her father had had a heart attack? She would never forgive herself for the year of silence if it ended like that.

She stepped onto the sun porch and breathed a sigh of relief. Her father, with his back to her, was staring out the window.

"Dad?"

He didn't turn around. She took a few steps toward him.

He spoke to the window. "I heard from that editor. They don't want my book."

"Oh, Dad, I'm so sorry. There will be other publishers."

He turned slowly. Shame clouded his expression. He held a glass in his hand. She recognized the amber liquid.

Jenna shook her head. Reality hit her like an icy gust of wind. This time was supposed to be different. Why had she let herself become hopeful? Her throat constricted, and her eyes warmed with tears. It was all a lie. People can't change.

Jenna turned and ran through the kitchen, out through the living room and back to her car. She fumbled with her keys, wiped her eyes and started the engine. She glanced at the door, thinking that maybe her father would come after her. She gritted her teeth. Why couldn't she let go of the idea that she could have a relationship with him?

She peeled out onto the street. Jenna drove for miles on country roads, losing track of where and when she turned. Thoughts charged at her from all directions. Anger and pain mixed together.

So what if some publisher didn't want his book? He was just looking for an excuse to drink. He probably wasn't even being honest about how long he had been sober. Lies, it was all lies.

She drove back to the center. She rested her head against the back of the car seat. She had no more tears left and no strength. She gripped the wheel. Why had she opened her heart to Keith? He was just like her father. It was probably just a matter of time before he drank again, too.

She closed her eyes and let her hands rest at her side. Every time she saw her father on the street, she would feel the pain all over again. Only now it would hurt even more. Keith had made things worse, not better.

Keith had been pleased to see Jenna's car pull into the center just ahead of him, but he was surprised when she didn't get out of the car. Stepping around to the driver's-side door, he tapped on her window.

Something about Jenna seemed off to Keith as she rolled down the window. There was a tightness to her features as if she were trying to hide something.

"What are you doing here?" Her voice sounded hoarse.

"I was just out driving and thinking after I went to early service at church," he said.

"What were you thinking about?" He caught a flash of anger in her voice.

Keith stepped back from her car. Something was definitely bothering her. "I was thinking about Eddie."

She opened her car door. He ambled back to his truck which now had a door a different color from the rest of the truck. He grabbed the piece of paper where he'd drawn the symbol he'd seen on Eddie's coffee cup. The sheriff had taken note of it but didn't think it was important. Keith hadn't stopped thinking about the symbol since he had seen it.

"This has to be a corporate logo or something."

She jabbed her finger at the piece of paper. "Didn't the sheriff say that Eddie's last name was Helms? The coffee cup has his initials on it—E.H." Her words were clipped, communicating impatience.

"Yeah, but what is with the weird symbol?"

"The sheriff will figure it out." Jenna pulled the keys for the center out of her purse. "I still have to do rounds with the birds. We don't have any volunteers come in on Sunday."

"I'll help you."

Her posture stiffened. "I can handle it, thanks."

Her coldness was confusing. Had he said or done something to upset her? "I want to help."

"Suit yourself." She shoved the key in the lock and twisted. The door swung open. "I just need to make sure there is no drama taking place with any of the birds and that they all have food and water. Everything else is paperwork I have to do on my own."

"We start here?" Keith asked, pointing to the birds next to the office.

She nodded. "Then the flight barn, then the education birds. Pretty simple." They both reached for the doorknob at the same time. Keith's hand brushed over hers. She pulled away and offered him an icy stare.

"Jenna, what is going on?"

"Nothing is going on. I'm tired and I need to get this work done." He detected a subtext of hurt beneath her words. No amount of probing on his part would get him a straight answer. Asking her directly just made her more bent out of shape. He wasn't a mind reader. Whatever was going on, it was her responsibility to tell him.

Eight of the ten cages next door to the office were occupied. Keith checked four of the cages, dealing with two spilled water dishes.

Keith trailed behind Jenna down the hill to the flight barn. She lifted the board and slid the door open. She turned to look at him. The icy veil over her wide brown eyes was like a stab to his heart. "I'm really used to doing this alone."

Was she rejecting him again? He took a step back. The coolness and calm of late summer in the mountains surrounded him. Here they were again at a crossroads. Was he staying in Hope Creek or not? He needed a clear answer from her. "I've got a job offer driving an ambulance in Denver that starts in the fall."

A shadow seemed to pass over her features. She offered him a single word response. "Oh."

"So do you think I should take it?" Anxiety wove through him as he waited for her to respond.

She turned away from him, resting her hand on the frame of the door. He traced the outline of her long slender fingers with his eyes. Her hair took on a golden sheen in the afternoon sun, and he longed to touch it.

She angled toward him. Her eyes drew him in, but

then she dropped her gaze and kicked at a rock on the ground. "It's your life, Keith. It always has been."

And she didn't want to be a part of it. She had made that pretty clear. He had his answer. "If you are used to doing this job by yourself, I will leave you to it."

She didn't look at him, didn't say anything, only gulped in a sudden shuddering breath before stepping inside the flight barn.

Inside the barn, wings fluttered, harmonizing with Jenna's soothing voice. Keith turned quickly and strode up the hill. Each step felt like a hammer blow to his heart. He and Jet could be packed and on the road by late afternoon tomorrow. The goodbye to his grandparents would be hard. His tie to them was the only thing holding him here. All other ties had been cut.

Jenna stood beside the open flight barn door and listened to the sound of Keith's Dodge starting up and fading into the distance. She stood for a long time, allowing the silence and loneliness to envelop her. Tears warmed her cheeks.

He had asked her straight out what was bothering her. Why couldn't she share what had happened with her father? Why hadn't she just told him about her fear that he would start drinking again? She had grown up in a home where she learned to talk around a problem, never stating anything directly. It was such an easy habit to fall back into.

She had nearly doubled over with pain when he had talked about leaving. She'd known all along that was the plan. But then hope had glimmered once again in her heart in the most cruel way. Even though they hadn't talked about it, after the kiss, she thought maybe things would be different...more permanent.

She should be happy. His leaving solved her problem and insured that the unbearable pain would not come again into her life.

She loved Keith. She knew that much. But being with him had the potential to bring so much hurt back into her life. With her father and with Keith, to open her heart was to risk being hurt. She had to let both of them go.

FIFTEEN

Jenna's cell phone rang just as she had tethered the bald eagle she was training to a post. Greta fluttered her wings and settled down. Jenna's mind was fogged from lack of sleep. She had stayed up most of the night thinking about Keith. It had been a long night and an even longer day. She pulled the phone off her belt and mustered up her best professional voice. "Hello. Bird of Prey Rescue Center, how may I help you?"

"This is Marybeth Helms. I'm Eddie Helms's wife." After a long pause on the other end of the line, Jenna thought she heard a sob. "The sheriff said you found my husband. He thought it would be okay if I called you."

"Yes."

"Was he alive when you found him? Did he say anything?" Even though Marybeth Helms chose her words carefully and spoke slowly, Jenna detected pain embedded in each syllable.

Jenna paced a few feet away from where she had tethered the eagle. This close to the flight barn, she had a nice view of the mountains. "I'm sorry, Mrs. Helms, but by the time I got to him…"

"I understand. I guess I was just looking for some closure, for an explanation."

Jenna stopped pacing and pressed the phone harder against her ear. "An explanation?"

"Eddie loved to hunt and find a new challenge with his hunting. He had done African safaris. We went to Alaska. I don't know what happened up there in Montana." Marybeth let out a faint cry.

"If this is too painful…"

"I want to talk. This last trip was different. He was afraid about something. He said things had gone too far."

So Eddie had been killed because he was going to blow the whistle.

"Did Eddie ever mention knowing someone named Craig Smith?"

"No…he never said any names." Silence filled the line for a moment. "He didn't talk much at all these last few months. My happy-go-lucky husband who loved the outdoors became this dark, brooding person."

"He felt guilty about something?"

"You know, the last time he got ready to go up to Montana, I remember thinking that this nightmare would be behind us." Her voice faltered. "And I would have my husband back." Marybeth sniffled.

Jenna could hear shuffling, water running, footsteps. Then she heard Marybeth talk to someone in the tone a person uses with a child. What could she say to comfort this poor woman? She said a quick prayer for guidance.

The hum of a car engine pulling into the center parking lot caught Jenna's attention. From where she stood, she couldn't see who it was.

"I need to go. I've got to go help my daughter. You've been very kind," Marybeth said.

With a heavy heart, Jenna said goodbye and hung up. Whoever had pulled into the center would have to come looking for her. She couldn't stop training. For a brief moment, she had wondered if it was Keith. Jenna shook her head. She had to let go of that hope.

She untied the eagle and set her on the fence post. "All right, Greta, let's try and get this right." She adjusted the glove. Greta had recovered enough for Jenna to start working with her. She would make a good education bird if she was responsive to training. Eagles with her wingspan were always a crowd pleaser, but she couldn't take Greta into schools if she was unpredictable. "You got to quit being such a teenage brat, okay?"

The bird tilted her head as though she understood.

Jenna offered the bird her gloved hand. "Up." Greta mounted onto Jenna's arm, rebalancing herself by flapping her wings. Even through the glove, Jenna could feel the strength of the eagle's talons. No matter how long she worked here, she couldn't become complacent about the kind of power she was dealing with. The dual ratcheting system of the talons that allowed this raptor to clamp down on its prey could just as easily dig into her. Eagles this size could topple a small deer if they wanted to. "Good." She pulled a treat from her pouch and offered it to the bird. "You like that part, don't you?"

"Ho, there." Peter Hickman waved at her from the top of the hill.

She signaled for him to come down. This would be a good test to see if Greta could keep her cool around another person. The bird shifted slightly on the glove.

When he arrived at the bottom of the hill, Peter waved an envelope in front of her. "I've got some post gala donations for you. Some people just need a while for their hearts to soften."

A tinge of pain rolled through her at the memory of her time with Keith at the fundraiser. How long would it be before this didn't hurt anymore? She forced a smile. "Peter, that's wonderful—we'll be able to get a security system and knock off some of that other stuff from our wish list."

"So you are serious about that security system." Peter's mouth twitched. His smile seemed forced. "That sounds terrific."

Greta flapped her wings as though preparing for takeoff. Jenna could feel air moving from the force of the wings. She held the tether a little tighter. "I got to get this bird inside. She's still a little nervous around people."

"I would be glad to help."

"I can just put her in the flight barn for now. Then we can go to the office. I assume the people want receipts for their donations."

Peter chuckled. "People like the tax write-off." He sauntered ahead of her, unlatched the flight barn door and pushed it open.

Jenna stepped into the barn. A red-tailed hawk sat on a perch post close to the door.

Peter came up behind her. "You seem preoccupied."

She turned to face him, but took a step back because he was standing so close. He narrowed his eyes and tilted his head.

She was preoccupied…about a lot of things. She

wasn't about to tell Peter about Keith, though. "I'm sure you heard about the shooting?"

"He nodded. Murder doesn't happen that often around here. The whole town is buzzing."

"Eddie's death is so disturbing. I just talked to his widow. I think he was trying to do the right thing. I think someone was making money off him and other out-of-state hunters, organizing these crazy illegal hunts."

"Oh, really?"

"Your place is right next to Craig Smith's. Have you seen anything?"

"Seen anything?"

Jenna shook her head. "I don't want to point fingers." She untethered the eagle and positioned her on a post. "But if you've noticed anything strange, like a helicopter parked on his land..."

Peter shook his head.

"You want to give me a hand? I need to take this guy in for a dose of antibiotics." She pointed toward an owl sleeping on a shelf by the windowsill. "If you could stand in the door and kind of block it, there is less risk of escapees. They are usually not that bold, but that red-tailed makes me nervous."

"Sure."

After attaching a tether, Jenna maneuvered the owl onto her gloved hand. The owl barely stirred. She strode over to the door. Peter stepped to one side so she could get out.

When she turned around, Peter was struggling to close the door. "It sticks sometimes. Give it a hard push."

He lunged at the door, and it slid into place. While he put the board into the hooks, Jenna noticed his keys had fallen on the ground. She leaned and picked them up with her free hand. Ice froze in her veins. Peter's key ring had the same symbol with the letters E.H. that had been on Eddie's coffee cup.

Peter turned to face her. Jenna managed a smile. "You dropped these."

He took the keys. His fingernails scraped across her palm. "Thank you."

Jenna's mouth went dry. "Why don't we head up to the office and get those receipts written up?" *And then you can be out of here, and I can call the police.*

"Everything all right, Jenna?"

Her heart pounded out a wild erratic beat. "I'm just shook up. Thinking about what happened to that poor man." She could tell that her voice sounded thin, like she was forcing the words out.

Peter offered her a smile. His teeth shone white in the sunlight. "The whole community has been shattered by this. It will be a while for healing to happen. I am thinking about opening up my home to the people in town, have some sort of get-together to help people process their feelings."

"I am sure the churches will do that, Peter." She struggled to keep the trembling out of her voice.

The owl flapped his wings, matching the rhythm of her own heartbeat. Her skin felt clammy.

Jenna turned and headed up the hill toward the office. The owl flew off her arm and landed on the ground. He bounced a few feet away from her. She raced after him, and he skittered a few feet more. Finally, she stopped him by stepping on the tether.

Peter materialized beside her. She could feel the heat of his body as he pressed against her arm. His fingers pinched the back of her neck.

"I think you and I need to go for a ride." He dug his fingers deeper into her nape.

The nerves in her neck muscles flared with pain. She gasped.

He spoke into her ear; his breath seared her skin. "But first, let's go to my car to get my gun."

Keith readjusted the suitcase on the seat of his truck as he drove through town. His goodbye to his grandparents had been bittersweet. He didn't deserve to be loved like they loved him. He could never repay them for what they had done for him. He would come back when he could to help out and to take care of them. Of course, that meant he might run into Jenna. The thought of even crossing paths with her made his chest ache.

Jet whimpered and rested his chin on the suitcase, staring up at Keith. They were nomads again. The lead on a job in Denver looked promising. He would land somewhere. He always did.

He parked and stared at the library as a young woman entered, holding the hand of a blond boy. The boy wasn't more than two feet tall and each step was a stretch for his tiny legs.

He had one more goodbye before he drove out of this place. Keith stepped out of his vehicle and strode across the street and took the library steps two at a time. He wove his way through the stacks, past a group of moms sitting in a circle with their children while one of them read aloud.

Richard Murphy's silver gray hair was visible above the high counter of the check-out desk. He smiled and lifted his chin when he saw Keith.

Richard sat at the computer, clicking through pages that were mostly text. As always, there was sadness in his eyes despite the smile. Richard focused on the screen as he spoke. "I hear you are headed out of town."

"I came to say goodbye and to wish you well with everything."

Richard swung his chair around to look up at Keith. The sadness in his eyes intensified. "Everything?"

Keith nodded, wondering what the older man meant by the one word response.

Richard managed a smile. "Your support has meant the world to me."

Keith rested his elbows on the counter. Beside him were a pile of children's books ready for check-in. The top book was about wolves. Keith stared at the cover photograph, a black wolf with intense yellow eyes.

He would be leaving Hope Creek with a lot of loose ends. Things with Jenna had ended so abruptly, so coldly. Maybe there was one thing he could resolve or at least help bring to a close. He brushed his hand over the picture of the wolf.

"Can we do a little looking around on that computer?" Keith grabbed a piece of paper and drew the logo he had seen on Eddie Helms's coffee cup. "Can we find out what this means?"

Richard took the piece of paper. "We can give it a try." Richard retrieved another chair for Keith.

Keith settled into the hard plastic chair while Richard studied the drawing. "What do you think it is, anyway?"

"I was thinking maybe it was some sort of corporate logo?" Keith examined his own crude drawing and tried to remember what the original had looked like.

Richard scratched his head. "Maybe some kind of club symbol like 4-H."

Keith chuckled. "I don't think these guys were into raising pigs for the county fair."

Richard released a soft laugh. He paged through several websites. "I'm not finding anything." He turned his attention back to the drawing, tapping his finger on it. "E.H." He repeated the letters three times.

"I think that stands for Eddie Helms. But it is the symbol that is bothering me. Maybe we are making this harder than it has to be. Why don't we see if Eddie Helms had a Facebook page?"

Richard clicked through until he found the Eddie Helms they were looking for. There were pictures of Eddie on a boat with his wife and two children. Pictures of Eddie at the motorcycle shop he owned.

"This symbol reminds me of a crossbow," Richard said.

Keith studied the pictures closer. There was one of Eddie standing over a lion carcass he had just shot. He was wearing a T-shirt with the crossbow logo, and the letters E.H. Several men stood beside Eddie while others milled around him. Some were unaware of the camera and others offered a thumbs-up. They were all wearing identical shirts. Keith leaned closer to the computer, studying the photograph. His attention was drawn to a figure in the background of the image.

Richard touched the photo Keith was examining. "Looks like someone went on safari. That's some high risk hunting if you ask me."

"Yeah, high risk, very extreme." Keith shifted in his chair. Now everything made sense. "E.H. doesn't stand for Eddie Helms, it stands for Extreme Hunters. I suspect that this guy is the club president." Keith pointed to a blurry figure in the background turned slightly away from the camera. "Peter Hickman knew Eddie Helms."

"They hunted together in Africa," Richard said.

Keith scooted his chair back. "I am going to tell the sheriff. Can you call Jenna and tell her for me?" It would be too heartbreaking to hear her voice.

A shadow fell across Richard's face. "I'm afraid my daughter isn't talking to me again and with good reason."

"But I thought—"

"Jenna came to visit me. I had gotten a letter from my potential publisher and waited until Sunday to open it. To celebrate the bad news, I had poured myself a drink. Guess I just wanted to feel it in my hand. I called my sponsor right after that. He assured me that this happens to everyone and I'm back on track, but none of that matters to Jenna. She is tired of being hurt by me, and I don't blame her."

"When was this?"

"Yesterday."

Keith's mind raced as he replayed his conversation with Jenna. "Sunday morning?"

Richard nodded.

Now he understood why she had been so cold to him. Seeing her father relapse had probably brought back old fears. She might have even blamed him since he was the one who had suggested reconciliation.

Richard gathered up the books off the counter. "For years, I could not see things from her perspective. She had to handle a lot as a child. I was too busy feeling sorry for myself to take care of her. Alcohol makes you selfish. I have put my daughter in the line of fire one too many times. Her hope has been built up, and I have dashed it to pieces."

"Do you want things to work out between you and your daughter?"

"More than anything." Richard's shoulders hunched. "But I wouldn't blame her if she never talked to me again."

"Don't give up, then. Sometimes you've just got to take these baby steps."

Keith's heart hammered in his chest. He had to find her, had to reassure her. "Why don't you take this information over to the sheriff? I think I am the one who needs to talk to Jenna."

Keith raced out of the library and across the street. He jumped into the cab of his Dodge. Jet yipped at him. "All is not lost, my friend." Could he promise Jenna that he would never drink again? No. But he knew with God's help, there was very little chance of it.

The truck charged to life, and he pulled onto the street. Fear mixed with excitement as he turned off the city street onto the country road. Now that he understood how afraid she was of having to relive the loneliness of her childhood, would his assurances be enough?

The top of the flight barn came into view and he accelerated. He could call her cell and let her know he was on the way, but no, this needed to be done face-to-face. Explaining over the phone wouldn't work, and it might make her not want to see him at all.

He pulled into the center lot and jumped out of his truck. A Lexus was parked in the lot. A hush had descended on the center. When he tried the door of the center, it was open. He stepped inside. "Hello?"

The clock said it was after five. The volunteers would have left by now. Keith walked down the hill. The wooden bar for the flight barn door lay on the ground. When he checked the carport by Jenna's cottage, her Subaru was gone. A chill blanketed Keith's skin. Given all that had happened, Jenna wouldn't take off and leave doors unlocked.

An owl on a tether came around the corner. The bird flapped its wings, but didn't take off. Something was going on here. Jenna would never leave a bird out like that.

He gathered up the bird. As he headed toward the hill to put the bird in a cage, he spotted Jenna's car winding up a mountain.

Keith found a cage for the bird, raced outside and jumped in his truck. He ripped out of the parking lot and sped toward the mountain road, saying a prayer for Jenna's safety.

SIXTEEN

Jenna couldn't get a deep breath. She adjusted her sticky hands on the steering wheel. Peter turned toward her, pointing the gun at her.

She pressed her lips together. "What are you going to do?"

"This one will have to look like an accident."

What did he mean by *this one?* "Please, Peter." Her mouth felt dry. Even without the gun, Peter was strong. With the gun, she was completely outmatched.

"Course, you are always running over hill and dale to save those precious birds. It is entirely believable that sooner or later you might slip off a mountain."

Jenna's heart thudded against her rib cage. She had just passed the last crossroads. At this point, the road only went one place, to the top of Mount Larson. Unless they met a car coming down the mountain, her chances of finding help had gone from slim to none.

One thought tumbled over another as she tried to come up with possibilities for escape. There was nothing in the car she could defend herself with. A pocketknife wasn't much of a match against a gun.

"Why are you going so slow?" Each word was like a knife jab in her skin.

"This is a single lane dirt road with a hundred foot drop-off." The speedometer read fifteen. She probably could have pushed it up to twenty or twenty-five, but going slower gave her time to think.

Peter faced forward, but still pointed the gun toward her. In her peripheral vision, she saw him reach down and tug on the seat belt as though it were uncomfortable.

She needed to buy some time. Maybe if she got him talking. "So all your talk about caring about the birds was just a big front?"

"What I care about is the game," he said.

She fought to keep her voice level. The one thing she had control over was her emotions. Letting him see her sense of betrayal would give him the upper hand in an even greater way. "The game? What are you talking about?"

"The challenge of the hunt. At some point, shooting an elk through the head at one hundred yards with a permit in your pocket doesn't give you the rush you crave."

Jenna swallowed the rising anger. This man had totally deceived her. Her teeth clenched. She couldn't say anything without revealing her rage. The car descended into the final dip before the road would end at the edge of a cliff.

"Fortunately, I found a group of men who felt the same way and were willing to pay for the thrill." Peter's chin jerked up in a show of pride.

Jenna squeezed the steering wheel. Her knuckles turned white. She couldn't contain her anger any longer. "Most hunters have respect for the landowners, for the land and for what they hunt."

Peter leaned toward her, placing the gun on her temple. "Don't go getting all self-righteous on me." He spat his words out.

The pressure of the barrel of the gun made her eyes water. Her throat constricted. She forced out her words anyway. "I have to say it." She spoke through gritted teeth. "You sir, are a hunter without honor."

Peter huffed. "Honor? Give me a break." He gave the gun a final push against her temple before pulling it away.

They reached the flat area at the top of the mountain. Jenna brought the car to a stop.

"You stay right there," Peter said as the gun jerked in his hand, "until I come around and open your door."

Jenna pulled her hands off the steering wheel. Her gaze traveled to the rearview mirror. Fifty yards behind her was the edge of the forest. Could she get to the cover of the trees fast enough? Probably not. Given his shooting abilities, he could put a bullet in her before she had run ten yards.

Her fingers hovered by the keys still in the ignition. Maybe she could get turned around and down the mountain before he had time to shoot. Her trembling fingers touched the key.

She saw a flash of movement in her rearview mirror as Peter passed around the back of the car. She sat up straight. He jerked the door open and grabbed her shirt at the shoulder.

"Go to the rear of your car and grab one of those empty cages."

Jenna scanned the area around her as she made her way to the hatch and opened it. Her hand touched the smaller carrier.

"Take a bigger one," Peter commanded. "Lots of eagle nests around here. We want it to look like you were trying to rescue one of your precious goldens, and in your enthusiasm, you fell to your death."

"You never cared about the birds."

"Of course not, it was just a front so no one would suspect me." He flashed a grin that made her blood run cold.

Jenna's pulse drummed in her ears. She closed her eyes, unable to think of a coherent prayer. Only two words came to mind.

Please, God.

Peter leaned toward her and grabbed her phone off her belt. "Now go over to the edge of the cliff and throw the carrier off."

Her own heartbeat sounded like a death march playing in her head. Jenna bit her lower lip. Her feet felt like they were encased in cement.

"Go," Peter barked.

Jenna walked to the edge of the cliff. The initial drop off was a gradual forty-five degrees of rocks. She and Keith had climbed this mountain; there were ledges and footholds, but for the most part, it was a straight down.

Jenna tossed the carrier across the broken shale. It bounced once and rolled toward the edge. Peter threw her phone in the same direction, which bounced off several rocks before coming to rest a few feet from the carrier. It was pretty clear what the next part of his plan was. Would he push her or make her jump?

Jenna stalked over to him. "You haven't thought this through. You can't take my car. You'll have to hike off this mountain. I wouldn't have walked all the way up here to get a bird."

He leaned toward her, pushing the gun against her stomach and standing so close that his spit hit her face. He waved his own phone at her. "I'll get a ride from one of my many hunter buddies who are sworn to silence and have a little more loyalty than Eddie Helms."

"So you did shoot him?"

"Quit stalling." He slapped her hard across the jaw.

The stinging on her face became a tingle. She touched her finger to her cheek. Tears welled.

He pointed toward the rocks. His voice was a low, husky whisper. "You know what you have to do now."

"If you shoot me, they will trace the bullet and know you were involved."

Rage exploded in his eyes. "Turn around and walk."

"I won't. You'll have to shoot me." Either way, she was going to die. She had no intention of Peter Hickman getting away with this.

His upper lip rippled. He spun her around and poked the gun in her back. "Walk."

"Shoot me."

The pressure of the gun against her spine lessened. Peter stepped away from her and then ran to the car. He glanced at her and then down the mountain. He grabbed something from the rear of the car and stalked toward her.

"Change of plans." He glanced back down the road.

Jenna tried to turn to see what he saw, but he spun her around so she faced the cliff.

In his hand, he held the leather rope she used to tether birds and the cloth she threw on them to calm them. He had also grabbed a long rope she kept in the car. He tied her hands together.

"What's going on?"

"You ask too many questions." He placed the blindfold over her eyes.

Only a sliver of light snuck in at the bottom of the cloth. "If they find me like this, it won't look like an accident."

"I'll deal with you later. Now walk." He pushed on her back. The hard metal of gun bruised her spine.

Why had Peter changed his plan? Jenna took a hesitant step forward, testing the ground in front of her. Solid.

Peter pushed on her back again. "Hurry."

Something had panicked him. She could hear it in his voice.

She took several more slow steps.

"You've got a good twenty yards. Come on, run."

She obeyed. She was breathless by the time he yelled "Stop." A second later he came up to her and tied the rope around her waist. She pulled away, resisted, but he cinched the rope tighter, causing it to dig into her stomach.

He spoke into her ear. "I'm going to lower you down. Any lack of cooperation from you, and you risk tumbling off this mountain and breaking into a million pieces."

Her own sense of self-preservation kept her from fighting when she slipped off the cliff face and he lowered her. Her head grazed against the side of the cliff as rocks crashed into each other and cascaded down the mountain.

His voice came from above her. "Hold very still."

Her feet touched solid surface. She crumpled to her knees. The wind brushed against her face. She detected the rush of a distant waterfall, reminding her that she was close to Eagle Falls where so many eagles nested.

She could barely make out the mechanical clang and hum of her car starting. The faint engine noises faded into the distance. Why on earth was Peter headed back down the mountain? Hope budded anew. Someone must be coming up the road.

Jenna inched her foot across the hard surface until she felt the drop off. If she moved, she would fall hundreds of feet.

SEVENTEEN

Keith was relieved to see Jenna's car parked at the last intersection before the road wound up the mountain. Maybe she had been called out on a big emergency, and she hadn't had time to lock the center.

He parked his truck beside her vehicle. No one was behind the wheel and the hatch was opened. Keith jumped out and circled the car. There were no carriers in the back. Jenna always had a small carrier and a large carrier with her. He studied the borders of the forest. The evergreens blended into dark shadows.

She wouldn't release a bird in such a thick forest anyway. It was usually easier to let them go in an open area or from a high place. He sauntered a few yards up the road. Wind blew through the grass of the meadow. He called her name. Fear crept into his awareness.

Something felt wrong.

A moment later, a man emerged from the trees holding one of the carriers. Maybe a volunteer. He wore a cowboy hat and dark glasses. The man shouted and waved. He drew closer.

Keith's stomach knotted. Peter Hickman.

Keith closed the distance between them. His feet pounded the hard earth. "Where is Jenna?"

Peter pulled off his sunglasses. "I imagine she is back at the center." He lifted the pet carrier. "I offered to help out with the release of a bird. She said I could take her car because it has all the needed equipment."

"You lie." Keith's blood boiled.

Peter took a step back and held up a hand. "Now hold on, just a minute."

Keith's hands curled into fists. He wanted to strangle this man. "Where. Is. Jenna?"

Peter stepped back again. "What is your problem? Calm down. I told you. She loaned me her car. Why don't you head to the center? I'm sure she is there."

"I was just there," Keith replied through clenched teeth. "The place was empty." Keith's heart pounded as adrenaline raged through him. Peter didn't know that Keith had linked him to the extreme hunters. Jenna was in danger. He knew it. Had Peter dragged her into the forest?

"Maybe she just stepped out." Peter offered Keith a crooked smile. "I've got to take the car back to the center. Are we good here?" His voice was patronizing.

Keith's mind reeled. Jenna must have made the same connections he had and now Peter had done something to her. "Where is she?" Keith lunged, hitting Peter across the jaw with a right hook. When Peter got back to his feet, he had a gun in his hand.

Keith swallowed hard to quell the storm brewing inside him. If Peter put the gun away, he might be able to jump him. If he played it cool, Peter might let his guard down. He struggled to keep the emotion out of his voice.

"You're right. I should calm down. I'm sorry I got so upset." Each beat of his heart was a tick on the clock.

Jenna, where are you? What has he done with you?

Peter continued to hold the gun on him. "You kind of scared me." He circled around Keith without turning his back.

A few seconds more and Peter would be in the car and gone. He stepped toward the driver's seat, edging along the front bumper, still not taking his eyes off Keith.

Wild drums beat inside Keith's head. He could not let this man go. Peter knew that Keith was on to him. He had the resources to be out of the country within hours. And Jenna?

Uncontrollable rage and desperation made Keith leap across the space between the two men and tackle Peter. A gunshot reverberated through the forest.

Jenna pressed close to the wall of the cliff. A branch brushed across her cheek. In the rush, Peter had not tied the blindfold very tight. She dipped her head so the branch hooked on the fabric. The branch was a centimeter from her eye. She leaned her head back, and the blindfold released from her eyes. The action caused her shoulder to brush against the loose rock of the cliff. A stone fell at her feet.

As the blindfold fell around her neck, she blinked. The ledge was even smaller than she had imagined. The view made her dizzy. Looking down only fueled her fear of heights.

Her arms strained from being tied behind her back. She tilted her head up. Peter had lowered her a good ten feet. The rope around her waist had been secured above her. A chill ran down her spine. Peter had said he wanted her death to look like an accident. He intended to come back for her.

He'd seen something down the mountain that had panicked him. Another car headed up this way, perhaps. But not Keith. Keith was on his way out of town. He was miles from here. Yet, he was the first person that came to mind. How many thousands of miles and how much time would there have to be between them before the strong connection died? She had to force herself to let it go. Just because he had rescued her so much in the past, saved her bacon in rivers and on the side of cliffs didn't mean he was good for her. He had saved her a thousand times from physical jeopardy but protecting her heart was a different thing altogether.

As much as she could without moving her legs, Jenna peered at the cliff face. She lifted her head. An eagle soared through the sky. The huge wingspan which always made her awestruck was the first clue that it was an eagle. As the bird drew closer, she could distinguish the white head of a mature baldy.

A hundred yards away and below her, the bird came in for a landing in a nest. The brown eaglet blended with the colors of the nest, but she could see slight movement. That guy needed to be pushed out of the nest and soon. This late in the summer most of the juveniles were out on their own. The older eagle flapped its wings before settling over her baby as the wind picked up.

What a picture of security.

Jenna held her breath as pieces of a psalm floated back into her head. Something about God protecting her with his wings. People, even good people like Keith, might let her down. Trusting in God was where the real safety in this world was. Her heart ached and she regretted her harsh words to Keith…and now it was too late.

The wind picked up even more. Her legs were starting to feel numb. She prayed. This was not the end. She was not without hope. Peter had seen someone coming up the mountain. They might get here before Peter could stop them. She was not about to give in to despair. She would do everything she could think of to get out of here.

She lifted her head as high as she could and shouted, "Hey, hey, somebody. I am down here."

Her foot slipped on the edge of the ledge.

Keith's body shuddered from the impact of falling on Peter. The two men rolled on the ground. Peter righted himself and subdued Keith by pinning his arm behind his back. The gun must have gone off. He saw Peter's hat and the crushed sunglasses but no gun.

Out of breath from the struggle, Keith wiggled to break free. "What have you done with Jenna?"

Peter didn't answer. He must be looking around for the gun. He released all the pressure off Keith's arm. Keith scrambled to his feet to see that Peter was pointing the gun at him again.

Behind him, Keith saw Jet racing through the tall grass. By the time Peter was aware of the noise, the dog had leaped up and grabbed Peter's shirttail. The attack was enough to throw Peter off balance, the gun fell out of his hand as he struggled to stay on his feet.

Keith scrambled for the gun and pointed it at Peter. Jet backed off but continued to bark, showing his teeth.

"Good boy, Jet." Keith tossed his cell phone to Peter. "Call the Sheriff."

With a wary glance toward Jet who released a low growl, Peter shook his head. "I haven't done anything wrong."

"We've linked you with the extreme hunters. No doubt you are the one setting things up. I am sure if we get some searchers out on your property, we can find that helicopter."

Peter's face blanched, and he took a step back.

Keith's head jerked up. "Now call the sheriff." He took in a breath. "And then...and then, tell me where Jenna is." His voice faltered. His thoughts jumbled. Was she still alive? What if Peter had done something to Jenna at the center and then hidden her somewhere? That didn't make sense. Why take her car and make himself look suspicious. "She is around here, isn't she? Tell me where she is."

Jenna's throat hurt from shouting. She pressed hard against the cliff face to keep from slipping again. She couldn't tell if the rope Peter had tied around her waist would hold her or not. Her legs had gone completely numb. She really needed to stretch out. The rope dug into her wrists and stomach.

She shifted slightly and more pebbles and dirt cascaded down the mountain. Slowly, carefully, she rose to her feet. Her legs tingled from lack of circulation. The view around her started to spin. She closed her eyes as a wave of despair washed through her. What if she died here? If she tumbled off this mountain, would the authorities even know Peter had done this?

Even as she was ready to give up, she heard that still small voice that told her to try one more time.

Her throat felt like someone had run sandpaper over it. Jenna gathered her remaining energy, lifted her head and shouted. "Hey, somebody! I'm down here!"

She thought she heard something. A humming noise like a car motor? She shook her head. Was she just so desperate that now she was imagining sounds?

She cried out again. The faint sound of a dog barking reached her ears. Mustering strength, she lifted her head and shouted again. "I'm here!"

A strong clear voice responded. "Jenna!"

Her heart burst with joy. Keith had found her. "Down here."

His head materialized above her and then Jet's head appeared. The dog offered a sympathetic whine for her predicament. "You seem to have gotten yourself into a pickle."

She uttered a strange sound that was meant to be the words *thank God,* but the power of the rush of emotion through her made her words come out garbled.

Keith knelt. "You have no idea how glad I am to see you, Jenna Murphy." His face glowed with affection.

"You came back."

"I never left," he said.

Was that because of her or some other reason? "My hands are tied."

"I see that." He angled his head side to side, assessing further. "Hold on, I think we can get you out of there."

Keith disappeared and returned a few minutes later.

He tossed a rope so it hung beside where she was. "I'm coming down to you."

"Where did you get the climbing gear?"

"After we talked about climbing again, I bought some gear and threw it in my truck." He buckled himself into the harness. "The sheriff is here to help. Peter is handcuffed in the car."

Keith rappelled down the mountain until he lined up with Jenna. Her back was to him. "Hold still. I'll cut the ties on your hands."

The pressure of the knife pressed against the rope. Her hands released, and she grabbed the rope tied around her waist as she wobbled backward. "Is this secure?"

Keith nodded. "This rope is not the best setup, but I'll help you. Come on, take your first foothold."

Her head buzzed and her pulse accelerated.

Keith positioned a hand on the middle of her back warming her to the core. The fogginess in her head cleared. If Keith was here, she wasn't afraid of falling.

"Like old times." She placed her foot on the tiny ledge.

"It would be nice if it was like old times for all time," Keith said.

Jenna reached up and found a handhold. Her foot searched for a ledge, and she pushed herself up. What was Keith saying? She bent her head to look down. "For all time? Are you serious?"

Her foothold gave way, and she slipped back down the rope to face Keith. They swung slightly, both of them hanging from their ropes. Keith angled his body, so he could rest his open palm on her cheek.

Jenna stared into the gentle gray eyes.

"For all time, for the rest of my life, with you," he whispered.

Keith wrapped the blanket the sheriff had given them tighter around Jenna's shoulders. The hard bench in the sheriff's office pressed against her back.

He leaned close to Jenna. "Are you okay?"

She nodded. She hadn't spoken much since they had gotten off the cliff face. He had proposed to her. What was her answer?

The sheriff clicked through pages on his computer. "If you folks will just wait a few minutes more, I will take your statements."

The deputy had already taken Peter Hickman into a holding cell.

The sheriff tapped his keyboard. "You'll be glad to know that we matched the bullet in the eagle to the bullet in Eddie Helms. We've got a warrant to search Hickman's place to find the rifle."

"I thought Craig Smith had something to do with all this?" Jenna said.

"We questioned Craig earlier today. He did get into a card game with Eddie. Eddie was trying to wrap up loose ends before he blew the whistle. He was on his way out to pay off his debt to Craig."

The sheriff walked over to the other side of the room to retrieve documents. The deputy returned. After speaking to the sheriff, he sauntered over to Jenna and Keith.

"Sheriff wants me to take your statements." The deputy sat at his computer.

"I'll go first." Keith pulled his arm away from Jenna.

Keith went through the deputy's questions. Jenna did the same thing. They walked out into the cool of the evening. A few people sauntered along the sidewalks. Lights from the steak house glowed as people stepped inside.

"Do you remember what I said to you on the mountain?" Keith wrapped his arm around Jenna.

This was it. Her heart raced. "Yes, I remember."

"To be together like old times...for all time. Is that something you'd want?"

She stopped. Her gaze traveled to the library. All the lights had been turned off and shadows covered the steps.

He placed a hand on her shoulder. "I know that he wants to patch things up."

"I miss him." Jenna shook her head. "But letting him back into my life means he could hurt me again."

"I can't promise you that he won't relapse. I can tell you he is serious about staying sober."

"You haven't had a drink in twelve years." She walked ahead of him a few steps.

"Everyone's recovery is different."

She turned back around to face him. "I will try."

"I do think it is worth it, risking the hurt." He placed his hands on her shoulders and brought her closer. "When I thought Peter had done something to you...I saw my life without you and that was more unbearable than any hurt you may have caused me in the past."

Her lips parted. She tilted her head, eyes searching. "I'll risk it if you'll risk it."

"Like old times for all time?" He looked at her, his expression filled with expectation.

"No, better than old times. No more secrets."

"I'll take that as a yes then." He gathered her into his arms and kissed her.

EPILOGUE

Jenna's stomach fluttered more than the wings of the doves her father would release during the wedding ceremony.

"Jenna, are you ready to go?" Her father stood at the door to the tent that had been set up as a changing room for the bride and bridesmaids.

Cassidy gave her a last hug. She stepped back and held Jenna's face in her hands. "You look beautiful. Now, I need to go find my escort down the aisle."

As Cassidy exited, her father stepped toward her. He looked handsome in his dress pants and white button-down shirt, but what she liked best was how clear and filled with love his eyes were. "Nervous?"

"A little. I'm glad you're here." He held out an elbow, and she wrapped her arm through his.

It was a short walk down the hill to the clearing in the forest where the wedding party had gathered. An acoustic guitar played the wedding march. The music swelled. Jenna took in a quick, sharp breath as the attendees turned to look at her. Her father patted her hand. Etta and Norm smiled at her from the first row.

Keith stood at the end of the aisle wearing jeans and a light blue button-down shirt. She smiled. He was dressed up for Montana. His expression brightened when he looked at her. Warmth spread through her from the top of her head to her toes.

As her father handed her over to Keith she heard him whisper, "Take care of her."

"I will," he mouthed, looking directly at Jenna as he gathered her hands in his.

As they said their vows, Jenna looked into Keith's eyes. She still saw some of the skinny, wild kid who could talk her into anything, but there was something deeper, more anchored there, too.

She loved the man Keith had become.

Jenna said the final words of her vows, "…and to a lifetime of love and adventure."

On either side of them two large cages were opened and six doves flew out and fluttered over them as the attendees applauded.

Overhead, Jenna thought she heard the plaintive cry of a red-tailed hawk.

* * * * *

WE HOPE YOU ENJOYED THIS BOOK FROM

LOVE INSPIRED SUSPENSE

INSPIRATIONAL ROMANCE

Courage. Danger. Faith.

Find strength and determination in stories
of faith and love in the face of danger.

6 NEW BOOKS AVAILABLE EVERY MONTH!

Lex Fielding drove, cutting down the narrow dirt path between the towering trees. Branches slapped the side of his park-ranger truck, and rocks spun beneath his wheels. All the while, words cascaded through his mind, clattering and colliding in a mass of disjointed ideas that didn't even begin to come close to what he wanted to say to Poppy. Years ago, he'd had no clue how to explain to the most incredible woman he'd ever known that he didn't think he was ready to get married and have a family. He might not have even had the guts to tell her all his doubts, if she hadn't called him out on it after he'd left a really unfortunate and accidental pocket-dial message on Poppy's voice mail admitting he wasn't ready to get married.

Something about being around Poppy had always made him feel like a better man than he had any right being. Even standing beside her made him feel an inch taller.

He just hadn't thought he'd been cut out to be anyone's husband. Something he'd then proved a couple of years later by marrying the wrong woman and surviving a couple of unhappy years together before she'd tragically died in a car crash.

He heard the chaos ahead before he could even see it through the thick forest. A dog was barking furiously, voices were shouting, and above it all was a loud and relentless banging sound, like something was trying to break down one of the cabins from the inside.

He whispered a prayer and asked God for wisdom. Hadn't been big on prayer outside of church on Sundays back when he'd been planning on marrying Poppy. But ever since Danny had been born, he'd been relying on it more and more to get through the day.

Then the trees parted, just in time for him to see the two figures directly in front of him dragging something across the road. His heart stopped.

Not something. *Someone.*

They had Poppy.

Don't miss
Wilderness Defender *by Maggie K. Black,*
available May 2021 wherever Love Inspired Suspense
books and ebooks are sold.

LoveInspired.com